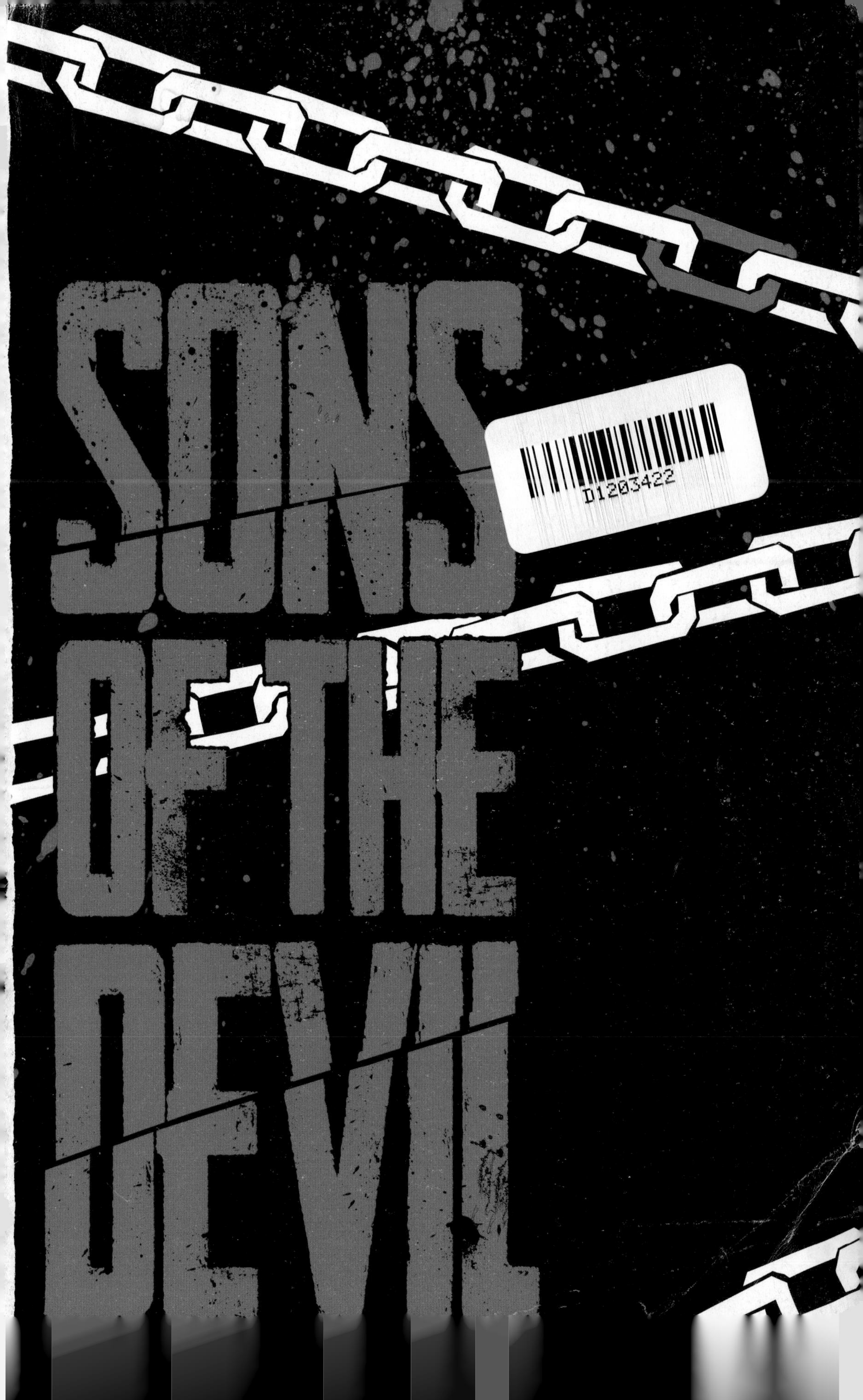
SONS
OF THE
DEVIL

IMAGE COMICS, INC.
Robert Kirkman - Chief Operating Officer
Erik Larsen - Chief Financial Officer
Todd McFarlane - President
Marc Silvestri - Chief Executive Officer
Jim Valentino - Vice-President

Eric Stephenson - Publisher
Corey Murphy - Director of Sales
Jeff Boison - Director of Publishing Planning & Book Trade Sales
Jeremy Sullivan - Director of Digital Sales
Kat Salazar - Director of PR & Marketing
Emily Miller - Director of Operations
Branwyn Bigglestone - Senior Accounts Manager
Sarah Mello - Accounts Manager
Drew Gill - Art Director
Jonathan Chan - Production Manager
Meredith Wallace - Print Manager
Briah Skelly - Publicity Assistant
Randy Okamura - Marketing Production Designer
David Brothers - Branding Manager
Ally Power - Content Manager
Addison Duke - Production Artist
Vincent Kukua - Production Artist
Sasha Head - Production Artist
Tricia Ramos - Production Artist
Jeff Stang - Direct Market Sales Representative
Emilio Bautista - Digital Sales Associate
Chloe Ramos-Peterson - Administrative Assistant
imagecomics.com

SONS OF THE DEVIL™
Volume 1
NOVEMBER 2015.
FIRST PRINTING.
Published by Image Comics, Inc.
Office of Publication: 2001 Center Street,
Sixth Floor, Berkeley, CA 94704. Copyright © 2015
Brian Buccellato. All Rights Reserved. Sons of the Devil™
and the Sons of the Devil logo, are the copyright and
trademarks of Brian Buccellato. The entire contents of this book, all
artwork, characters and their likenesses of all characters herein are
© 2015 Brian Buccellato. Image Comics® is a trademark of Image Comics, Inc.
Originally published in single magazine form as SONS OF THE DEVIL #1-5.
All Rights Reserved. Any similarities between names, characters, events,
persons, and/or institutions in this magazine with persons (living or dead) or
institutions is unintended and is purely coincidental. With the exception of
artwork used for review purposes, none of the contents of this book may be
reprinted, reproduced or transmitted by any means or in any form without the
express written consent of Brian Buccellato. Printed in the USA.
For information regarding the CPSIA on this printed material call:
203-595-3636 and provide reference #RICH -652145. ISBN: 978-1-63215-552-8
For international rights, please contact: foreignlicensing@imagecomics.com

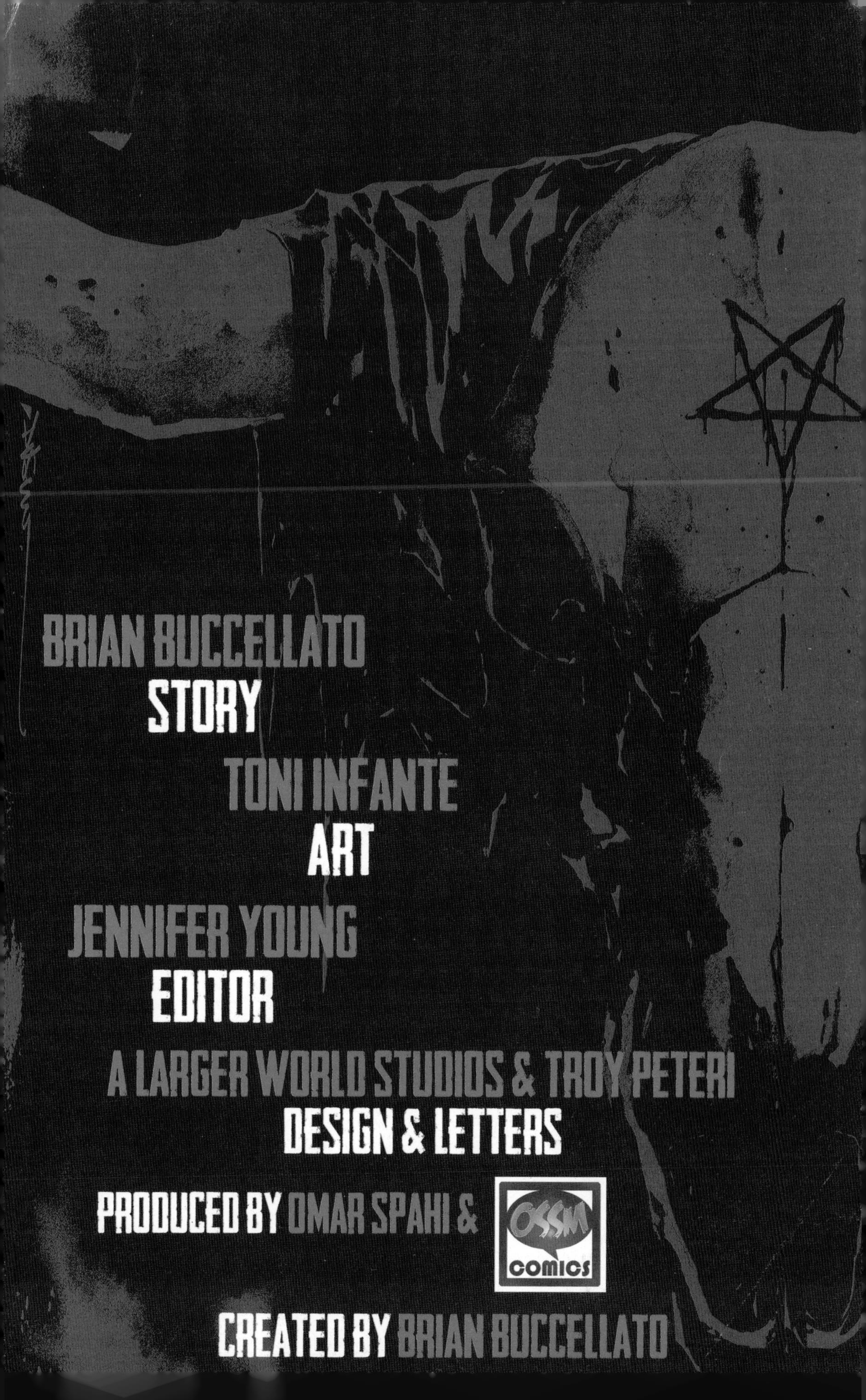

BRIAN BUCCELLATO
STORY

TONI INFANTE
ART

JENNIFER YOUNG
EDITOR

A LARGER WORLD STUDIOS & TROY PETERI
DESIGN & LETTERS

PRODUCED BY OMAR SPAHI & OSSM COMICS

CREATED BY BRIAN BUCCELLATO

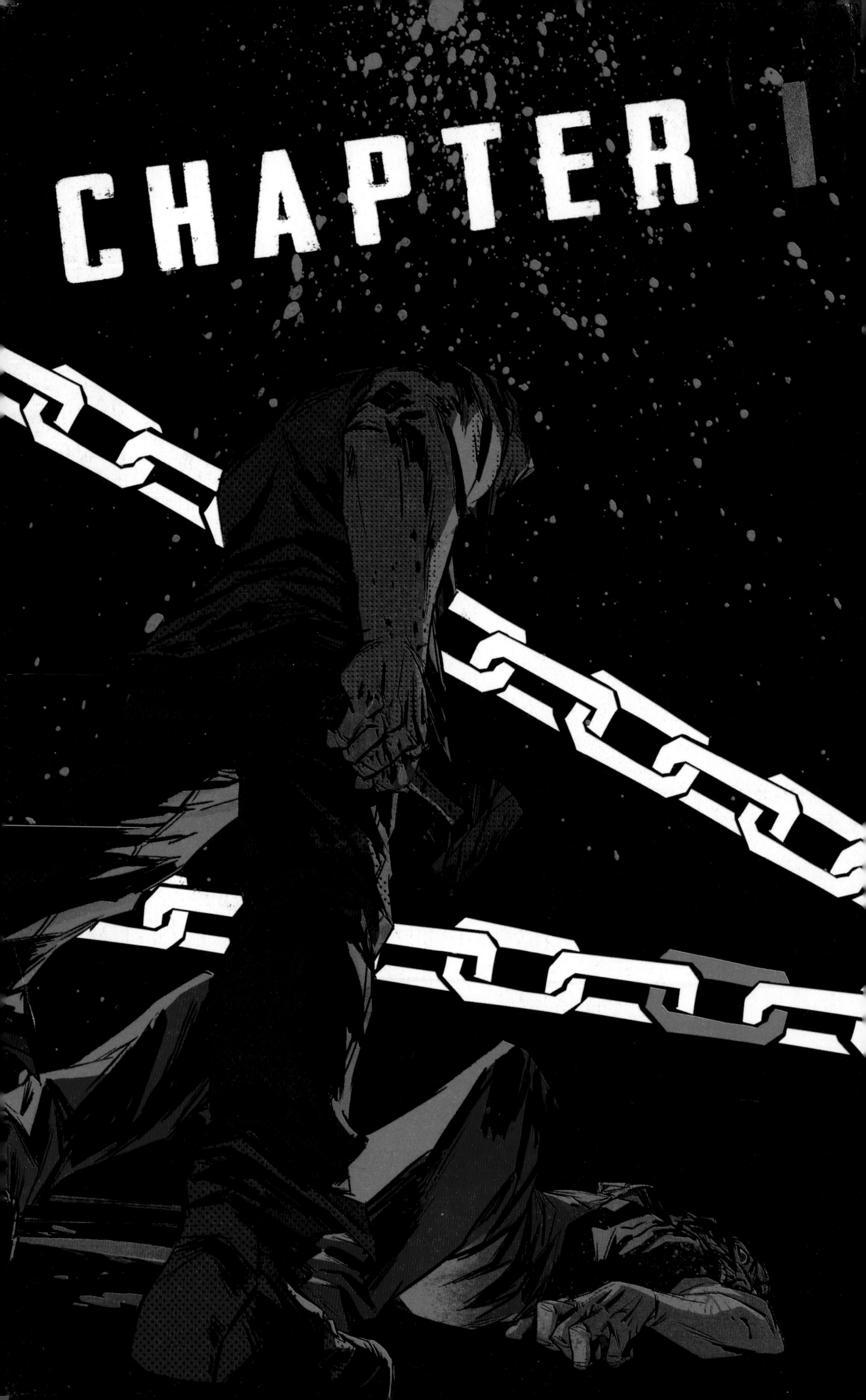
CHAPTER 1

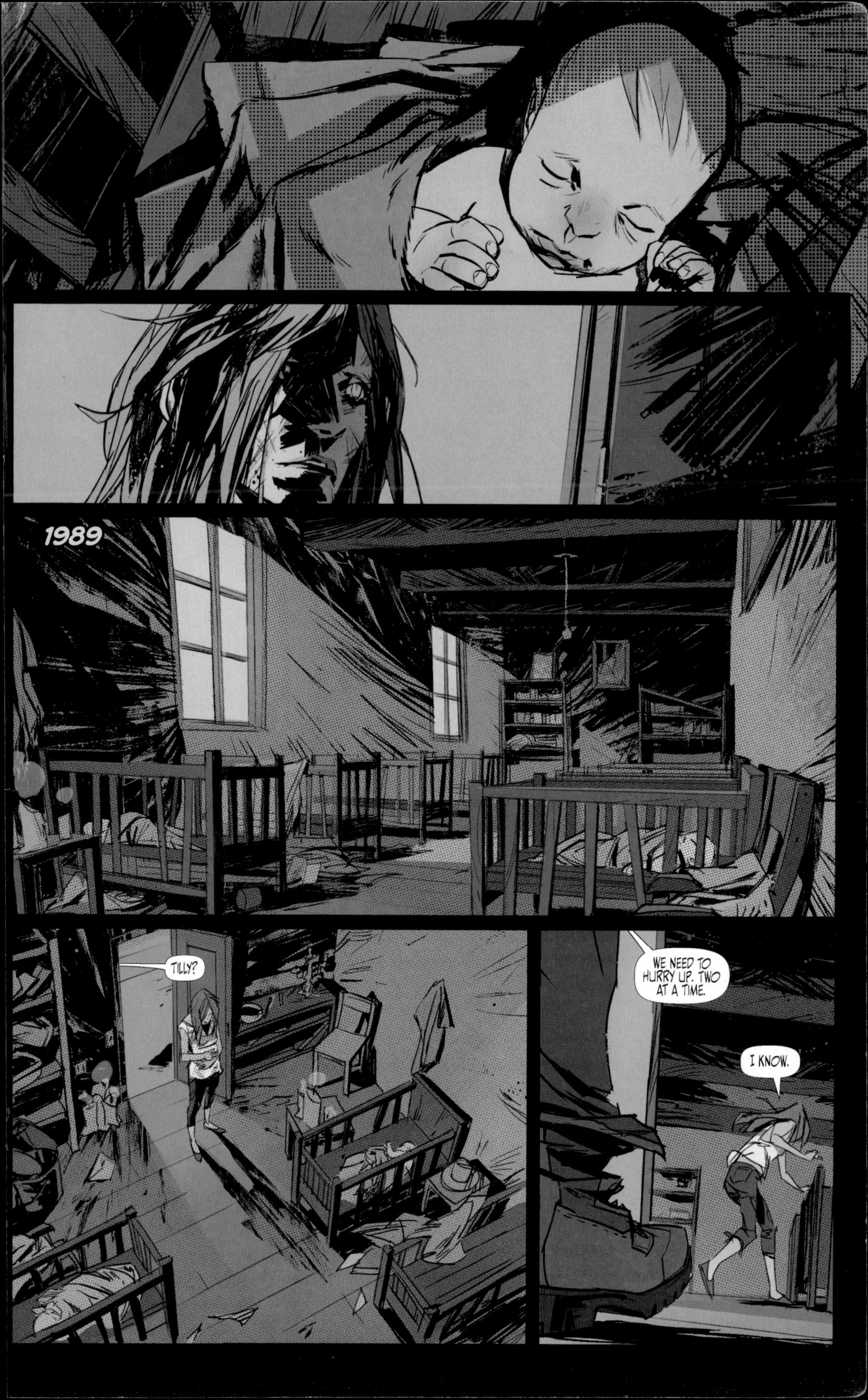
1989
TILLY?
WE NEED TO HURRY UP. TWO AT A TIME.
I KNOW.

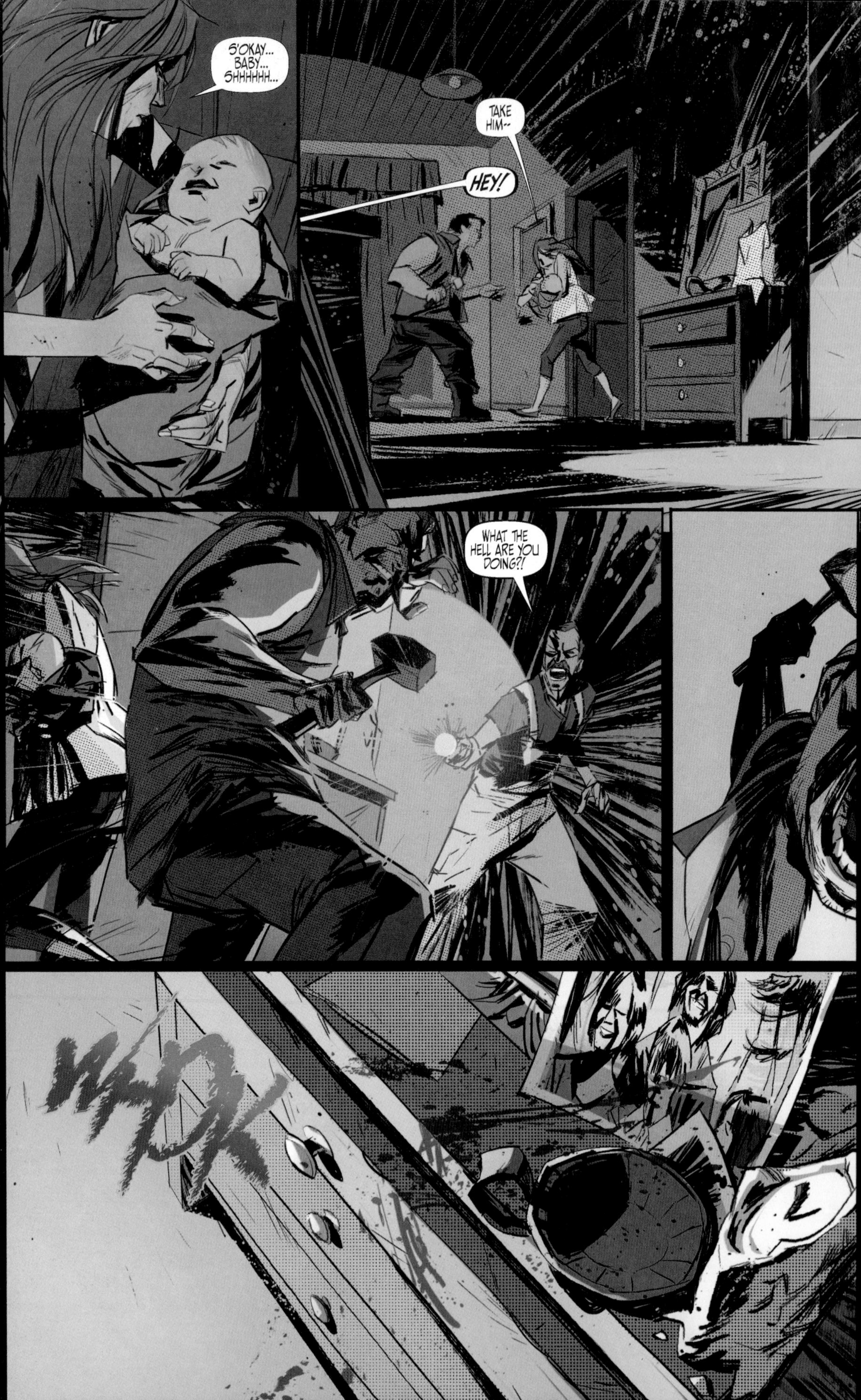
S'OKAY... BABY... SHHHHHH...
TAKE HIM--
HEY!
WHAT THE HELL ARE YOU DOING?!

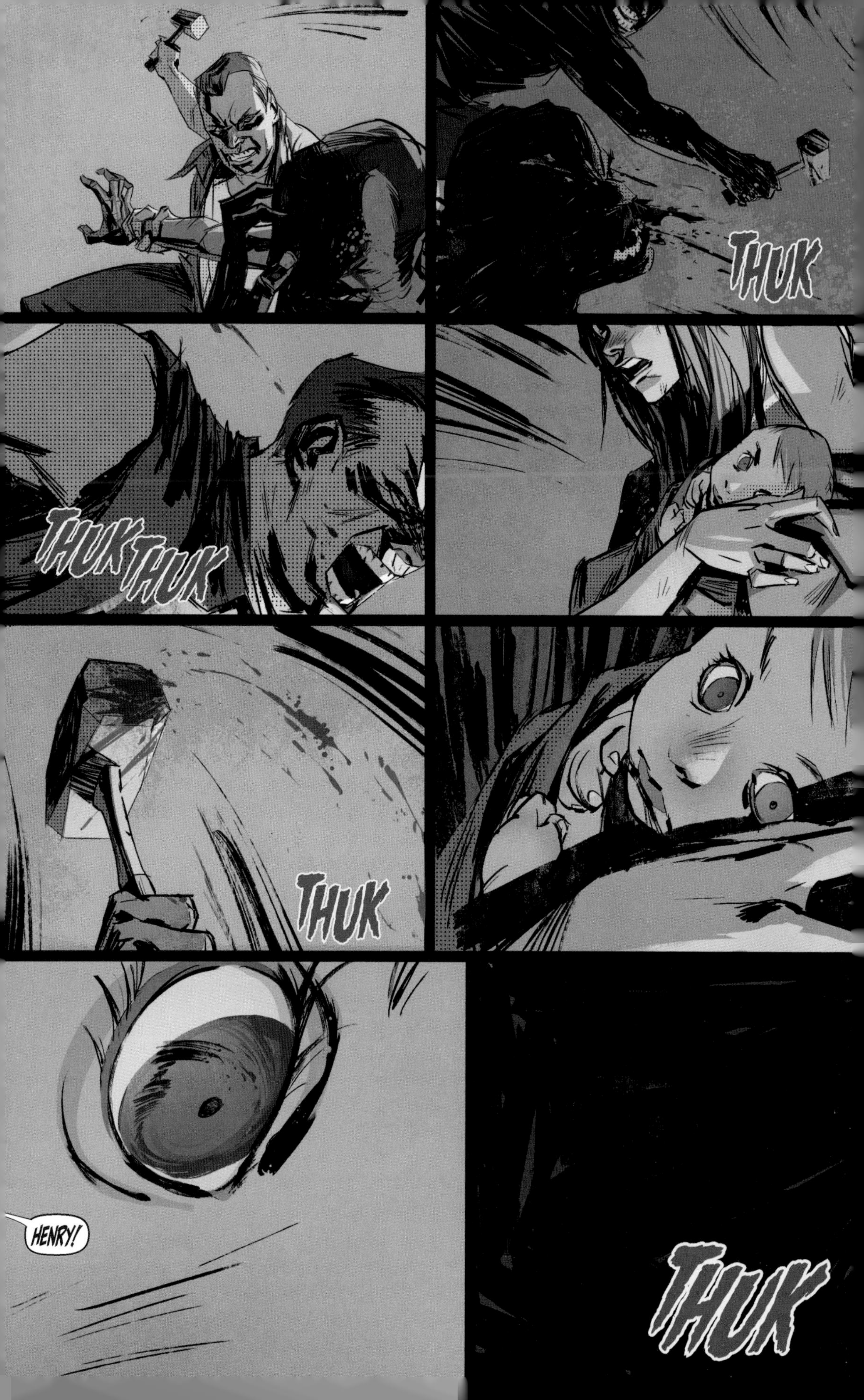
THUK
THUK THUK
THUK
HENRY!
THUK

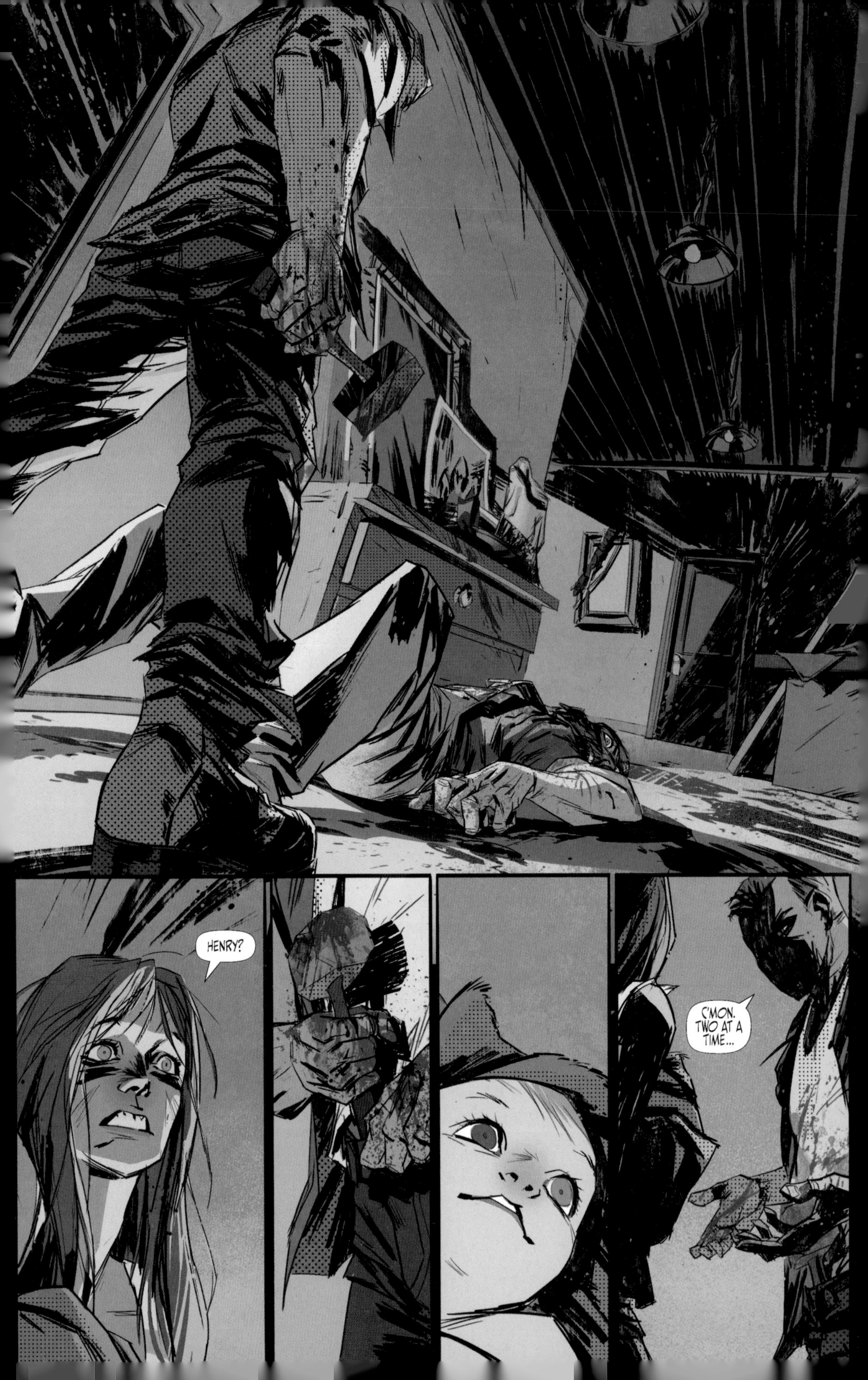
HENRY?
C'MON. TWO AT A TIME...

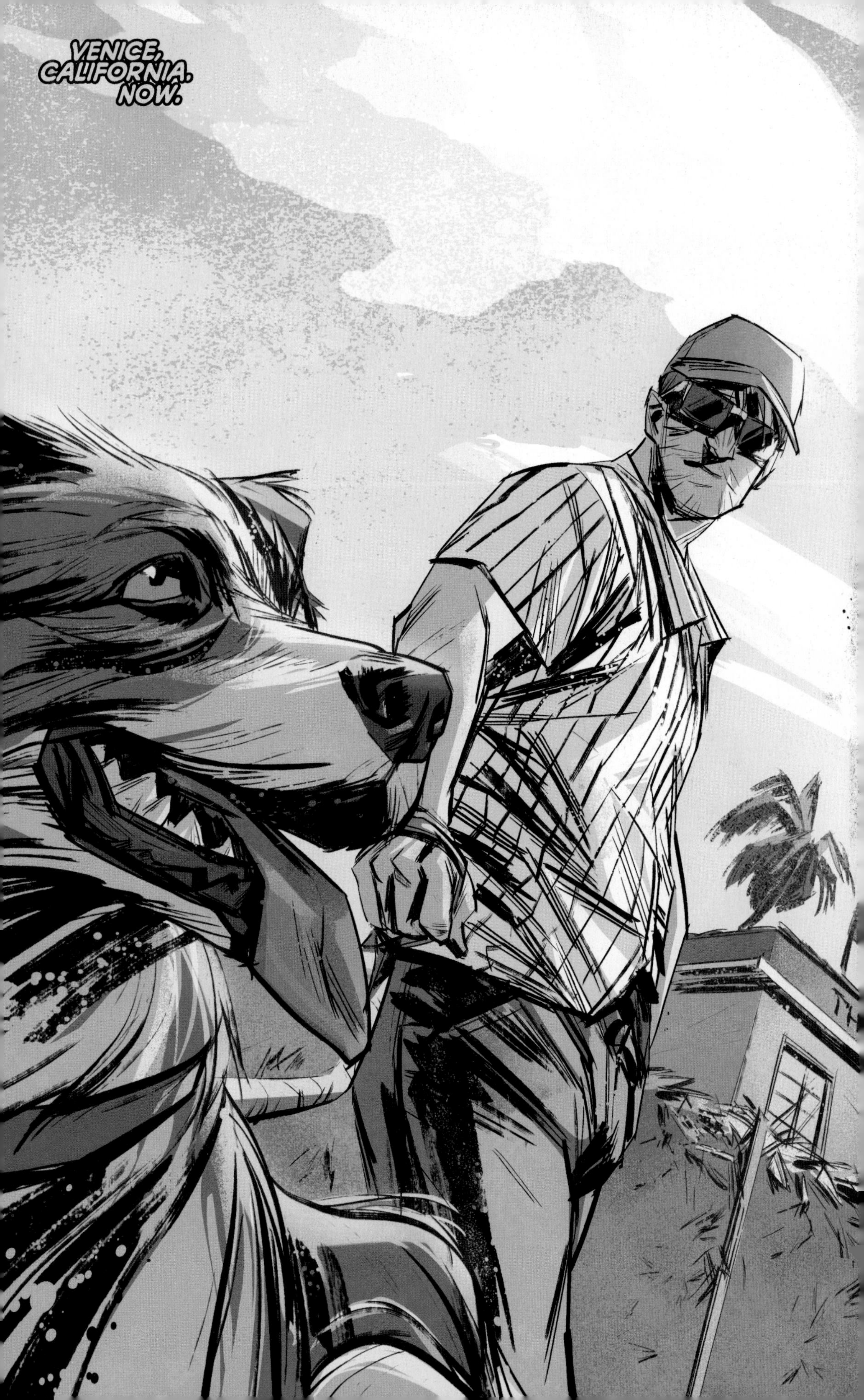
VENICE, CALIFORNIA. NOW.

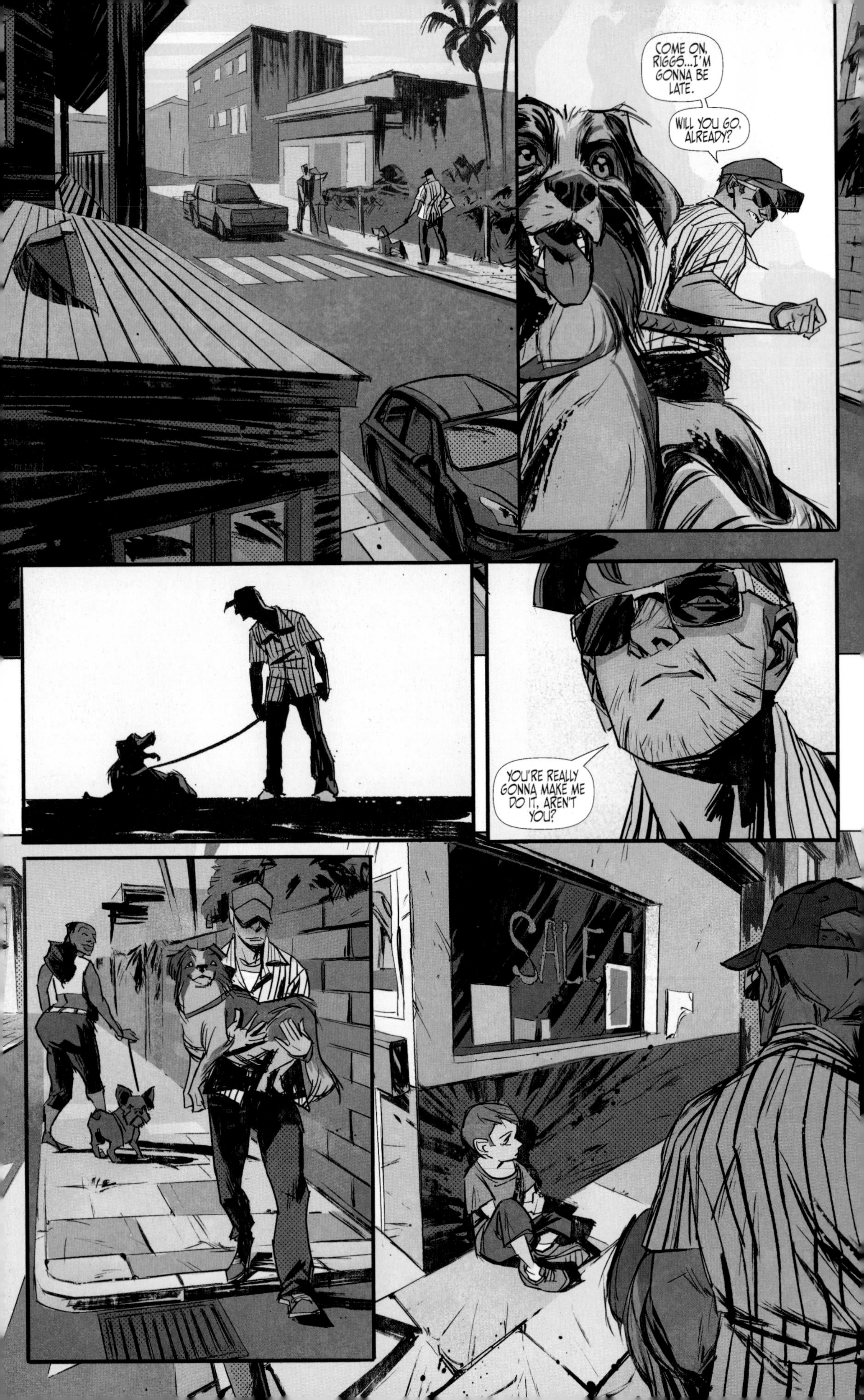
COME ON, RIGGS...I'M GONNA BE LATE.
WILL YOU GO, ALREADY?
YOU'RE REALLY GONNA MAKE ME DO IT, AREN'T YOU?
SALE

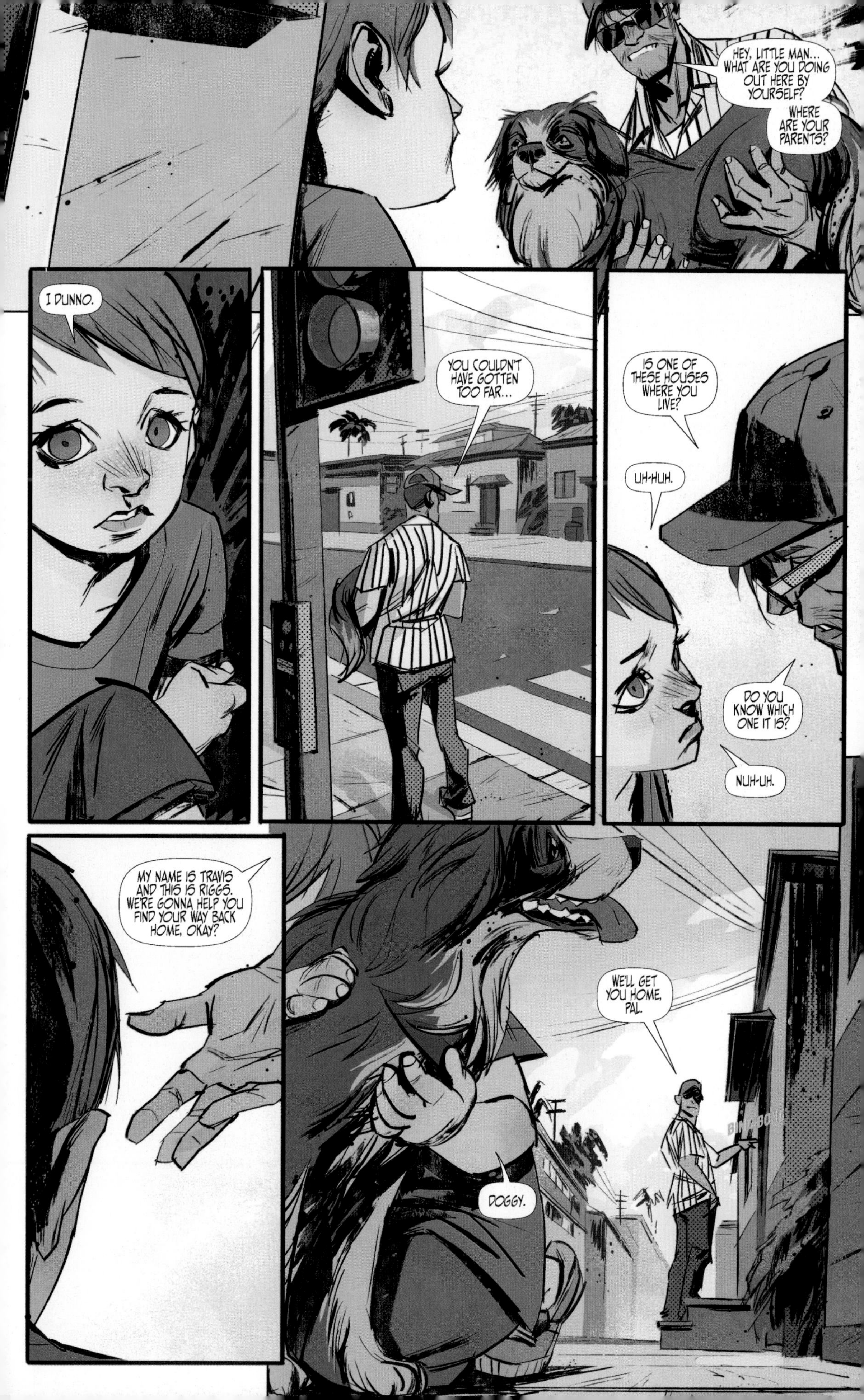
HEY, LITTLE MAN... WHAT ARE YOU DOING OUT HERE BY YOURSELF?
WHERE ARE YOUR PARENTS?
I DUNNO.
YOU COULDN'T HAVE GOTTEN TOO FAR...
IS ONE OF THESE HOUSES WHERE YOU LIVE?
UH-HUH.
DO YOU KNOW WHICH ONE IT IS?
NUH-UH.
MY NAME IS TRAVIS AND THIS IS RIGGS. WE'RE GONNA HELP YOU FIND YOUR WAY BACK HOME, OKAY?
WE'LL GET YOU HOME, PAL.
DOGGY.

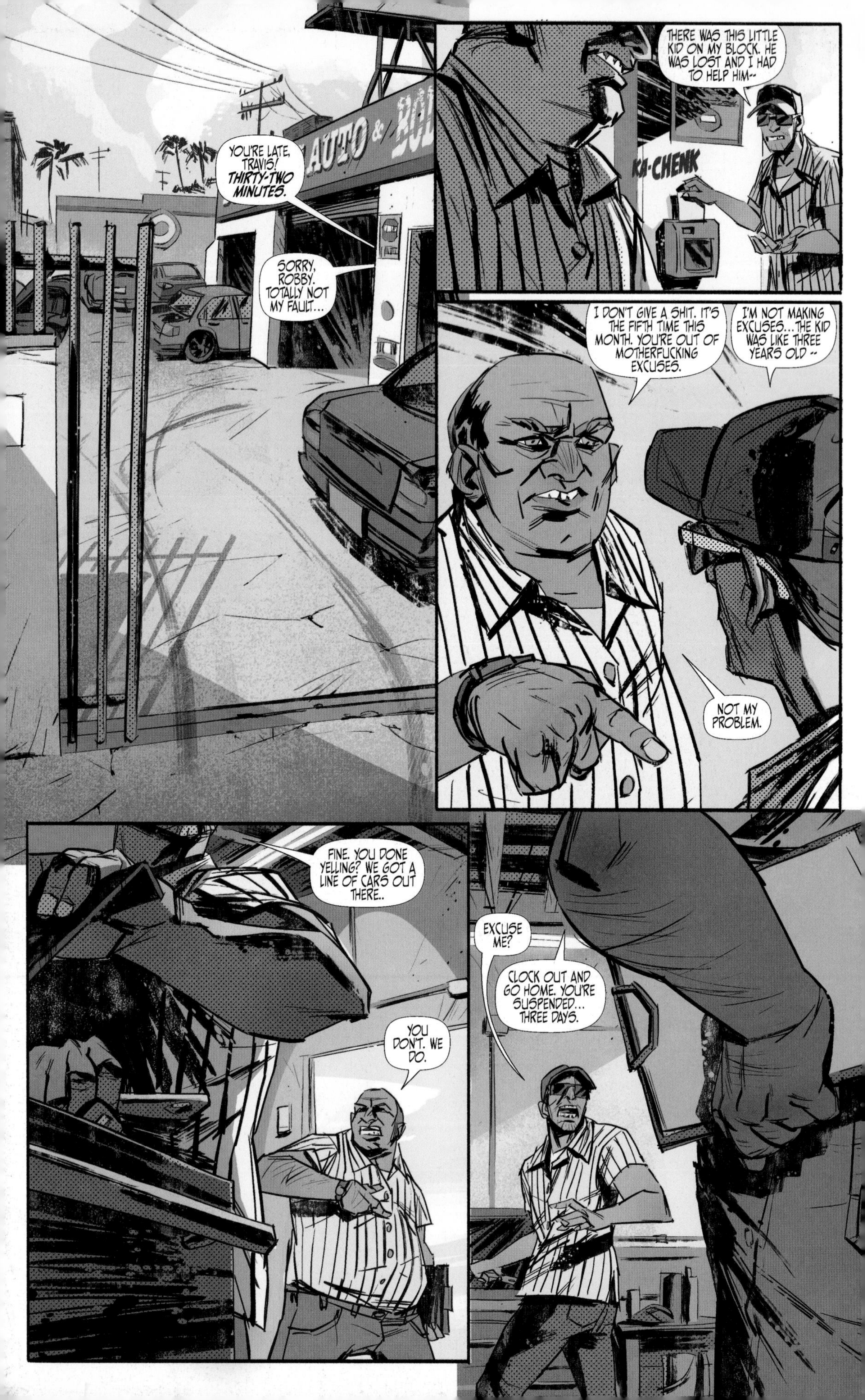
YOU'RE LATE, TRAVIS! THIRTY-TWO MINUTES.
SORRY, ROBBY. TOTALLY NOT MY FAULT...
THERE WAS THIS LITTLE KID ON MY BLOCK. HE WAS LOST AND I HAD TO HELP HIM--
KA-CHENK
I DON'T GIVE A SHIT. IT'S THE FIFTH TIME THIS MONTH. YOU'RE OUT OF MOTHERFUCKING EXCUSES.
I'M NOT MAKING EXCUSES... THE KID WAS LIKE THREE YEARS OLD --
NOT MY PROBLEM.
FINE. YOU DONE YELLING? WE GOT A LINE OF CARS OUT THERE..
YOU DON'T. WE DO.
EXCUSE ME?
CLOCK OUT AND GO HOME. YOU'RE SUSPENDED... THREE DAYS.

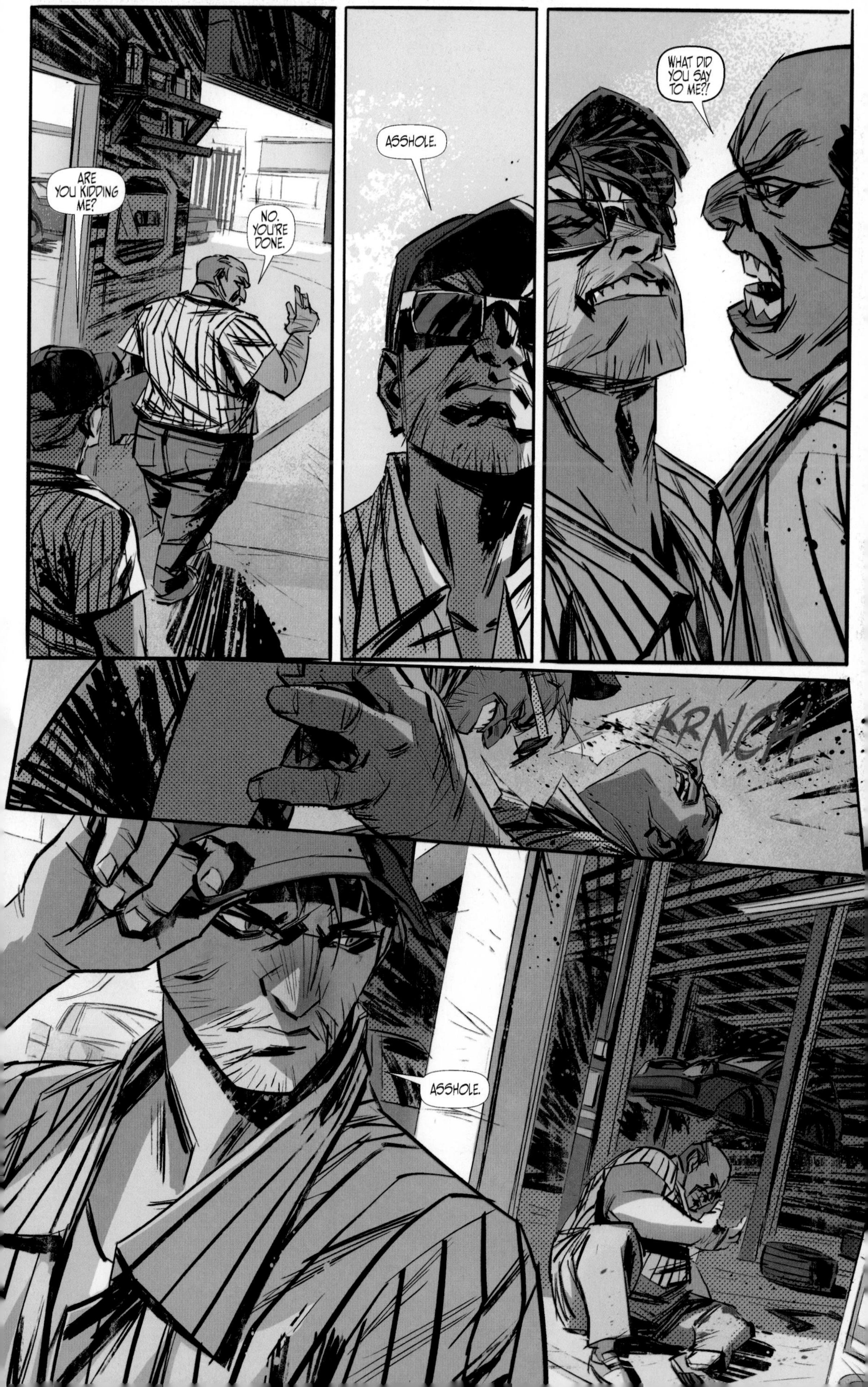
ARE YOU KIDDING ME?
NO. YOU'RE DONE.
ASSHOLE.
WHAT DID YOU SAY TO ME?!
KRNCH
ASSHOLE.

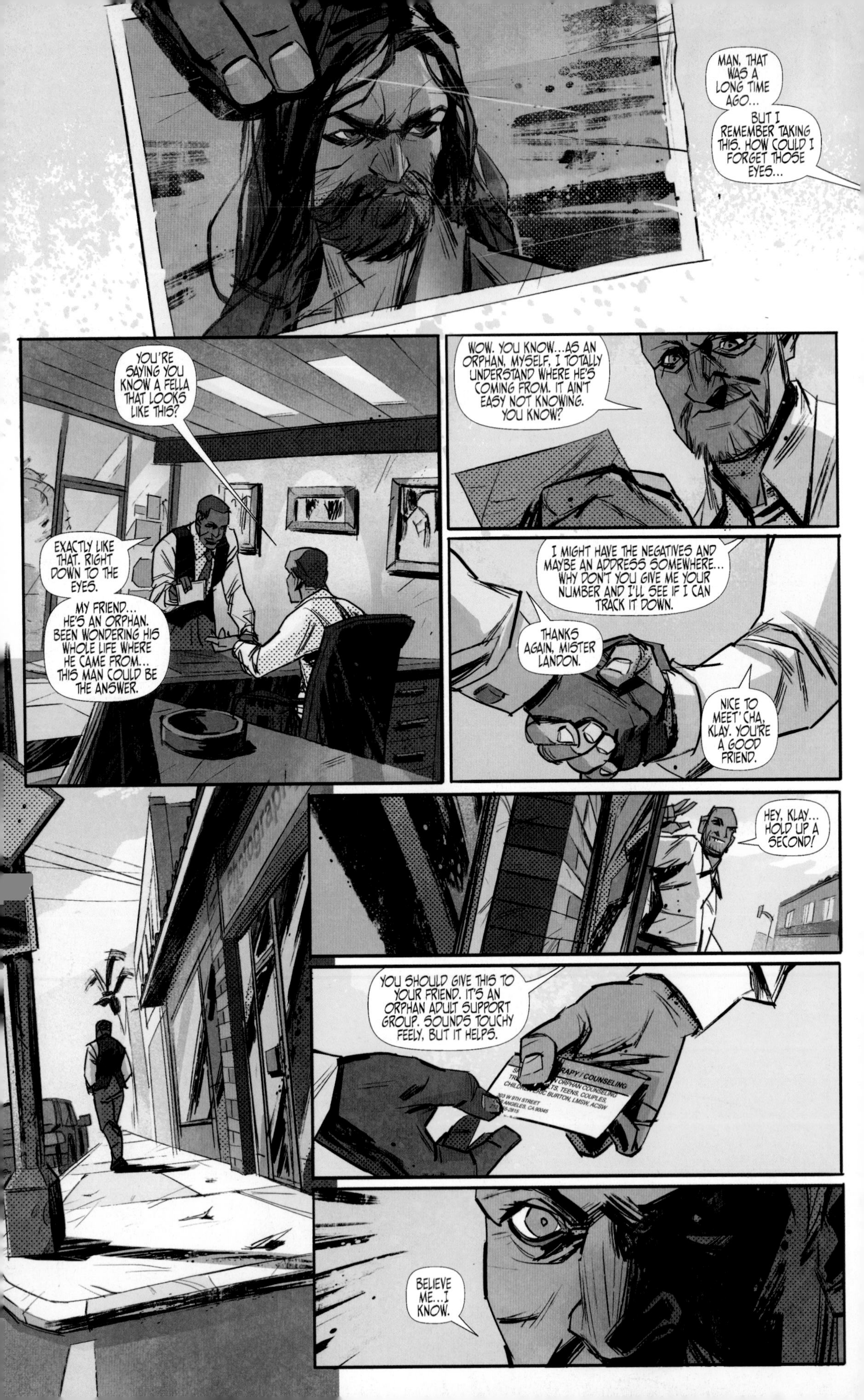

MAN, THAT WAS A LONG TIME AGO...
BUT I REMEMBER TAKING THIS. HOW COULD I FORGET THOSE EYES...
YOU'RE SAYING YOU KNOW A FELLA THAT LOOKS LIKE THIS?
EXACTLY LIKE THAT. RIGHT DOWN TO THE EYES.
MY FRIEND... HE'S AN ORPHAN. BEEN WONDERING HIS WHOLE LIFE WHERE HE CAME FROM... THIS MAN COULD BE THE ANSWER.
WOW. YOU KNOW...AS AN ORPHAN, MYSELF, I TOTALLY UNDERSTAND WHERE HE'S COMING FROM. IT AIN'T EASY NOT KNOWING. YOU KNOW?
I MIGHT HAVE THE NEGATIVES AND MAYBE AN ADDRESS SOMEWHERE... WHY DON'T YOU GIVE ME YOUR NUMBER AND I'LL SEE IF I CAN TRACK IT DOWN.
THANKS AGAIN, MISTER LANDON.
NICE TO MEET' CHA, KLAY. YOU'RE A GOOD FRIEND.
HEY, KLAY... HOLD UP A SECOND!
YOU SHOULD GIVE THIS TO YOUR FRIEND. IT'S AN ORPHAN ADULT SUPPORT GROUP. SOUNDS TOUCHY FEELY, BUT IT HELPS.
BELIEVE ME...I KNOW.

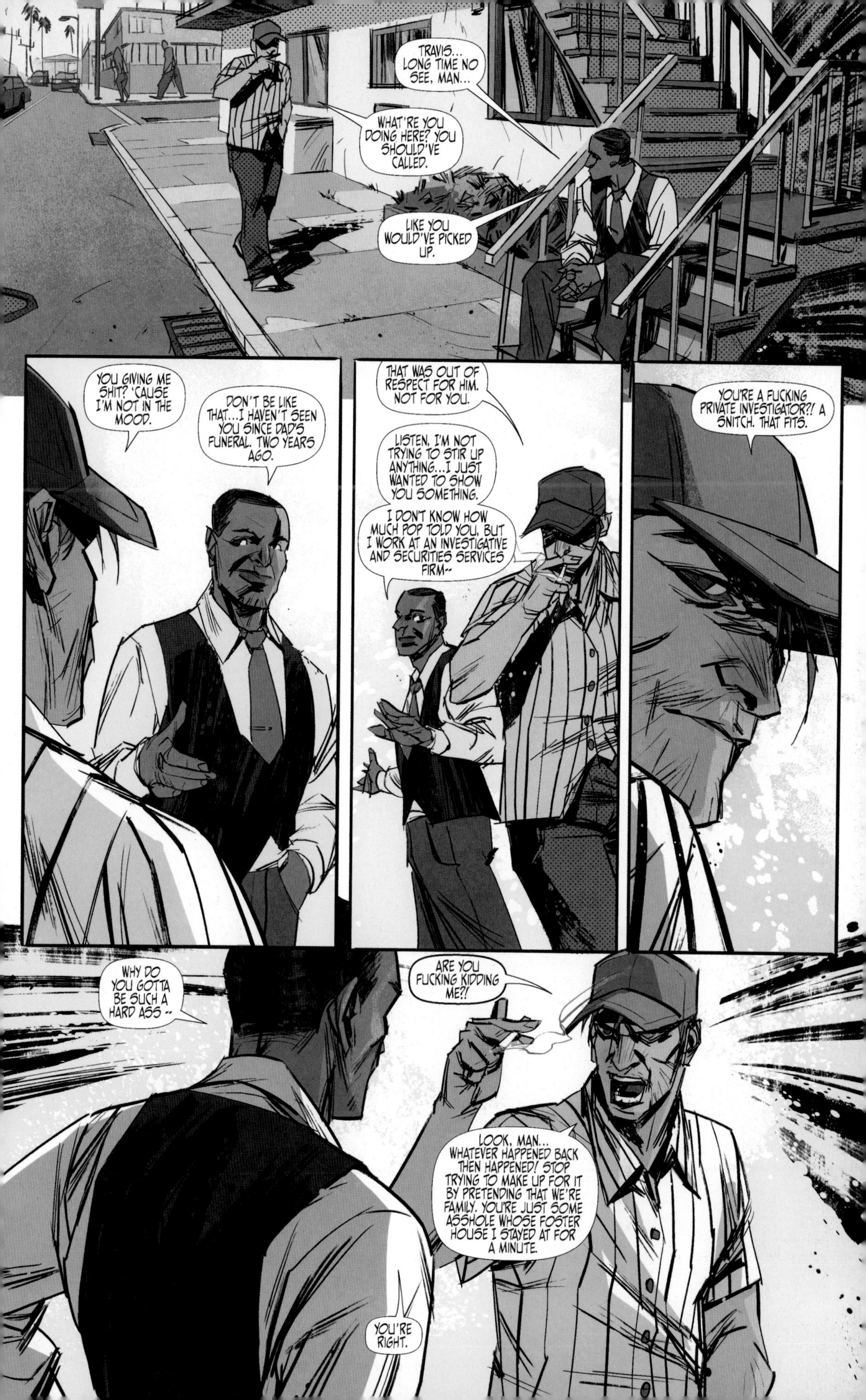
TRAVIS... LONG TIME NO SEE, MAN...
WHAT'RE YOU DOING HERE? YOU SHOULD'VE CALLED.
LIKE YOU WOULD'VE PICKED UP.
YOU GIVING ME SHIT? 'CAUSE I'M NOT IN THE MOOD.
DON'T BE LIKE THAT...I HAVEN'T SEEN YOU SINCE DAD'S FUNERAL. TWO YEARS AGO.
THAT WAS OUT OF RESPECT FOR HIM. NOT FOR YOU.
LISTEN, I'M NOT TRYING TO STIR UP ANYTHING...I JUST WANTED TO SHOW YOU SOMETHING.
I DON'T KNOW HOW MUCH POP TOLD YOU, BUT I WORK AT AN INVESTIGATIVE AND SECURITIES SERVICES FIRM--
YOU'RE A FUCKING PRIVATE INVESTIGATOR?! A SNITCH. THAT FITS.
WHY DO YOU GOTTA BE SUCH A HARD ASS --
ARE YOU FUCKING KIDDING ME?!
LOOK, MAN... WHATEVER HAPPENED BACK THEN HAPPENED! STOP TRYING TO MAKE UP FOR IT BY PRETENDING THAT WE'RE FAMILY. YOU'RE JUST SOME ASSHOLE WHOSE FOSTER HOUSE I STAYED AT FOR A MINUTE.
YOU'RE RIGHT.

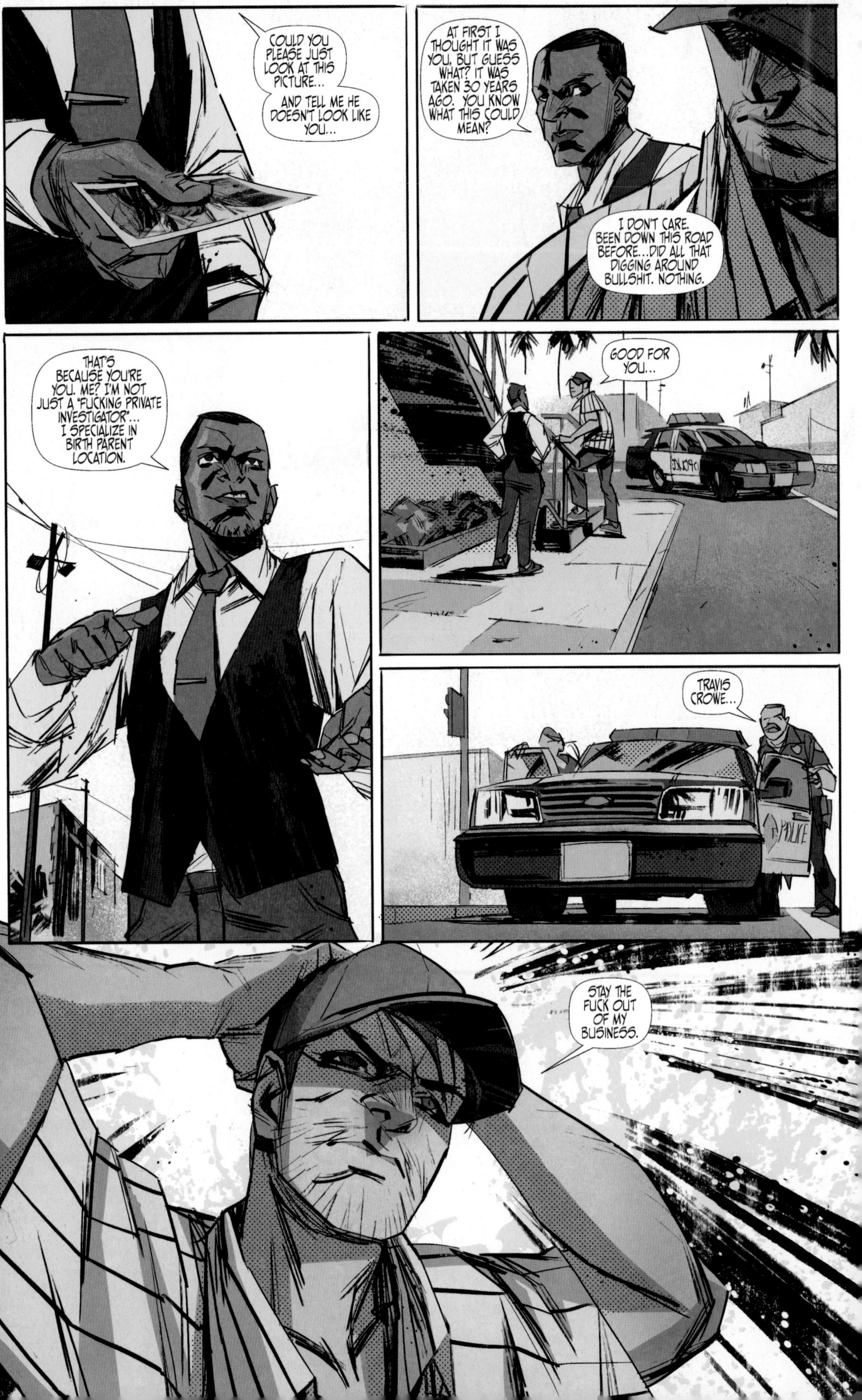
COULD YOU PLEASE JUST LOOK AT THIS PICTURE...
AND TELL ME HE DOESN'T LOOK LIKE YOU...
AT FIRST I THOUGHT IT WAS YOU, BUT GUESS WHAT? IT WAS TAKEN 30 YEARS AGO. YOU KNOW WHAT THIS COULD MEAN?
I DON'T CARE. BEEN DOWN THIS ROAD BEFORE...DID ALL THAT DIGGING AROUND BULLSHIT. NOTHING.
THAT'S BECAUSE YOU'RE YOU. ME? I'M NOT JUST A "FUCKING PRIVATE INVESTIGATOR"... I SPECIALIZE IN BIRTH PARENT LOCATION.
GOOD FOR YOU...
POLICE
TRAVIS CROWE...
POLICE
STAY THE FUCK OUT OF MY BUSINESS.

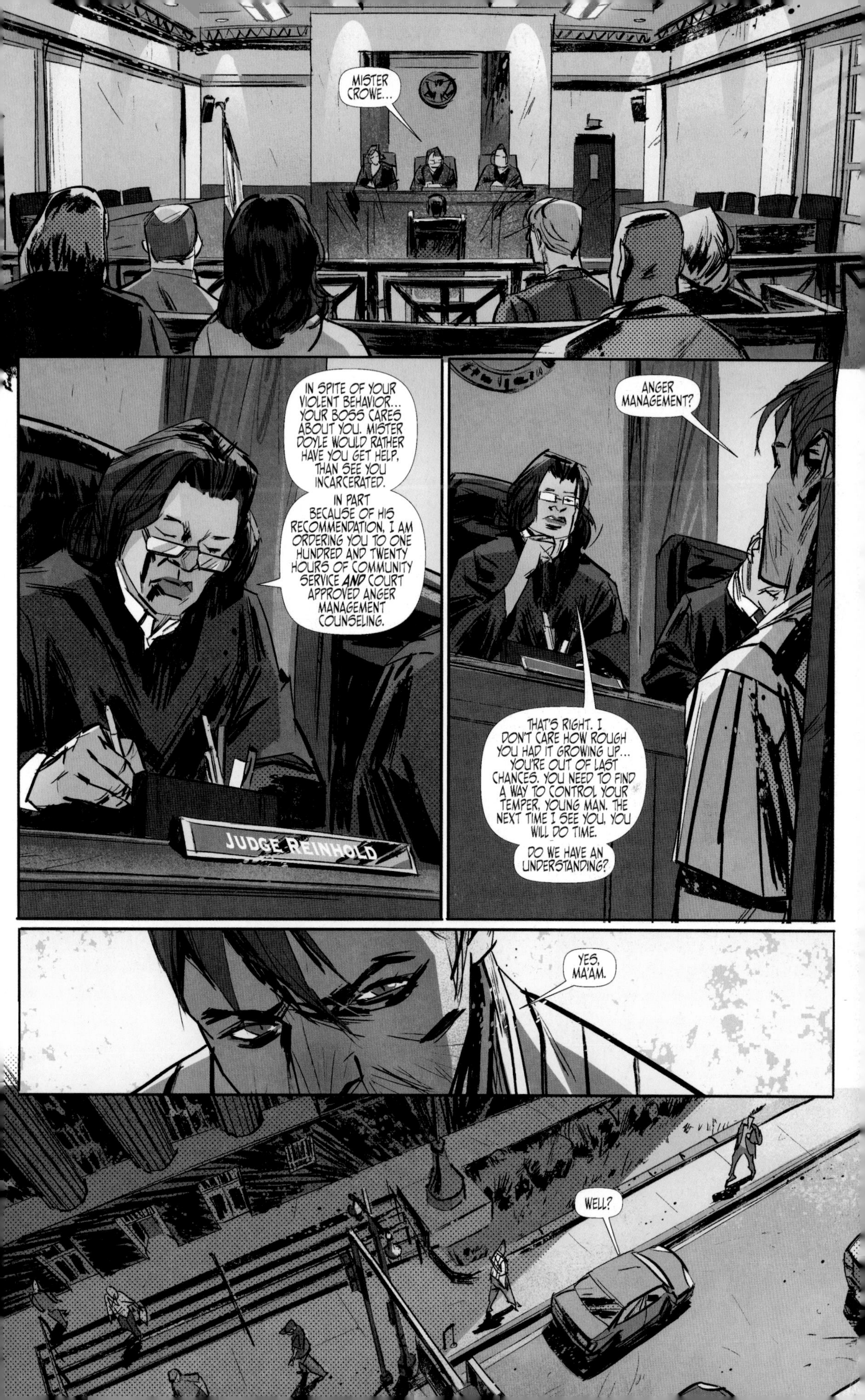
MISTER CROWE...
IN SPITE OF YOUR VIOLENT BEHAVIOR... YOUR BOSS CARES ABOUT YOU. MISTER DOYLE WOULD RATHER HAVE YOU GET HELP, THAN SEE YOU INCARCERATED.
IN PART BECAUSE OF HIS RECOMMENDATION, I AM ORDERING YOU TO ONE HUNDRED AND TWENTY HOURS OF COMMUNITY SERVICE AND COURT APPROVED ANGER MANAGEMENT COUNSELING.
JUDGE REINHOLD
ANGER MANAGEMENT?
THAT'S RIGHT. I DON'T CARE HOW ROUGH YOU HAD IT GROWING UP... YOU'RE OUT OF LAST CHANCES. YOU NEED TO FIND A WAY TO CONTROL YOUR TEMPER, YOUNG MAN. THE NEXT TIME I SEE YOU, YOU WILL DO TIME.
DO WE HAVE AN UNDERSTANDING?
YES, MA'AM.
WELL?

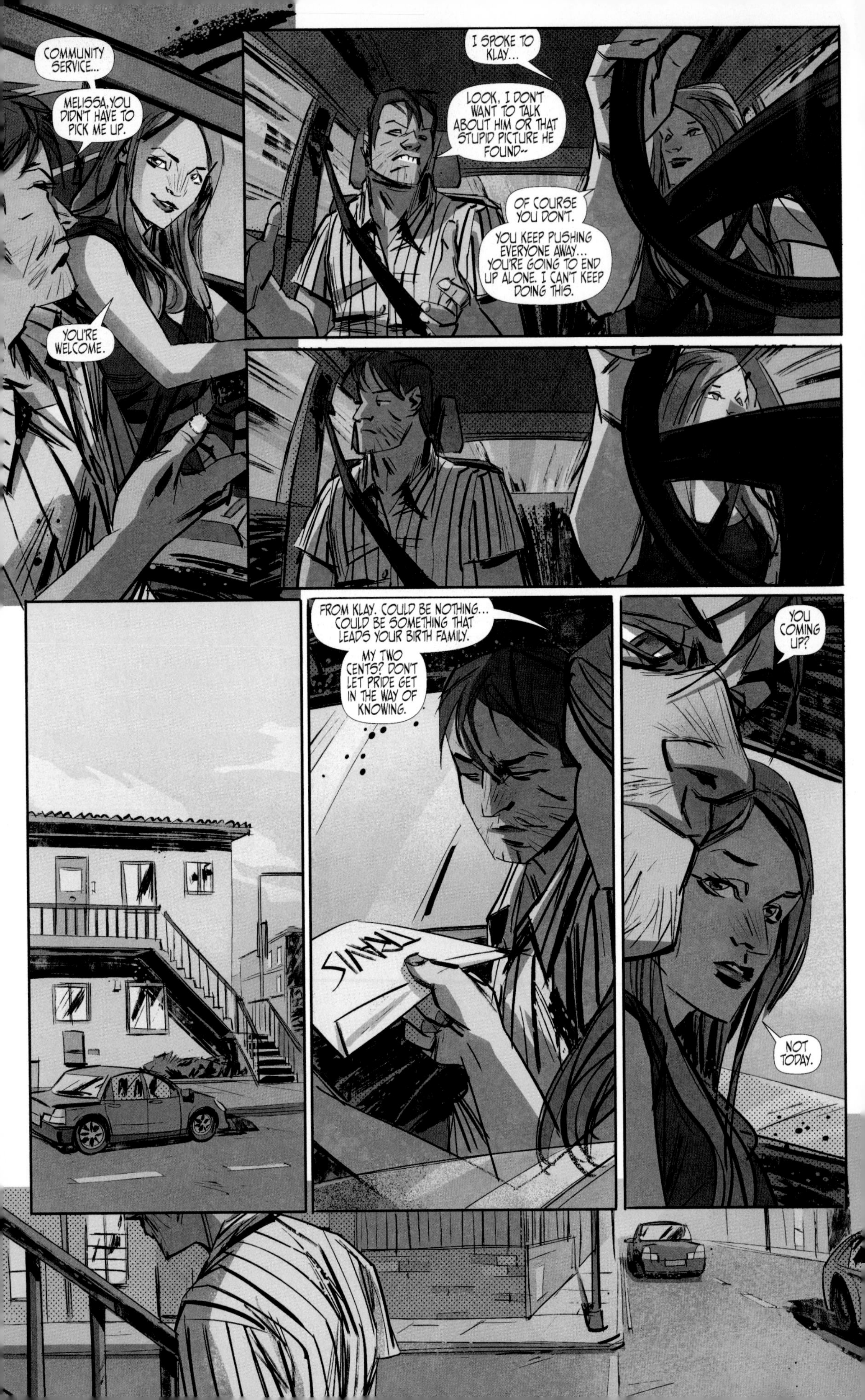
COMMUNITY SERVICE...
MELISSA, YOU DIDN'T HAVE TO PICK ME UP.
YOU'RE WELCOME.
I SPOKE TO KLAY...
LOOK, I DON'T WANT TO TALK ABOUT HIM OR THAT STUPID PICTURE HE FOUND--
OF COURSE YOU DON'T.
YOU KEEP PUSHING EVERYONE AWAY... YOU'RE GOING TO END UP ALONE. I CAN'T KEEP DOING THIS.
FROM KLAY. COULD BE NOTHING... COULD BE SOMETHING THAT LEADS YOUR BIRTH FAMILY.
MY TWO CENTS? DON'T LET PRIDE GET IN THE WAY OF KNOWING.
TRAVIS
YOU COMING UP?
NOT TODAY.

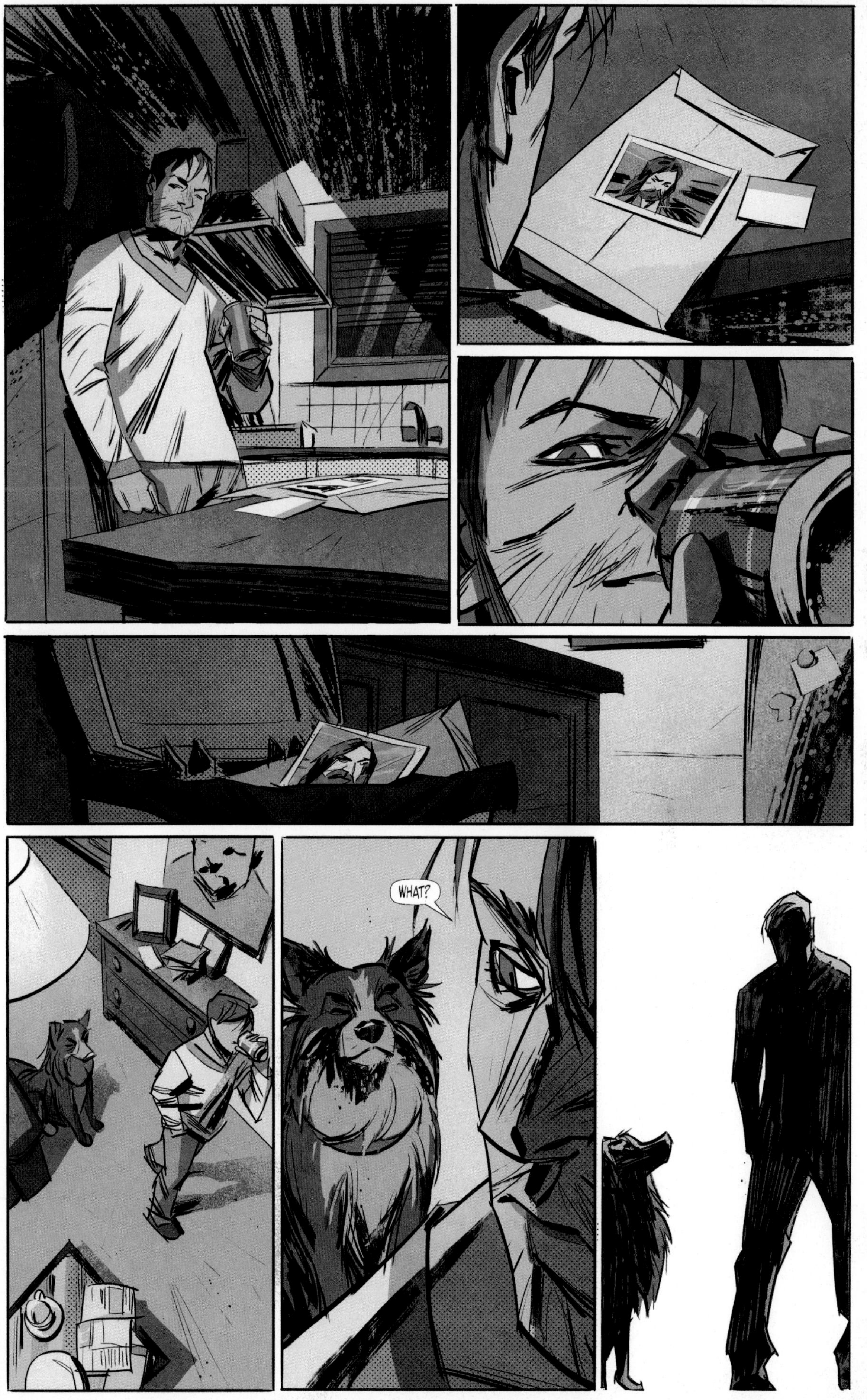
WHAT?

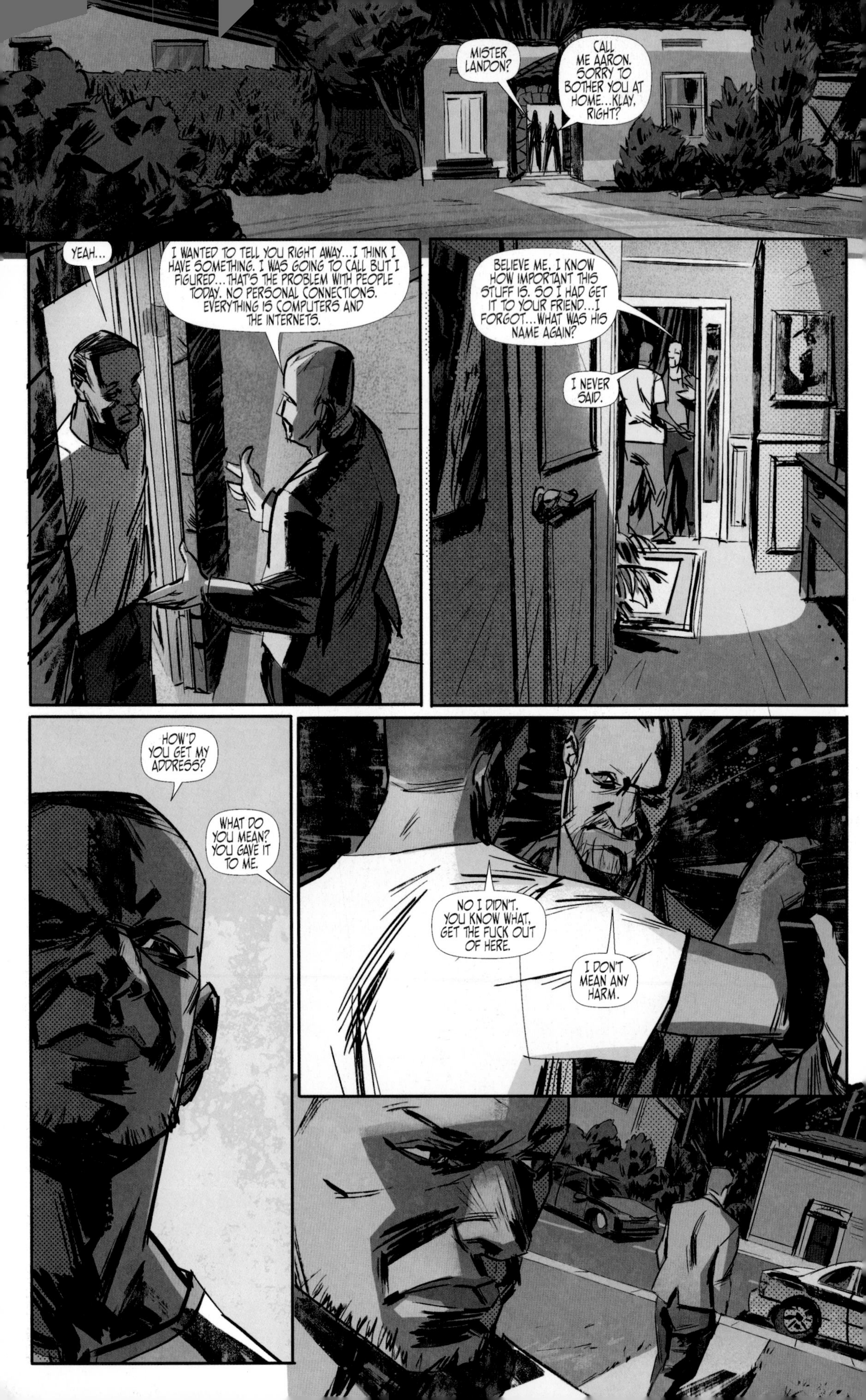
MISTER LANDON?
CALL ME AARON. SORRY TO BOTHER YOU AT HOME...KLAY, RIGHT?
YEAH...
I WANTED TO TELL YOU RIGHT AWAY...I THINK I HAVE SOMETHING. I WAS GOING TO CALL BUT I FIGURED...THAT'S THE PROBLEM WITH PEOPLE TODAY. NO PERSONAL CONNECTIONS. EVERYTHING IS COMPUTERS AND THE INTERNETS.
BELIEVE ME, I KNOW HOW IMPORTANT THIS STUFF IS. SO I HAD GET IT TO YOUR FRIEND...I FORGOT...WHAT WAS HIS NAME AGAIN?
I NEVER SAID.
HOW'D YOU GET MY ADDRESS?
WHAT DO YOU MEAN? YOU GAVE IT TO ME.
NO I DIDN'T. YOU KNOW WHAT, GET THE FUCK OUT OF HERE.
I DON'T MEAN ANY HARM.

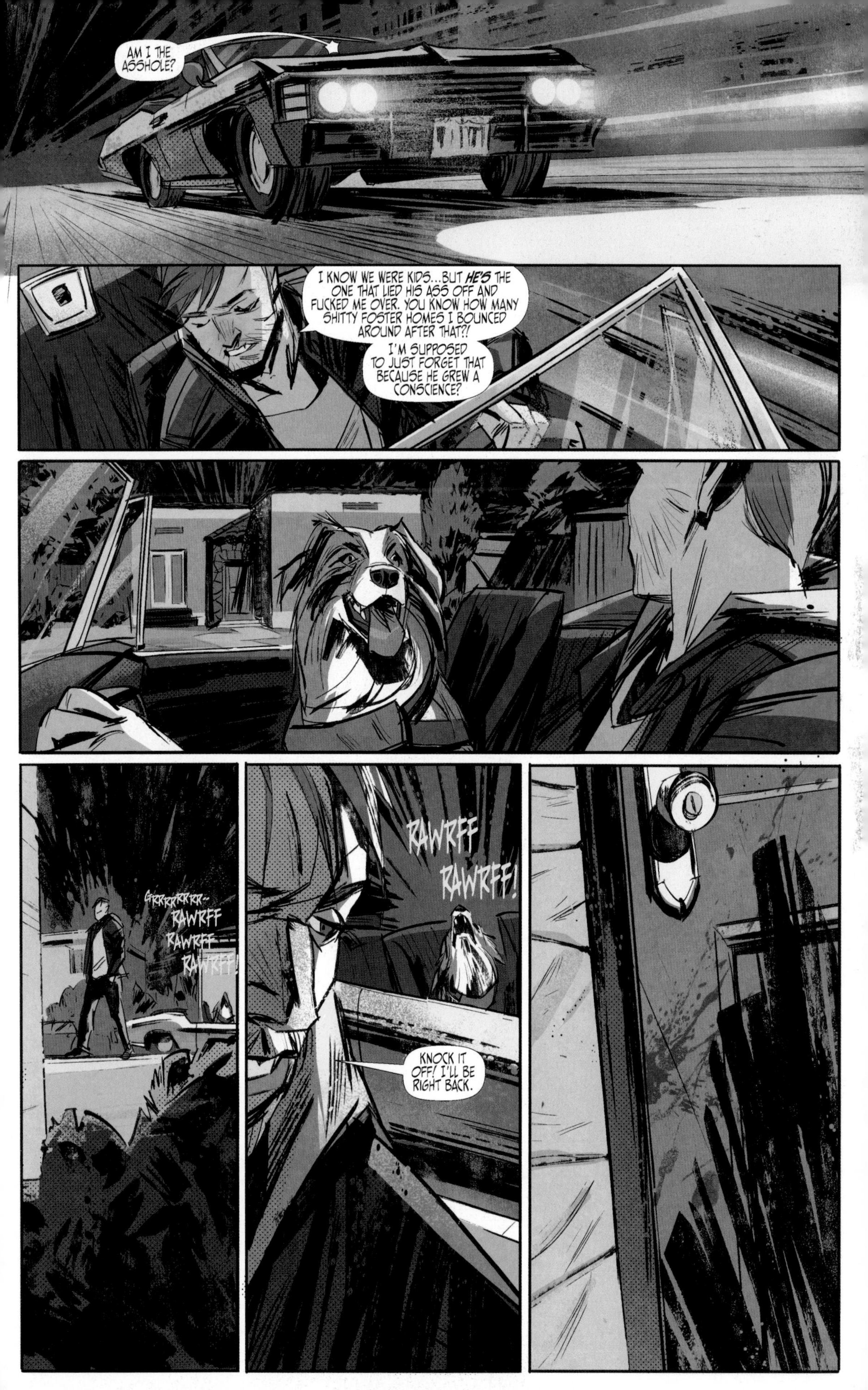
AM I THE ASSHOLE?
I KNOW WE WERE KIDS...BUT HE'S THE ONE THAT LIED HIS ASS OFF AND FUCKED ME OVER. YOU KNOW HOW MANY SHITTY FOSTER HOMES I BOUNCED AROUND AFTER THAT?!
I'M SUPPOSED TO JUST FORGET THAT BECAUSE HE GREW A CONSCIENCE?
GRRRRRRRR-
RAWRFF
RAWRFF
RAWRFF!
RAWRFF
RAWRFF!
KNOCK IT OFF! I'LL BE RIGHT BACK.

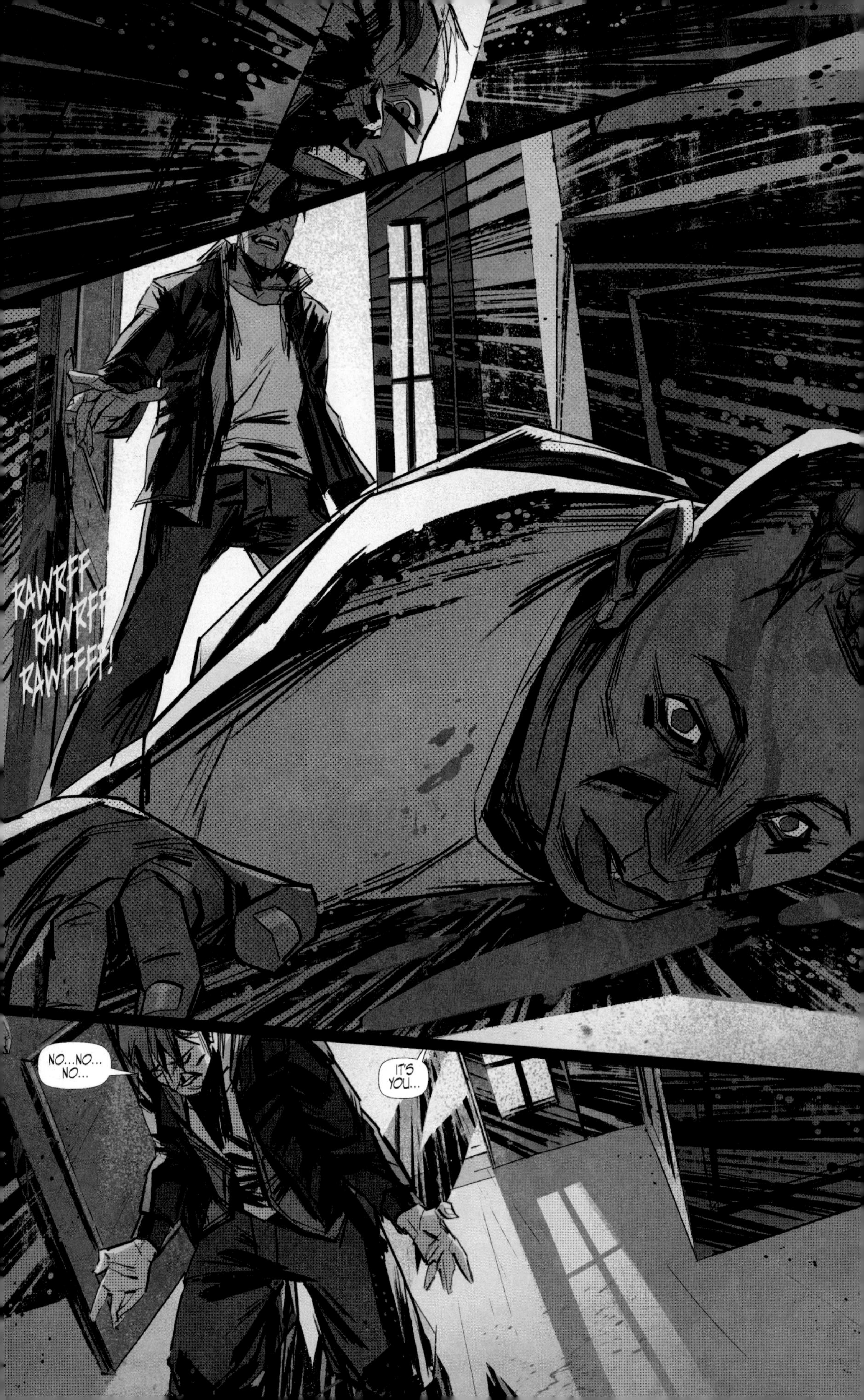
RAWRFF
RAWRFF
RAWFFFF!
NO...NO...
NO...
IT'S
YOU...

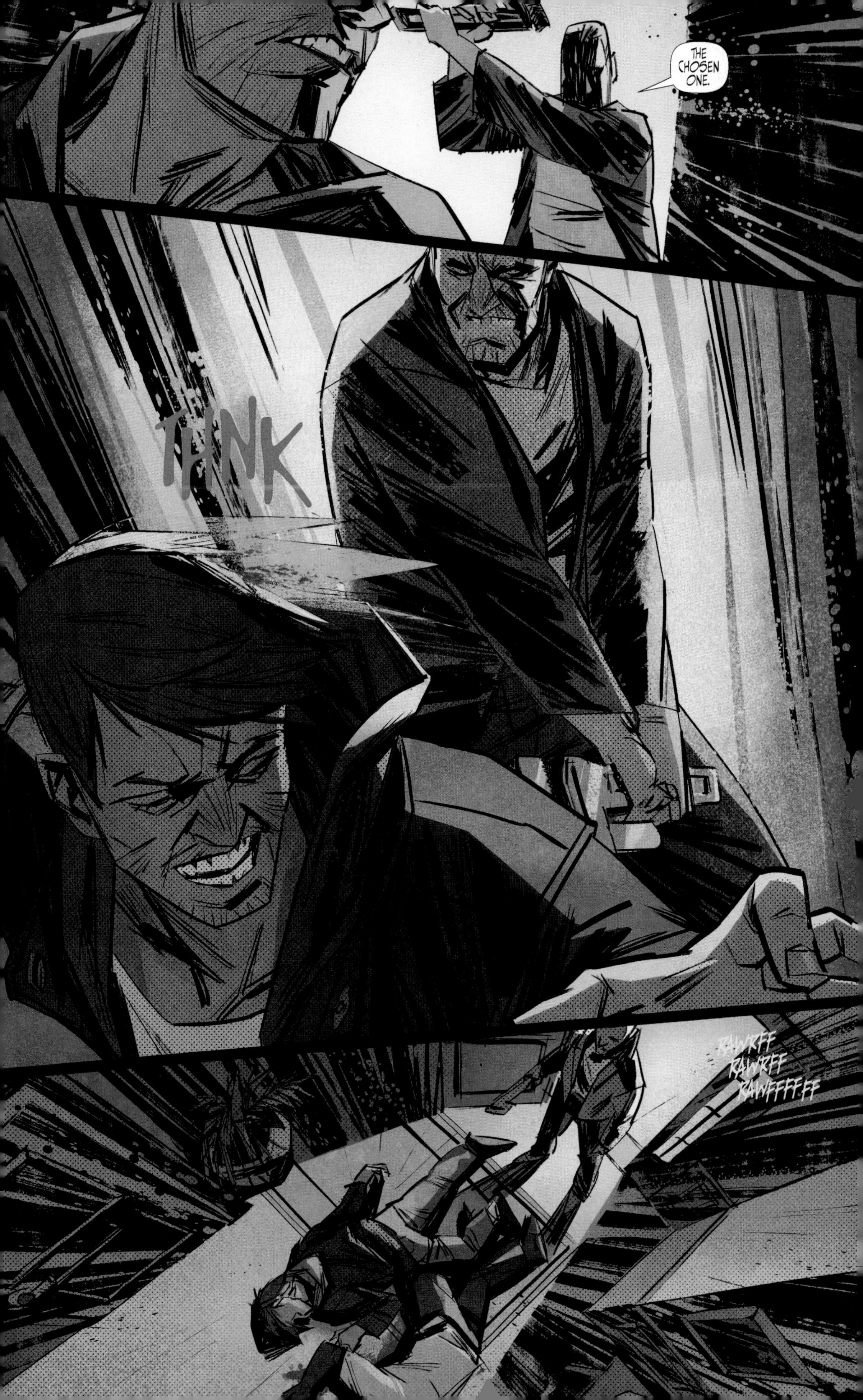
THE CHOSEN ONE.
THNK
RAWRFF
RAWRFF
RAWFFFF FF

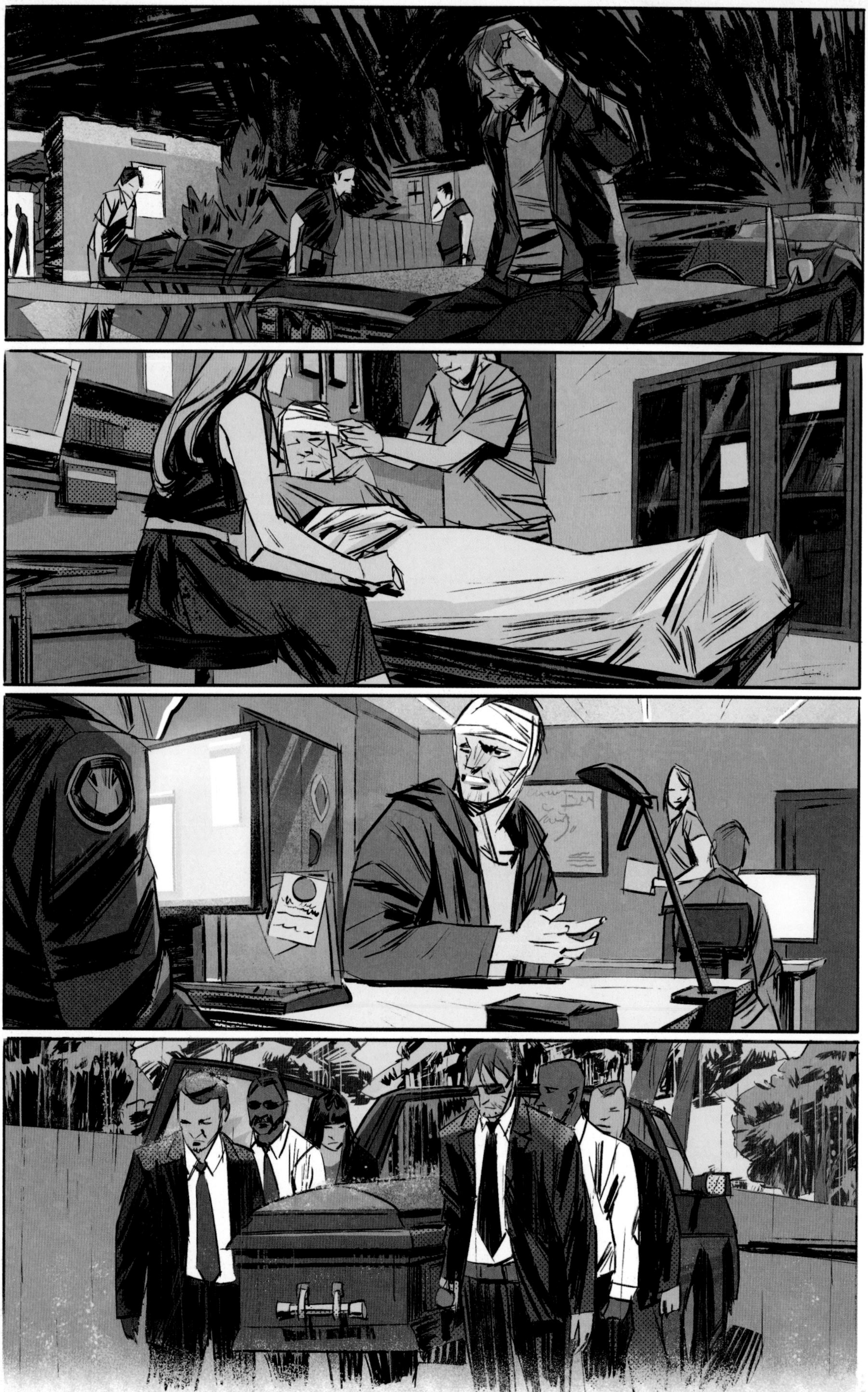

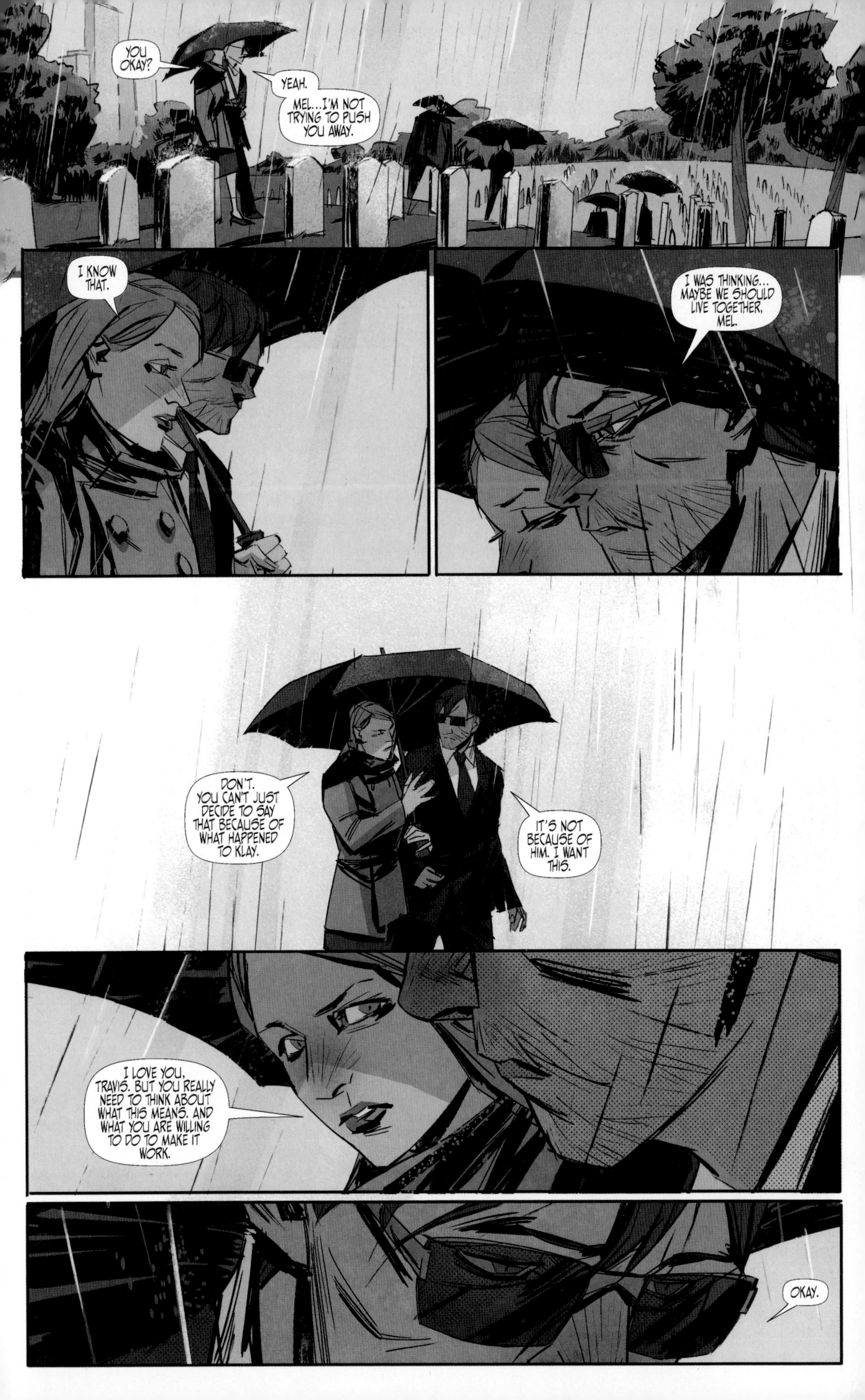
YOU OKAY?
YEAH.
MEL...I'M NOT TRYING TO PUSH YOU AWAY.
I KNOW THAT.
I WAS THINKING... MAYBE WE SHOULD LIVE TOGETHER, MEL.
DON'T. YOU CAN'T JUST DECIDE TO SAY THAT BECAUSE OF WHAT HAPPENED TO KLAY.
IT'S NOT BECAUSE OF HIM. I WANT THIS.
I LOVE YOU, TRAVIS. BUT YOU REALLY NEED TO THINK ABOUT WHAT THIS MEANS. AND WHAT YOU ARE WILLING TO DO TO MAKE IT WORK.
OKAY.

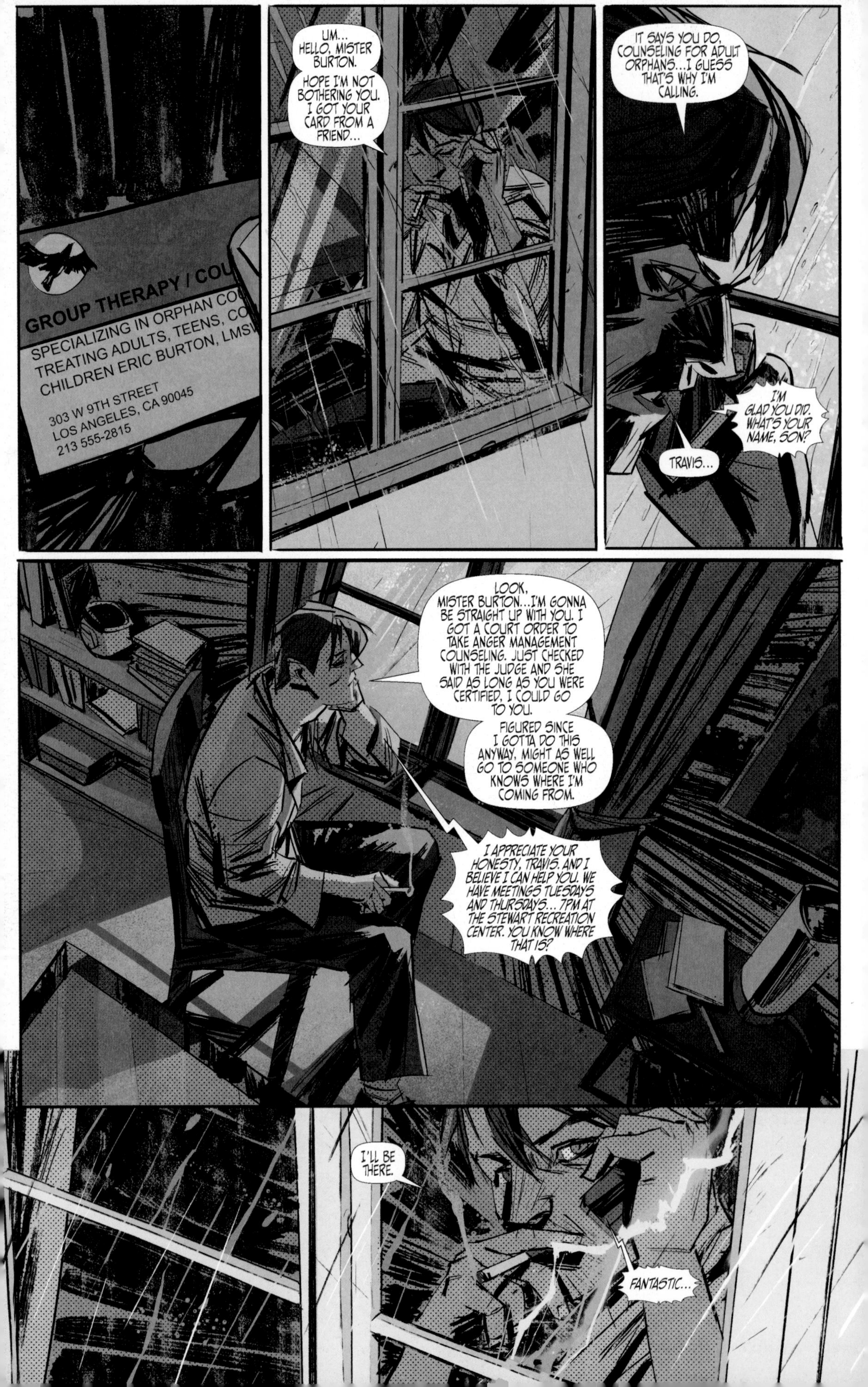
GROUP THERAPY / COU
SPECIALIZING IN ORPHAN COU
TREATING ADULTS, TEENS, CO
CHILDREN ERIC BURTON, LMSW
303 W 9TH STREET
LOS ANGELES, CA 90045
213 555-2815
UM... HELLO, MISTER BURTON.
HOPE I'M NOT BOTHERING YOU. I GOT YOUR CARD FROM A FRIEND...
IT SAYS YOU DO, COUNSELING FOR ADULT ORPHANS...I GUESS THAT'S WHY I'M CALLING.
I'M GLAD YOU DID. WHAT'S YOUR NAME, SON?
TRAVIS...
LOOK, MISTER BURTON...I'M GONNA BE STRAIGHT UP WITH YOU. I GOT A COURT ORDER TO TAKE ANGER MANAGEMENT COUNSELING. JUST CHECKED WITH THE JUDGE AND SHE SAID AS LONG AS YOU WERE CERTIFIED, I COULD GO TO YOU.
FIGURED SINCE I GOTTA DO THIS ANYWAY, MIGHT AS WELL GO TO SOMEONE WHO KNOWS WHERE I'M COMING FROM.
I APPRECIATE YOUR HONESTY, TRAVIS. AND I BELIEVE I CAN HELP YOU. WE HAVE MEETINGS TUESDAYS AND THURSDAYS... 7PM AT THE STEWART RECREATION CENTER. YOU KNOW WHERE THAT IS?
I'LL BE THERE.
FANTASTIC...

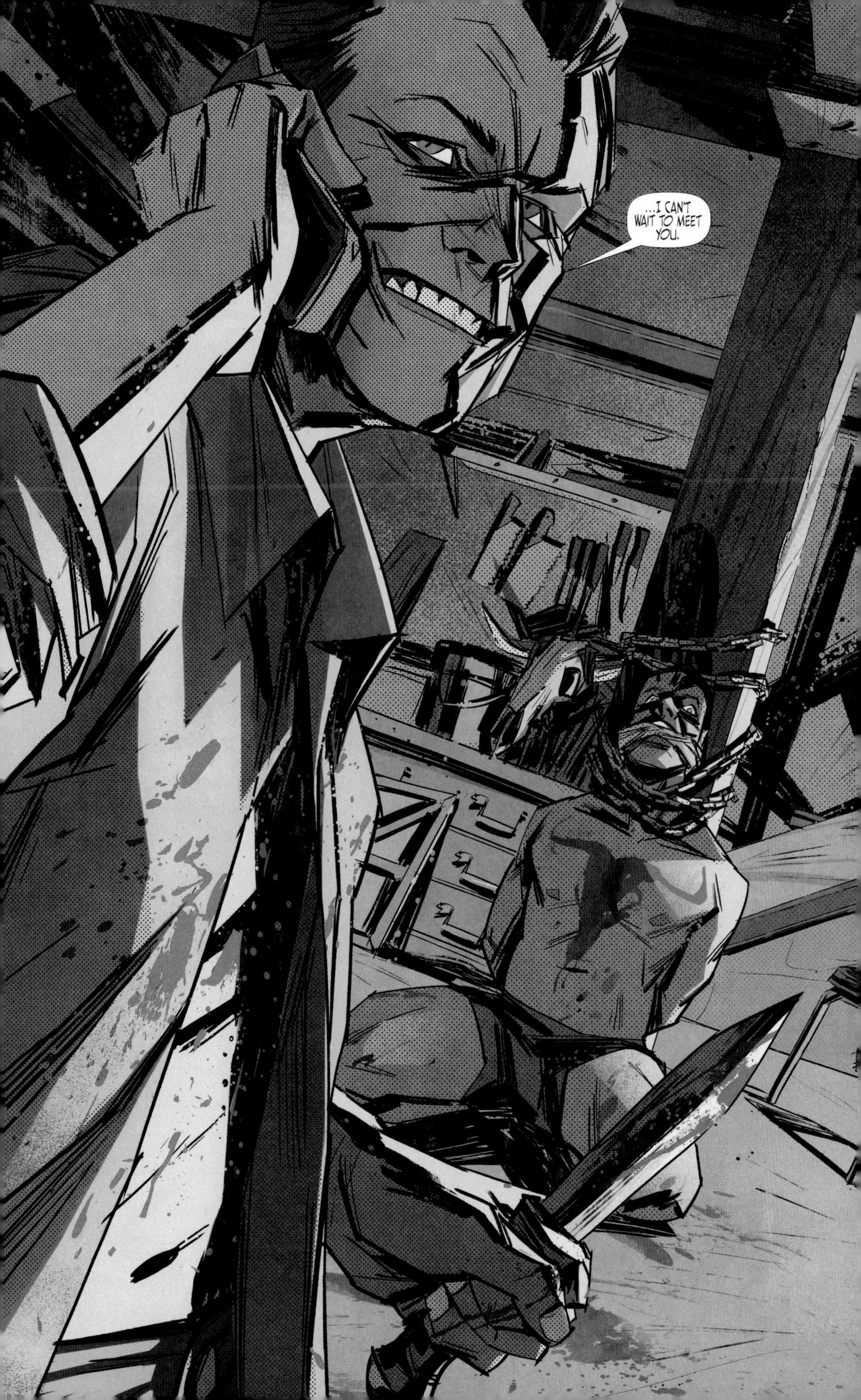
...I CAN'T WAIT TO MEET YOU.

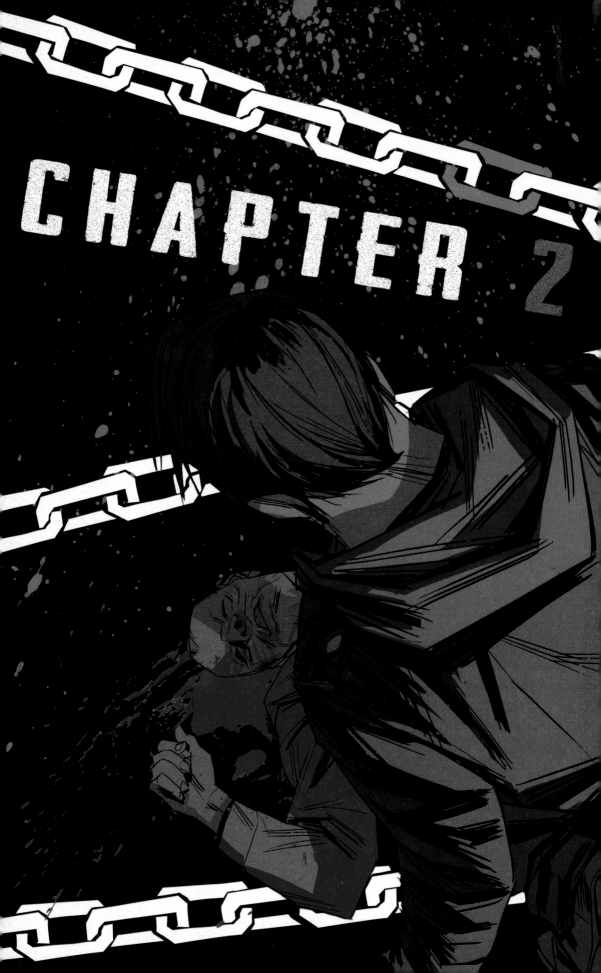

CHAPTER 2

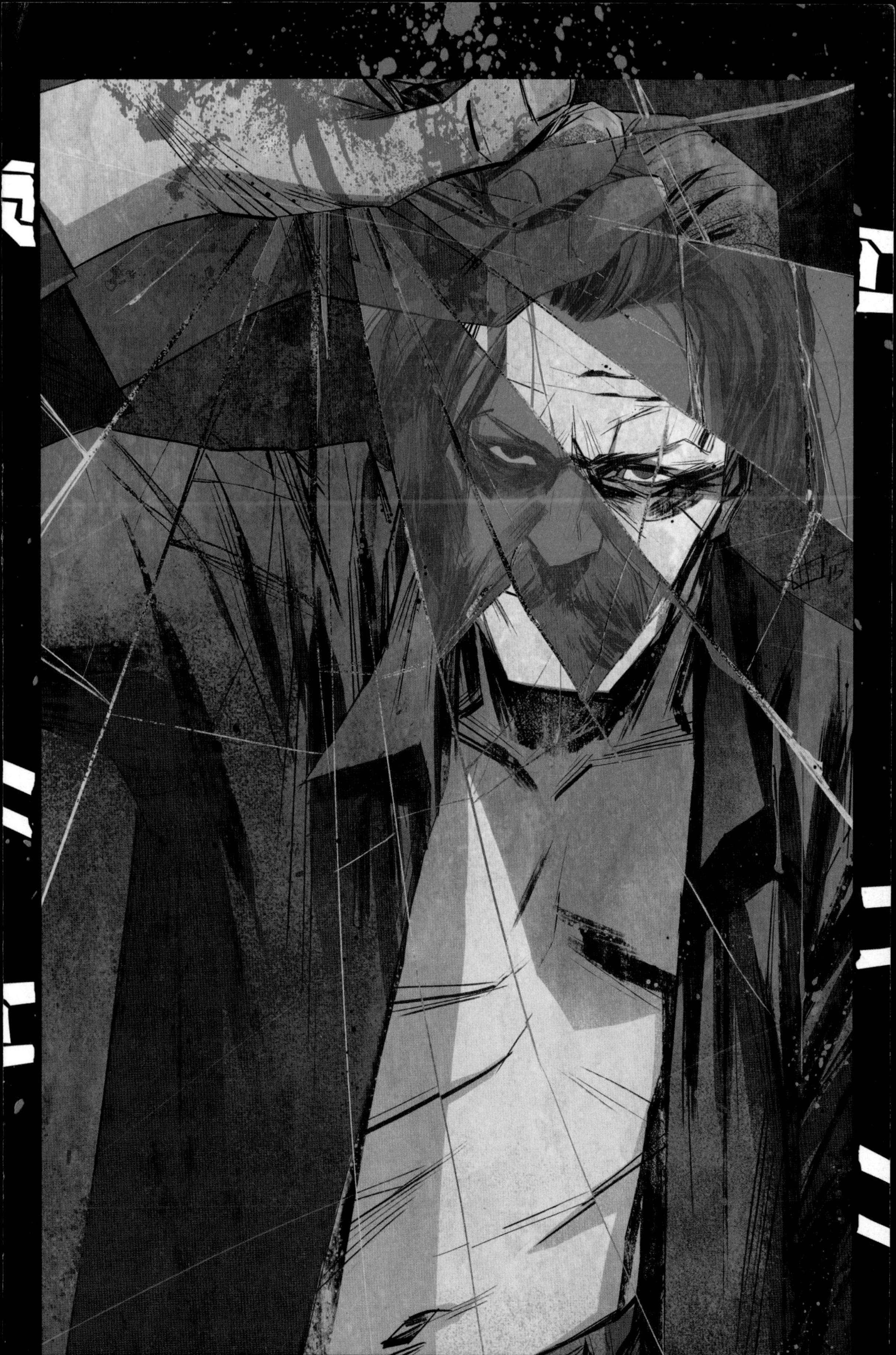

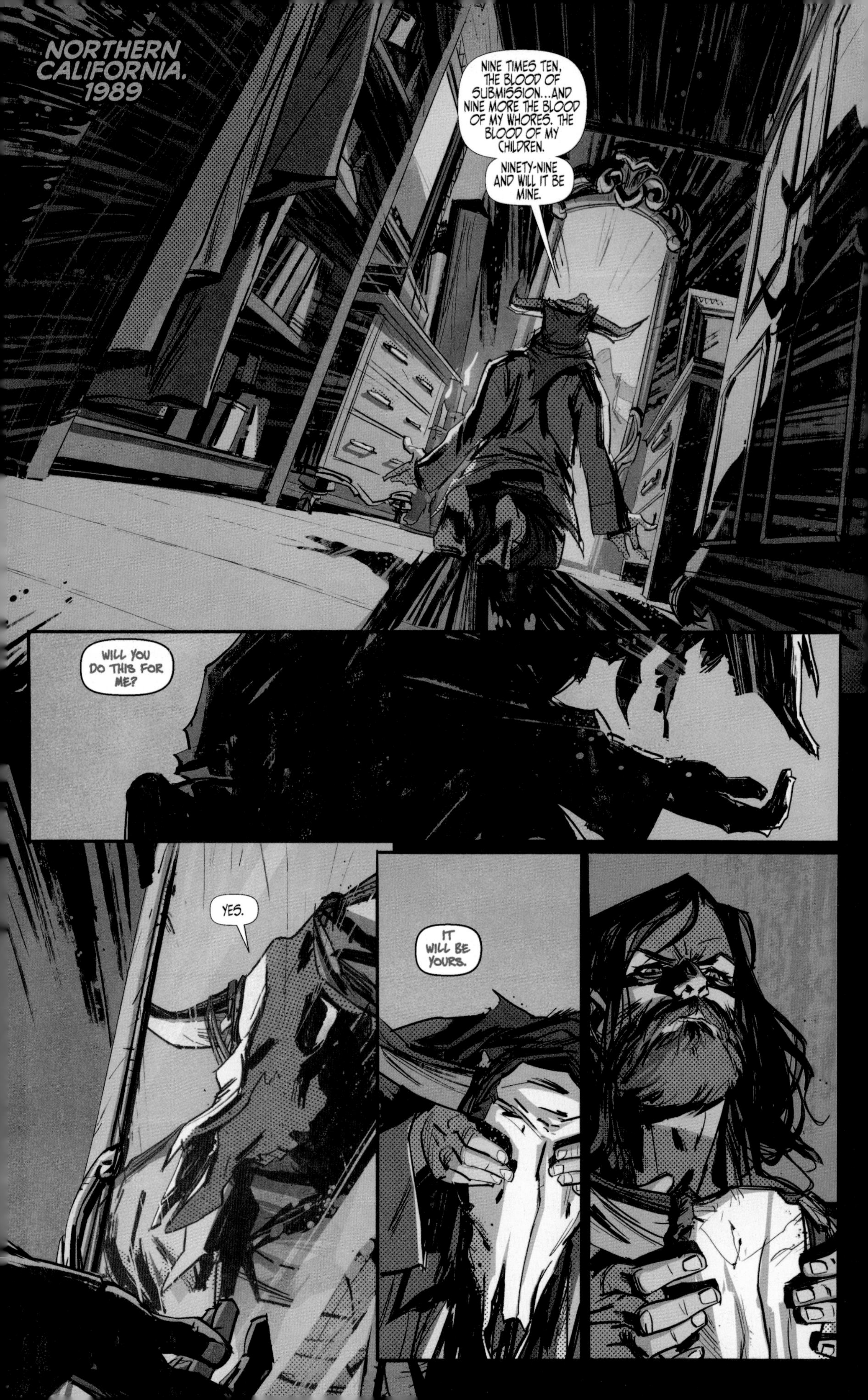
NORTHERN CALIFORNIA. 1989
NINE TIMES TEN, THE BLOOD OF SUBMISSION...AND NINE MORE THE BLOOD OF MY WHORES. THE BLOOD OF MY CHILDREN.
NINETY-NINE AND WILL IT BE MINE.
WILL YOU DO THIS FOR ME?
YES.
IT WILL BE YOURS.

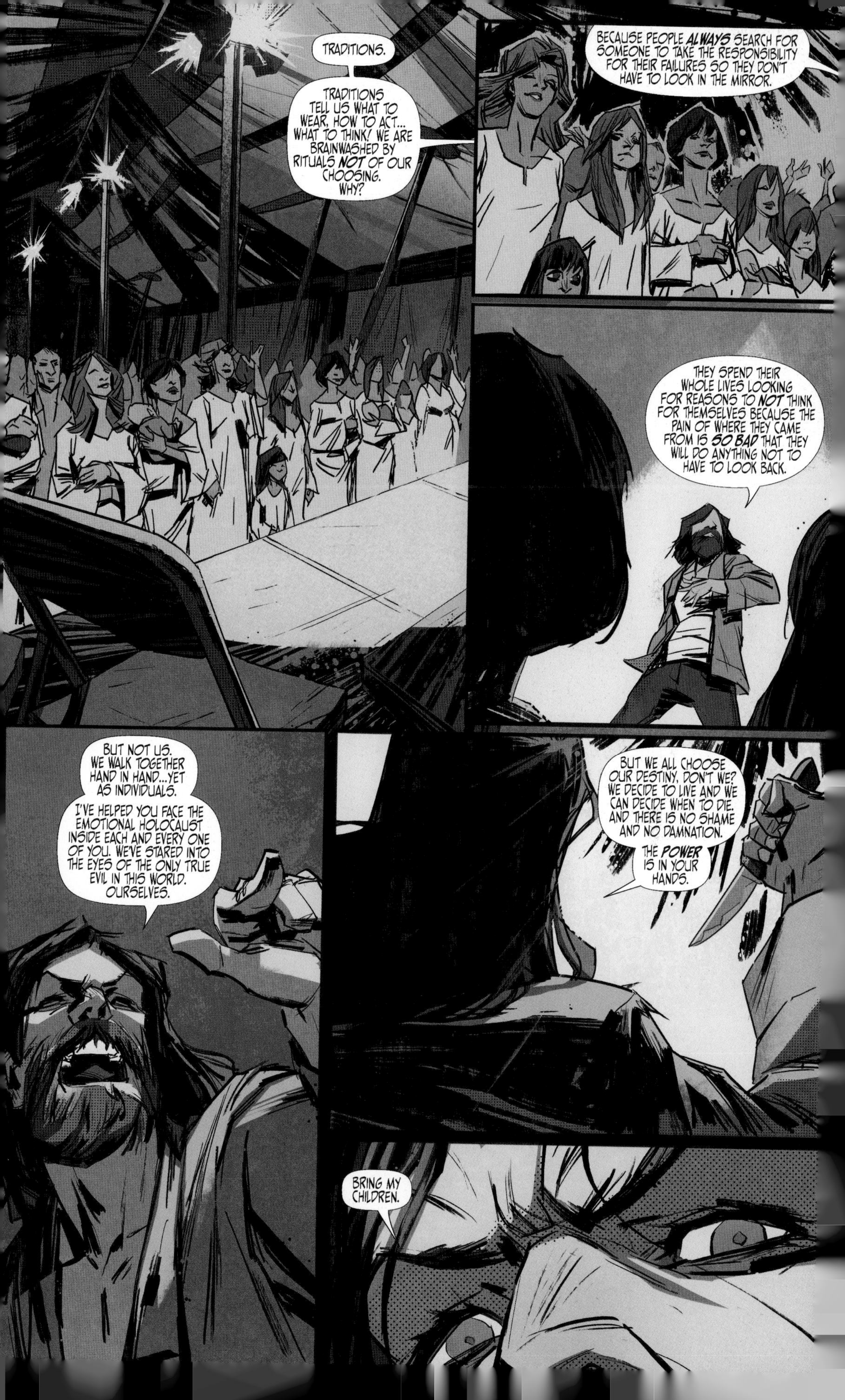
TRADITIONS.
TRADITIONS TELL US WHAT TO WEAR, HOW TO ACT... WHAT TO THINK! WE ARE BRAINWASHED BY RITUALS NOT OF OUR CHOOSING. WHY?
BECAUSE PEOPLE ALWAYS SEARCH FOR SOMEONE TO TAKE THE RESPONSIBILITY FOR THEIR FAILURES SO THEY DON'T HAVE TO LOOK IN THE MIRROR.
THEY SPEND THEIR WHOLE LIVES LOOKING FOR REASONS TO NOT THINK FOR THEMSELVES BECAUSE THE PAIN OF WHERE THEY CAME FROM IS SO BAD THAT THEY WILL DO ANYTHING NOT TO HAVE TO LOOK BACK.
BUT NOT US. WE WALK TOGETHER HAND IN HAND...YET AS INDIVIDUALS.
I'VE HELPED YOU FACE THE EMOTIONAL HOLOCAUST INSIDE EACH AND EVERY ONE OF YOU. WE'VE STARED INTO THE EYES OF THE ONLY TRUE EVIL IN THIS WORLD. OURSELVES.
BUT WE ALL CHOOSE OUR DESTINY, DON'T WE? WE DECIDE TO LIVE AND WE CAN DECIDE WHEN TO DIE. AND THERE IS NO SHAME AND NO DAMNATION.
THE POWER IS IN YOUR HANDS.
BRING MY CHILDREN.

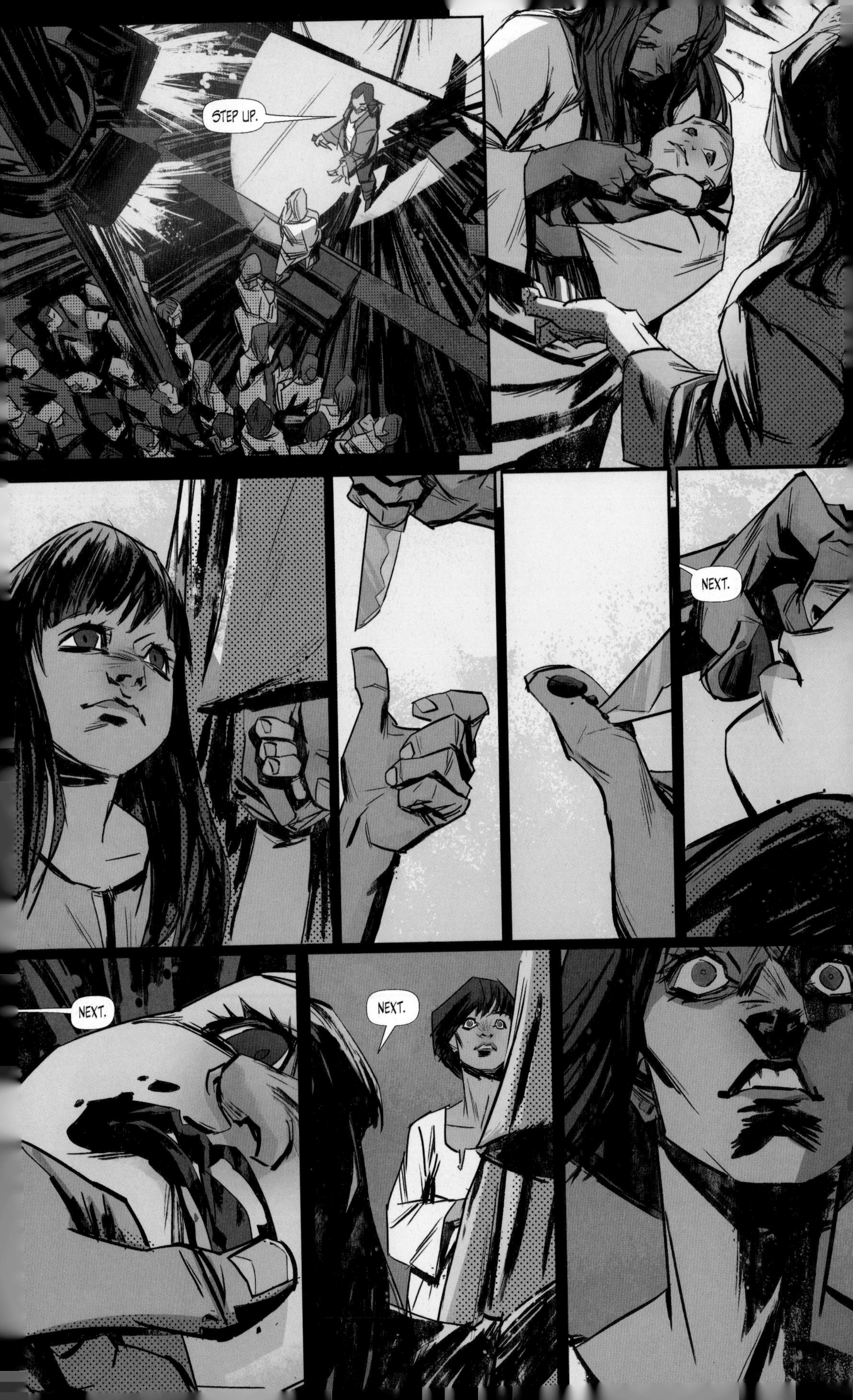
STEP UP.
NEXT.
NEXT.
NEXT.

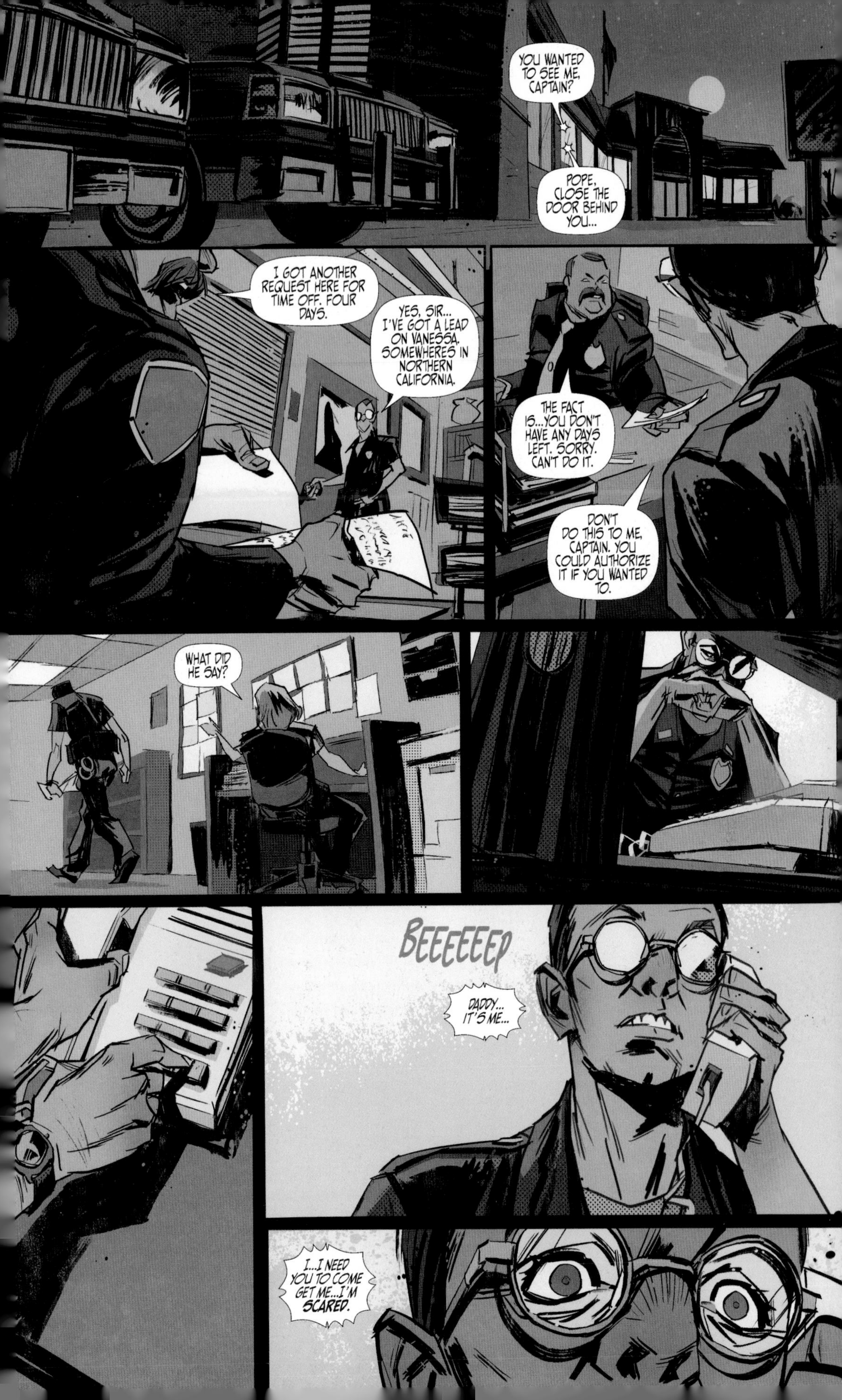
YOU WANTED TO SEE ME, CAPTAIN?
POPE, CLOSE THE DOOR BEHIND YOU...
I GOT ANOTHER REQUEST HERE FOR TIME OFF. FOUR DAYS.
YES, SIR... I'VE GOT A LEAD ON VANESSA. SOMEWHERES IN NORTHERN CALIFORNIA.
THE FACT IS...YOU DON'T HAVE ANY DAYS LEFT. SORRY. CAN'T DO IT.
DON'T DO THIS TO ME, CAPTAIN. YOU COULD AUTHORIZE IT IF YOU WANTED TO.
WHAT DID HE SAY?
BEEEEEEP
DADDY... IT'S ME...
I...I NEED YOU TO COME GET ME...I'M SCARED.

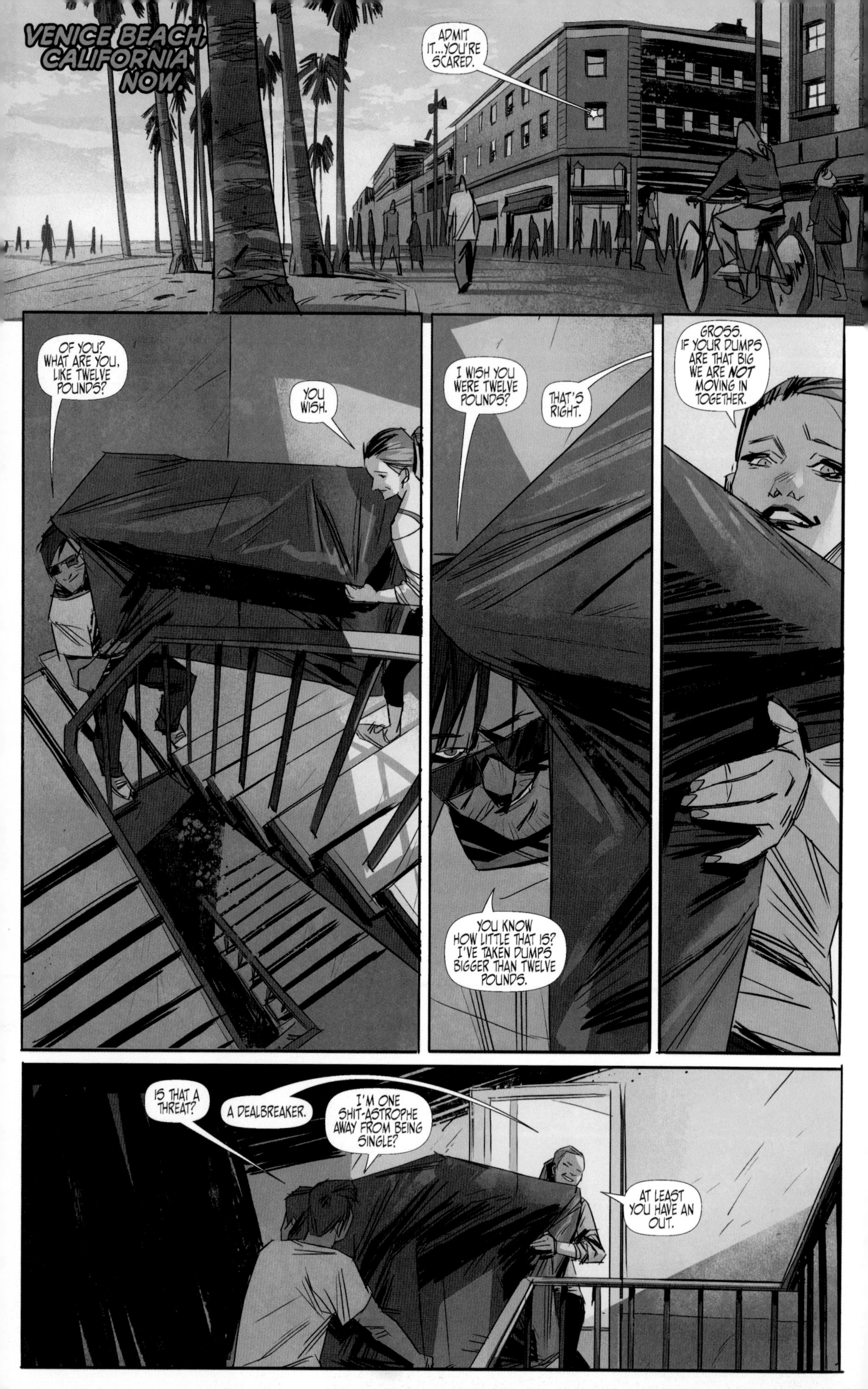
VENICE BEACH, CALIFORNIA NOW.
ADMIT IT...YOU'RE SCARED.
OF YOU? WHAT ARE YOU, LIKE TWELVE POUNDS?
YOU WISH.
I WISH YOU WERE TWELVE POUNDS?
THAT'S RIGHT.
YOU KNOW HOW LITTLE THAT IS? I'VE TAKEN DUMPS BIGGER THAN TWELVE POUNDS.
GROSS. IF YOUR DUMPS ARE THAT BIG WE ARE NOT MOVING IN TOGETHER.
IS THAT A THREAT?
A DEALBREAKER.
I'M ONE SHIT-ASTROPHE AWAY FROM BEING SINGLE?
AT LEAST YOU HAVE AN OUT.

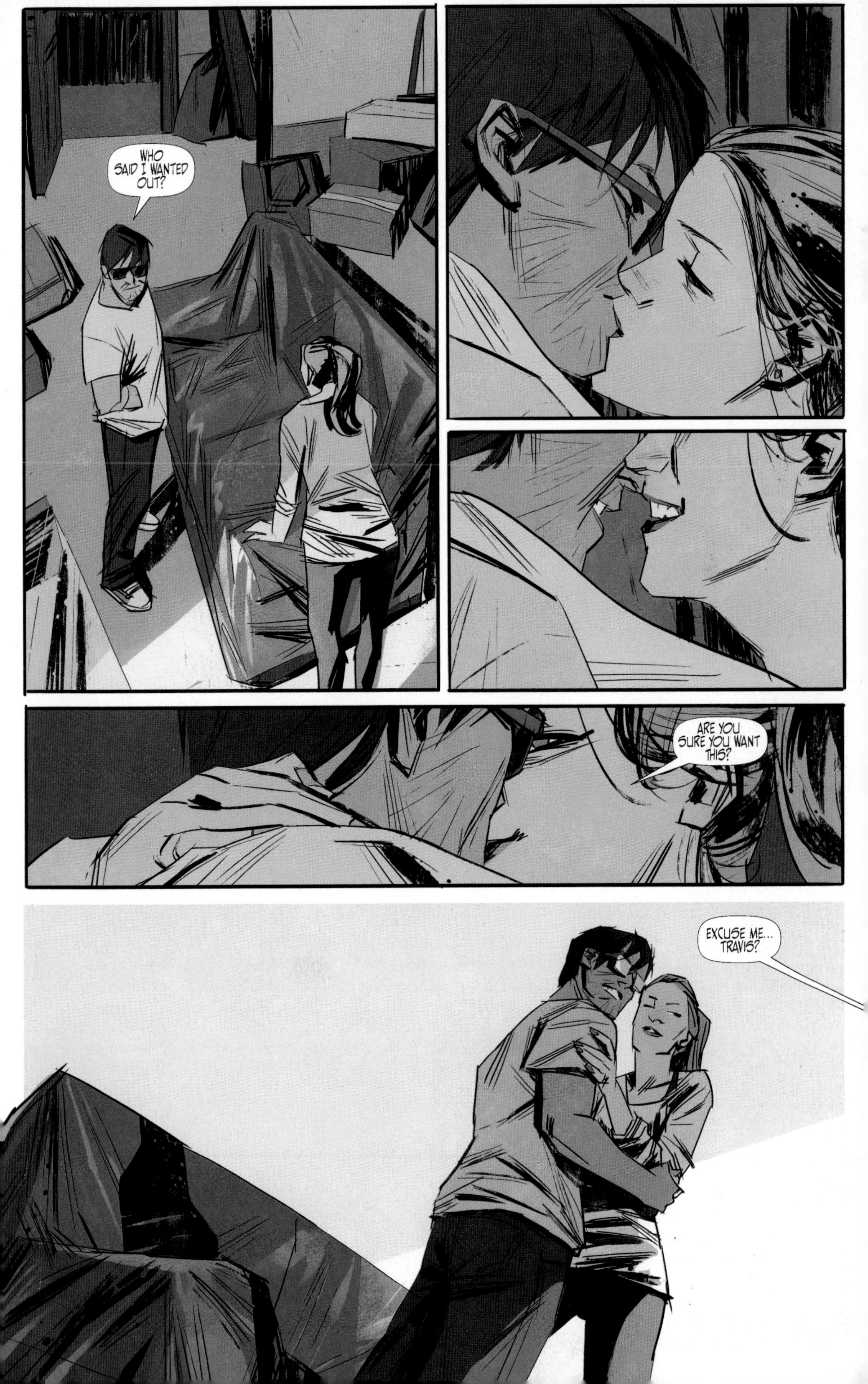
WHO SAID I WANTED OUT?
ARE YOU SURE YOU WANT THIS?
EXCUSE ME... TRAVIS?

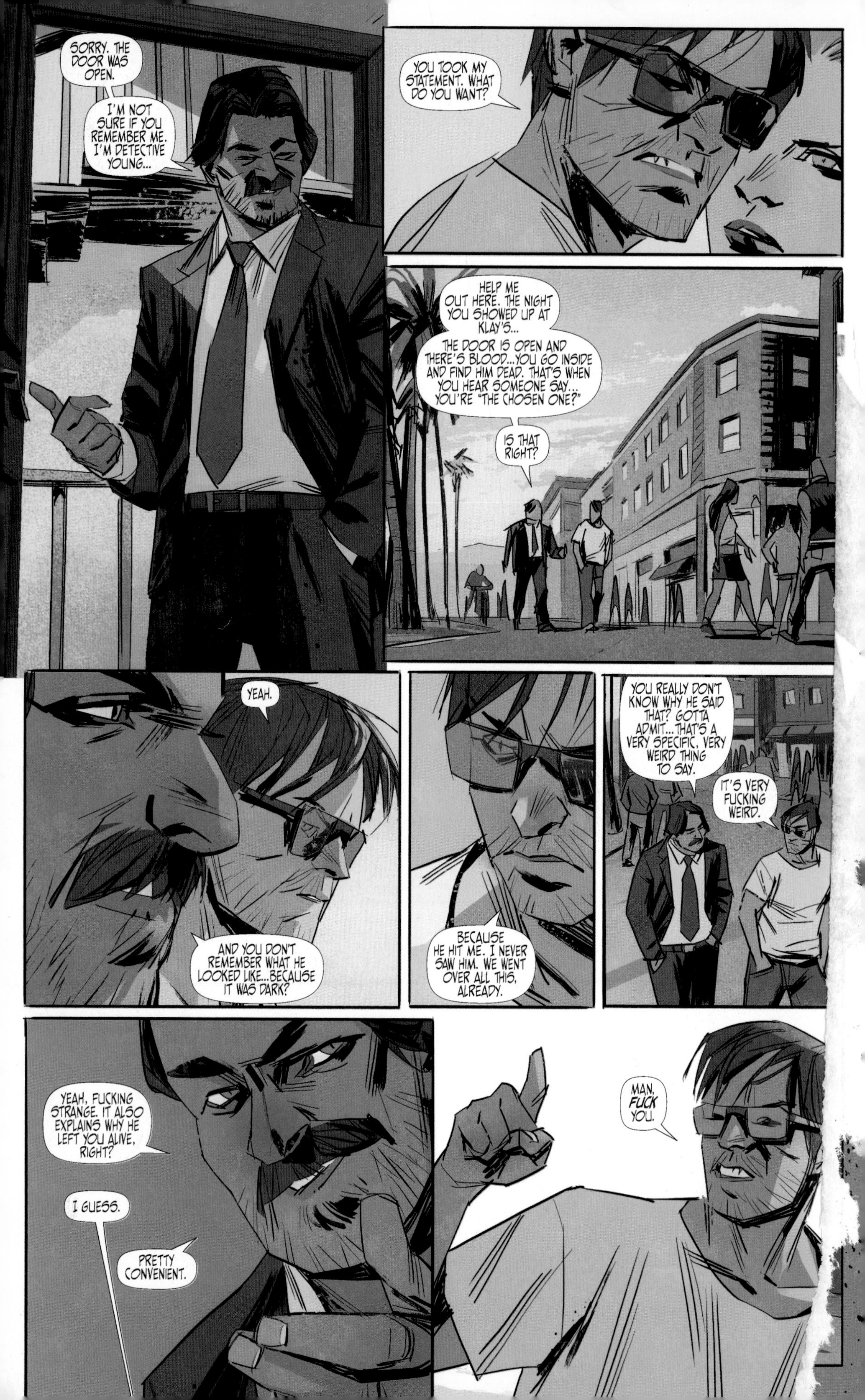
SORRY. THE DOOR WAS OPEN.
I'M NOT SURE IF YOU REMEMBER ME. I'M DETECTIVE YOUNG...
YOU TOOK MY STATEMENT. WHAT DO YOU WANT?
HELP ME OUT HERE. THE NIGHT YOU SHOWED UP AT KLAY'S...
THE DOOR IS OPEN AND THERE'S BLOOD...YOU GO INSIDE AND FIND HIM DEAD. THAT'S WHEN YOU HEAR SOMEONE SAY... YOU'RE "THE CHOSEN ONE?"
IS THAT RIGHT?
YEAH.
AND YOU DON'T REMEMBER WHAT HE LOOKED LIKE...BECAUSE IT WAS DARK?
BECAUSE HE HIT ME. I NEVER SAW HIM. WE WENT OVER ALL THIS, ALREADY.
YOU REALLY DON'T KNOW WHY HE SAID THAT? GOTTA ADMIT...THAT'S A VERY SPECIFIC, VERY WEIRD THING TO SAY.
IT'S VERY FUCKING WEIRD.
YEAH, FUCKING STRANGE. IT ALSO EXPLAINS WHY HE LEFT YOU ALIVE, RIGHT?
I GUESS.
PRETTY CONVENIENT.
MAN, **FUCK** YOU.

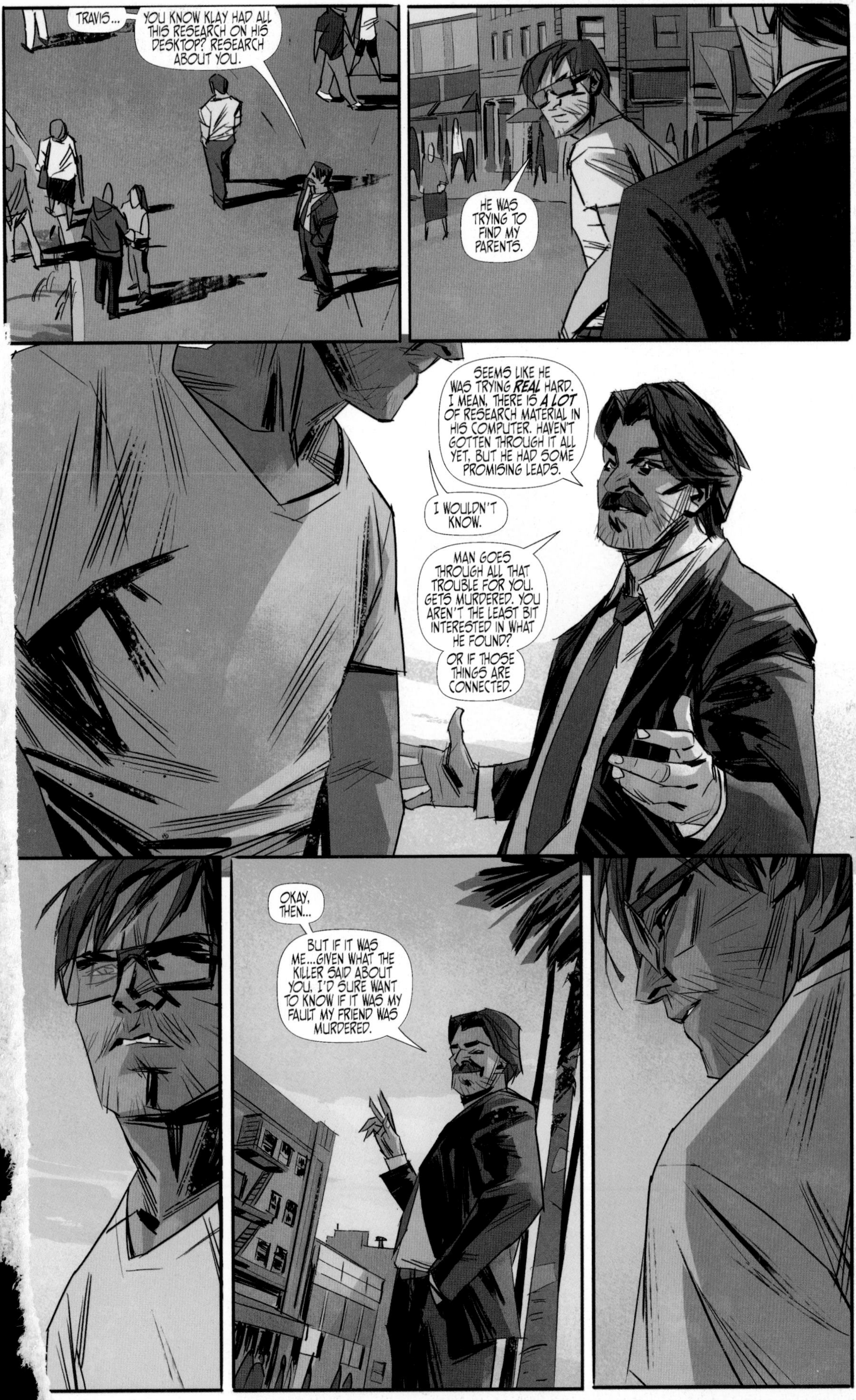
TRAVIS...
YOU KNOW KLAY HAD ALL THIS RESEARCH ON HIS DESKTOP? RESEARCH ABOUT YOU.
HE WAS TRYING TO FIND MY PARENTS.
SEEMS LIKE HE WAS TRYING *REAL* HARD. I MEAN, THERE IS *A LOT* OF RESEARCH MATERIAL IN HIS COMPUTER. HAVEN'T GOTTEN THROUGH IT ALL YET, BUT HE HAD SOME PROMISING LEADS.
I WOULDN'T KNOW.
MAN GOES THROUGH ALL THAT TROUBLE FOR YOU. GETS MURDERED. YOU AREN'T THE LEAST BIT INTERESTED IN WHAT HE FOUND?
OR IF THOSE THINGS ARE CONNECTED.
OKAY, THEN...
BUT IF IT WAS ME...GIVEN WHAT THE KILLER SAID ABOUT YOU, I'D SURE WANT TO KNOW IF IT WAS MY FAULT MY FRIEND WAS MURDERED.

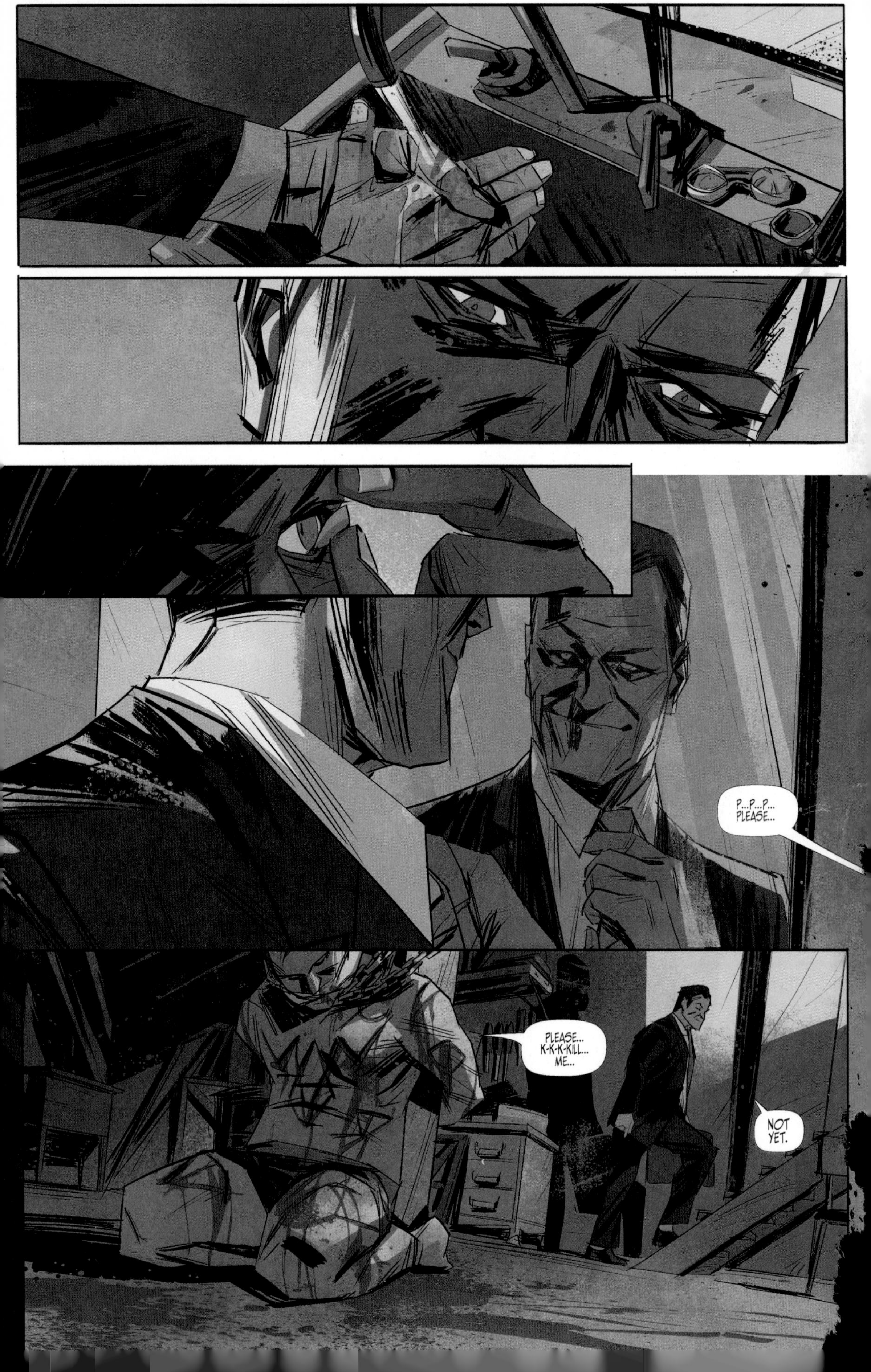
P...P...P...
PLEASE...
PLEASE...
K-K-K-KILL...
ME...
NOT
YET.

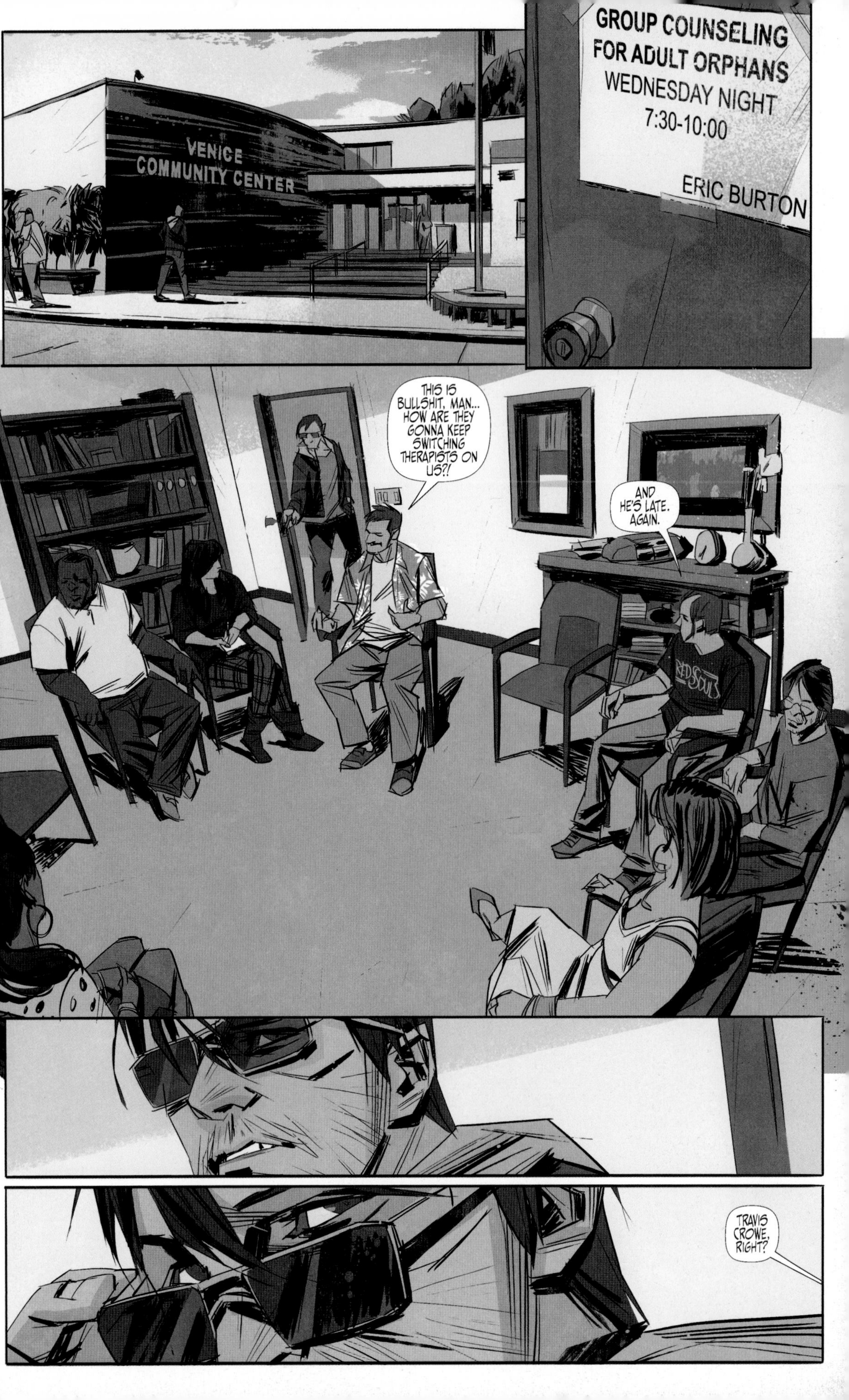
VENICE
COMMUNITY CENTER
GROUP COUNSELING
FOR ADULT ORPHANS
WEDNESDAY NIGHT
7:30-10:00
ERIC BURTON
THIS IS BULLSHIT, MAN... HOW ARE THEY GONNA KEEP SWITCHING THERAPISTS ON US?!
AND HE'S LATE. AGAIN.
TRAVIS CROWE, RIGHT?

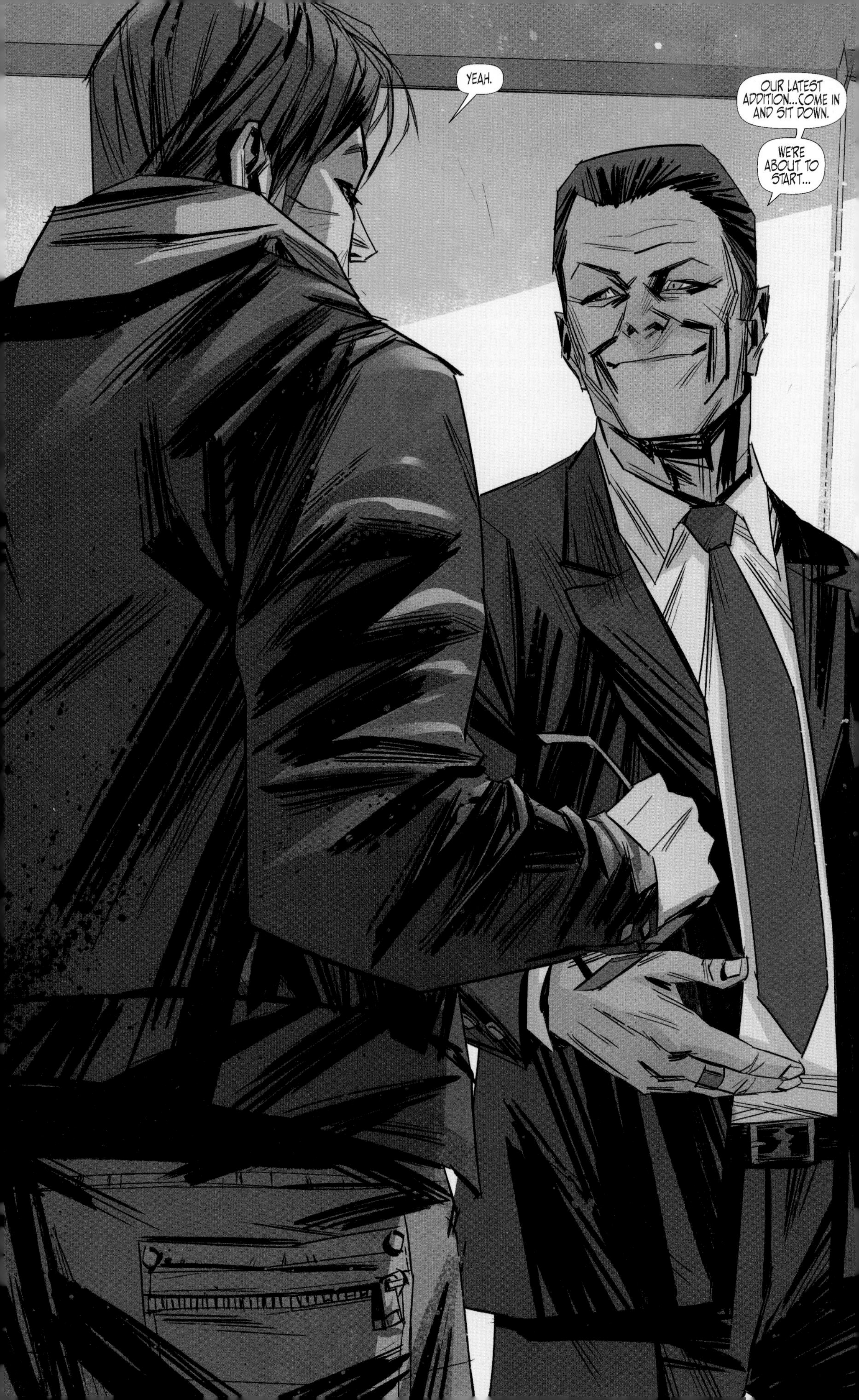
YEAH.
OUR LATEST ADDITION...COME IN AND SIT DOWN.
WE'RE ABOUT TO START...

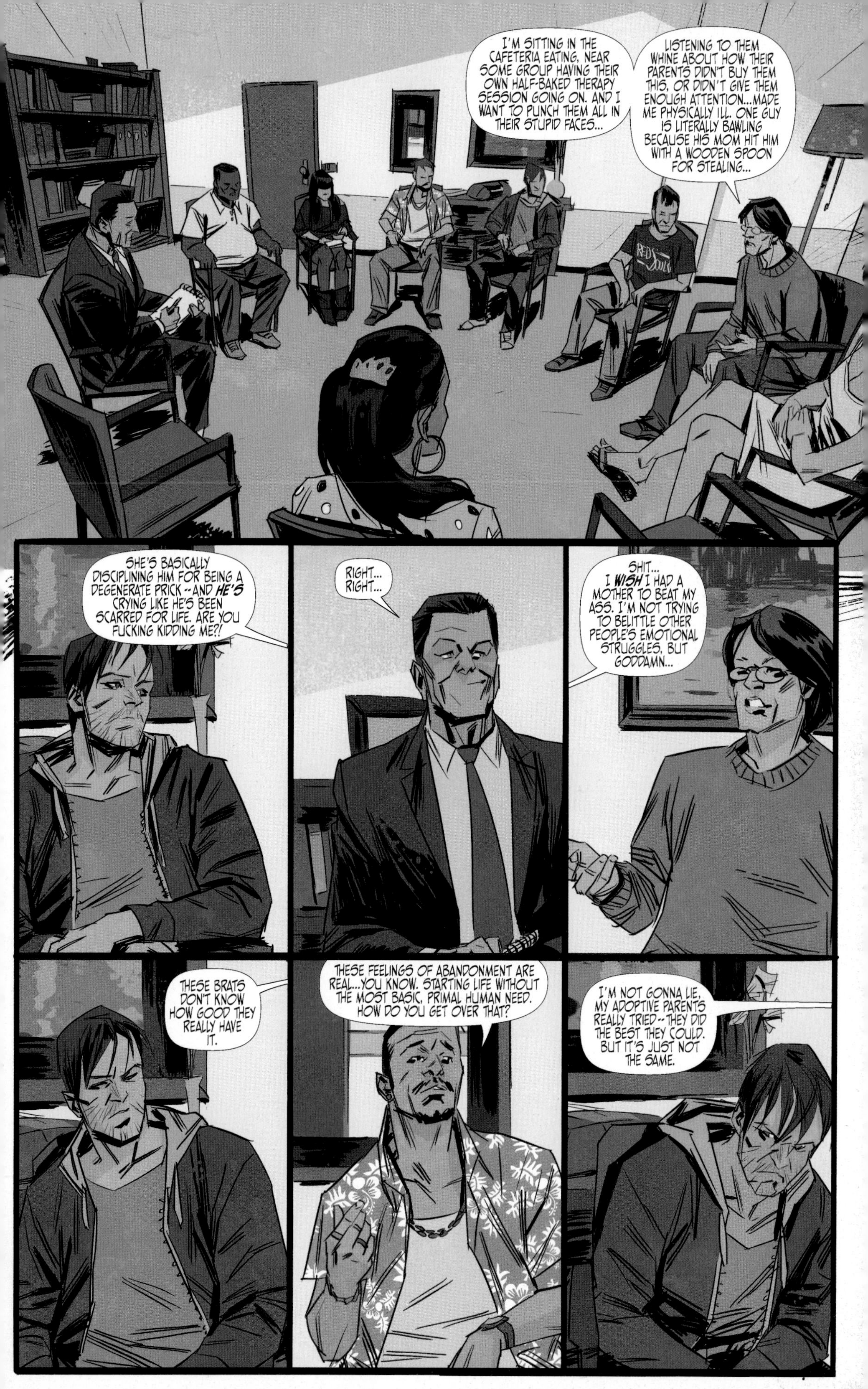
I'M SITTING IN THE CAFETERIA EATING, NEAR SOME GROUP HAVING THEIR OWN HALF-BAKED THERAPY SESSION GOING ON. AND I WANT TO PUNCH THEM ALL IN THEIR STUPID FACES...
LISTENING TO THEM WHINE ABOUT HOW THEIR PARENTS DIDN'T BUY THEM THIS, OR DIDN'T GIVE THEM ENOUGH ATTENTION...MADE ME PHYSICALLY ILL. ONE GUY IS LITERALLY BAWLING BECAUSE HIS MOM HIT HIM WITH A WOODEN SPOON FOR STEALING...
SHE'S BASICALLY DISCIPLINING HIM FOR BEING A DEGENERATE PRICK --AND HE'S CRYING LIKE HE'S BEEN SCARRED FOR LIFE. ARE YOU FUCKING KIDDING ME?!
RIGHT... RIGHT...
SHIT... I WISH I HAD A MOTHER TO BEAT MY ASS. I'M NOT TRYING TO BELITTLE OTHER PEOPLE'S EMOTIONAL STRUGGLES, BUT GODDAMN...
THESE BRATS DON'T KNOW HOW GOOD THEY REALLY HAVE IT.
THESE FEELINGS OF ABANDONMENT ARE REAL...YOU KNOW. STARTING LIFE WITHOUT THE MOST BASIC, PRIMAL HUMAN NEED. HOW DO YOU GET OVER THAT?
I'M NOT GONNA LIE, MY ADOPTIVE PARENTS REALLY TRIED--THEY DID THE BEST THEY COULD. BUT IT'S JUST NOT THE SAME.

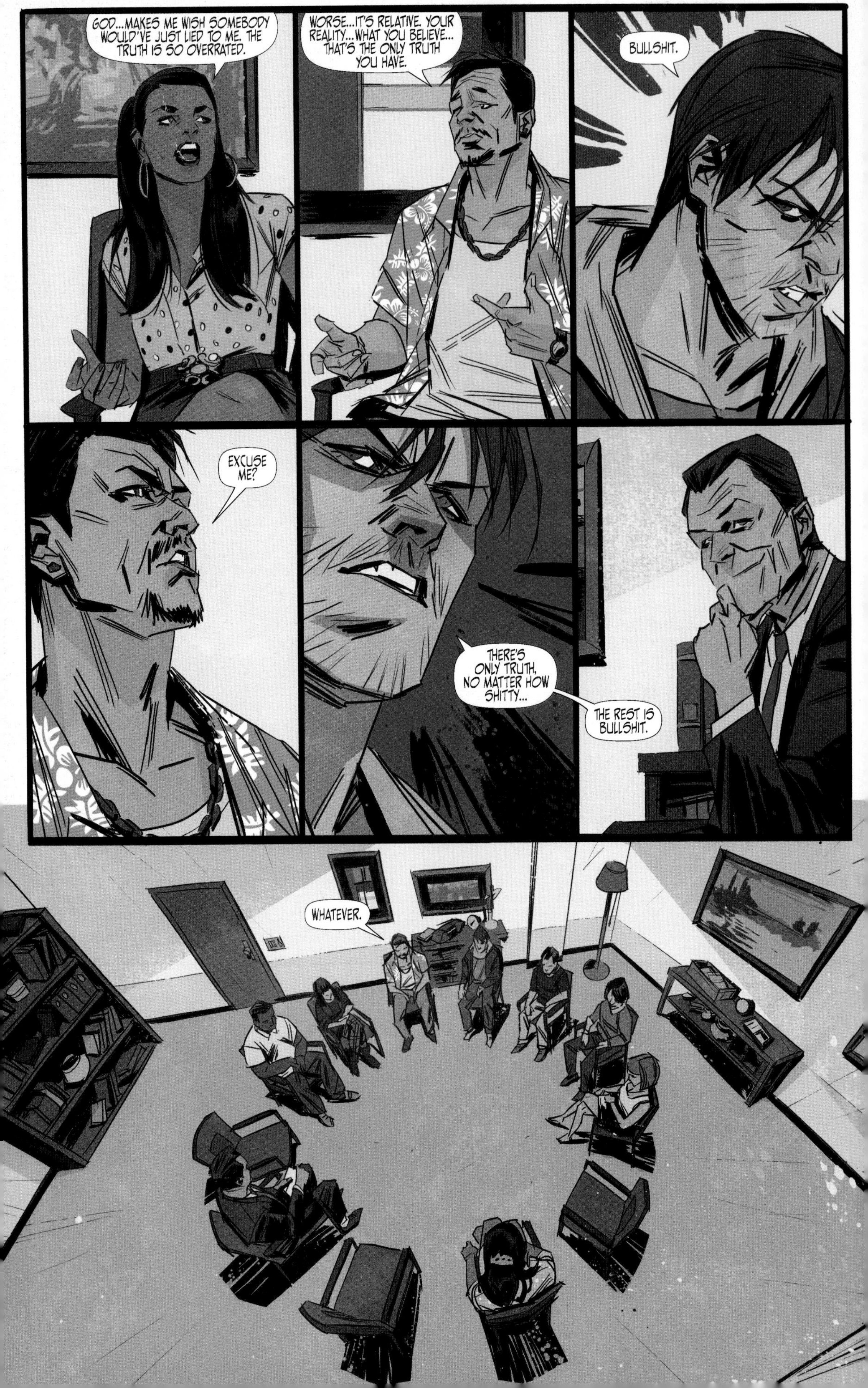
GOD...MAKES ME WISH SOMEBODY WOULD'VE JUST LIED TO ME. THE TRUTH IS SO OVERRATED.
WORSE...IT'S RELATIVE. YOUR REALITY...WHAT YOU BELIEVE... THAT'S THE ONLY TRUTH YOU HAVE.
BULLSHIT.
EXCUSE ME?
THERE'S ONLY TRUTH, NO MATTER HOW SHITTY...
THE REST IS BULLSHIT.
WHATEVER.

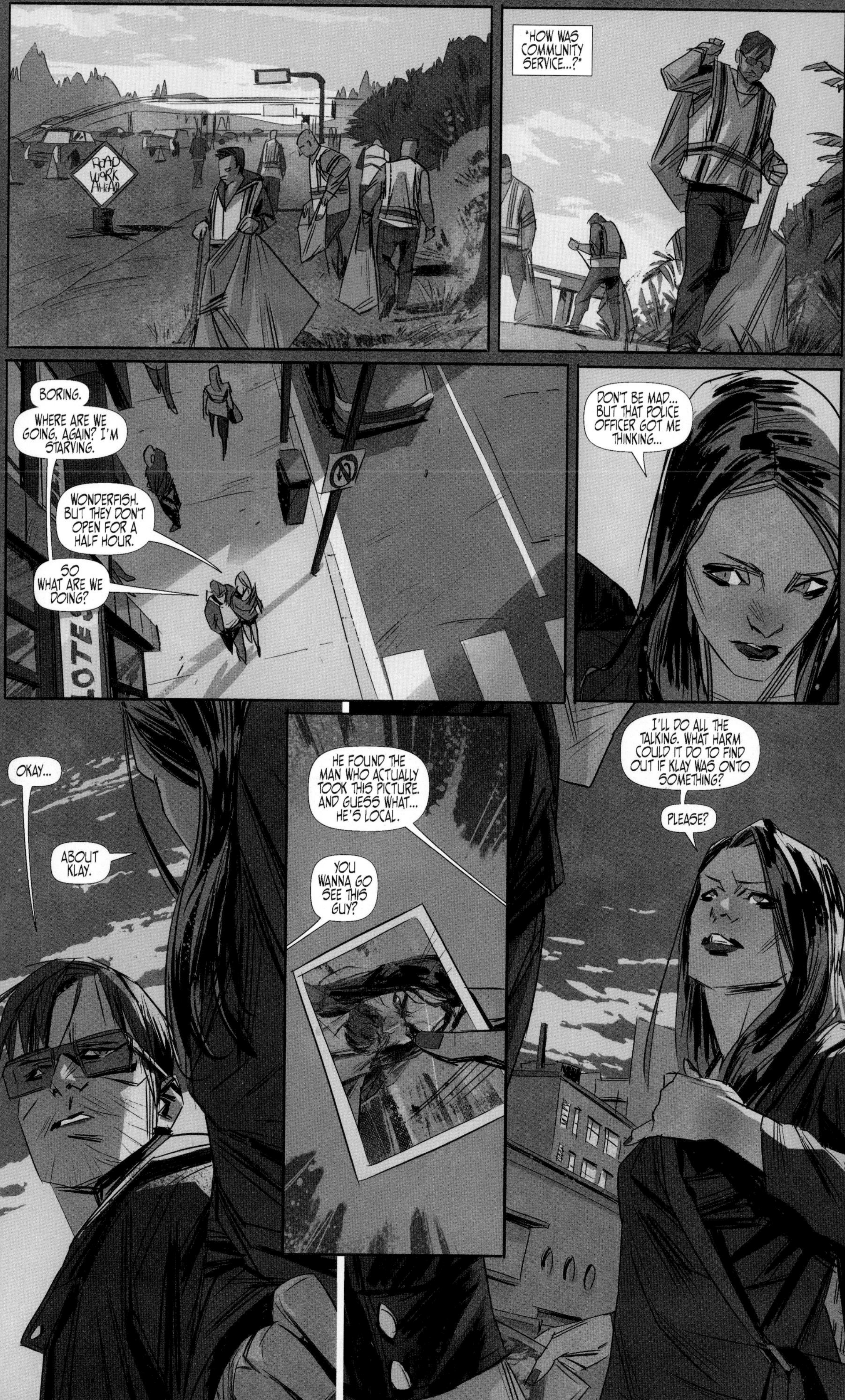

ROAD WORK AHEAD
"HOW WAS COMMUNITY SERVICE...?"
BORING.
WHERE ARE WE GOING, AGAIN? I'M STARVING.
WONDERFISH. BUT THEY DON'T OPEN FOR A HALF HOUR.
SO WHAT ARE WE DOING?
DON'T BE MAD... BUT THAT POLICE OFFICER GOT ME THINKING...
OKAY...
ABOUT KLAY.
HE FOUND THE MAN WHO ACTUALLY TOOK THIS PICTURE. AND GUESS WHAT... HE'S LOCAL.
YOU WANNA GO SEE THIS GUY?
I'LL DO ALL THE TALKING. WHAT HARM COULD IT DO TO FIND OUT IF KLAY WAS ONTO SOMETHING?
PLEASE?

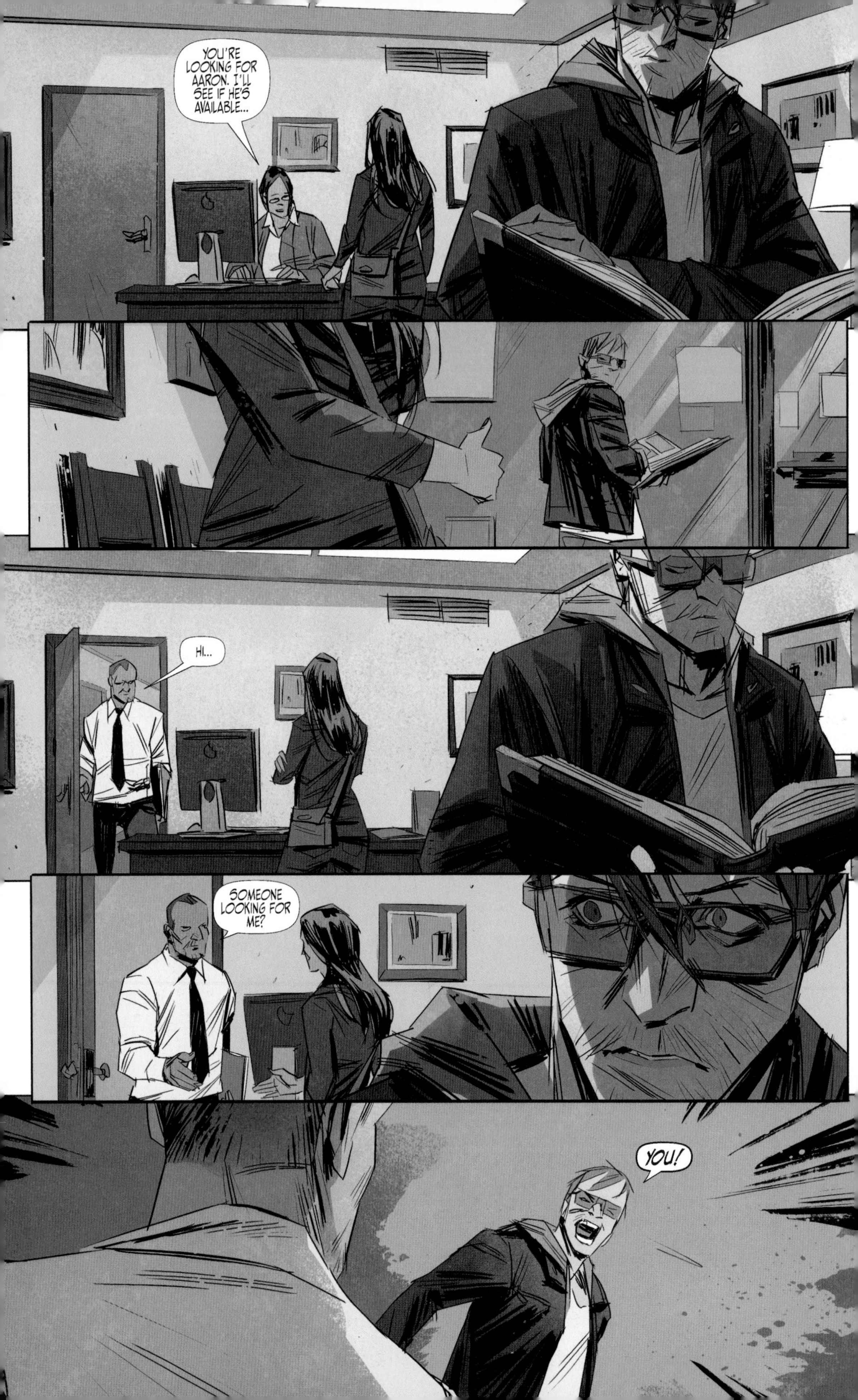
YOU'RE LOOKING FOR AARON. I'LL SEE IF HE'S AVAILABLE...
HI...
SOMEONE LOOKING FOR ME?
YOU!

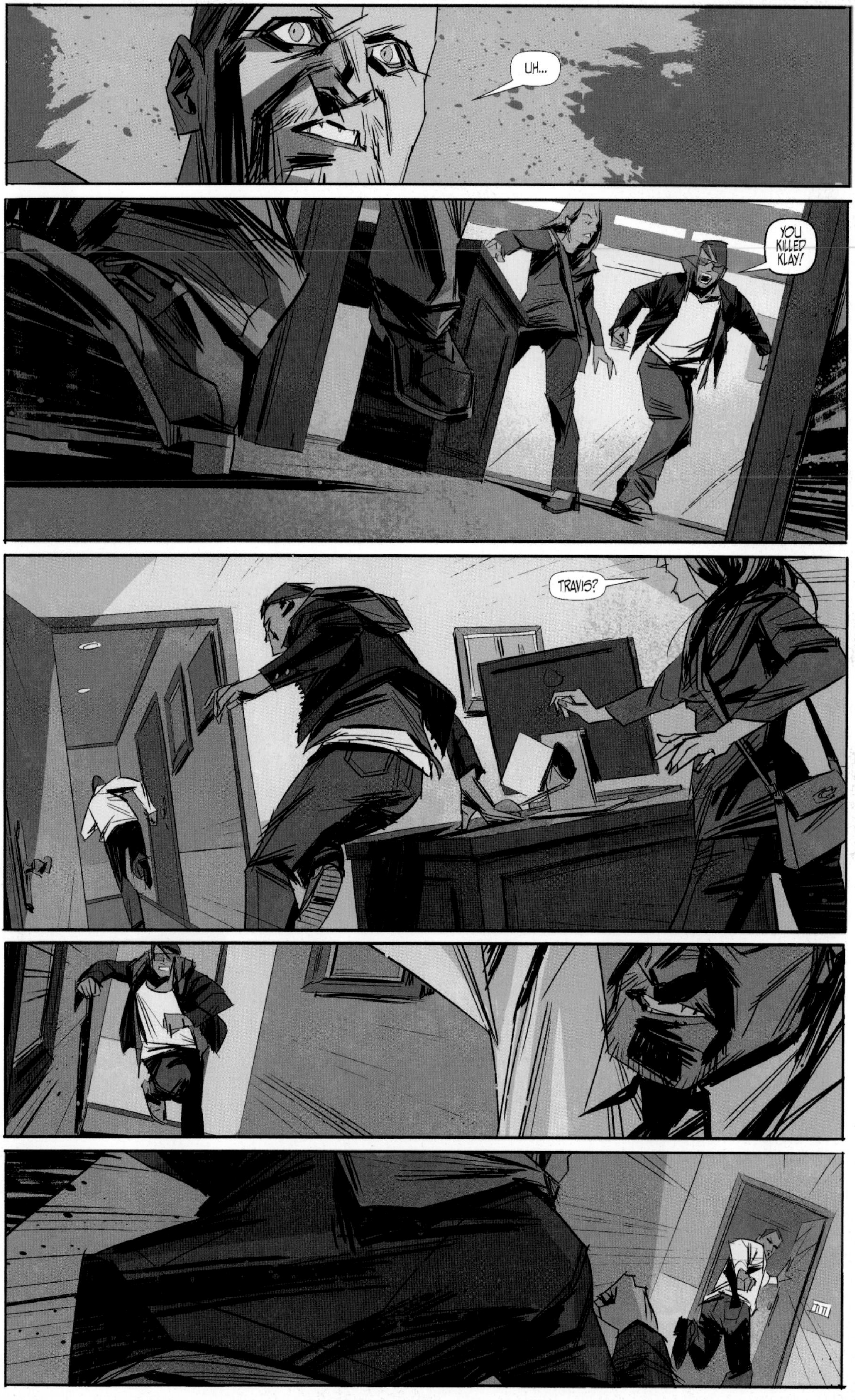
UH...
YOU KILLED KLAY!
TRAVIS?

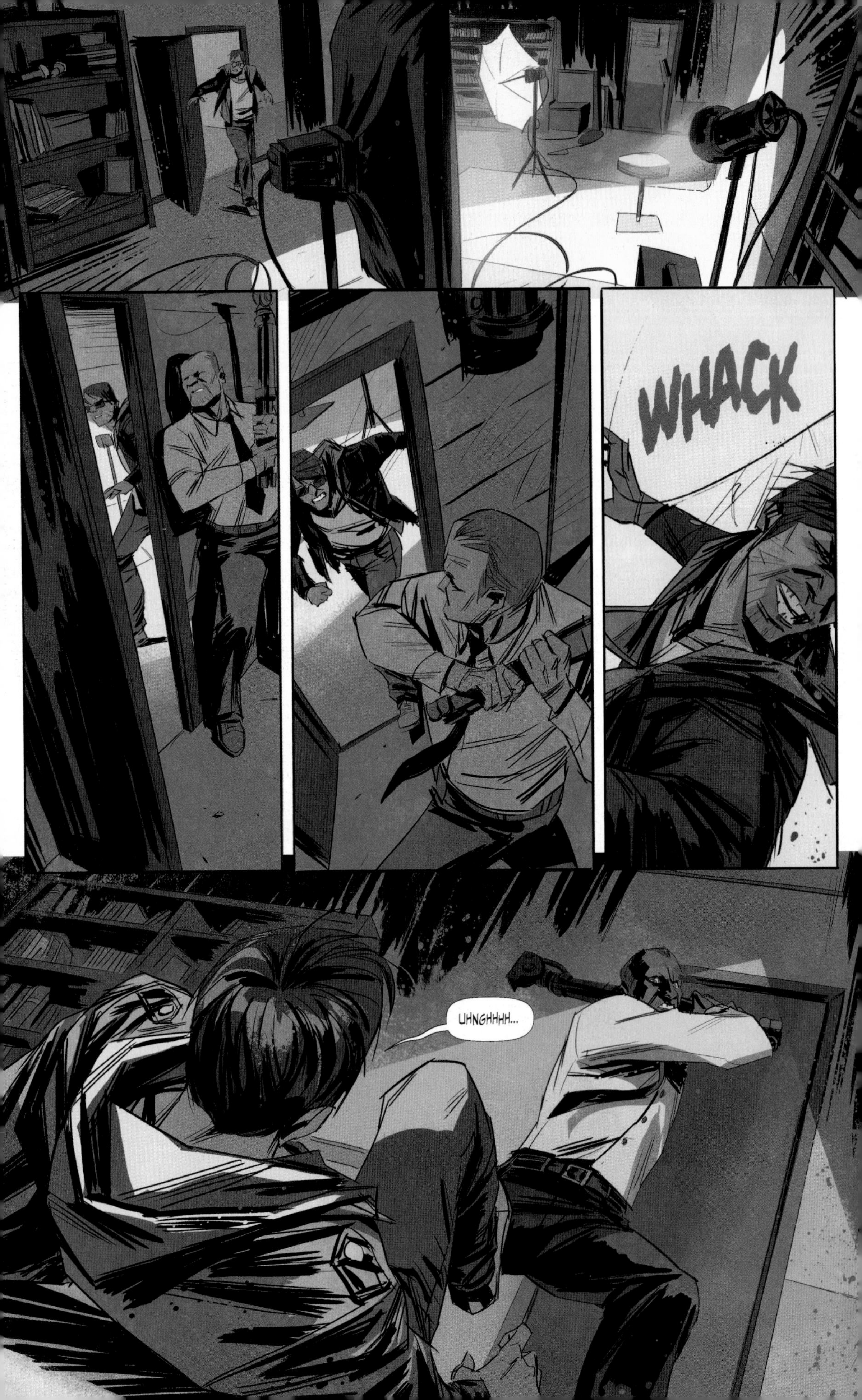
WHACK
UHNGHHHH...

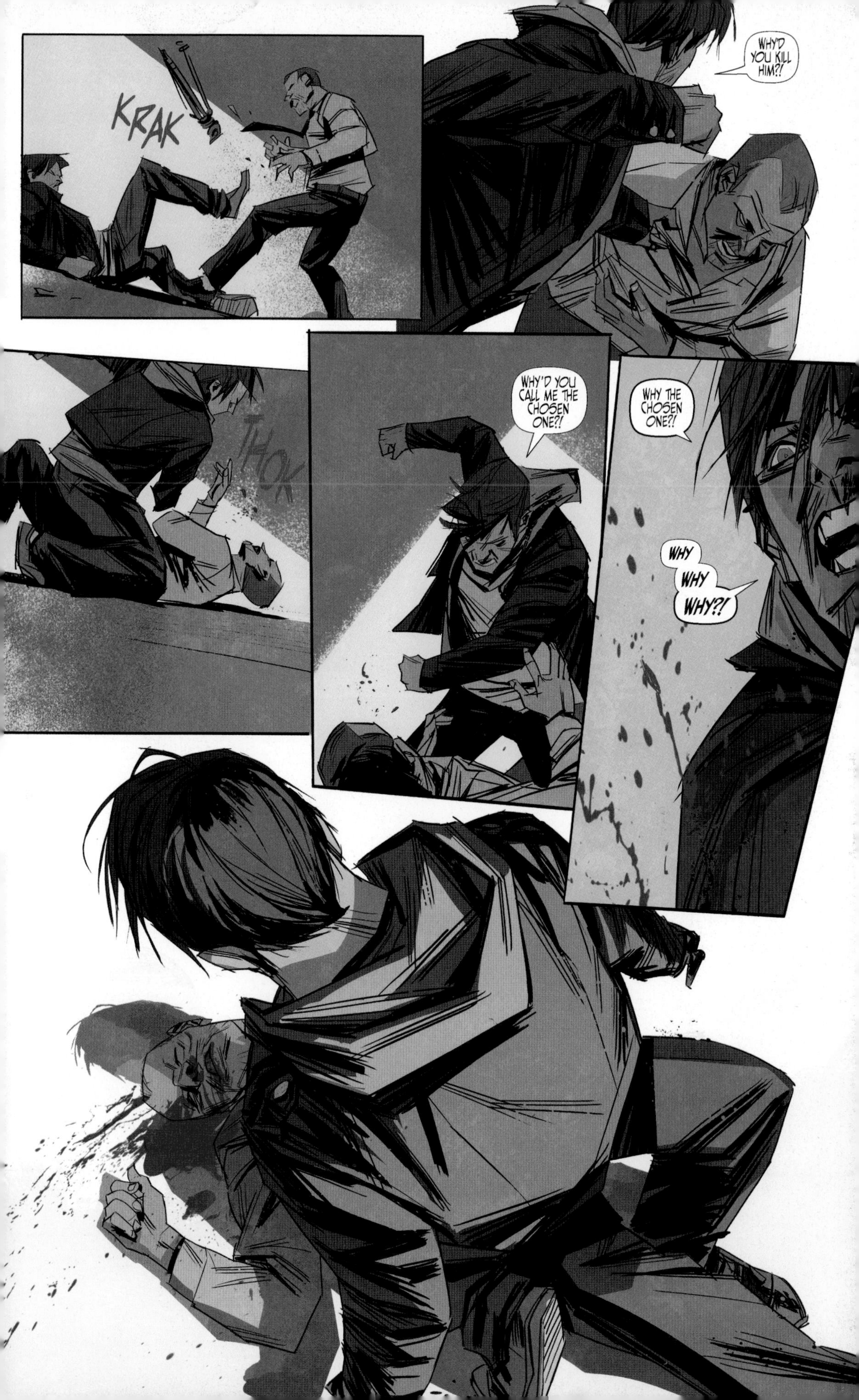
KRAK
WHY'D YOU KILL HIM?!
THOK
WHY'D YOU CALL ME THE CHOSEN ONE?!
WHY THE CHOSEN ONE?!
WHY
WHY
WHY?!

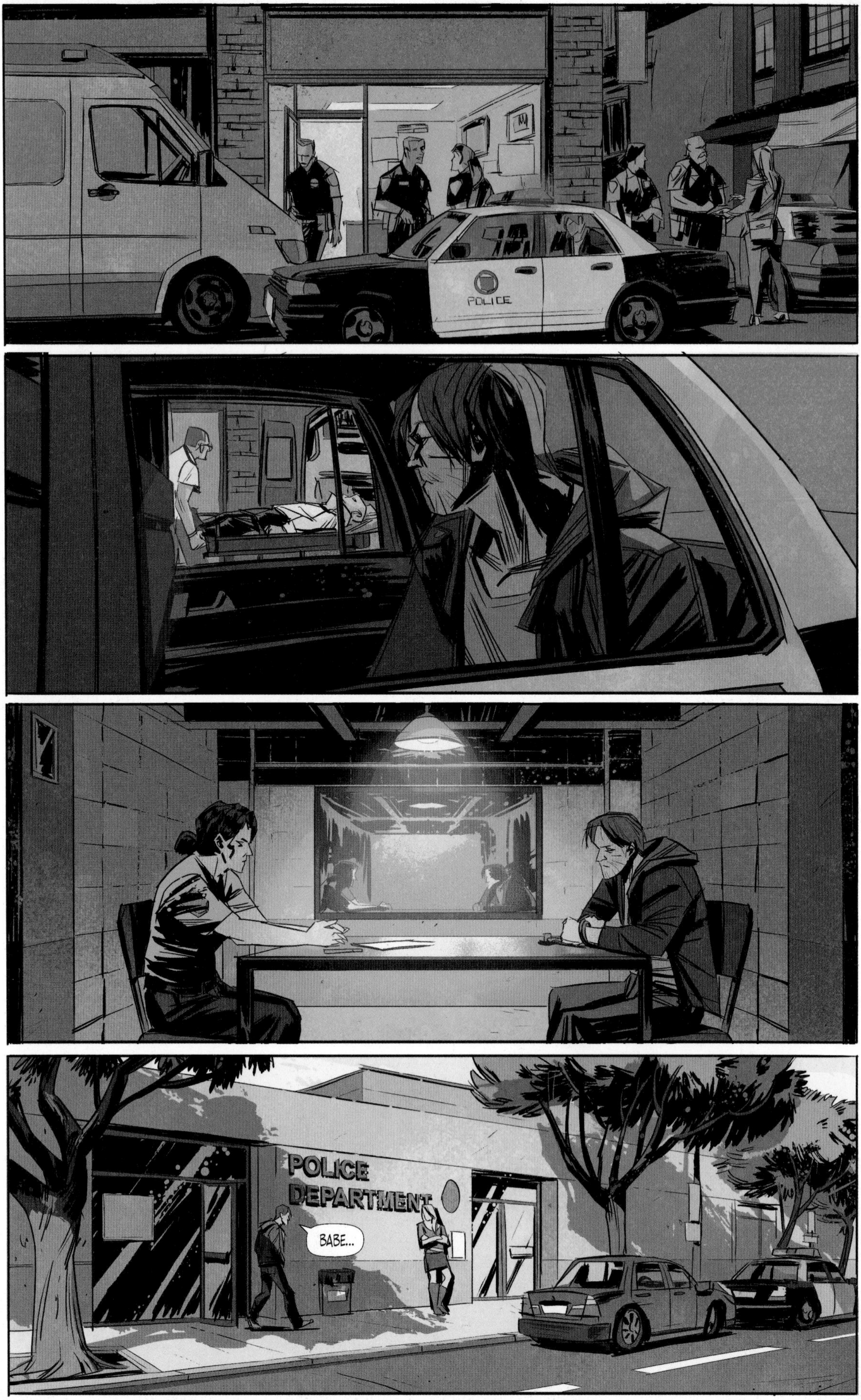
POLICE
POLICE DEPARTMENT
BABE...

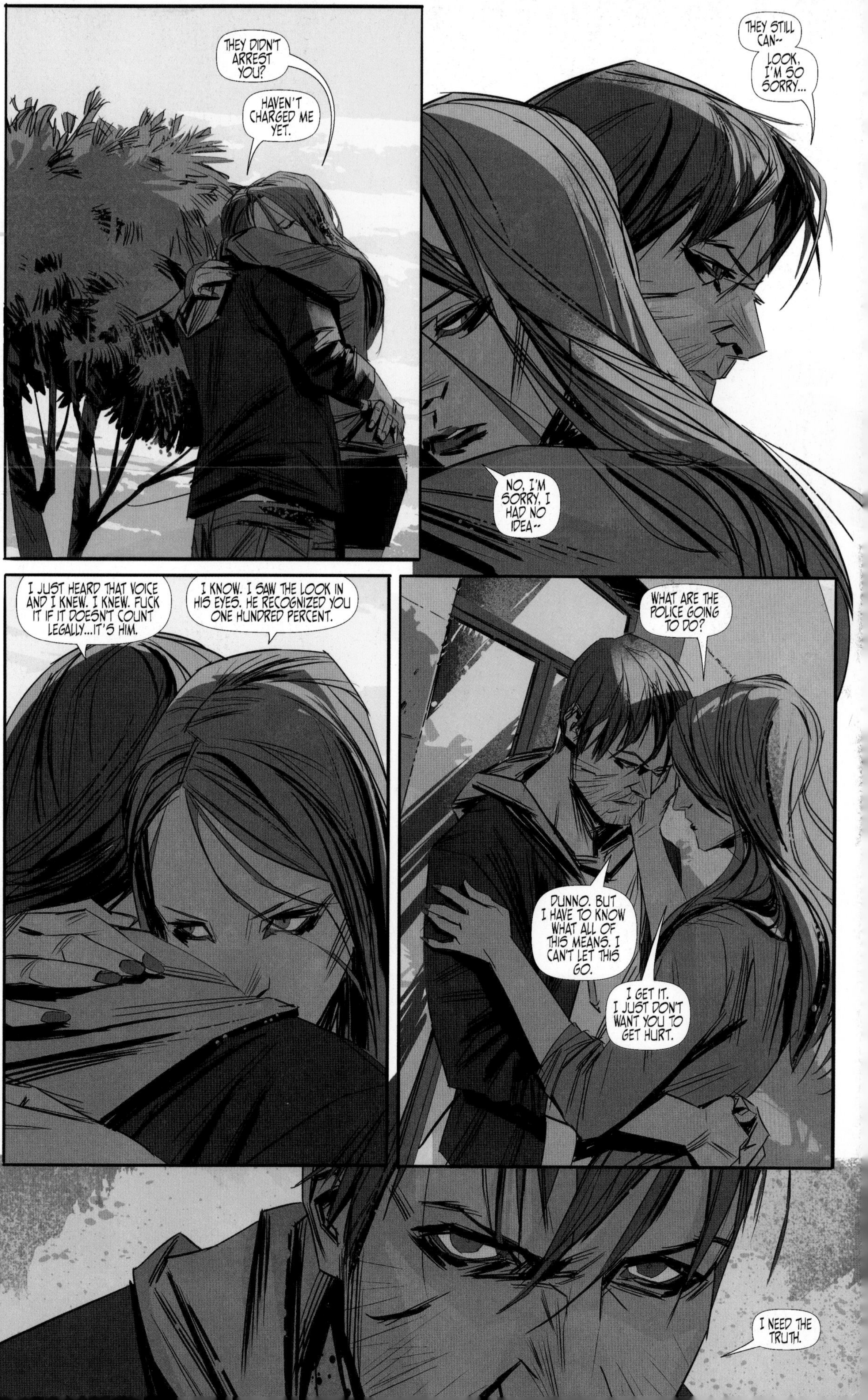
THEY DIDN'T ARREST YOU?
HAVEN'T CHARGED ME YET.
THEY STILL CAN--
LOOK, I'M SO SORRY...
NO, I'M SORRY, I HAD NO IDEA--
I JUST HEARD THAT VOICE AND I KNEW. I KNEW. FUCK IT IF IT DOESN'T COUNT LEGALLY...IT'S HIM.
I KNOW. I SAW THE LOOK IN HIS EYES. HE RECOGNIZED YOU ONE HUNDRED PERCENT.
WHAT ARE THE POLICE GOING TO DO?
DUNNO. BUT I HAVE TO KNOW WHAT ALL OF THIS MEANS. I CAN'T LET THIS GO.
I GET IT. I JUST DON'T WANT YOU TO GET HURT.
I NEED THE TRUTH.

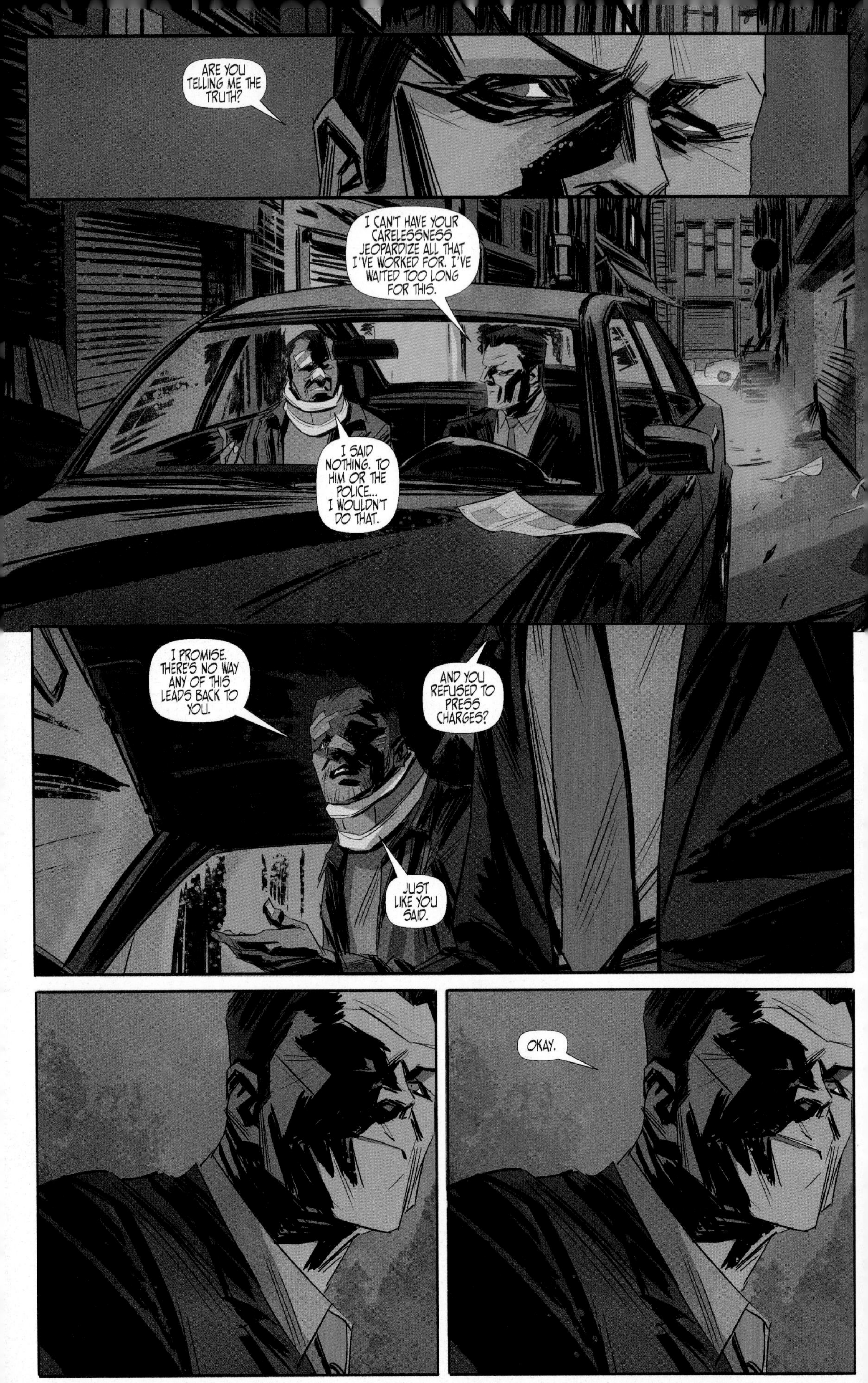
ARE YOU TELLING ME THE TRUTH?
I CAN'T HAVE YOUR CARELESSNESS JEOPARDIZE ALL THAT I'VE WORKED FOR. I'VE WAITED TOO LONG FOR THIS.
I SAID NOTHING. TO HIM OR THE POLICE... I WOULDN'T DO THAT.
I PROMISE. THERE'S NO WAY ANY OF THIS LEADS BACK TO YOU.
AND YOU REFUSED TO PRESS CHARGES?
JUST LIKE YOU SAID.
OKAY.

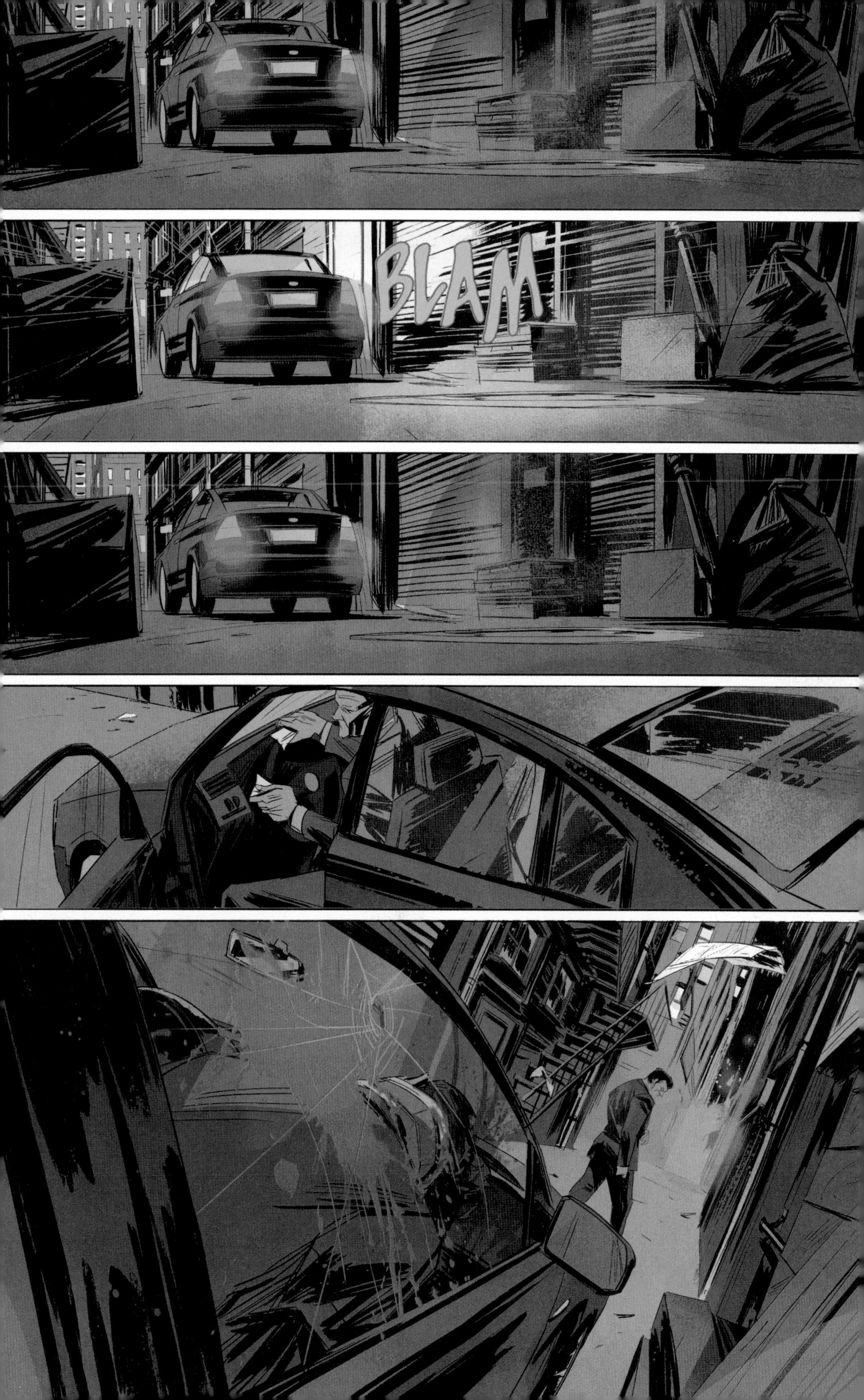
BLAM

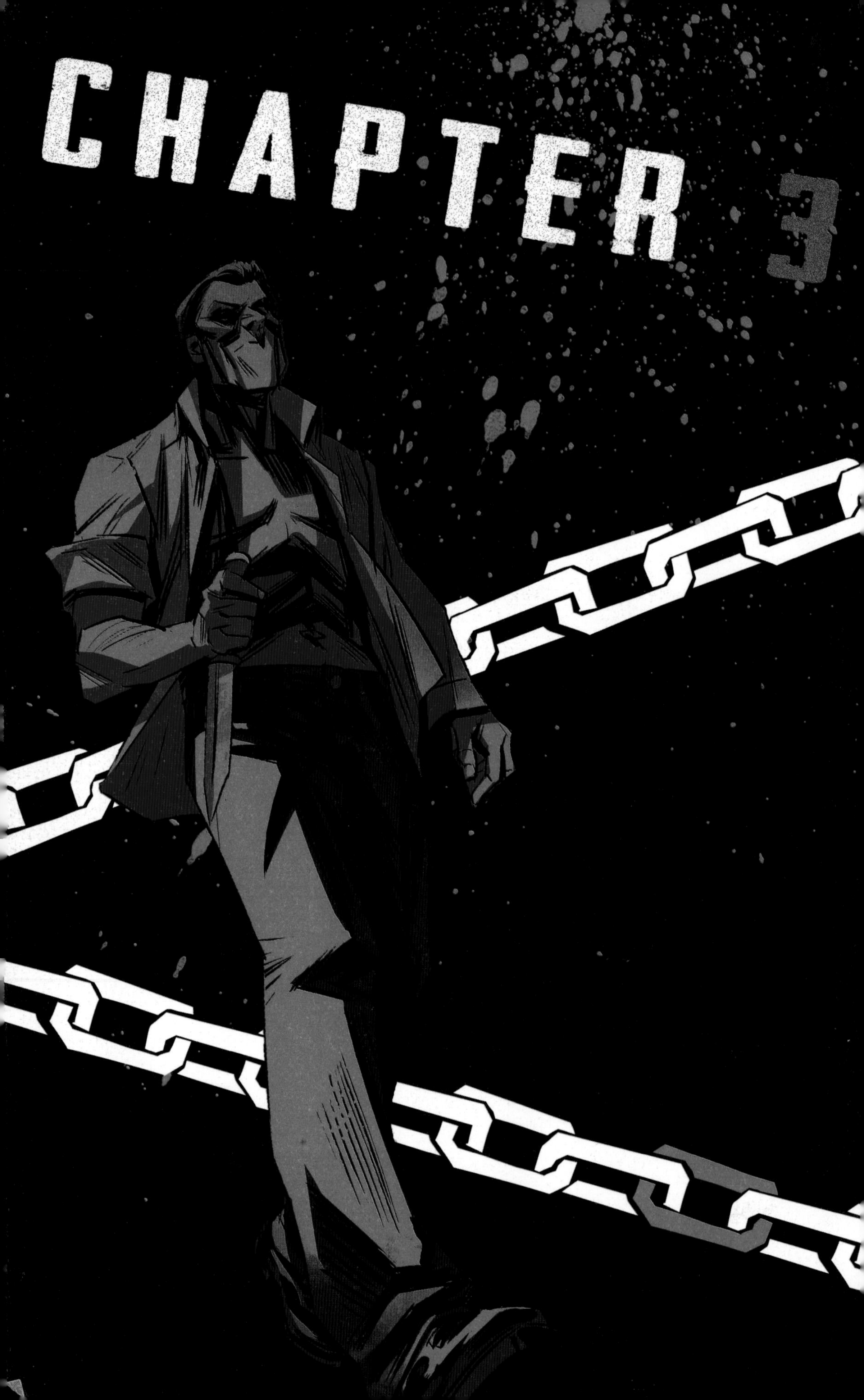
CHAPTER 3

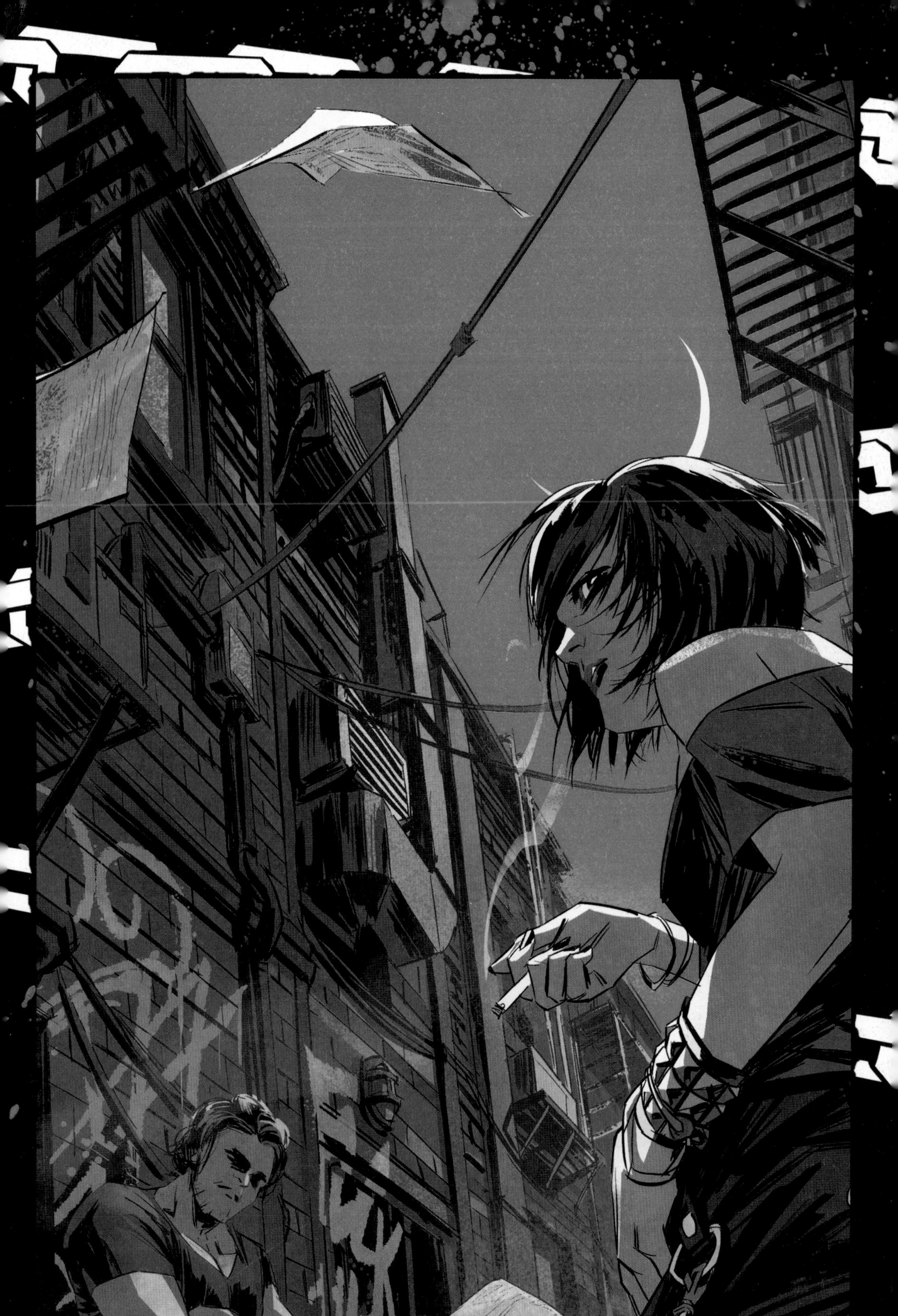

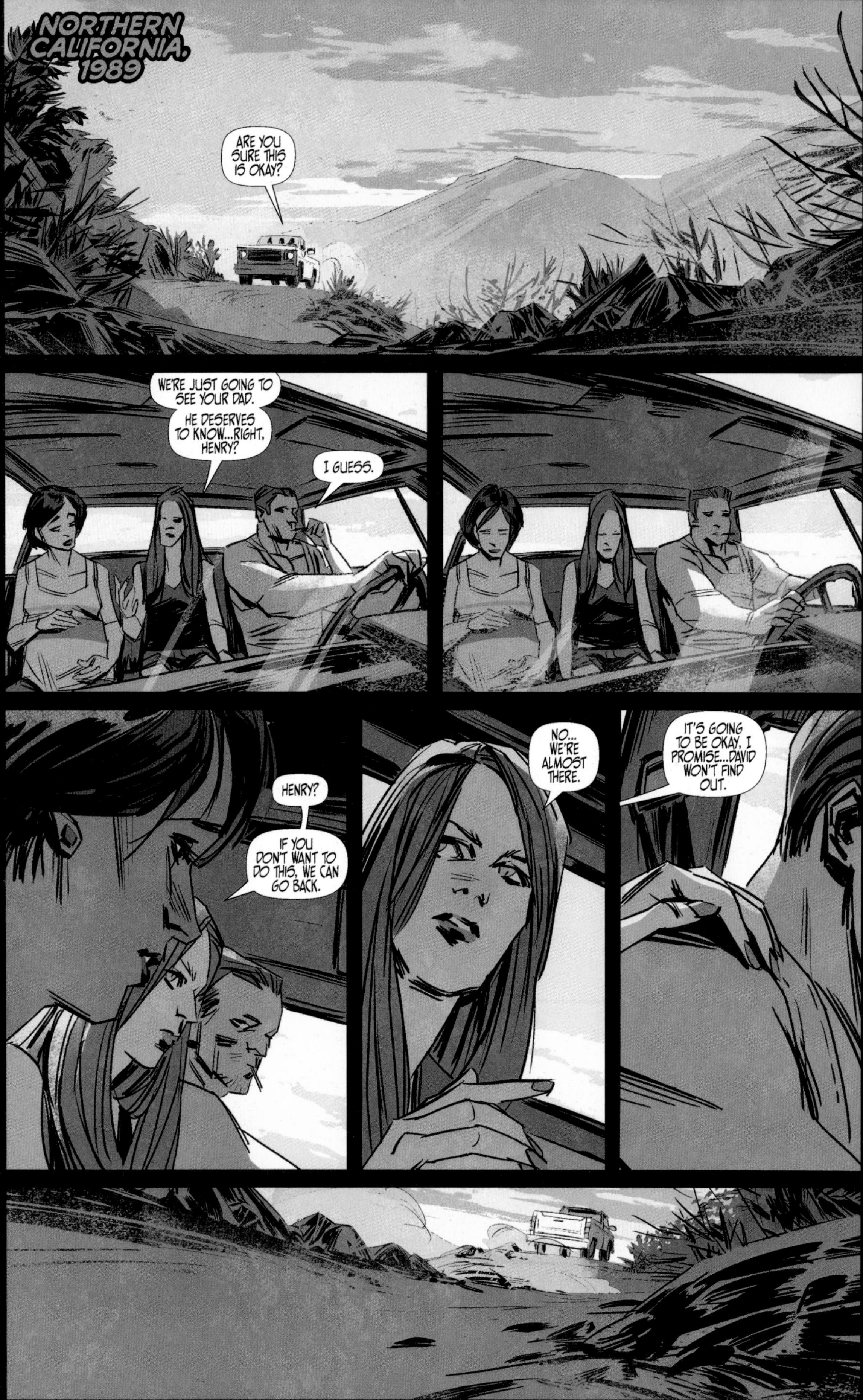
NORTHERN CALIFORNIA. 1989
ARE YOU SURE THIS IS OKAY?
WE'RE JUST GOING TO SEE YOUR DAD.
HE DESERVES TO KNOW...RIGHT, HENRY?
I GUESS.
HENRY?
IF YOU DON'T WANT TO DO THIS, WE CAN GO BACK.
NO... WE'RE ALMOST THERE.
IT'S GOING TO BE OKAY, I PROMISE...DAVID WON'T FIND OUT.

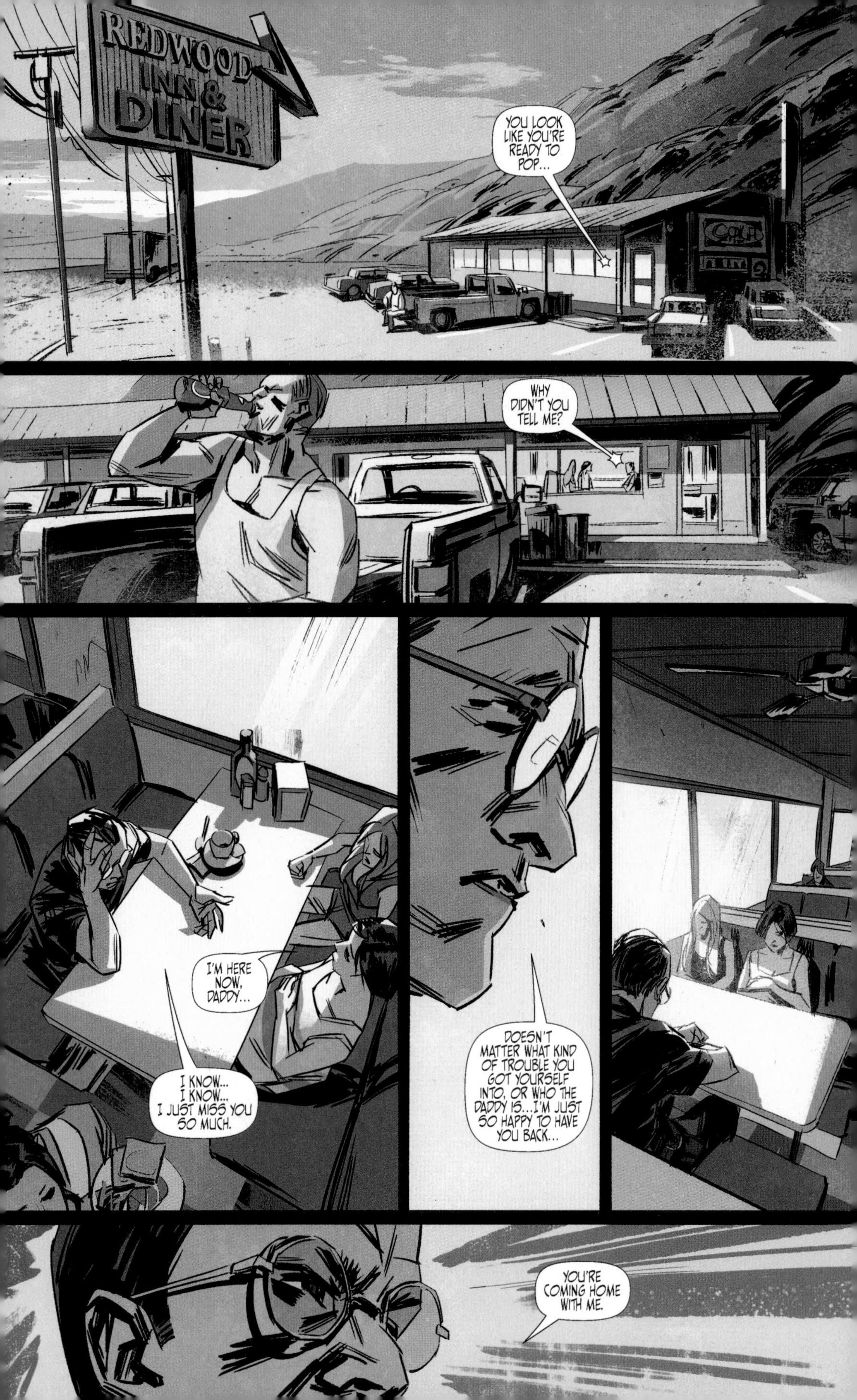
REDWOOD INN & DINER
YOU LOOK LIKE YOU'RE READY TO POP...
WHY DIDN'T YOU TELL ME?
I'M HERE NOW, DADDY...
I KNOW... I KNOW... I JUST MISS YOU SO MUCH.
DOESN'T MATTER WHAT KIND OF TROUBLE YOU GOT YOURSELF INTO, OR WHO THE DADDY IS...I'M JUST SO HAPPY TO HAVE YOU BACK...
YOU'RE COMING HOME WITH ME.

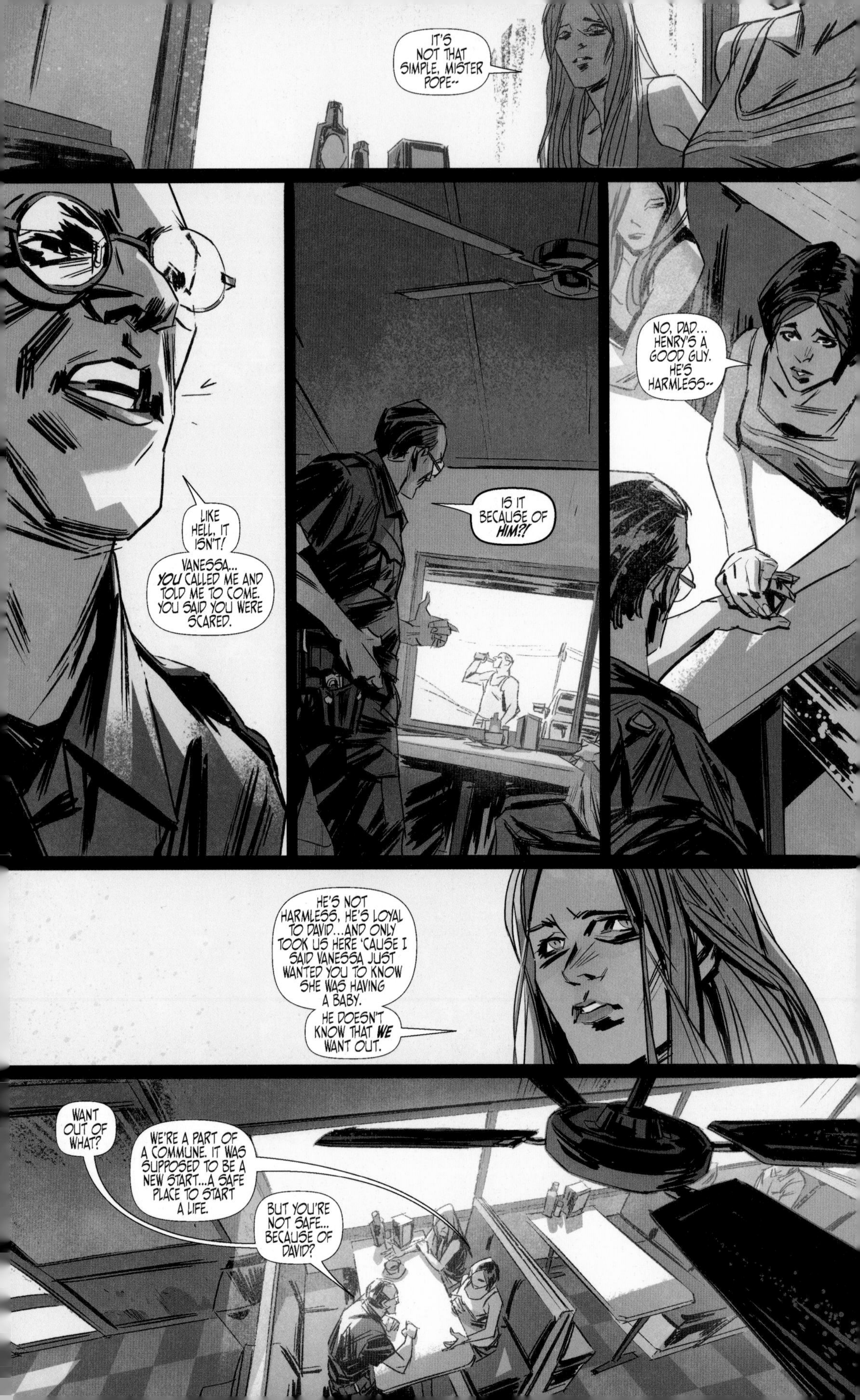
IT'S NOT THAT SIMPLE, MISTER POPE--
LIKE HELL, IT ISN'T!
VANESSA... **YOU** CALLED ME AND TOLD ME TO COME. YOU SAID YOU WERE SCARED.
IS IT BECAUSE OF **HIM?!**
NO, DAD... HENRY'S A GOOD GUY. HE'S HARMLESS--
HE'S NOT HARMLESS, HE'S LOYAL TO DAVID...AND ONLY TOOK US HERE 'CAUSE I SAID VANESSA JUST WANTED YOU TO KNOW SHE WAS HAVING A BABY.
HE DOESN'T KNOW THAT **WE** WANT OUT.
WANT OUT OF WHAT?
WE'RE A PART OF A COMMUNE. IT WAS SUPPOSED TO BE A NEW START...A SAFE PLACE TO START A LIFE.
BUT YOU'RE NOT SAFE... BECAUSE OF DAVID?

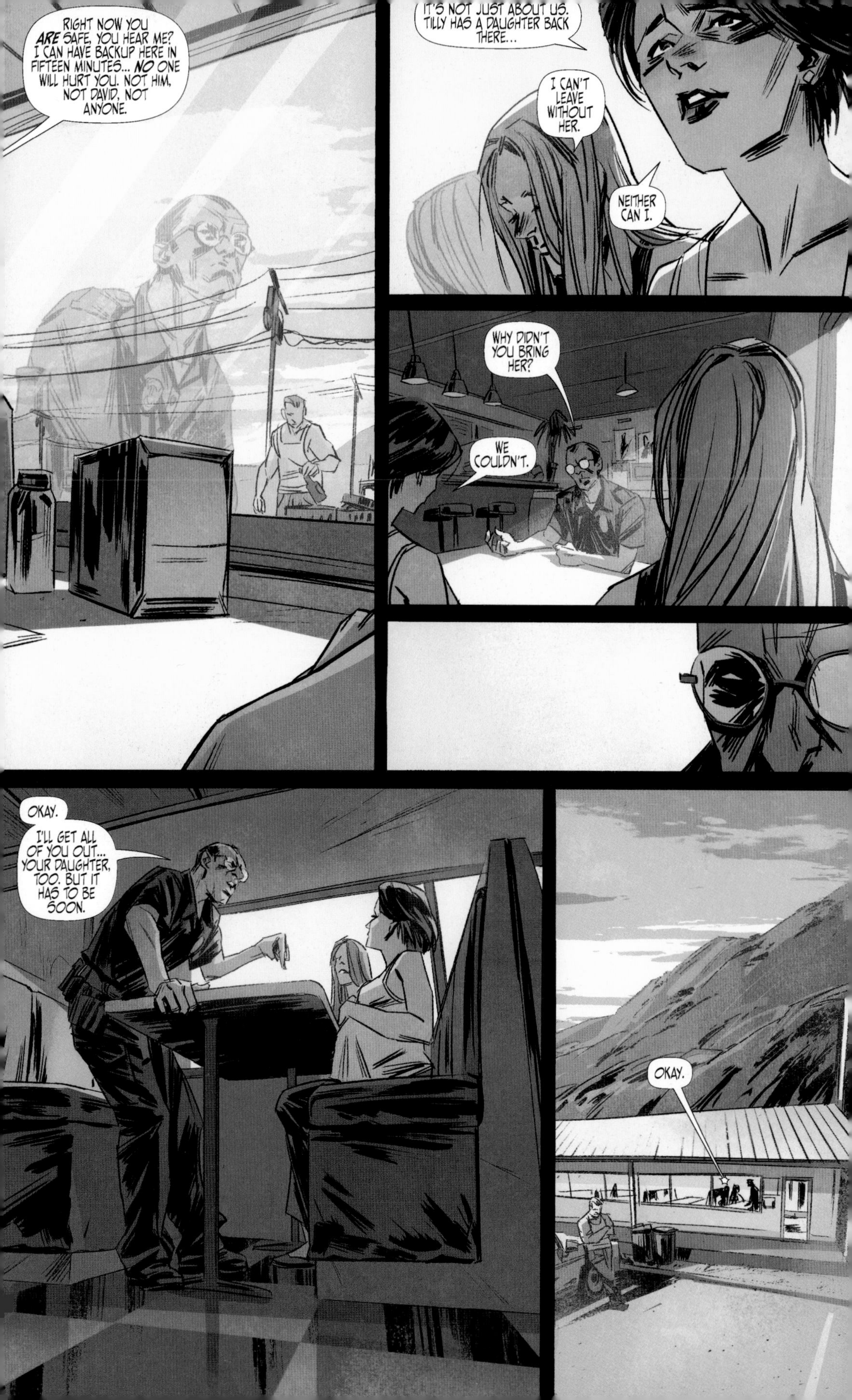
RIGHT NOW YOU ARE SAFE, YOU HEAR ME? I CAN HAVE BACKUP HERE IN FIFTEEN MINUTES... NO ONE WILL HURT YOU. NOT HIM, NOT DAVID, NOT ANYONE.
IT'S NOT JUST ABOUT US. TILLY HAS A DAUGHTER BACK THERE...
I CAN'T LEAVE WITHOUT HER.
NEITHER CAN I.
WHY DIDN'T YOU BRING HER?
WE COULDN'T.
OKAY.
I'LL GET ALL OF YOU OUT... YOUR DAUGHTER, TOO. BUT IT HAS TO BE SOON.
OKAY.

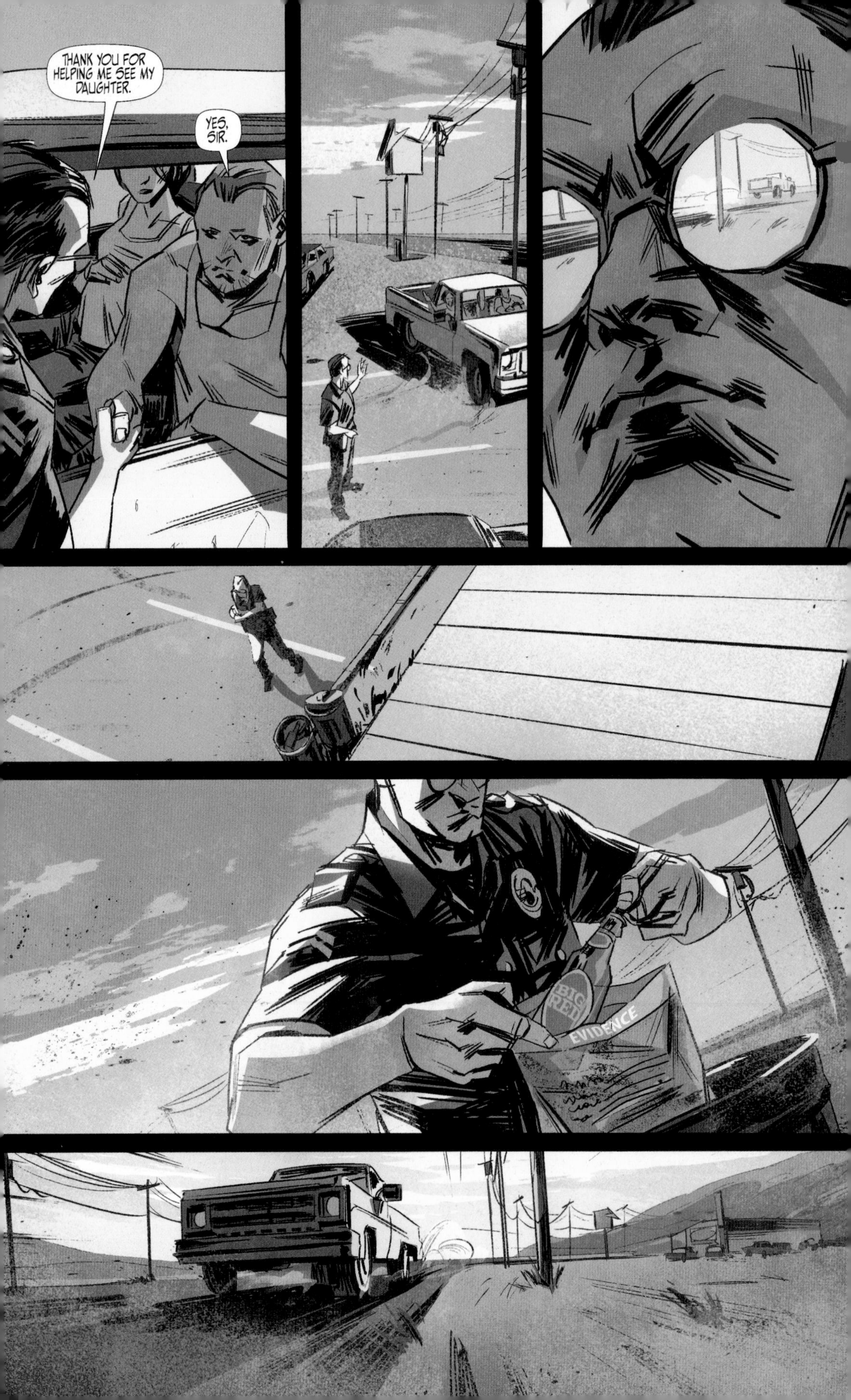
THANK YOU FOR HELPING ME SEE MY DAUGHTER.
YES, SIR.
BIG RED
EVIDENCE

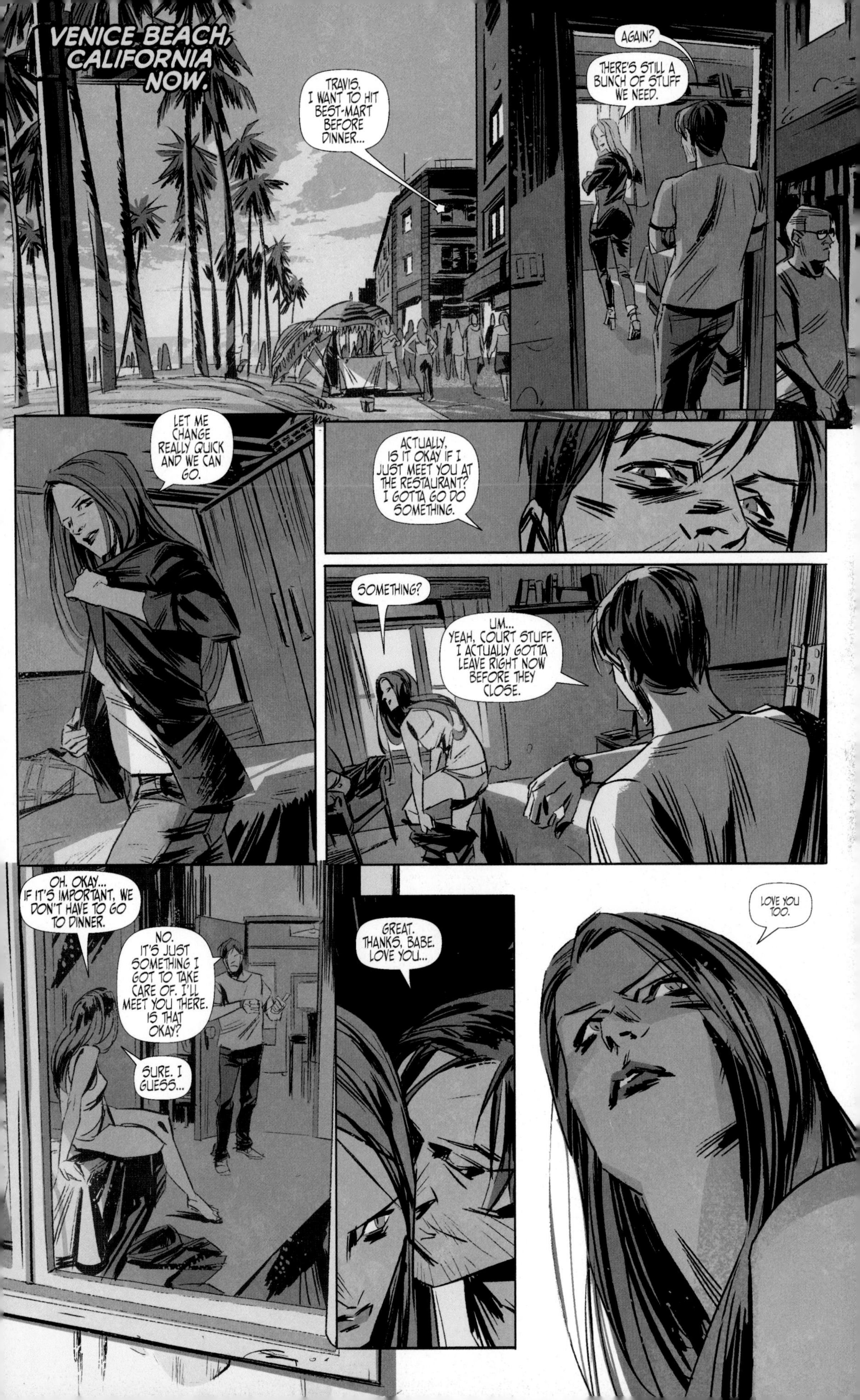
VENICE BEACH, CALIFORNIA NOW.
TRAVIS, I WANT TO HIT BEST-MART BEFORE DINNER...
AGAIN?
THERE'S STILL A BUNCH OF STUFF WE NEED.
LET ME CHANGE REALLY QUICK AND WE CAN GO.
ACTUALLY, IS IT OKAY IF I JUST MEET YOU AT THE RESTAURANT? I GOTTA GO DO SOMETHING.
SOMETHING?
UM... YEAH, COURT STUFF. I ACTUALLY GOTTA LEAVE RIGHT NOW BEFORE THEY CLOSE.
OH. OKAY... IF IT'S IMPORTANT, WE DON'T HAVE TO GO TO DINNER.
NO. IT'S JUST SOMETHING I GOT TO TAKE CARE OF. I'LL MEET YOU THERE. IS THAT OKAY?
SURE. I GUESS...
GREAT. THANKS, BABE. LOVE YOU...
LOVE YOU TOO.

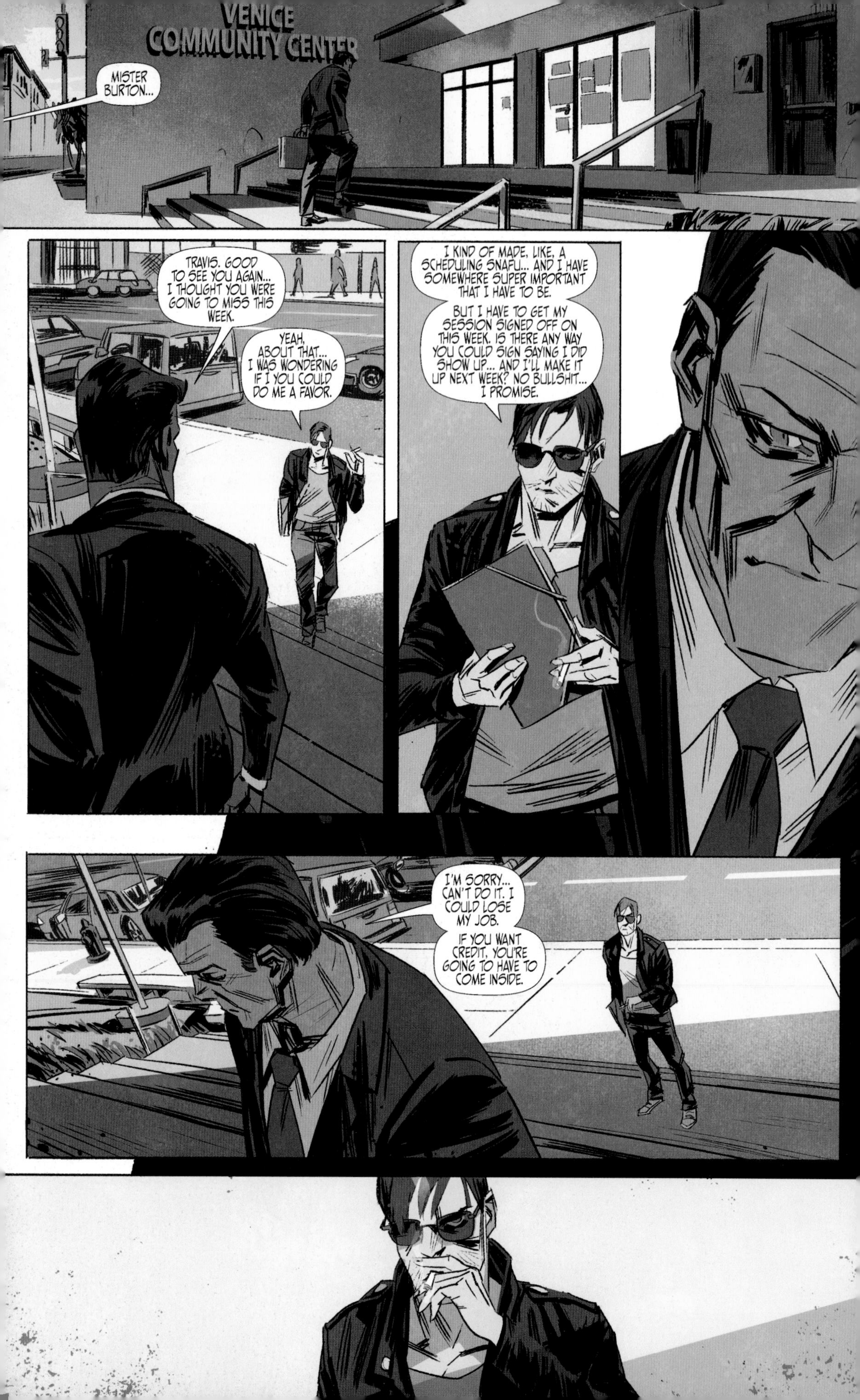
VENICE COMMUNITY CENTER
MISTER BURTON...
TRAVIS. GOOD TO SEE YOU AGAIN... I THOUGHT YOU WERE GOING TO MISS THIS WEEK.
YEAH, ABOUT THAT... I WAS WONDERING IF I YOU COULD DO ME A FAVOR.
I KIND OF MADE, LIKE, A SCHEDULING SNAFU... AND I HAVE SOMEWHERE SUPER IMPORTANT THAT I HAVE TO BE.
BUT I HAVE TO GET MY SESSION SIGNED OFF ON THIS WEEK. IS THERE ANY WAY YOU COULD SIGN SAYING I DID SHOW UP... AND I'LL MAKE IT UP NEXT WEEK? NO BULLSHIT... I PROMISE.
I'M SORRY... CAN'T DO IT. I COULD LOSE MY JOB.
IF YOU WANT CREDIT, YOU'RE GOING TO HAVE TO COME INSIDE.

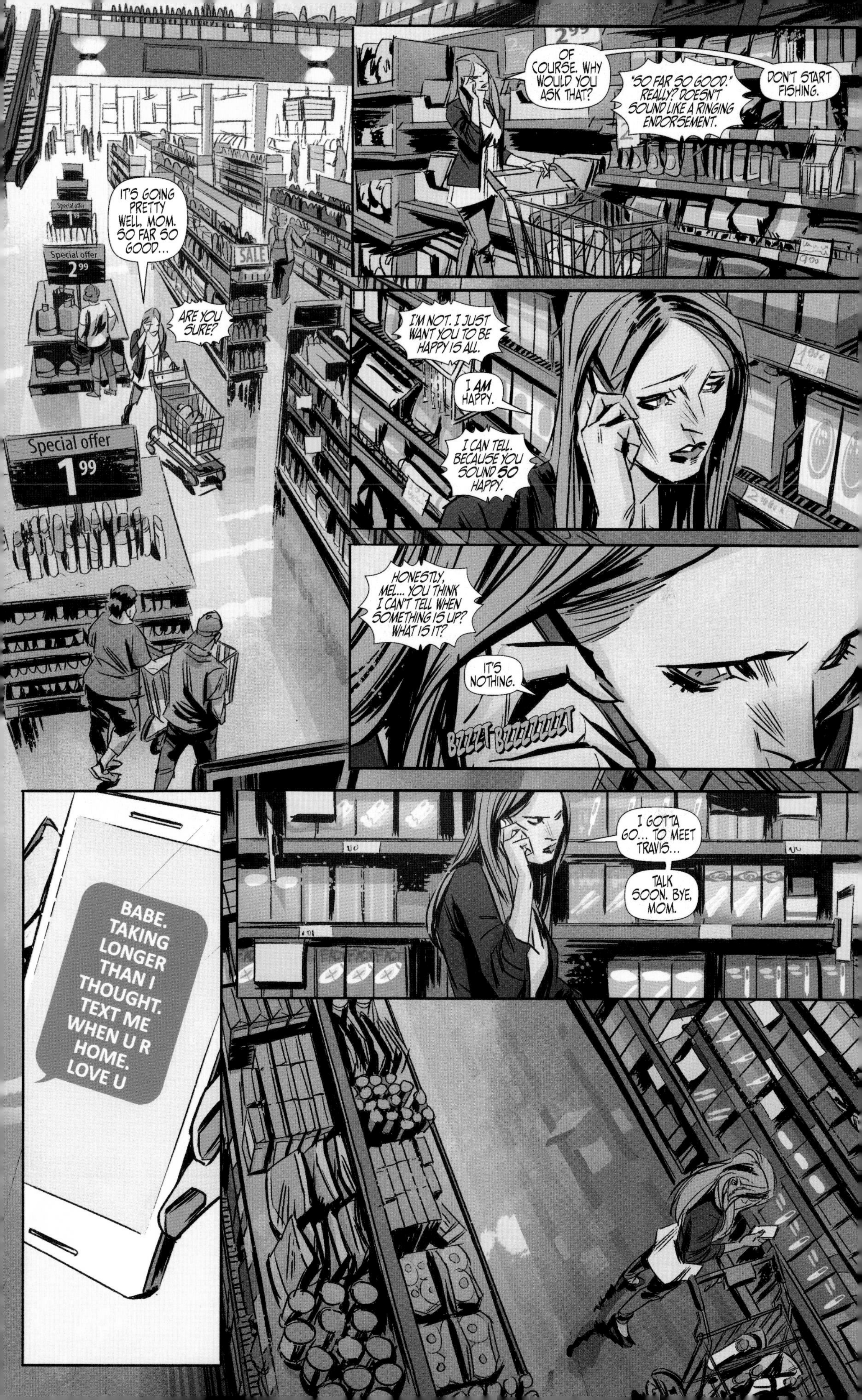
Special offer
2.99
Special offer
1.99
SALE
IT'S GOING PRETTY WELL, MOM. SO FAR SO GOOD...
ARE YOU SURE?
OF COURSE. WHY WOULD YOU ASK THAT?
"SO FAR SO GOOD." REALLY? DOESN'T SOUND LIKE A RINGING ENDORSEMENT.
DON'T START FISHING.
I'M NOT. I JUST WANT YOU TO BE HAPPY IS ALL.
I AM HAPPY.
I CAN TELL. BECAUSE YOU SOUND SO HAPPY.
HONESTLY, MEL... YOU THINK I CAN'T TELL WHEN SOMETHING IS UP? WHAT IS IT?
IT'S NOTHING.
BZZZT BZZZZZZZT
I GOTTA GO... TO MEET TRAVIS...
TALK SOON. BYE, MOM.
BABE. TAKING LONGER THAN I THOUGHT. TEXT ME WHEN U R HOME. LOVE U

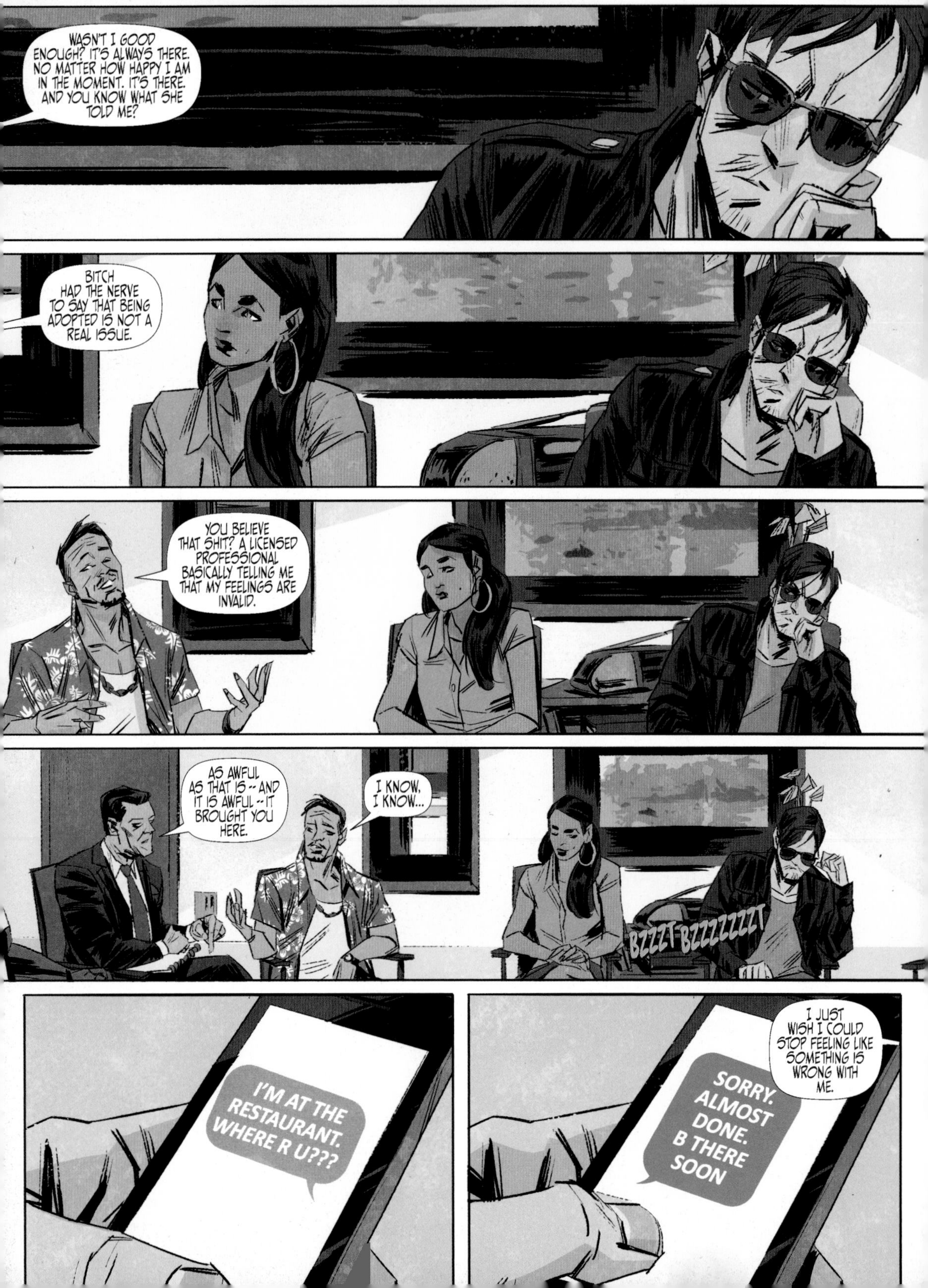
WASN'T I GOOD ENOUGH? IT'S ALWAYS THERE. NO MATTER HOW HAPPY I AM IN THE MOMENT. IT'S THERE. AND YOU KNOW WHAT SHE TOLD ME?
BITCH HAD THE NERVE TO SAY THAT BEING ADOPTED IS NOT A REAL ISSUE.
YOU BELIEVE THAT SHIT? A LICENSED PROFESSIONAL BASICALLY TELLING ME THAT MY FEELINGS ARE INVALID.
AS AWFUL AS THAT IS -- AND IT IS AWFUL -- IT BROUGHT YOU HERE.
I KNOW. I KNOW...
BZZZT BZZZZZZZT
I'M AT THE RESTAURANT. WHERE R U???
I JUST WISH I COULD STOP FEELING LIKE SOMETHING IS WRONG WITH ME.
SORRY. ALMOST DONE. B THERE SOON

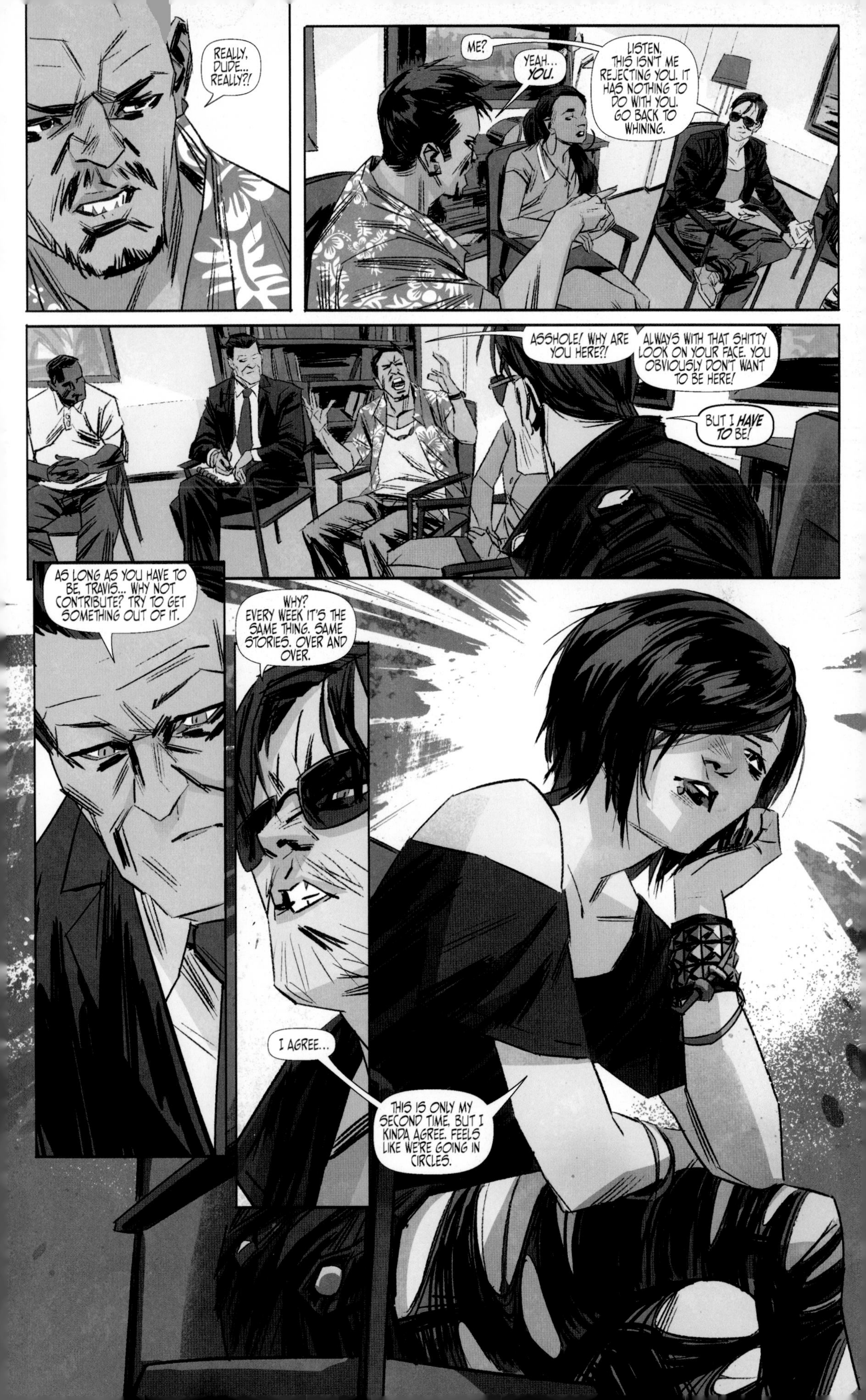
REALLY, DUDE... REALLY?!
ME?
YEAH... *YOU.*
LISTEN, THIS ISN'T ME REJECTING YOU. IT HAS NOTHING TO DO WITH YOU. GO BACK TO WHINING.
ASSHOLE! WHY ARE YOU HERE?!
ALWAYS WITH THAT SHITTY LOOK ON YOUR FACE. YOU OBVIOUSLY DON'T WANT TO BE HERE!
BUT I *HAVE TO* BE!
AS LONG AS YOU HAVE TO BE, TRAVIS... WHY NOT CONTRIBUTE? TRY TO GET SOMETHING OUT OF IT.
WHY? EVERY WEEK IT'S THE SAME THING. SAME STORIES. OVER AND OVER.
I AGREE...
THIS IS ONLY MY SECOND TIME, BUT I KINDA AGREE. FEELS LIKE WE'RE GOING IN CIRCLES.

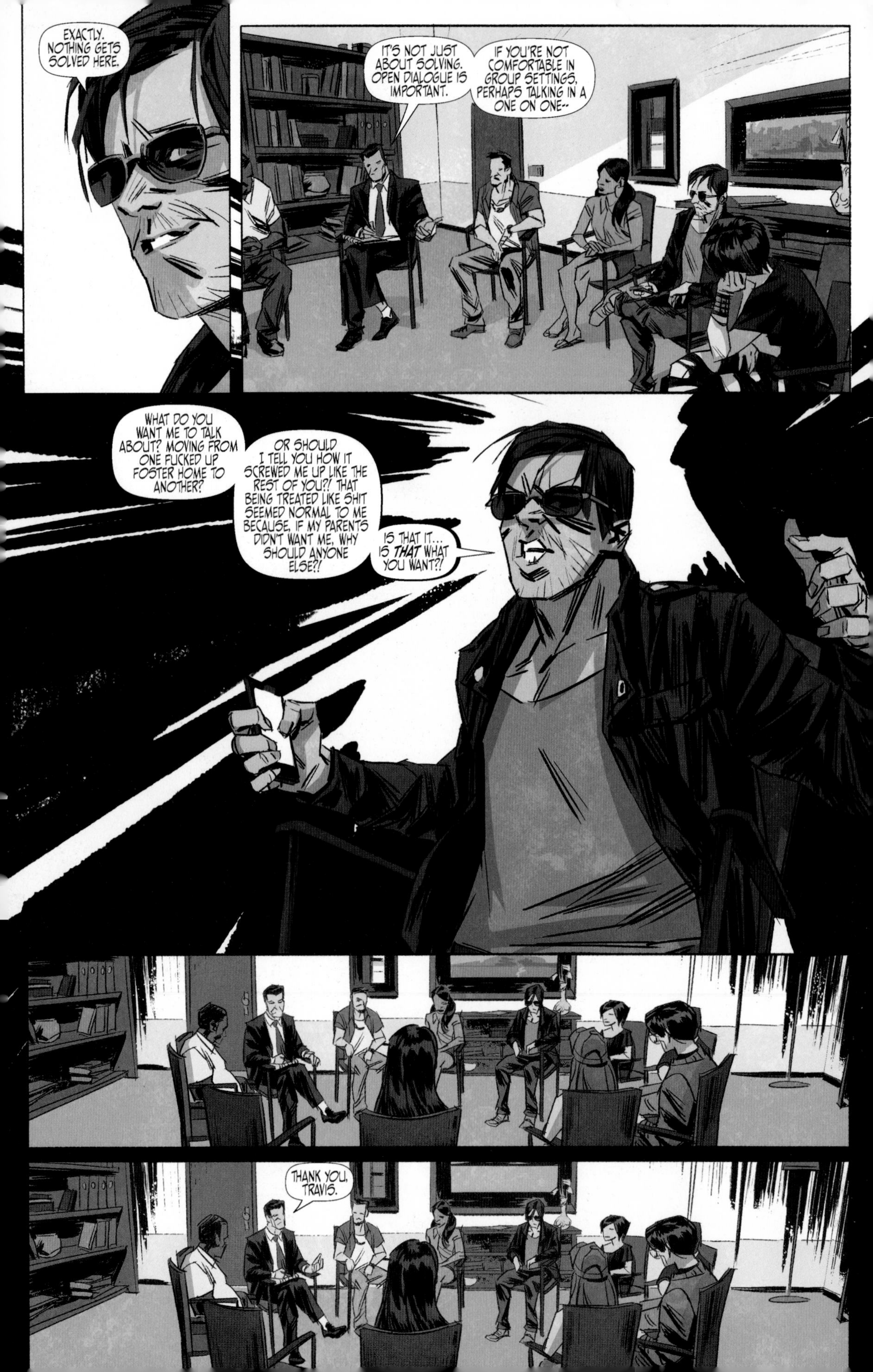
EXACTLY. NOTHING GETS SOLVED HERE.
IT'S NOT JUST ABOUT SOLVING. OPEN DIALOGUE IS IMPORTANT.
IF YOU'RE NOT COMFORTABLE IN GROUP SETTINGS, PERHAPS TALKING IN A ONE ON ONE--
WHAT DO YOU WANT ME TO TALK ABOUT? MOVING FROM ONE FUCKED UP FOSTER HOME TO ANOTHER?
OR SHOULD I TELL YOU HOW IT SCREWED ME UP LIKE THE REST OF YOU?! THAT BEING TREATED LIKE SHIT SEEMED NORMAL TO ME BECAUSE, IF MY PARENTS DIDN'T WANT ME, WHY SHOULD ANYONE ELSE?!
IS THAT IT... IS *THAT* WHAT YOU WANT?!
THANK YOU, TRAVIS.

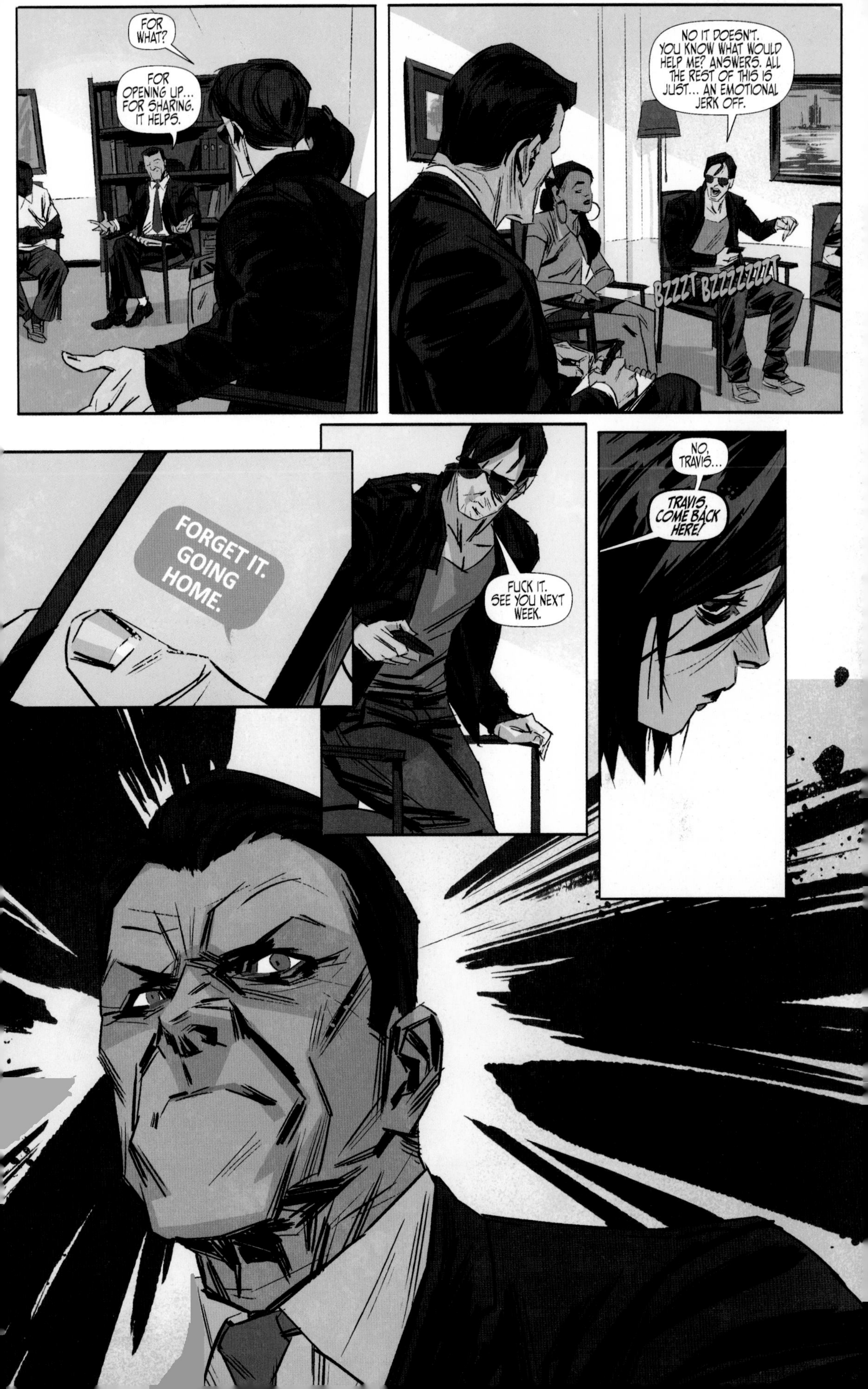

FOR WHAT?
FOR OPENING UP... FOR SHARING. IT HELPS.
NO IT DOESN'T. YOU KNOW WHAT WOULD HELP ME? ANSWERS. ALL THE REST OF THIS IS JUST... AN EMOTIONAL JERK OFF.
BZZZT BZZZZZZZT
FORGET IT. GOING HOME.
FUCK IT. SEE YOU NEXT WEEK.
NO, TRAVIS...
TRAVIS, COME BACK HERE!

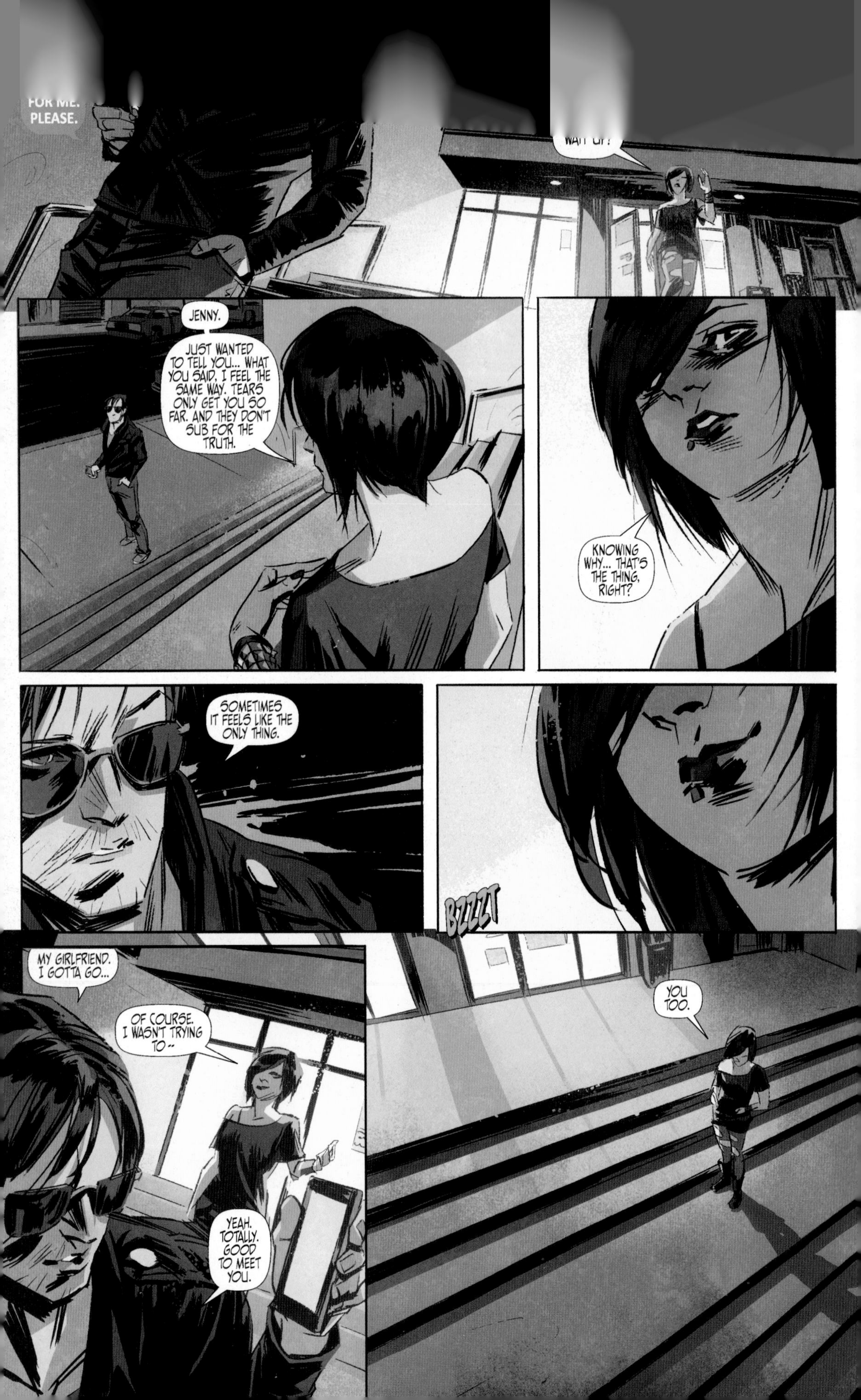
FOR ME. PLEASE.
WAIT UP?
JENNY.
JUST WANTED TO TELL YOU... WHAT YOU SAID, I FEEL THE SAME WAY. TEARS ONLY GET YOU SO FAR. AND THEY DON'T SUB FOR THE TRUTH.
KNOWING WHY... THAT'S THE THING, RIGHT?
SOMETIMES IT FEELS LIKE THE ONLY THING.
BZZZT
MY GIRLFRIEND. I GOTTA GO...
OF COURSE. I WASN'T TRYING TO --
YEAH. TOTALLY. GOOD TO MEET YOU.
YOU TOO.

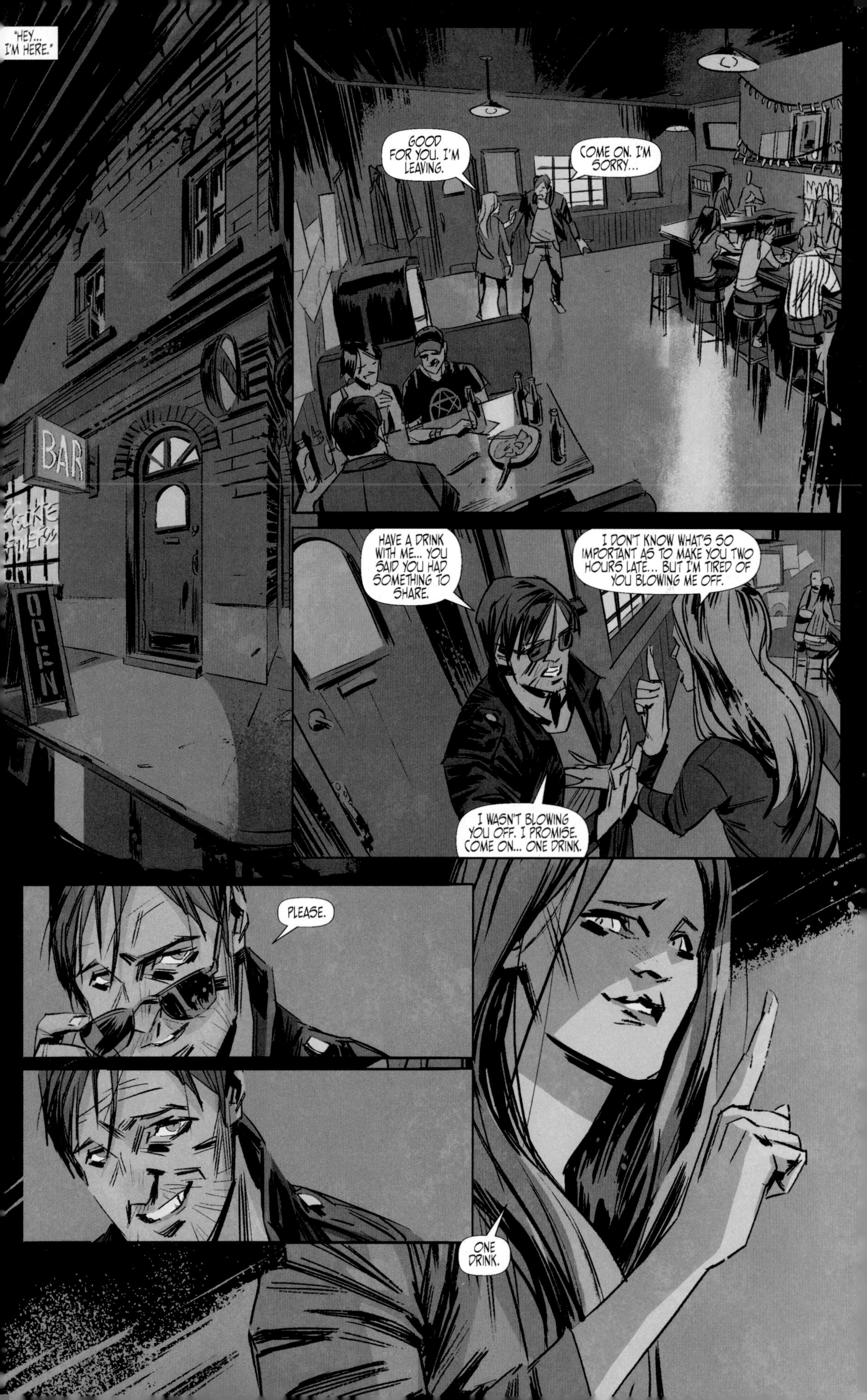
"HEY... I'M HERE."
GOOD FOR YOU. I'M LEAVING.
COME ON. I'M SORRY...
BAR
OPEN
HAVE A DRINK WITH ME... YOU SAID YOU HAD SOMETHING TO SHARE.
I DON'T KNOW WHAT'S SO IMPORTANT AS TO MAKE YOU TWO HOURS LATE... BUT I'M TIRED OF YOU BLOWING ME OFF.
I WASN'T BLOWING YOU OFF. I PROMISE. COME ON... ONE DRINK.
PLEASE.
ONE DRINK.

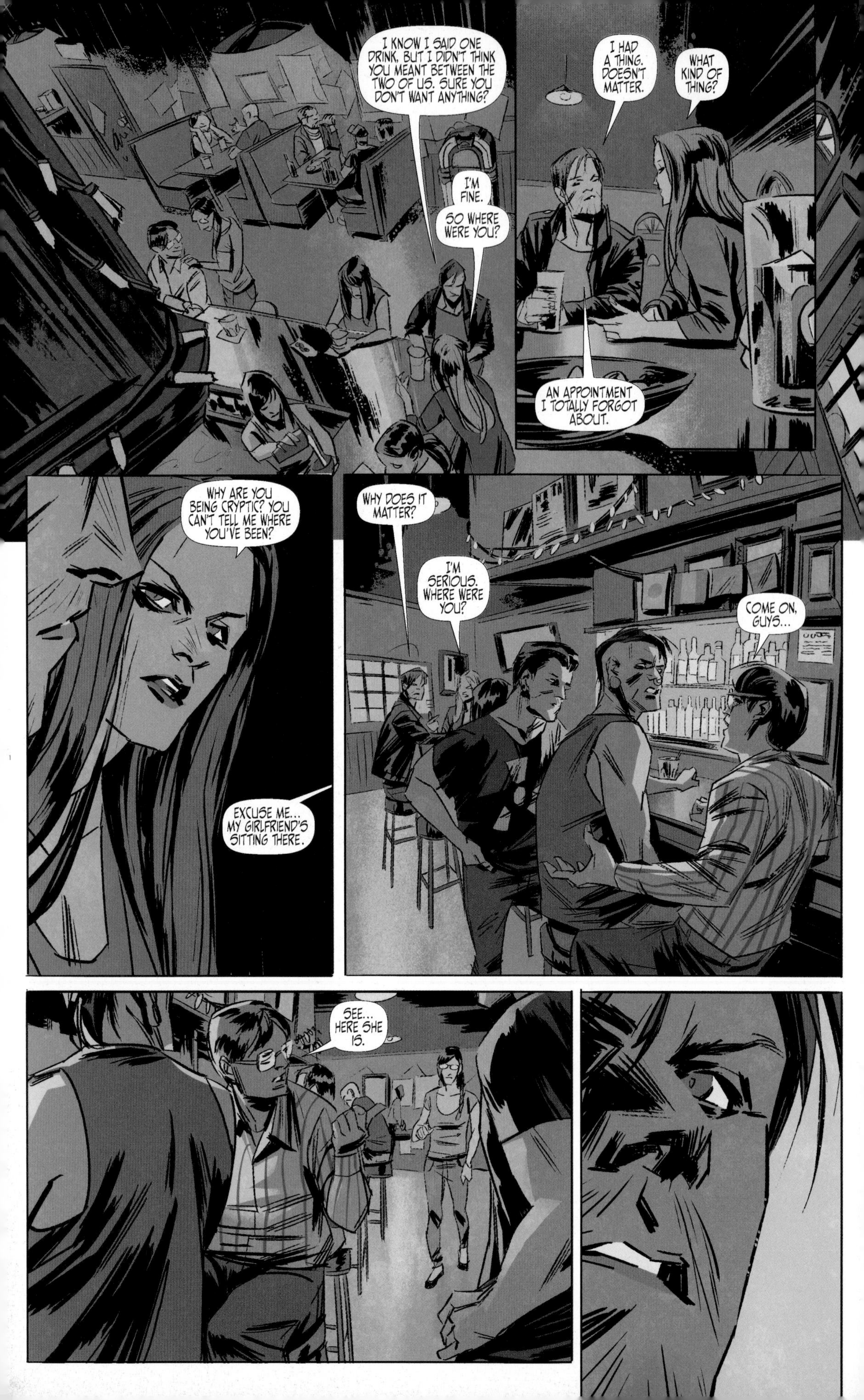

I KNOW I SAID ONE DRINK, BUT I DIDN'T THINK YOU MEANT BETWEEN THE TWO OF US. SURE YOU DON'T WANT ANYTHING?
I'M FINE.
SO WHERE WERE YOU?
I HAD A THING. DOESN'T MATTER.
WHAT KIND OF THING?
AN APPOINTMENT I TOTALLY FORGOT ABOUT.
WHY ARE YOU BEING CRYPTIC? YOU CAN'T TELL ME WHERE YOU'VE BEEN?
EXCUSE ME... MY GIRLFRIEND'S SITTING THERE.
WHY DOES IT MATTER?
I'M SERIOUS. WHERE WERE YOU?
COME ON, GUYS...
SEE... HERE SHE IS.

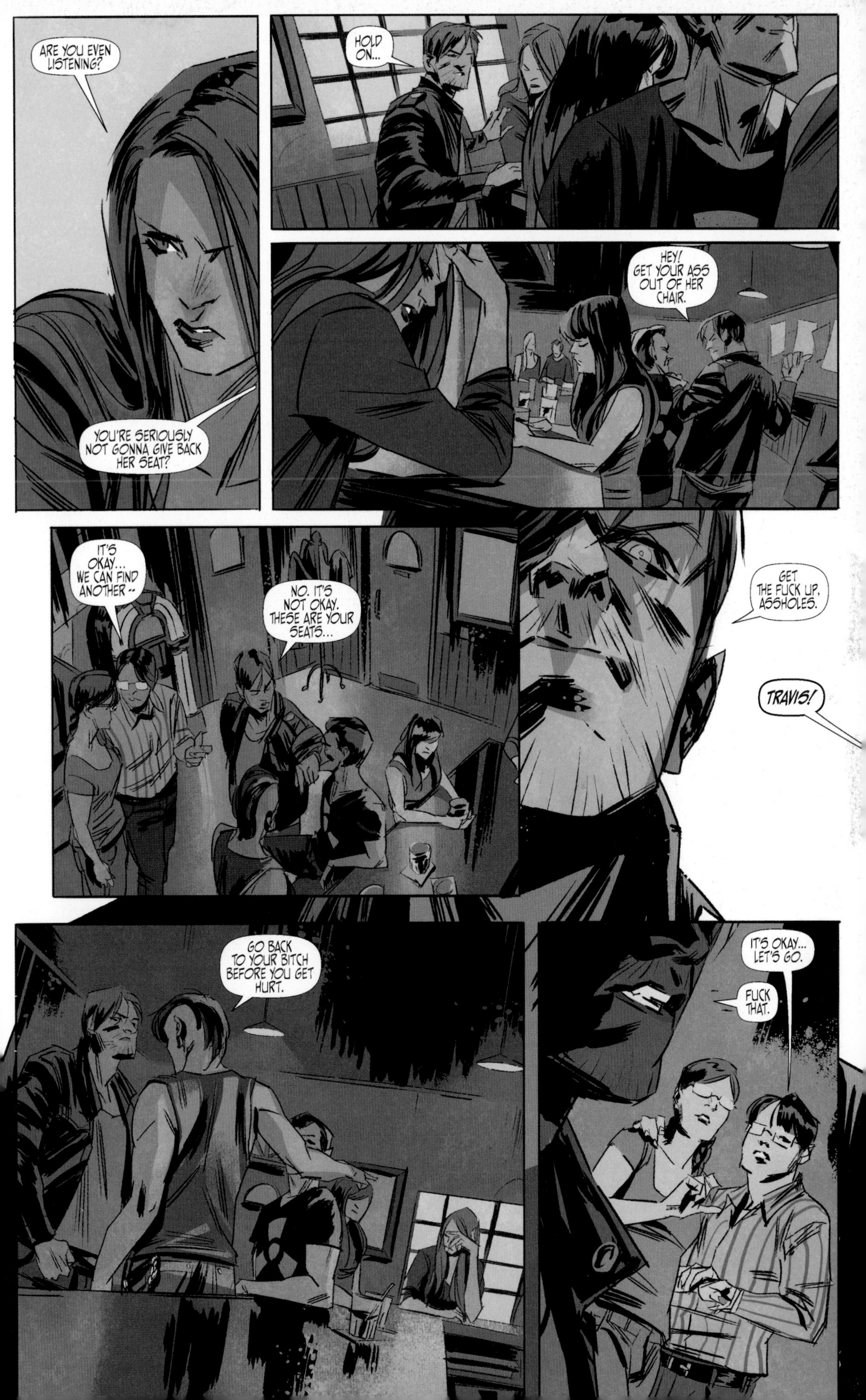
ARE YOU EVEN LISTENING?
YOU'RE SERIOUSLY NOT GONNA GIVE BACK HER SEAT?
HOLD ON...
HEY! GET YOUR ASS OUT OF HER CHAIR.
IT'S OKAY... WE CAN FIND ANOTHER --
NO. IT'S NOT OKAY. THESE ARE YOUR SEATS...
GET THE FUCK UP, ASSHOLES.
TRAVIS!
GO BACK TO YOUR BITCH BEFORE YOU GET HURT.
IT'S OKAY... LET'S GO.
FUCK THAT.

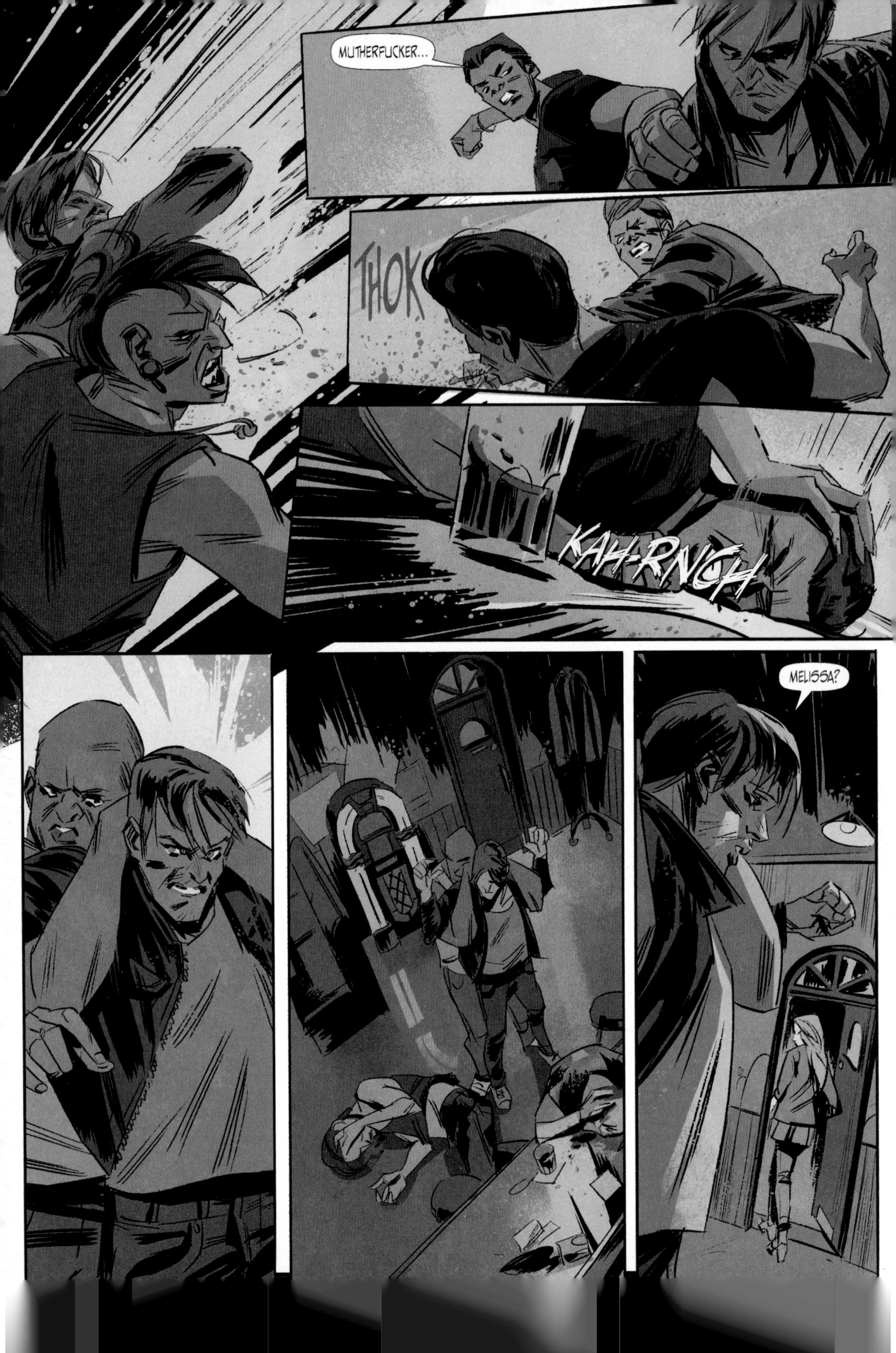
MUTHERFUCKER...
THOK
KAH-RNCH
MELISSA?

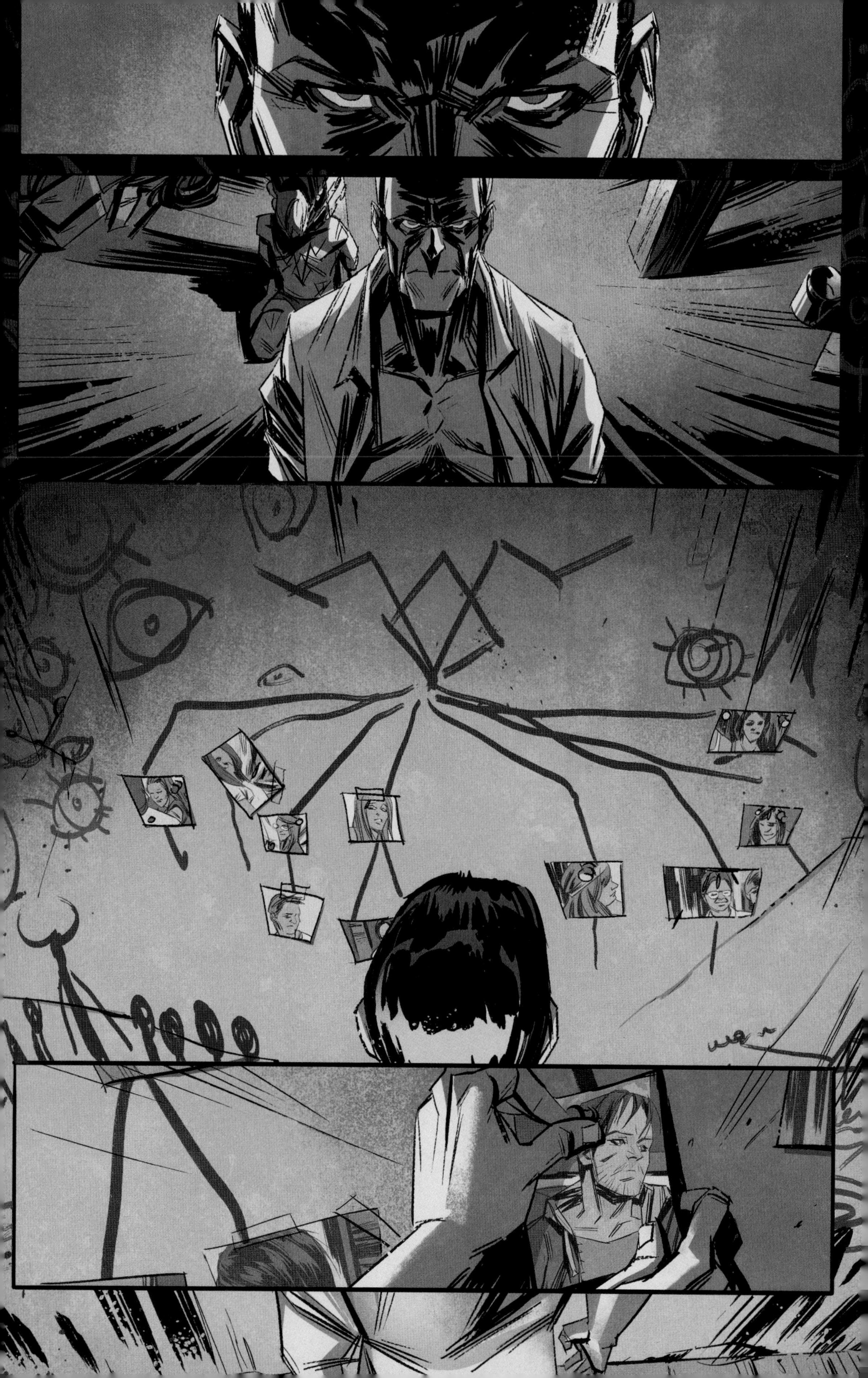

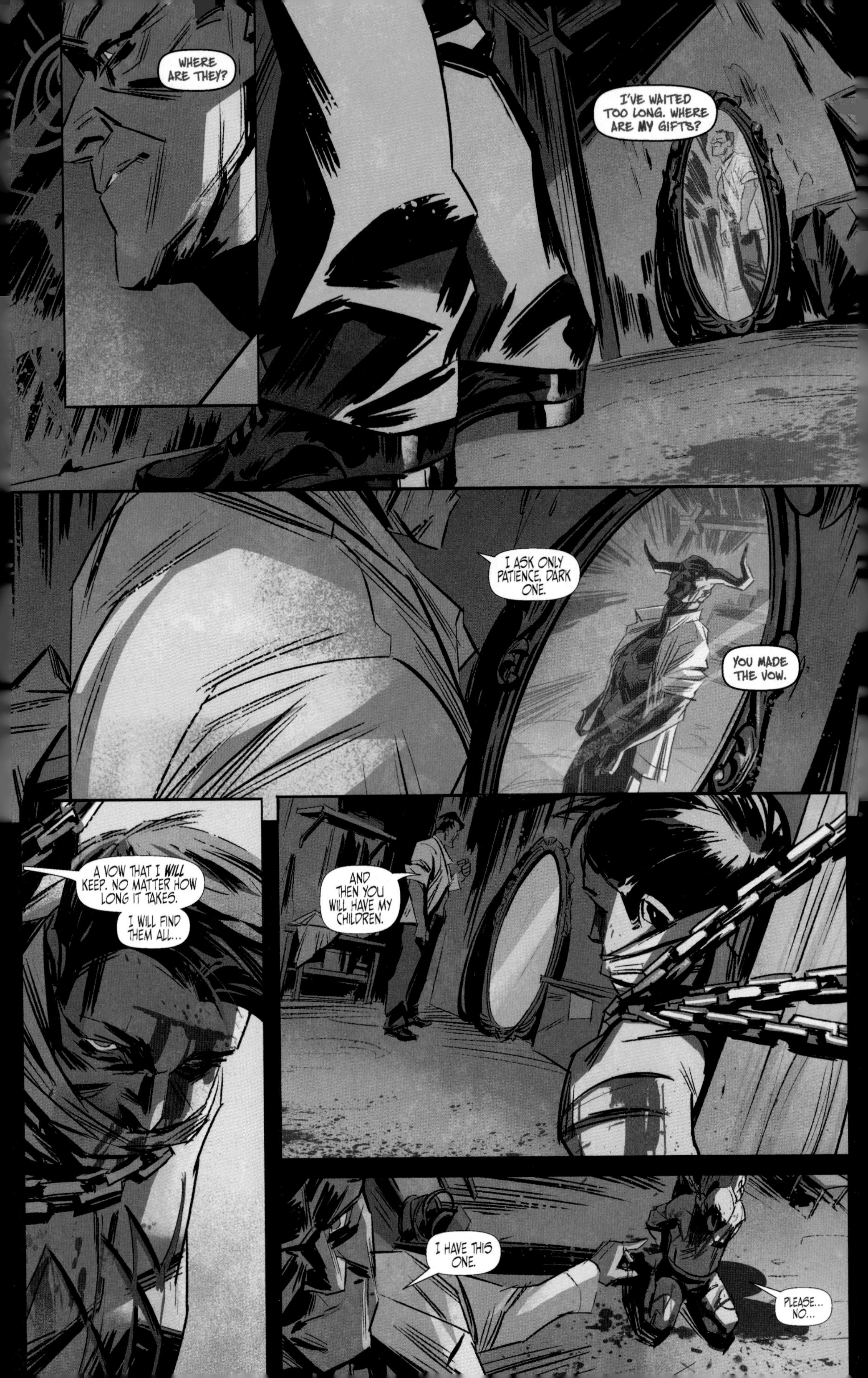
WHERE ARE THEY?
I'VE WAITED TOO LONG. WHERE ARE MY GIFTS?
I ASK ONLY PATIENCE, DARK ONE.
YOU MADE THE VOW.
A VOW THAT I *WILL* KEEP. NO MATTER HOW LONG IT TAKES.
I WILL FIND THEM ALL...
AND THEN YOU WILL HAVE MY CHILDREN.
I HAVE THIS ONE.
PLEASE... NO...

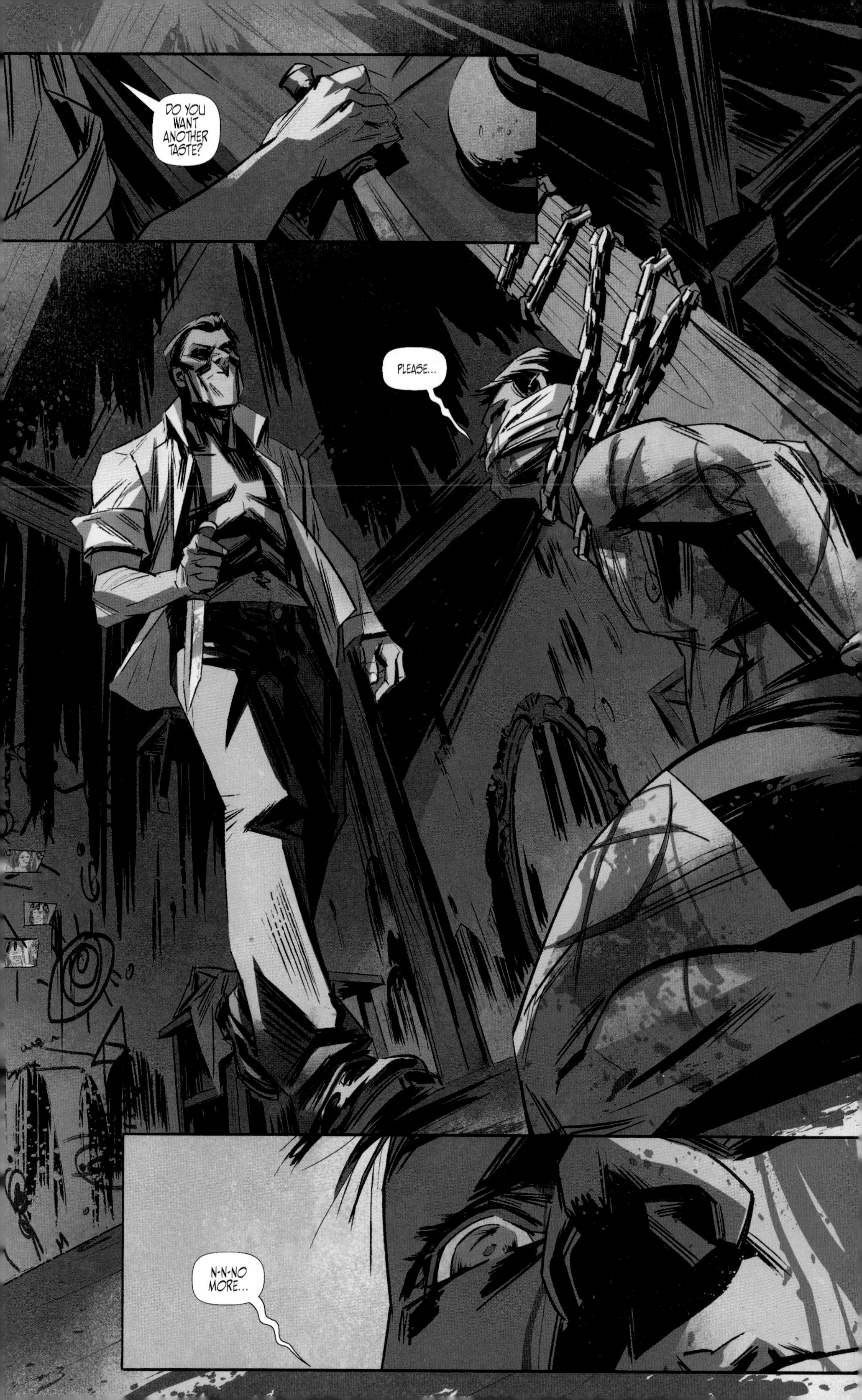
DO YOU WANT ANOTHER TASTE?
PLEASE...
N-N-NO MORE...

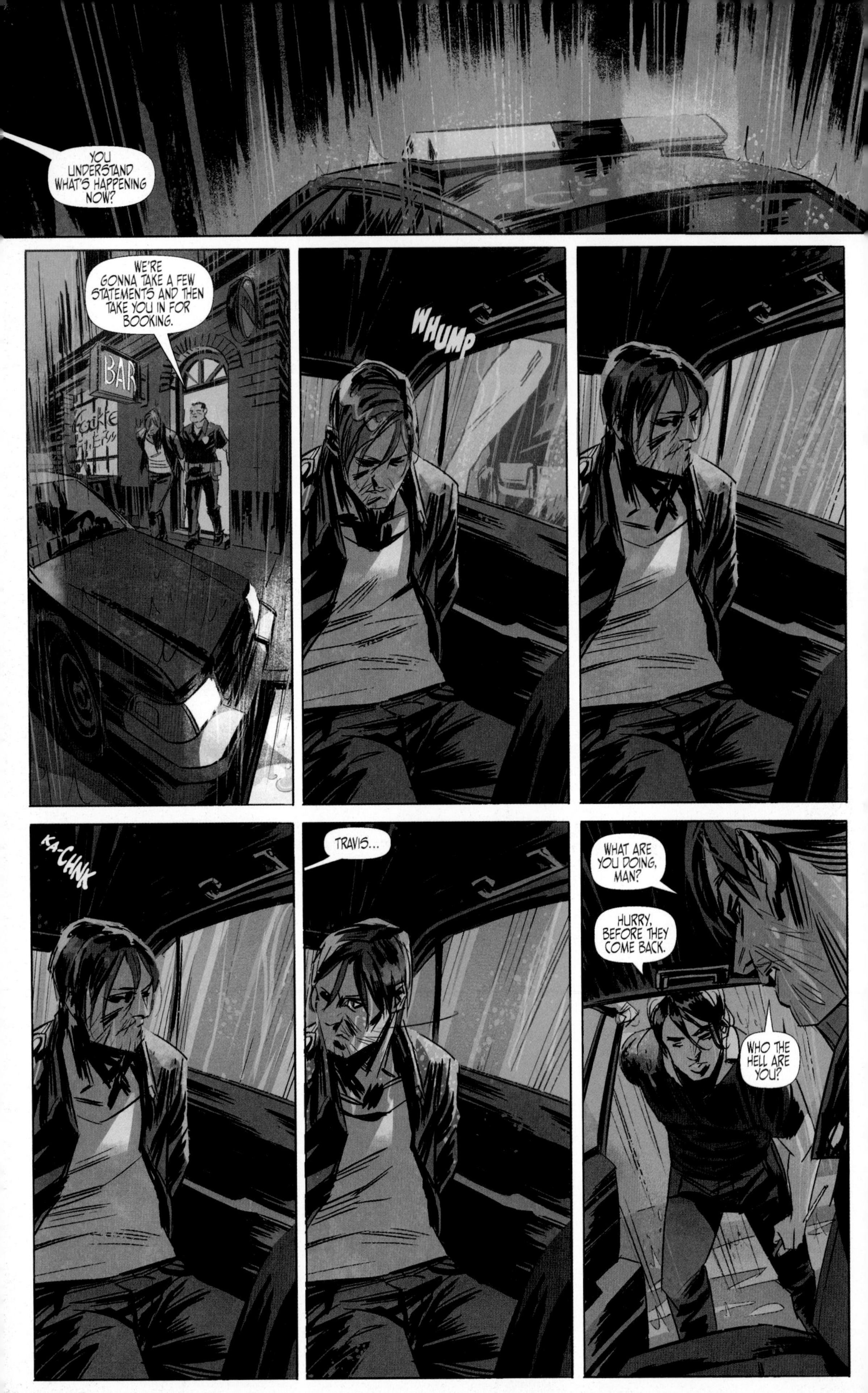
YOU UNDERSTAND WHAT'S HAPPENING NOW?
WE'RE GONNA TAKE A FEW STATEMENTS AND THEN TAKE YOU IN FOR BOOKING.
BAR
WHUMP
KA-CHNK
TRAVIS...
WHAT ARE YOU DOING, MAN?
HURRY, BEFORE THEY COME BACK.
WHO THE HELL ARE YOU?

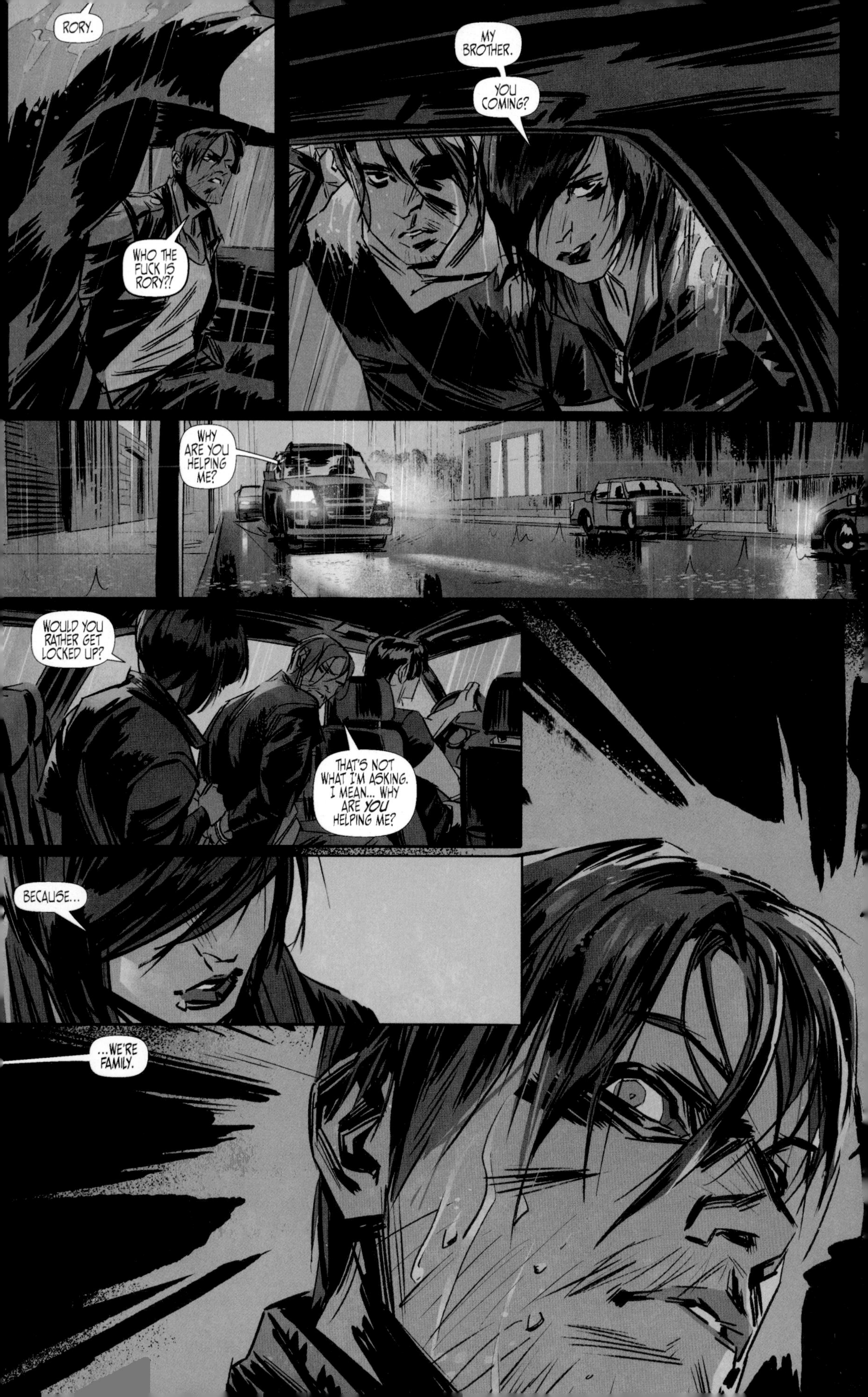
RORY.
WHO THE FUCK IS RORY?!
MY BROTHER.
YOU COMING?
WHY ARE YOU HELPING ME?
WOULD YOU RATHER GET LOCKED UP?
THAT'S NOT WHAT I'M ASKING. I MEAN... WHY ARE *YOU* HELPING ME?
BECAUSE...
...WE'RE FAMILY.

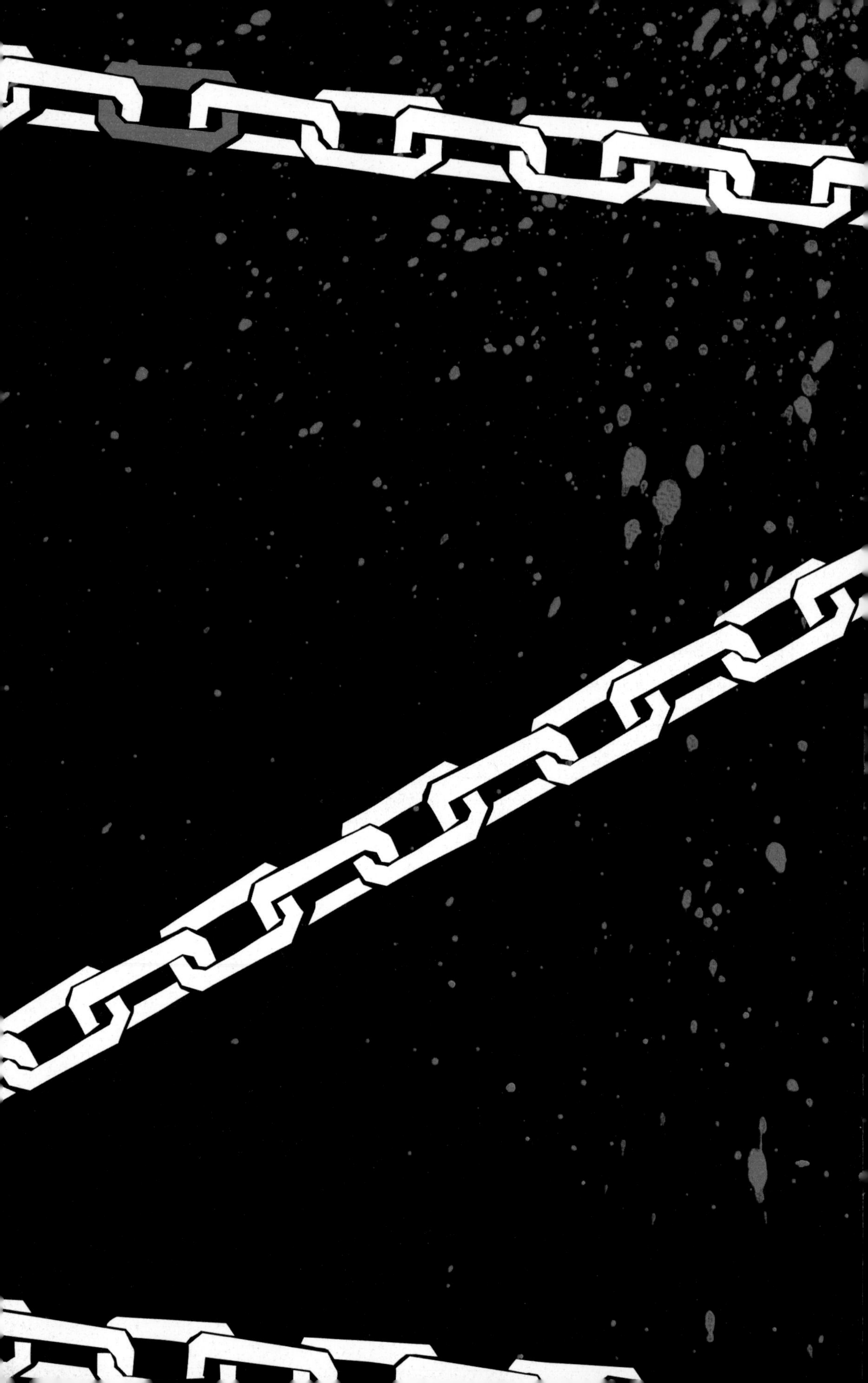

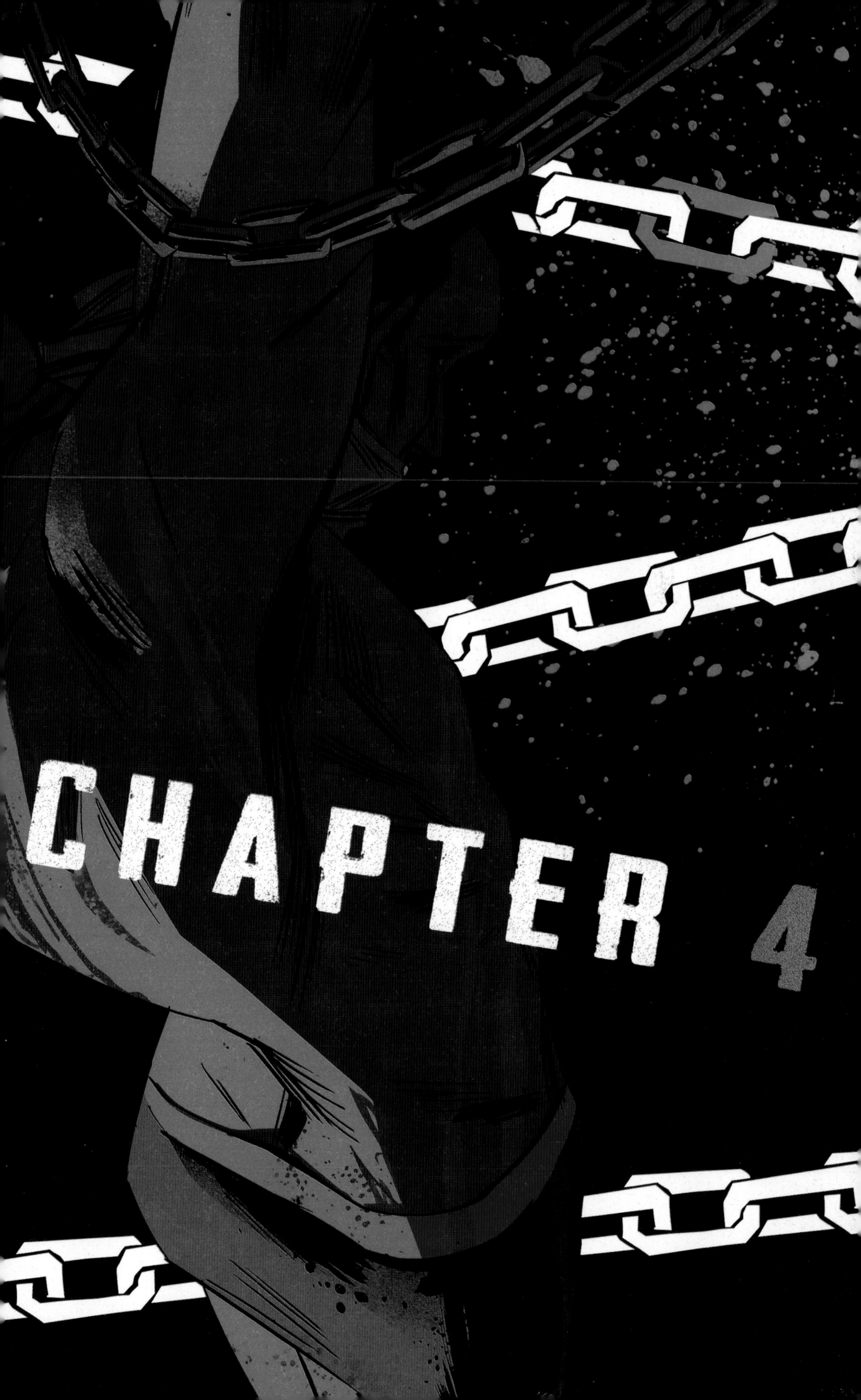
CHAPTER 4

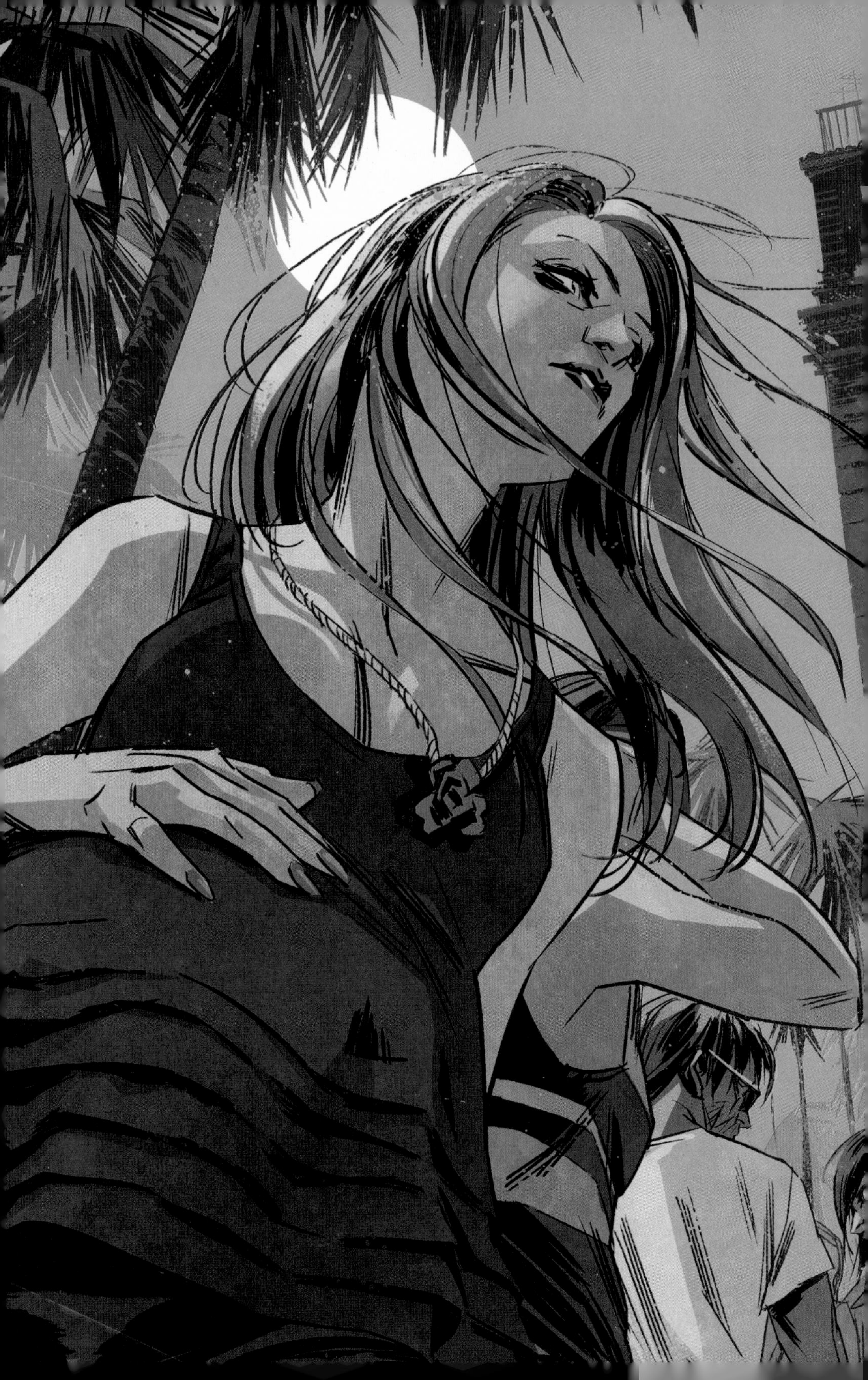

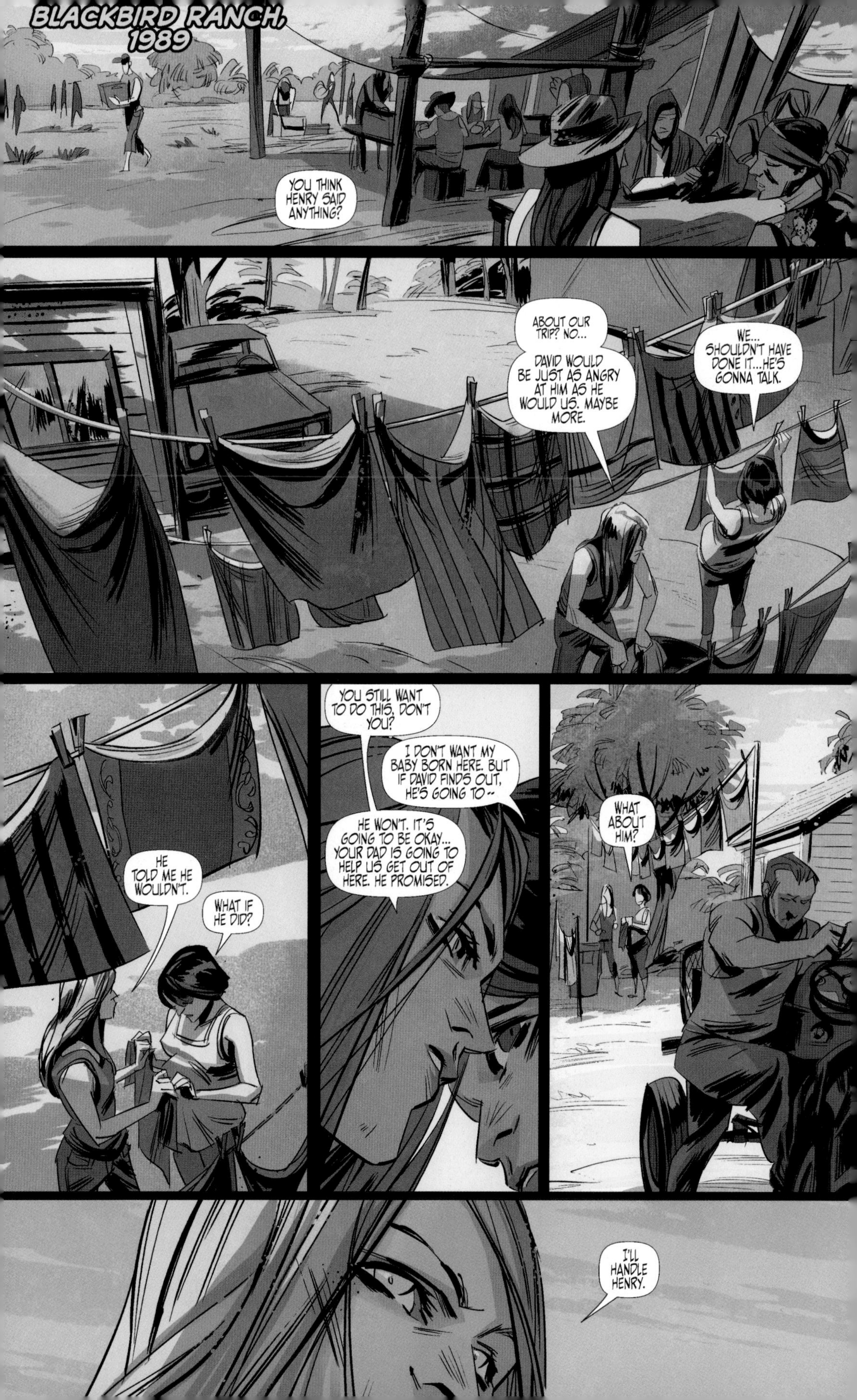
BLACKBIRD RANCH, 1989
YOU THINK HENRY SAID ANYTHING?
ABOUT OUR TRIP? NO...
DAVID WOULD BE JUST AS ANGRY AT HIM AS HE WOULD US. MAYBE MORE.
WE... SHOULDN'T HAVE DONE IT...HE'S GONNA TALK.
HE TOLD ME HE WOULDN'T.
WHAT IF HE DID?
YOU STILL WANT TO DO THIS, DON'T YOU?
I DON'T WANT MY BABY BORN HERE. BUT IF DAVID FINDS OUT, HE'S GOING TO--
HE WON'T. IT'S GOING TO BE OKAY... YOUR DAD IS GOING TO HELP US GET OUT OF HERE. HE PROMISED.
WHAT ABOUT HIM?
I'LL HANDLE HENRY.

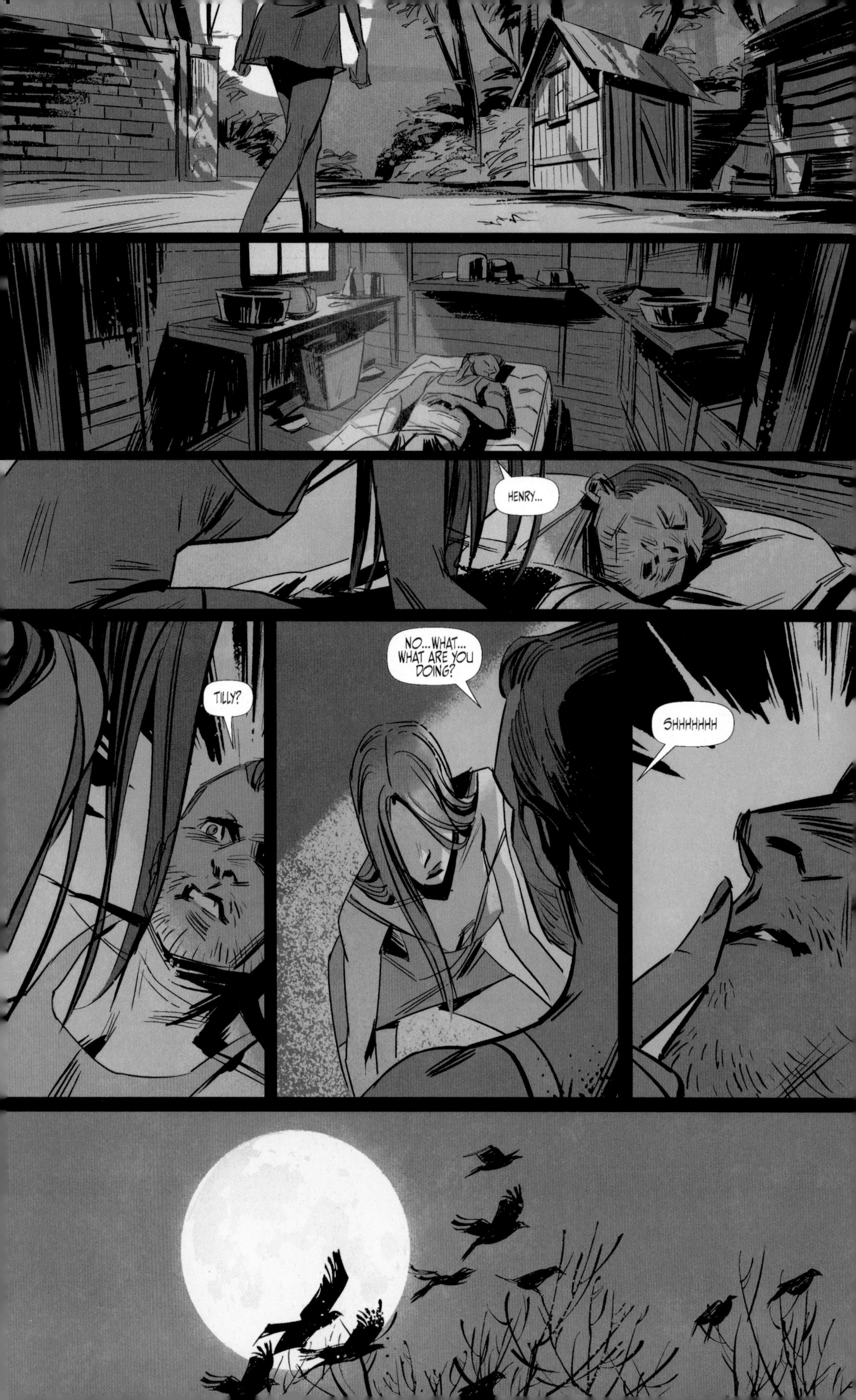
HENRY...
TILLY?
NO... WHAT... WHAT ARE YOU DOING?
SHHHHHHH

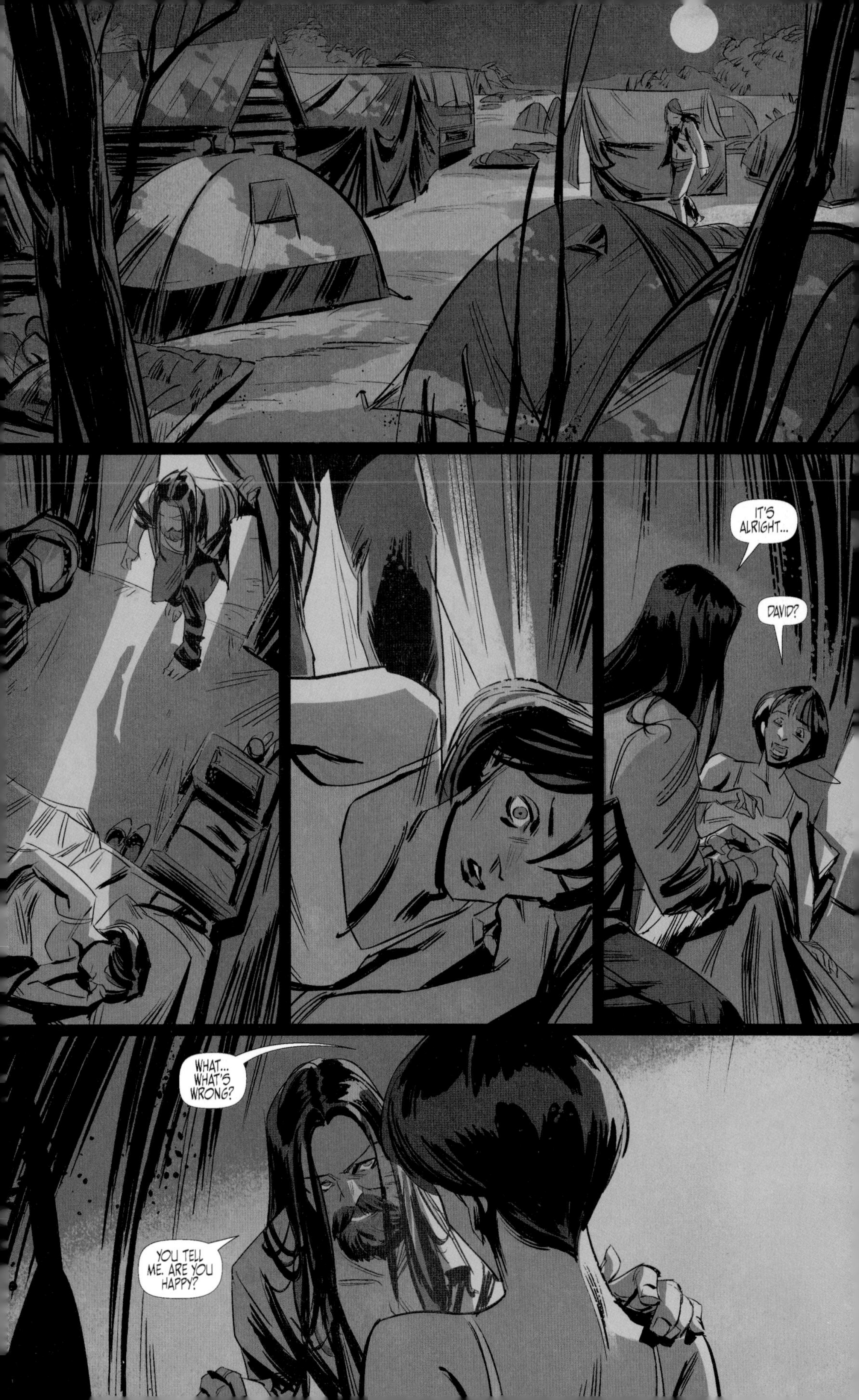
IT'S ALRIGHT...
DAVID?
WHAT... WHAT'S WRONG?
YOU TELL ME. ARE YOU HAPPY?

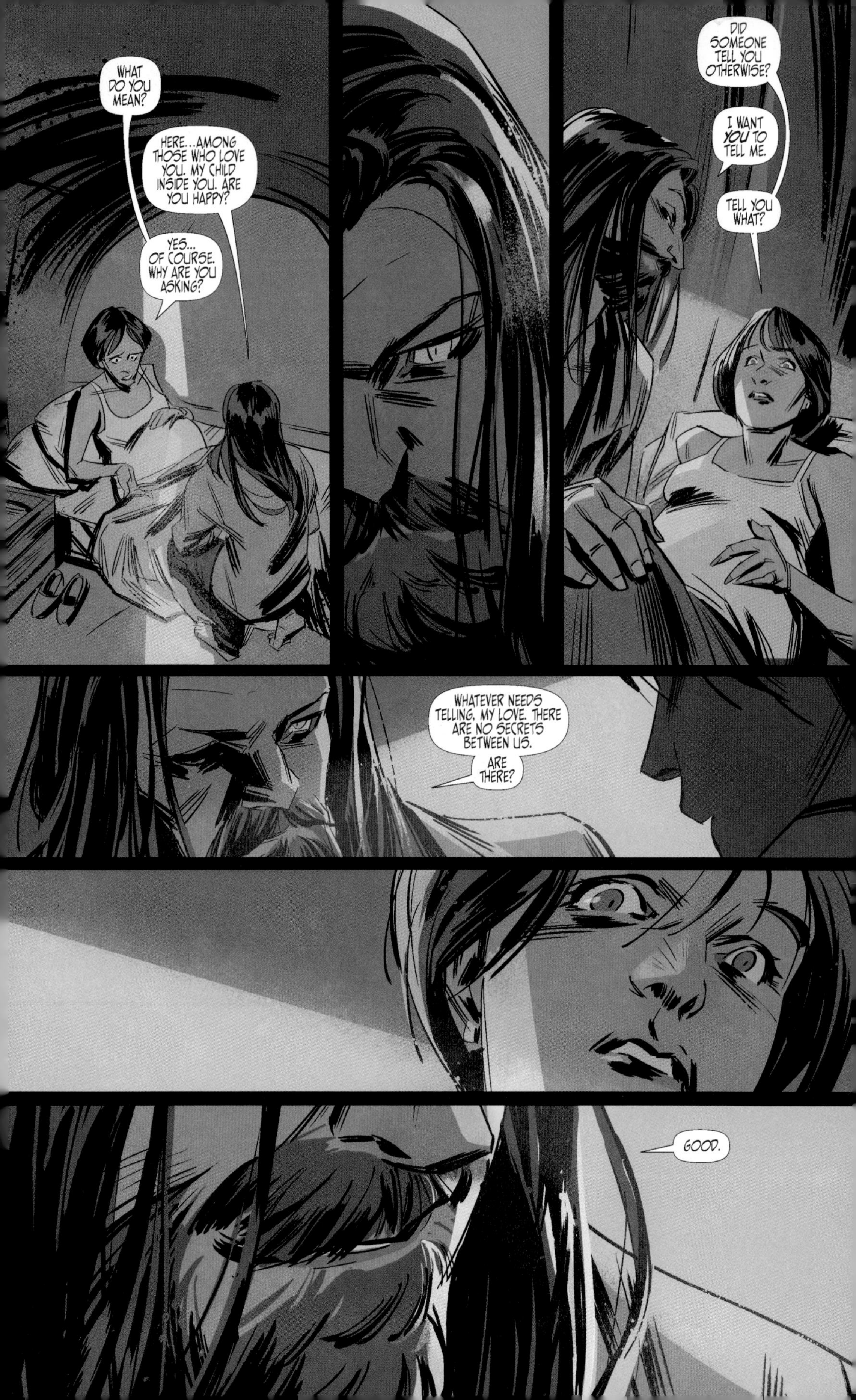
WHAT DO YOU MEAN?
HERE...AMONG THOSE WHO LOVE YOU. MY CHILD INSIDE YOU. ARE YOU HAPPY?
YES... OF COURSE. WHY ARE YOU ASKING?
DID SOMEONE TELL YOU OTHERWISE?
I WANT *YOU* TO TELL ME.
TELL YOU WHAT?
WHATEVER NEEDS TELLING, MY LOVE. THERE ARE NO SECRETS BETWEEN US.
ARE THERE?
GOOD.

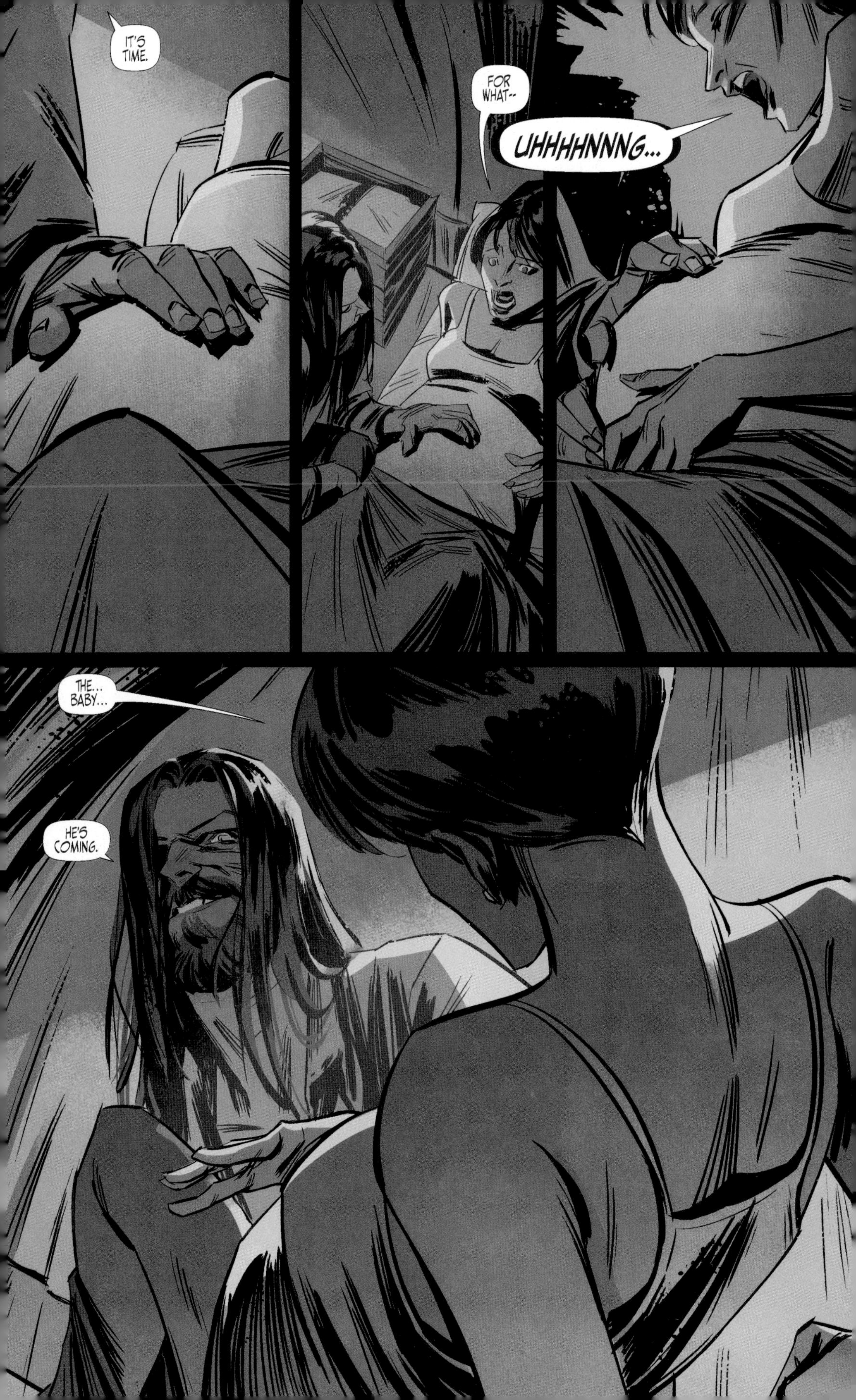
IT'S TIME.
FOR WHAT--
UHHHHNNNG...
THE... BABY...
HE'S COMING.

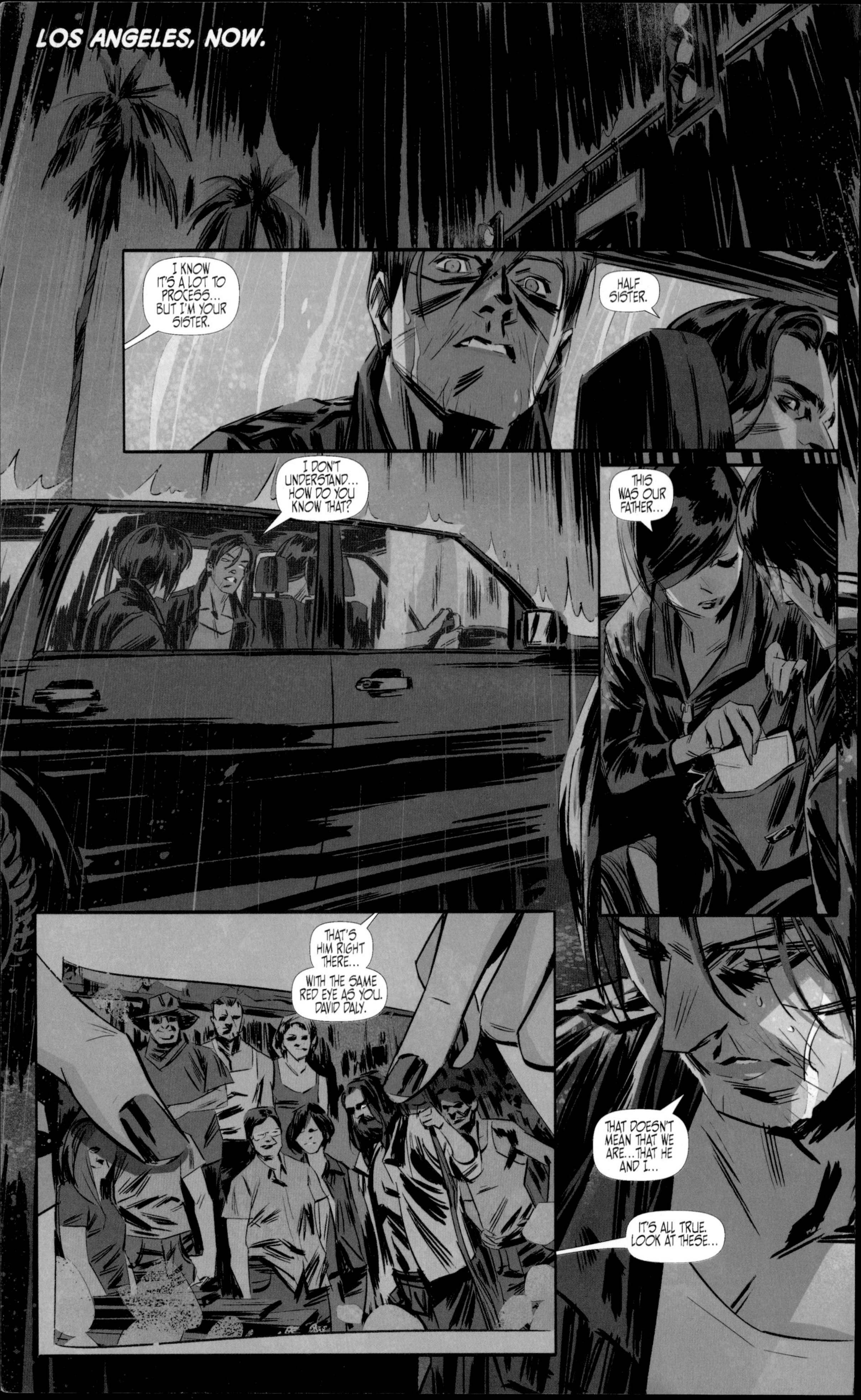
LOS ANGELES, NOW.
I KNOW IT'S A LOT TO PROCESS... BUT I'M YOUR SISTER.
HALF SISTER.
I DON'T UNDERSTAND... HOW DO YOU KNOW THAT?
THIS WAS OUR FATHER...
THAT'S HIM RIGHT THERE...
WITH THE SAME RED EYE AS YOU. DAVID DALY.
THAT DOESN'T MEAN THAT WE ARE... THAT HE AND I...
IT'S ALL TRUE. LOOK AT THESE...

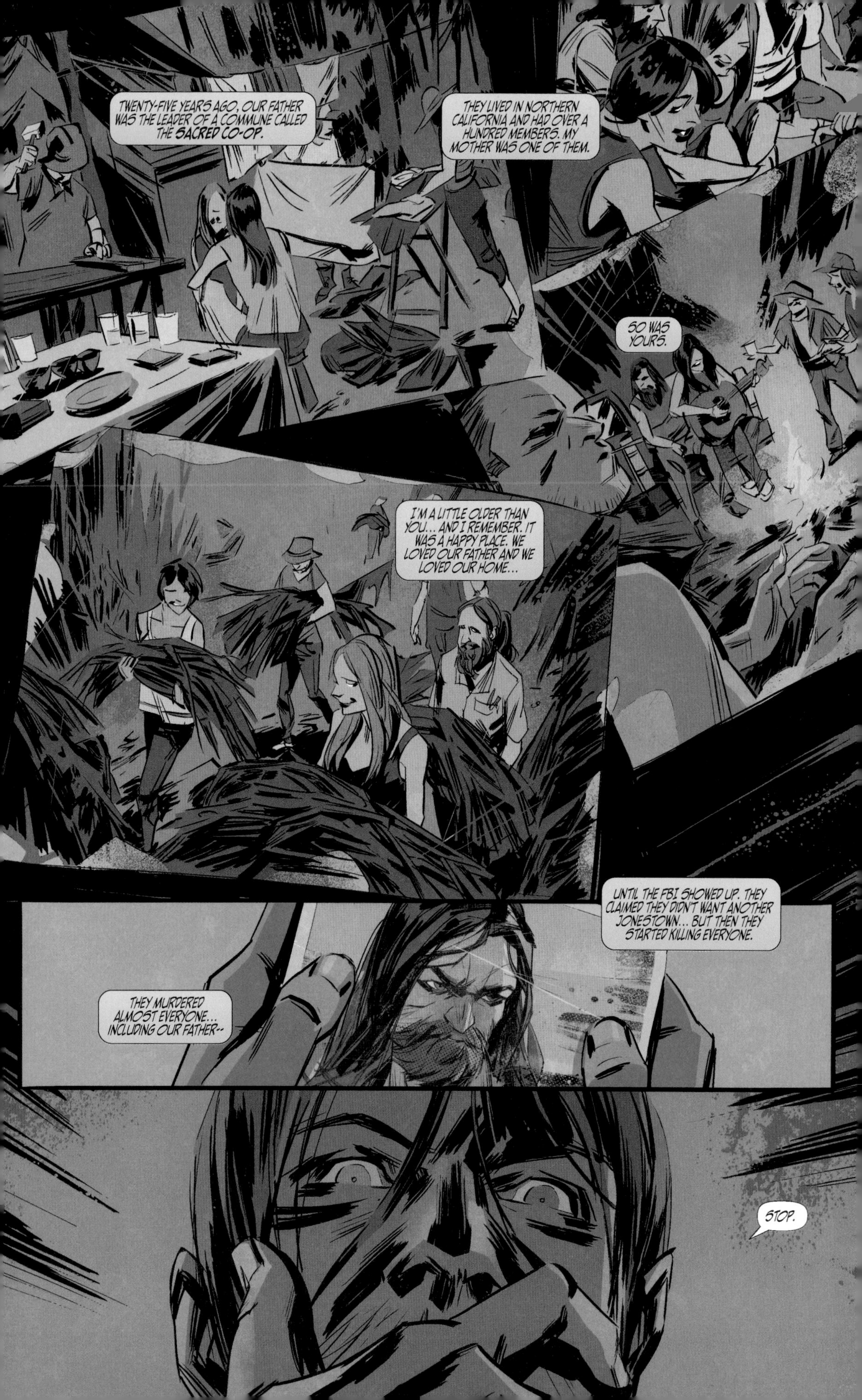
TWENTY-FIVE YEARS AGO, OUR FATHER WAS THE LEADER OF A COMMUNE CALLED THE SACRED CO-OP.
THEY LIVED IN NORTHERN CALIFORNIA AND HAD OVER A HUNDRED MEMBERS. MY MOTHER WAS ONE OF THEM.
SO WAS YOURS.
I'M A LITTLE OLDER THAN YOU... AND I REMEMBER. IT WAS A HAPPY PLACE. WE LOVED OUR FATHER AND WE LOVED OUR HOME...
UNTIL THE FBI SHOWED UP. THEY CLAIMED THEY DIDN'T WANT ANOTHER JONESTOWN... BUT THEN THEY STARTED KILLING EVERYONE.
THEY MURDERED ALMOST EVERYONE... INCLUDING OUR FATHER--
STOP.

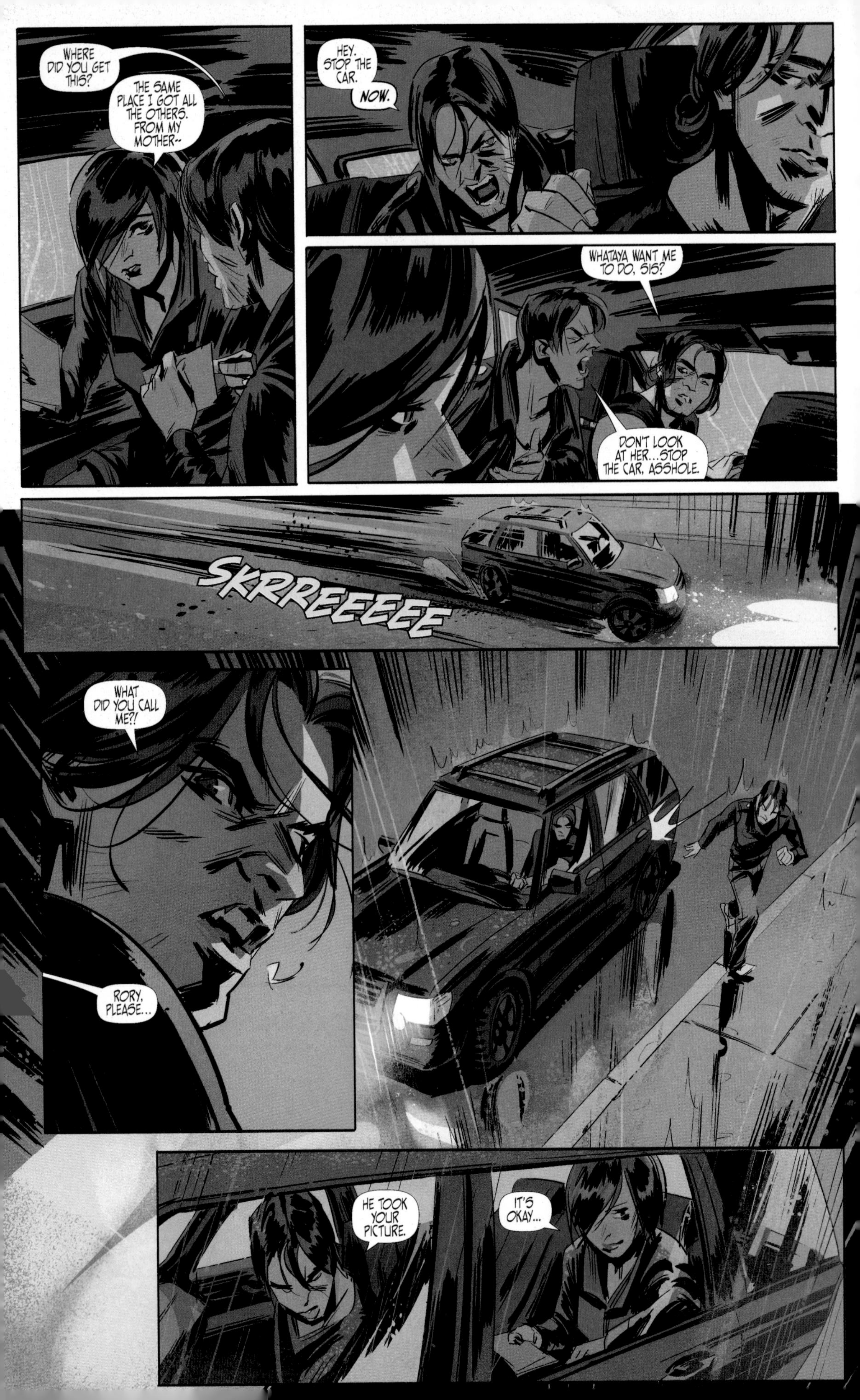
WHERE DID YOU GET THIS?
THE SAME PLACE I GOT ALL THE OTHERS. FROM MY MOTHER--
HEY. STOP THE CAR. NOW.
WHATAYA WANT ME TO DO, SIS?
DON'T LOOK AT HER...STOP THE CAR, ASSHOLE.
SKRREEEEEE
WHAT DID YOU CALL ME?!
RORY, PLEASE...
HE TOOK YOUR PICTURE.
IT'S OKAY...

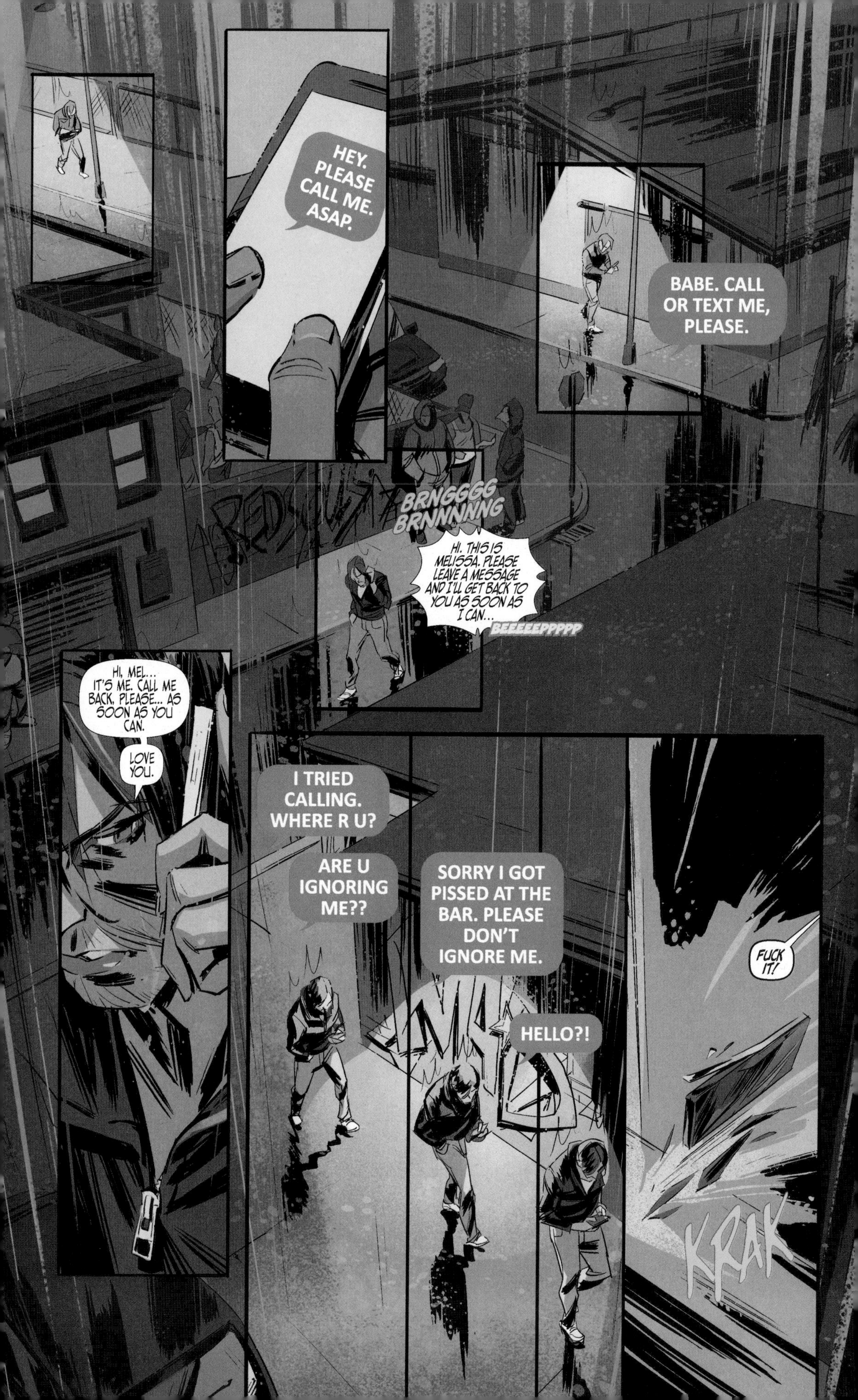
HEY. PLEASE CALL ME. ASAP.
BABE. CALL OR TEXT ME, PLEASE.
BRNGGGG BRNNNNNG
HI. THIS IS MELISSA. PLEASE LEAVE A MESSAGE AND I'LL GET BACK TO YOU AS SOON AS I CAN...
BEEEEEPPPPP
HI, MEL... IT'S ME. CALL ME BACK, PLEASE... AS SOON AS YOU CAN.
LOVE YOU.
I TRIED CALLING. WHERE R U?
ARE U IGNORING ME??
SORRY I GOT PISSED AT THE BAR. PLEASE DON'T IGNORE ME.
HELLO?!
FUCK IT!
KRAK

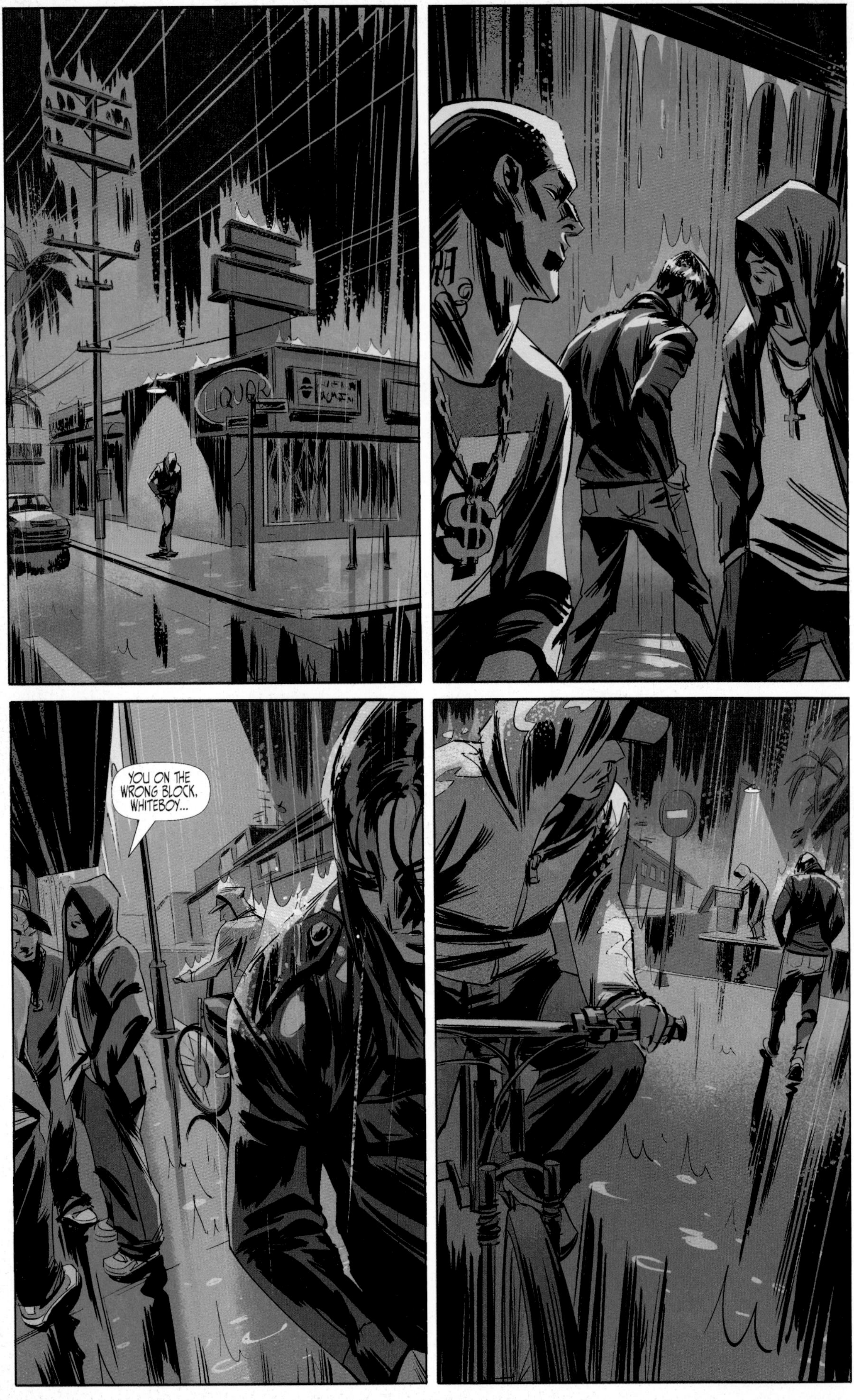
YOU ON THE WRONG BLOCK, WHITEBOY...

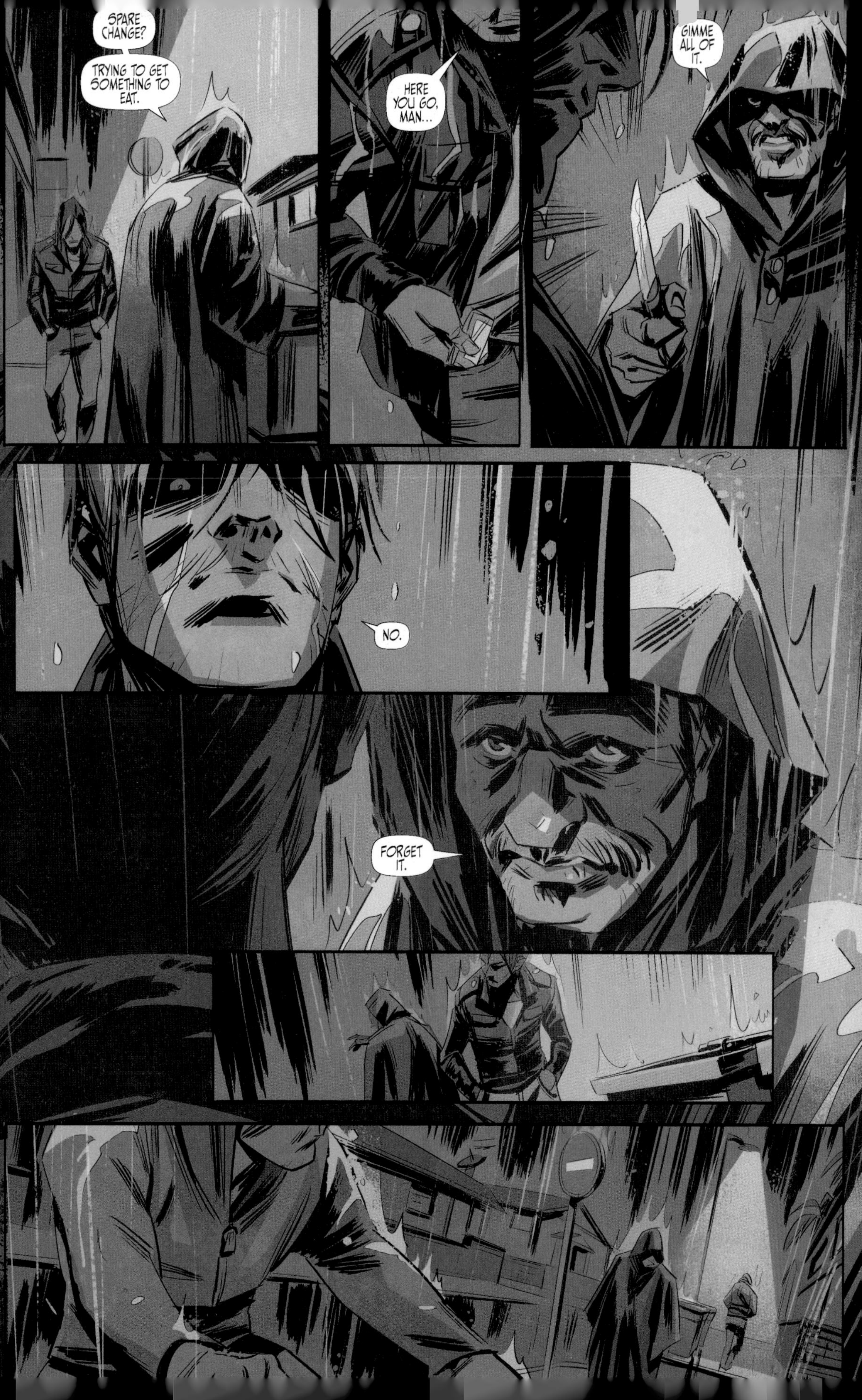
SPARE CHANGE?
TRYING TO GET SOMETHING TO EAT.
HERE YOU GO, MAN...
GIMME ALL OF IT.
NO.
FORGET IT.

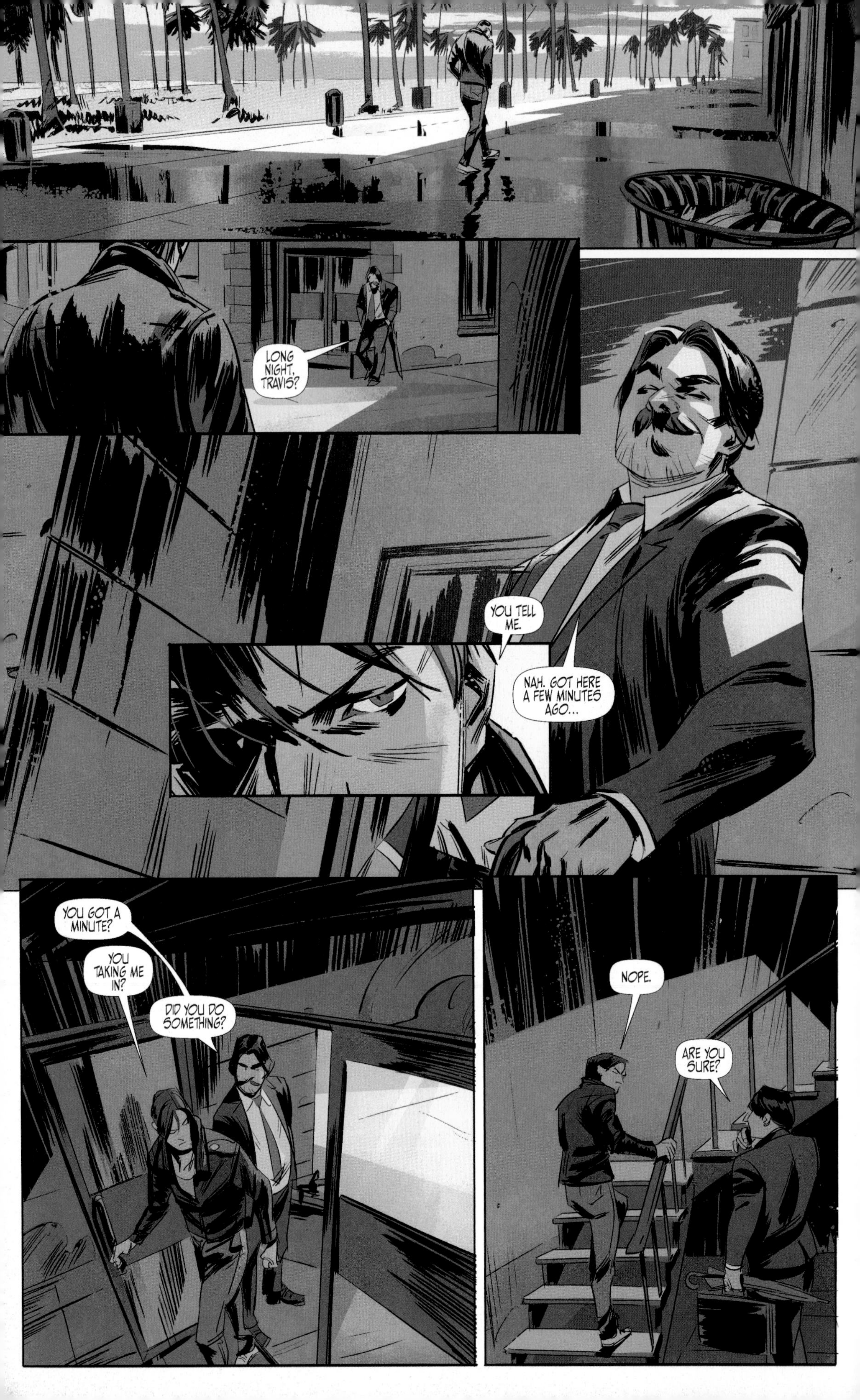
LONG NIGHT, TRAVIS?
YOU TELL ME.
NAH. GOT HERE A FEW MINUTES AGO...
YOU GOT A MINUTE?
YOU TAKING ME IN?
DID YOU DO SOMETHING?
NOPE.
ARE YOU SURE?

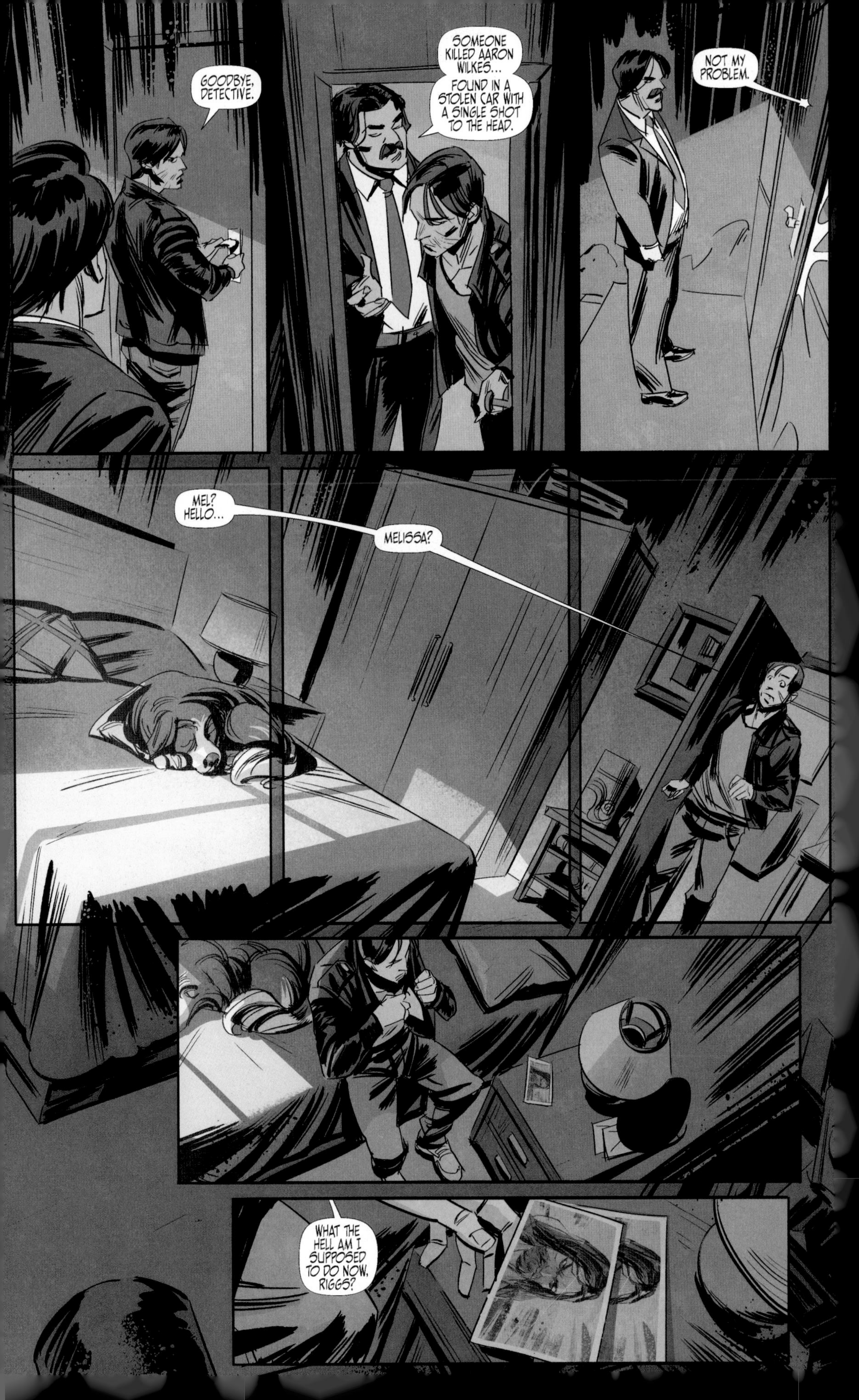
GOODBYE, DETECTIVE.
SOMEONE KILLED AARON WILKES...
FOUND IN A STOLEN CAR WITH A SINGLE SHOT TO THE HEAD.
NOT MY PROBLEM.
MEL? HELLO...
MELISSA?
WHAT THE HELL AM I SUPPOSED TO DO NOW, RIGGS?

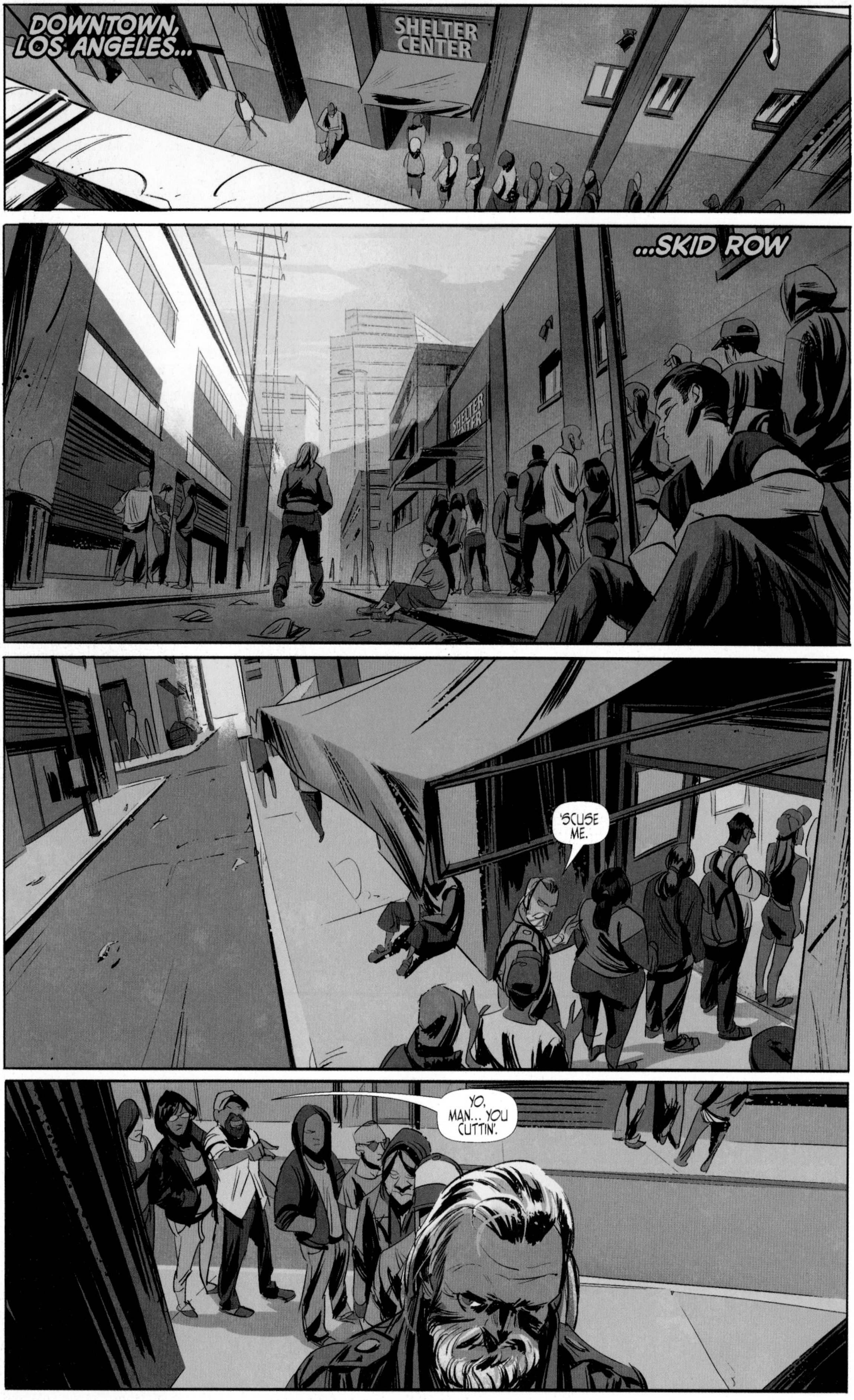
DOWNTOWN, LOS ANGELES...
SHELTER CENTER
...SKID ROW
SHELTER CENTER
'SCUSE ME.
YO, MAN... YOU CUTTIN'.

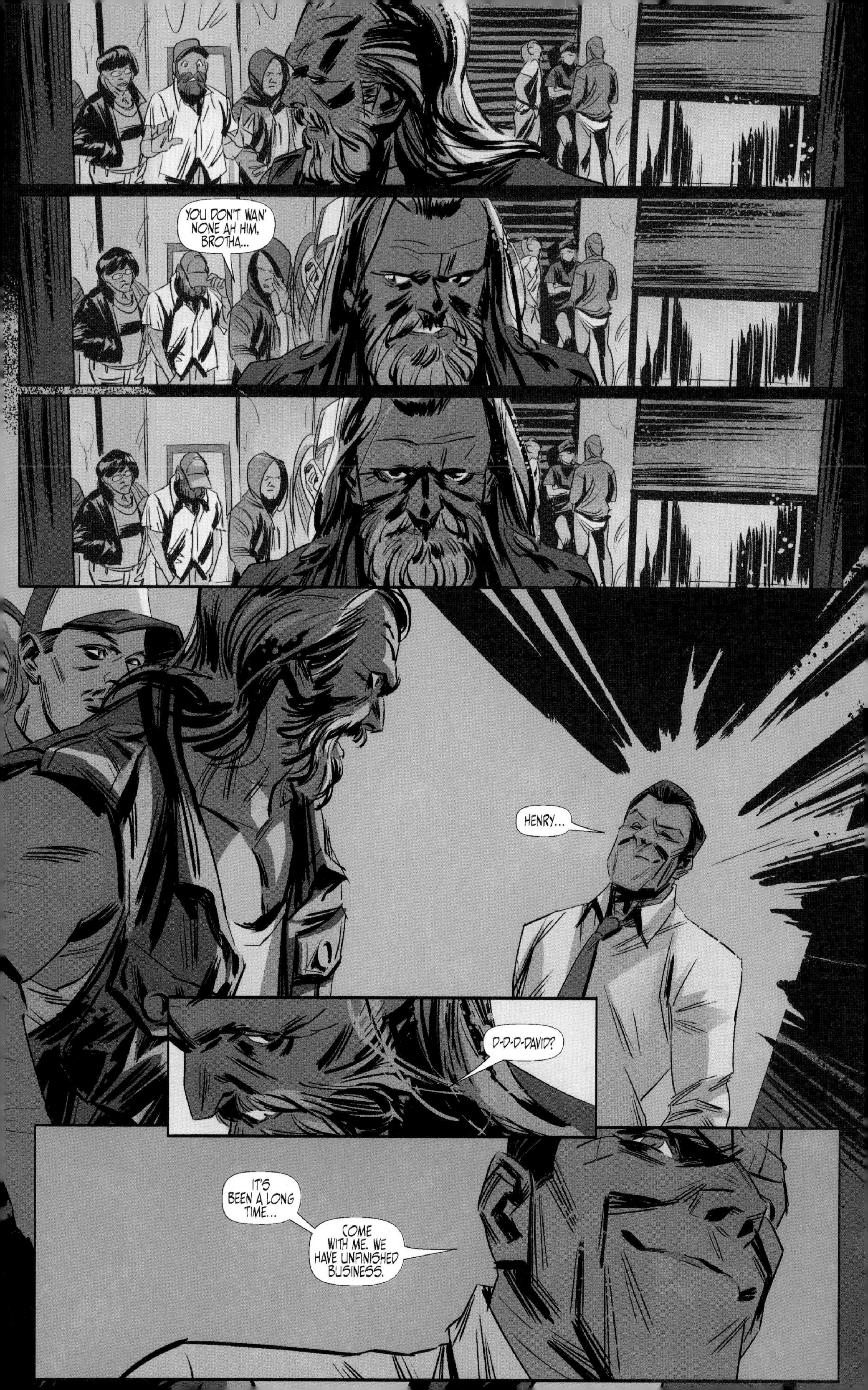
YOU DON'T WAN' NONE AH HIM, BROTHA...
HENRY...
D-D-D-DAVID?
IT'S BEEN A LONG TIME...
COME WITH ME. WE HAVE UNFINISHED BUSINESS.

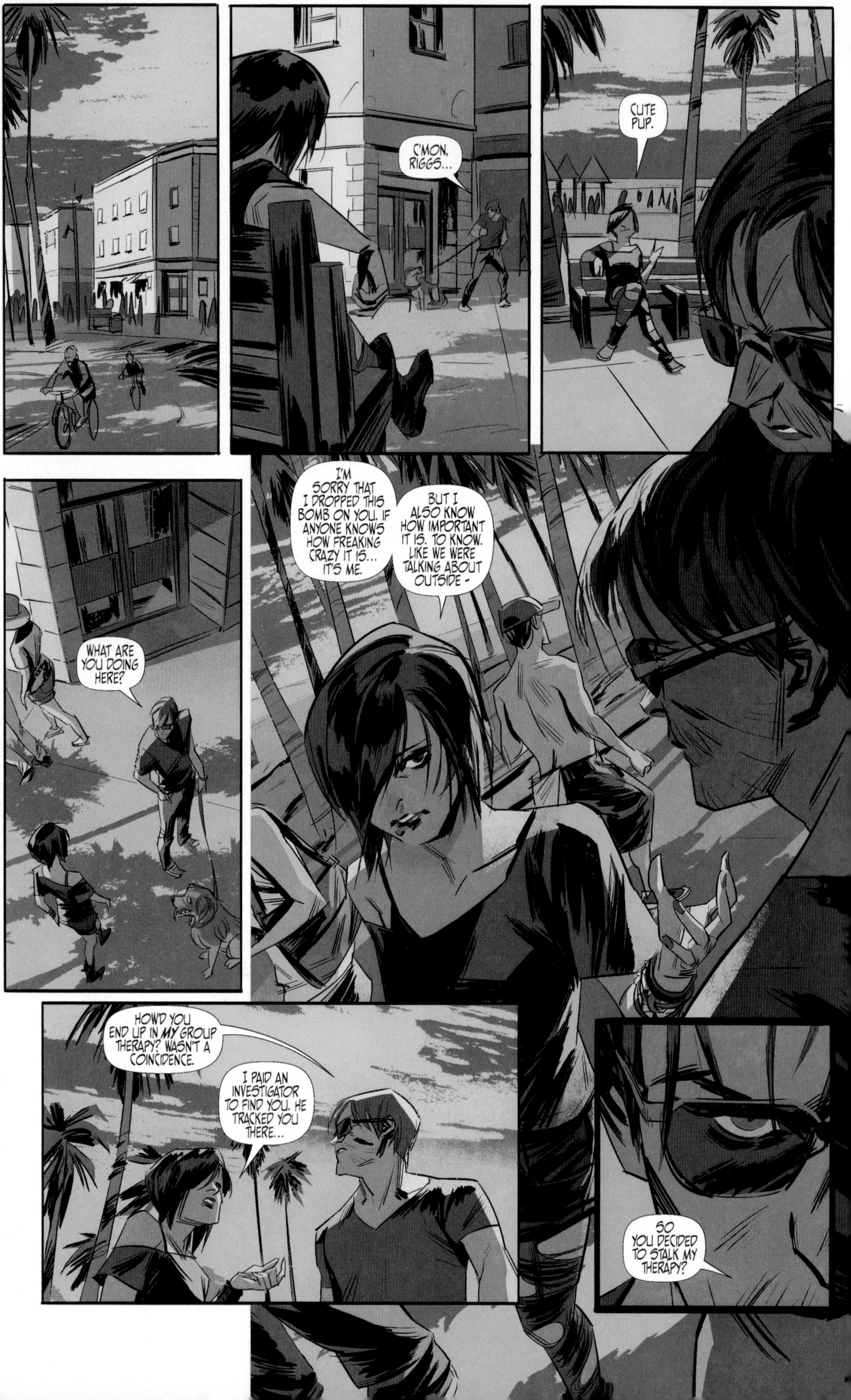
C'MON, RIGGS...
CUTE PUP.
WHAT ARE YOU DOING HERE?
I'M SORRY THAT I DROPPED THIS BOMB ON YOU. IF ANYONE KNOWS HOW FREAKING CRAZY IT IS... IT'S ME.
BUT I ALSO KNOW HOW IMPORTANT IT IS. TO KNOW. LIKE WE WERE TALKING ABOUT OUTSIDE -
HOW'D YOU END UP IN MY GROUP THERAPY? WASN'T A COINCIDENCE.
I PAID AN INVESTIGATOR TO FIND YOU. HE TRACKED YOU THERE...
SO YOU DECIDED TO STALK MY THERAPY?

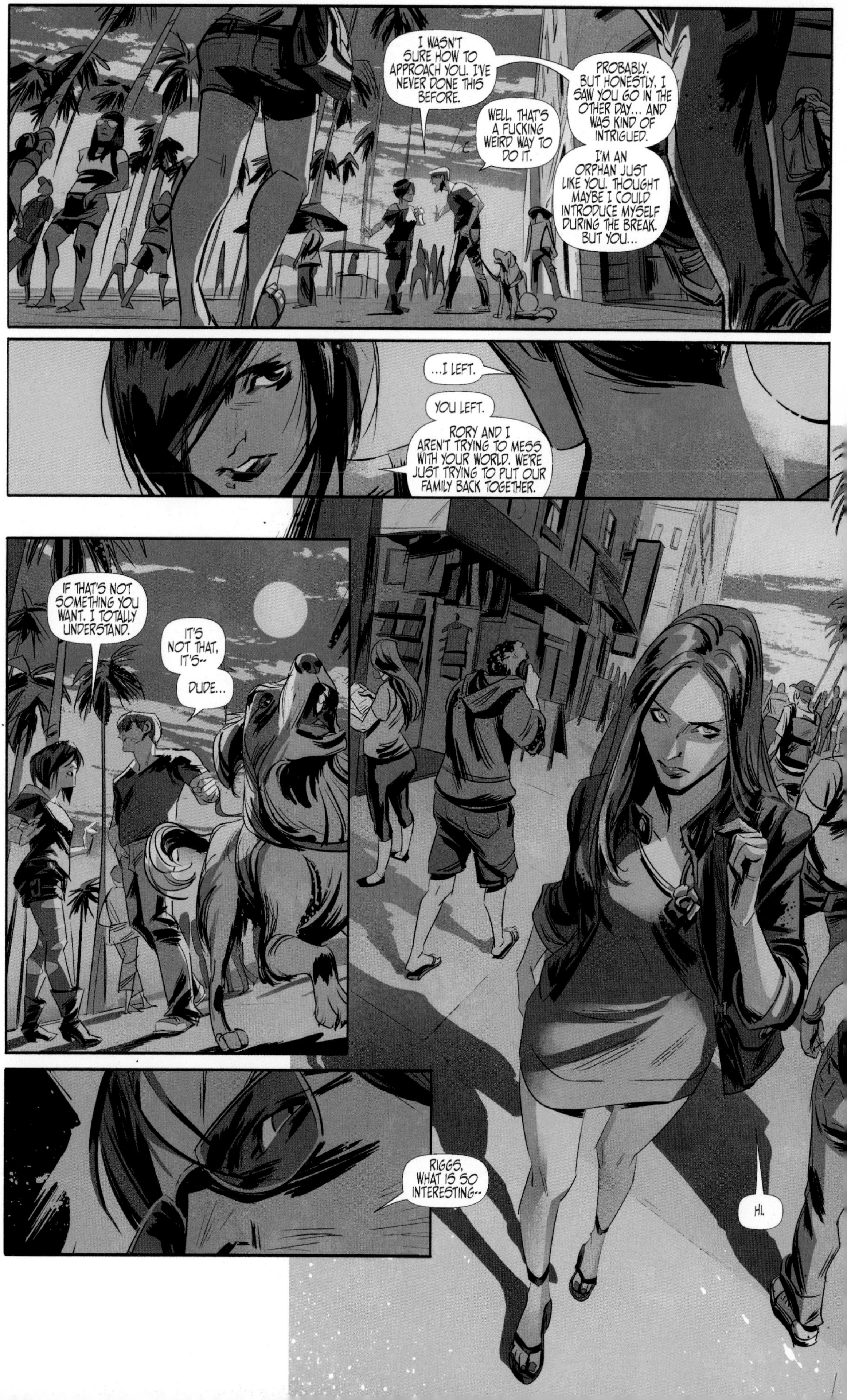
I WASN'T SURE HOW TO APPROACH YOU. I'VE NEVER DONE THIS BEFORE.
WELL, THAT'S A FUCKING WEIRD WAY TO DO IT.
PROBABLY. BUT HONESTLY, I SAW YOU GO IN THE OTHER DAY... AND WAS KIND OF INTRIGUED.
I'M AN ORPHAN JUST LIKE YOU. THOUGHT MAYBE I COULD INTRODUCE MYSELF DURING THE BREAK. BUT YOU...
...I LEFT.
YOU LEFT.
RORY AND I AREN'T TRYING TO MESS WITH YOUR WORLD. WE'RE JUST TRYING TO PUT OUR FAMILY BACK TOGETHER.
IF THAT'S NOT SOMETHING YOU WANT. I TOTALLY UNDERSTAND.
IT'S NOT THAT, IT'S--
DUDE...
RIGGS, WHAT IS SO INTERESTING--
HI.

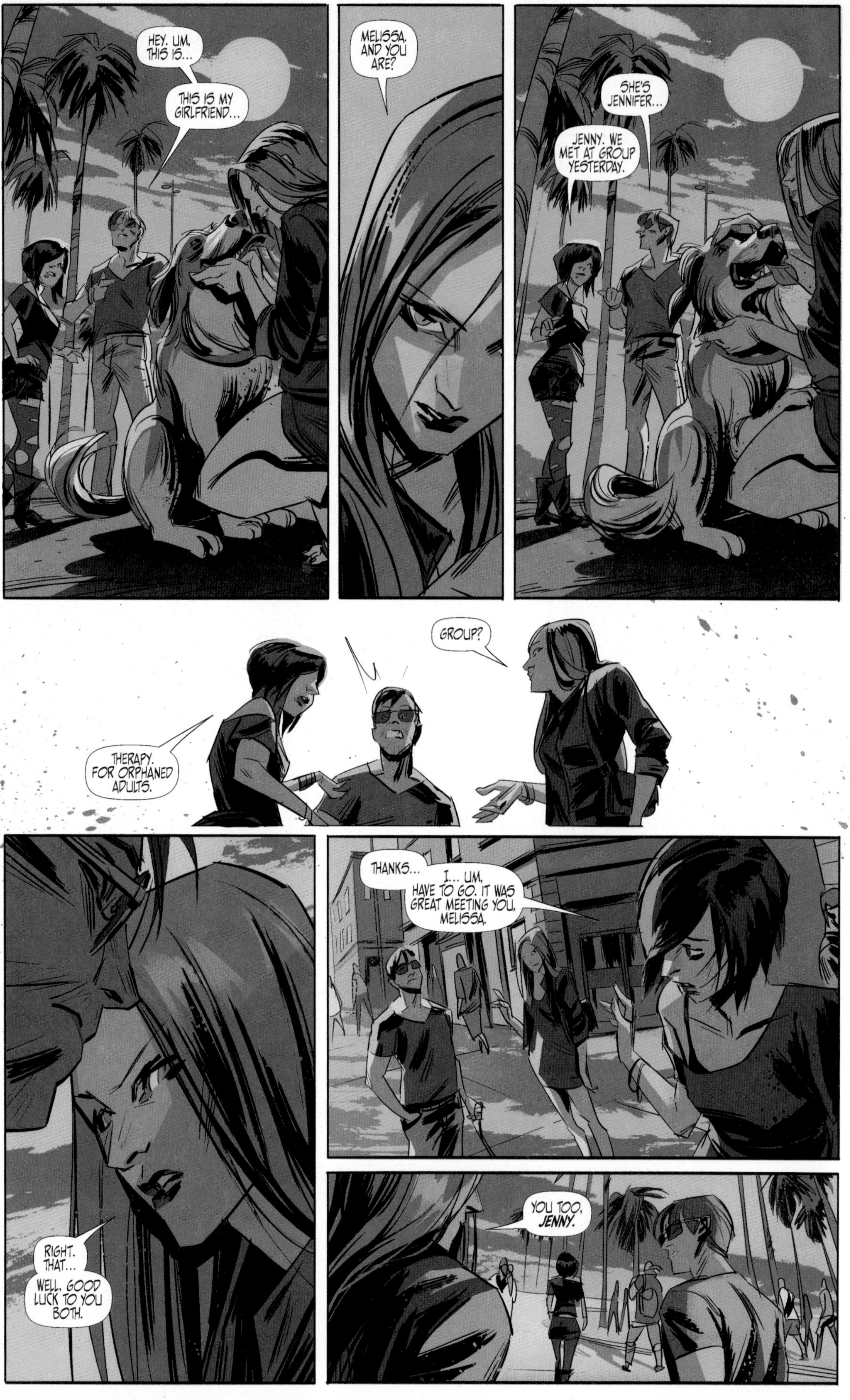
HEY. UM, THIS IS...
THIS IS MY GIRLFRIEND...
MELISSA. AND YOU ARE?
SHE'S JENNIFER...
JENNY. WE MET AT GROUP YESTERDAY.
GROUP?
THERAPY. FOR ORPHANED ADULTS.
RIGHT. THAT...
WELL, GOOD LUCK TO YOU BOTH.
THANKS...
I... UM, HAVE TO GO. IT WAS GREAT MEETING YOU, MELISSA.
YOU TOO, JENNY.

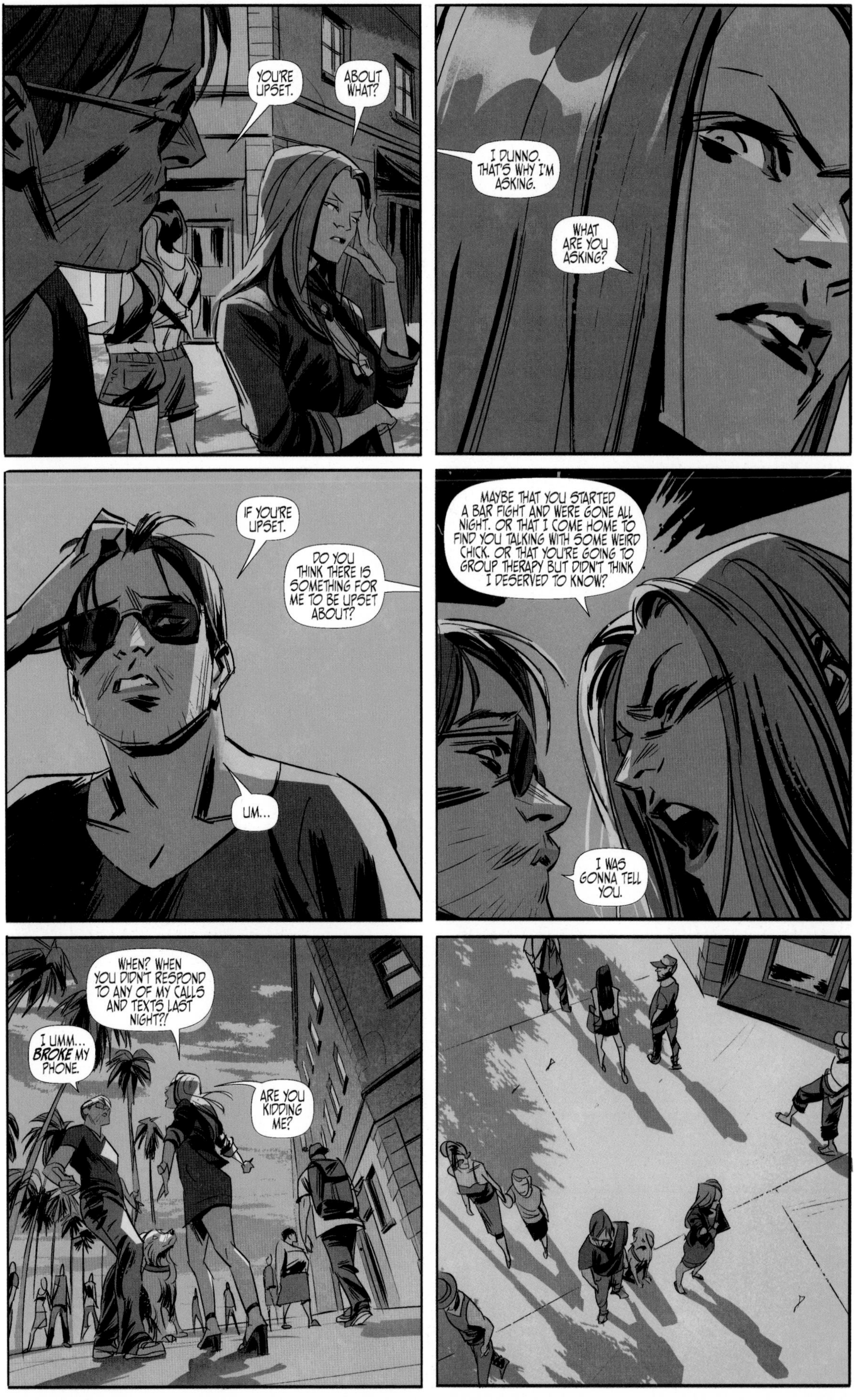
YOU'RE UPSET.
ABOUT WHAT?
I DUNNO. THAT'S WHY I'M ASKING.
WHAT ARE YOU ASKING?
IF YOU'RE UPSET.
DO YOU THINK THERE IS SOMETHING FOR ME TO BE UPSET ABOUT?
UM...
MAYBE THAT YOU STARTED A BAR FIGHT AND WERE GONE ALL NIGHT. OR THAT I COME HOME TO FIND YOU TALKING WITH SOME WEIRD CHICK. OR THAT YOU'RE GOING TO GROUP THERAPY BUT DIDN'T THINK I DESERVED TO KNOW?
I WAS GONNA TELL YOU.
WHEN? WHEN YOU DIDN'T RESPOND TO ANY OF MY CALLS AND TEXTS LAST NIGHT?!
I UMM... **BROKE** MY PHONE.
ARE YOU KIDDING ME?

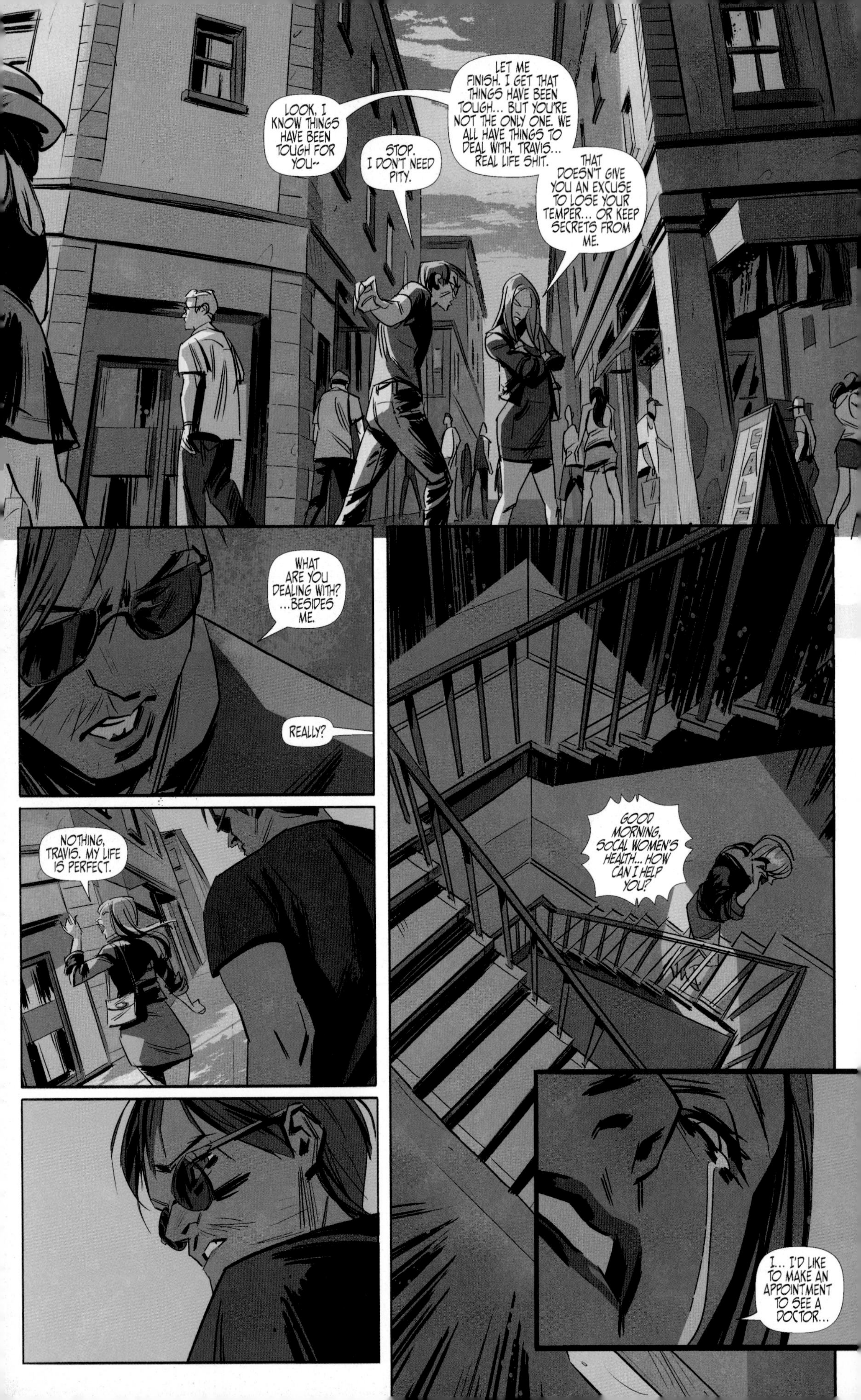
LOOK, I KNOW THINGS HAVE BEEN TOUGH FOR YOU--
STOP. I DON'T NEED PITY.
LET ME FINISH. I GET THAT THINGS HAVE BEEN TOUGH... BUT YOU'RE NOT THE ONLY ONE. WE ALL HAVE THINGS TO DEAL WITH, TRAVIS... REAL LIFE SHIT.
THAT DOESN'T GIVE YOU AN EXCUSE TO LOSE YOUR TEMPER... OR KEEP SECRETS FROM ME.
WHAT ARE YOU DEALING WITH? ...BESIDES ME.
REALLY?
NOTHING, TRAVIS. MY LIFE IS PERFECT.
GOOD MORNING, SOCAL WOMEN'S HEALTH... HOW CAN I HELP YOU?
I... I'D LIKE TO MAKE AN APPOINTMENT TO SEE A DOCTOR...

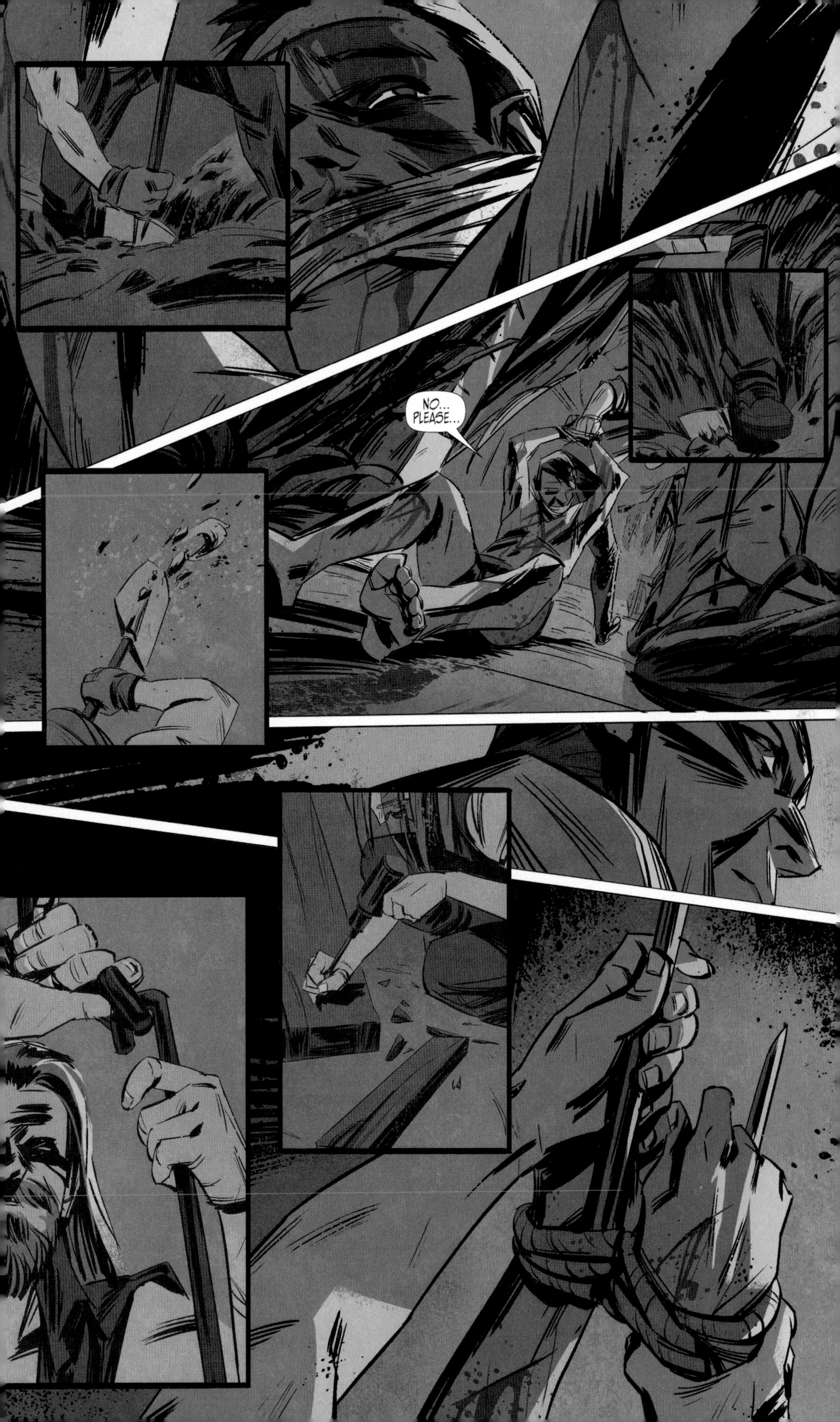
NO... PLEASE...

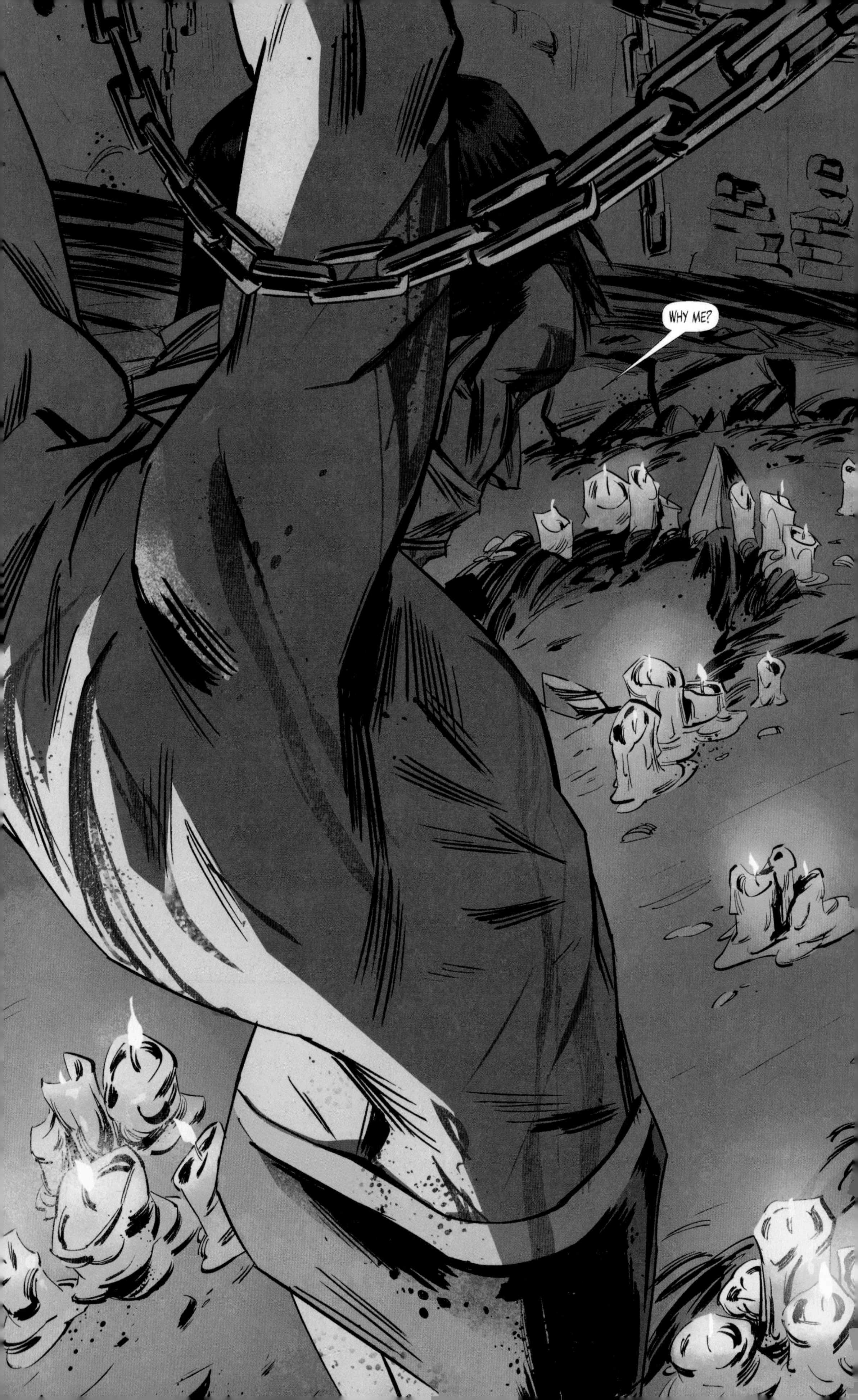
WHY ME?

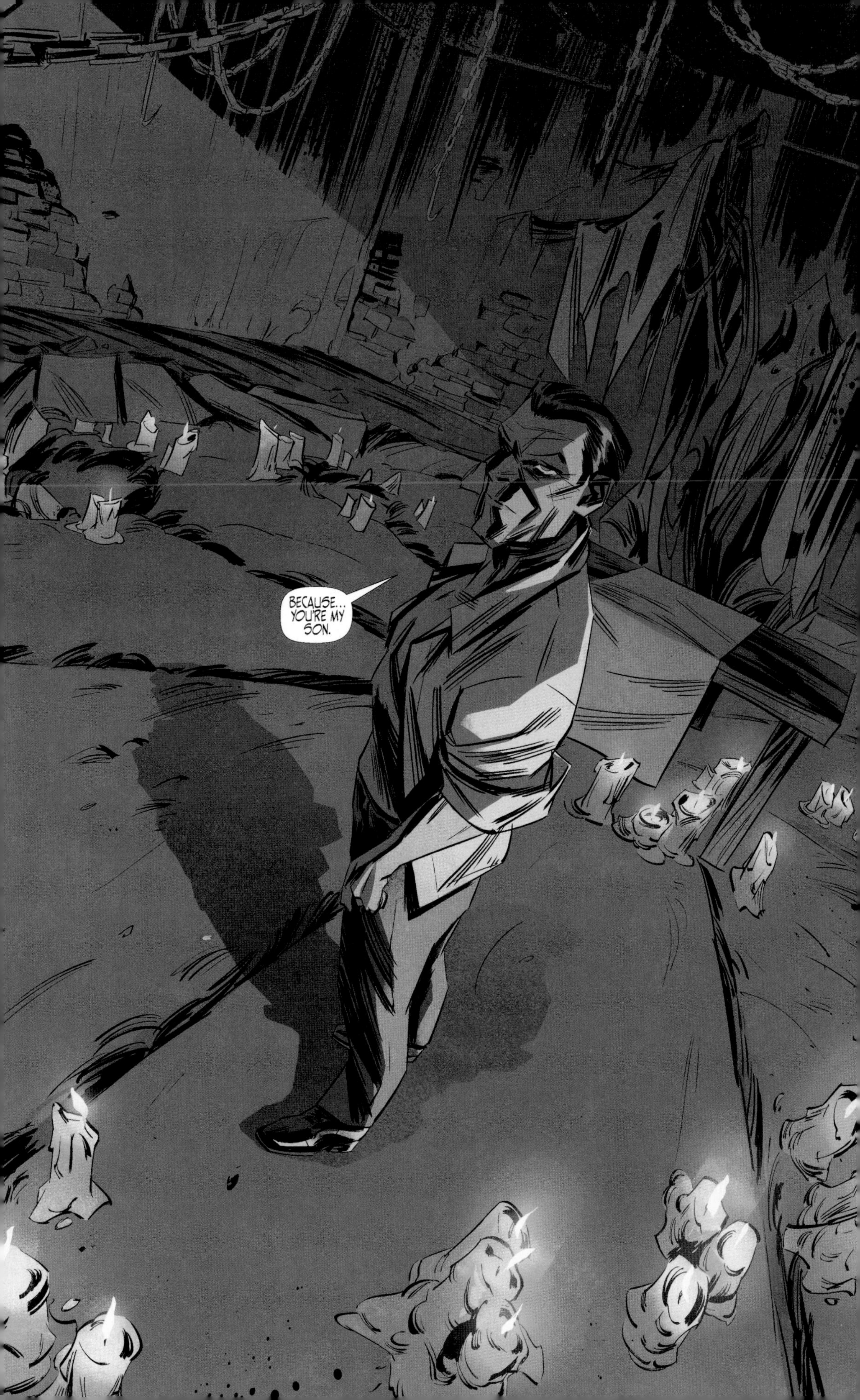
BECAUSE... YOU'RE MY SON.

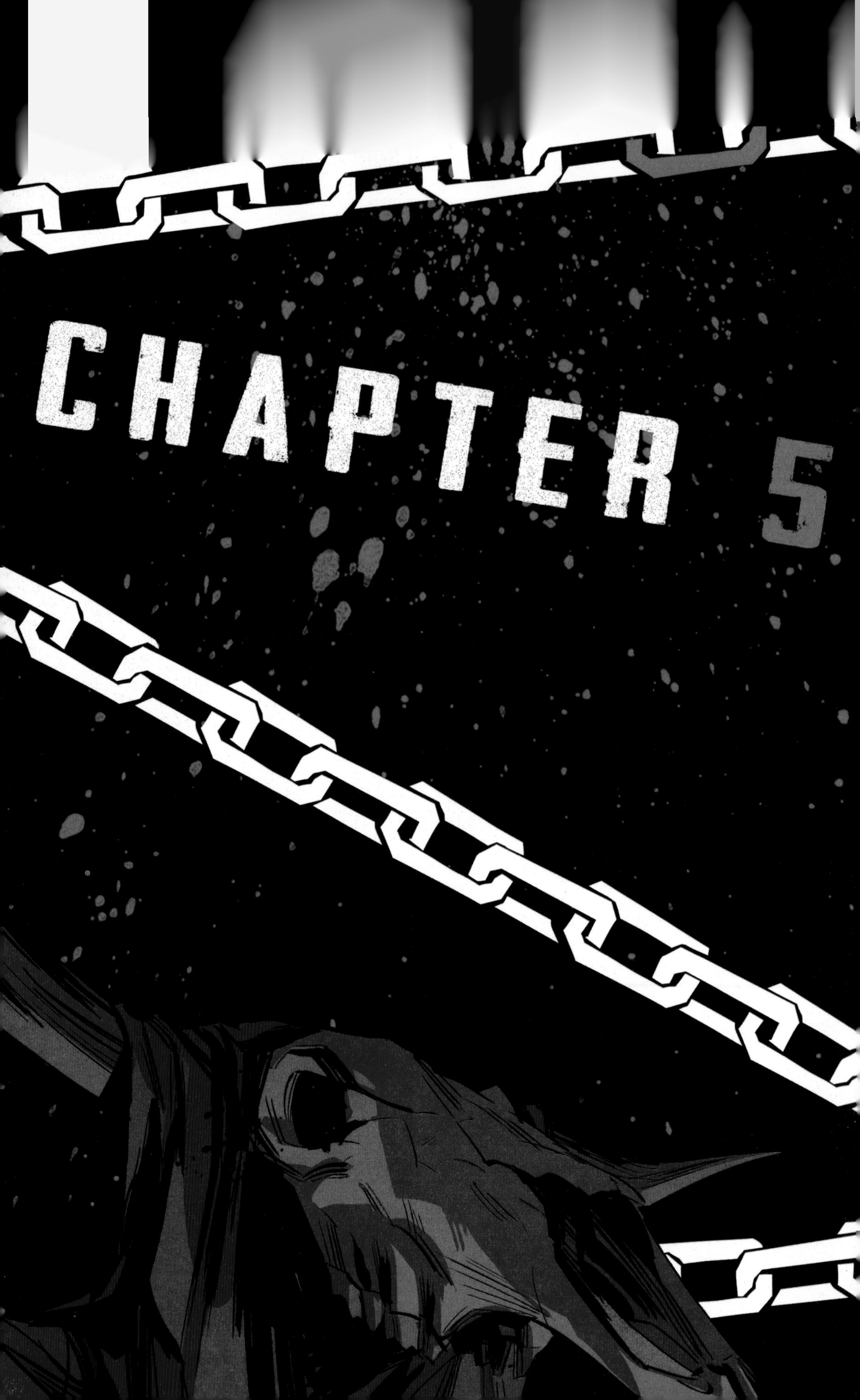
CHAPTER 5

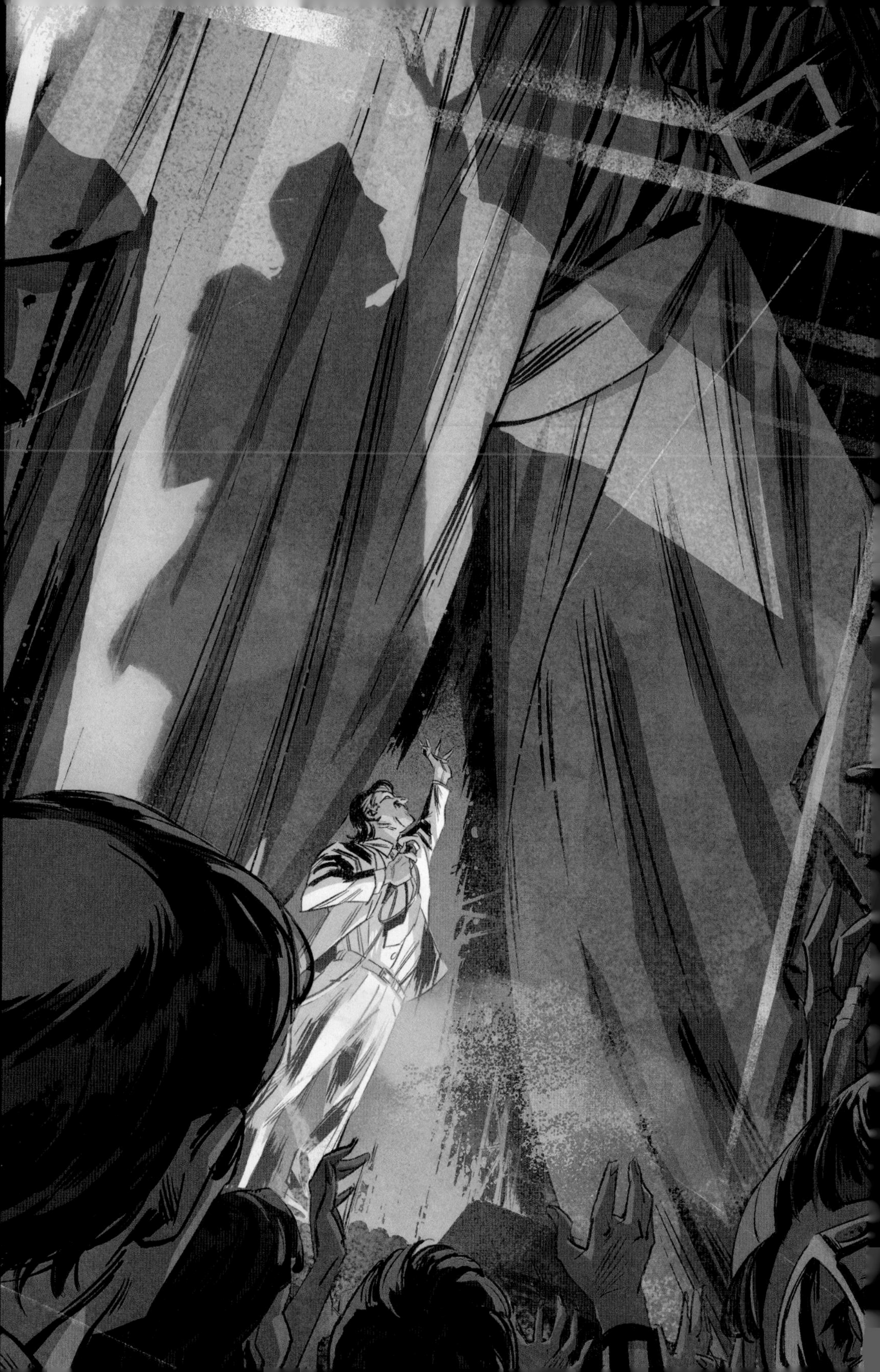

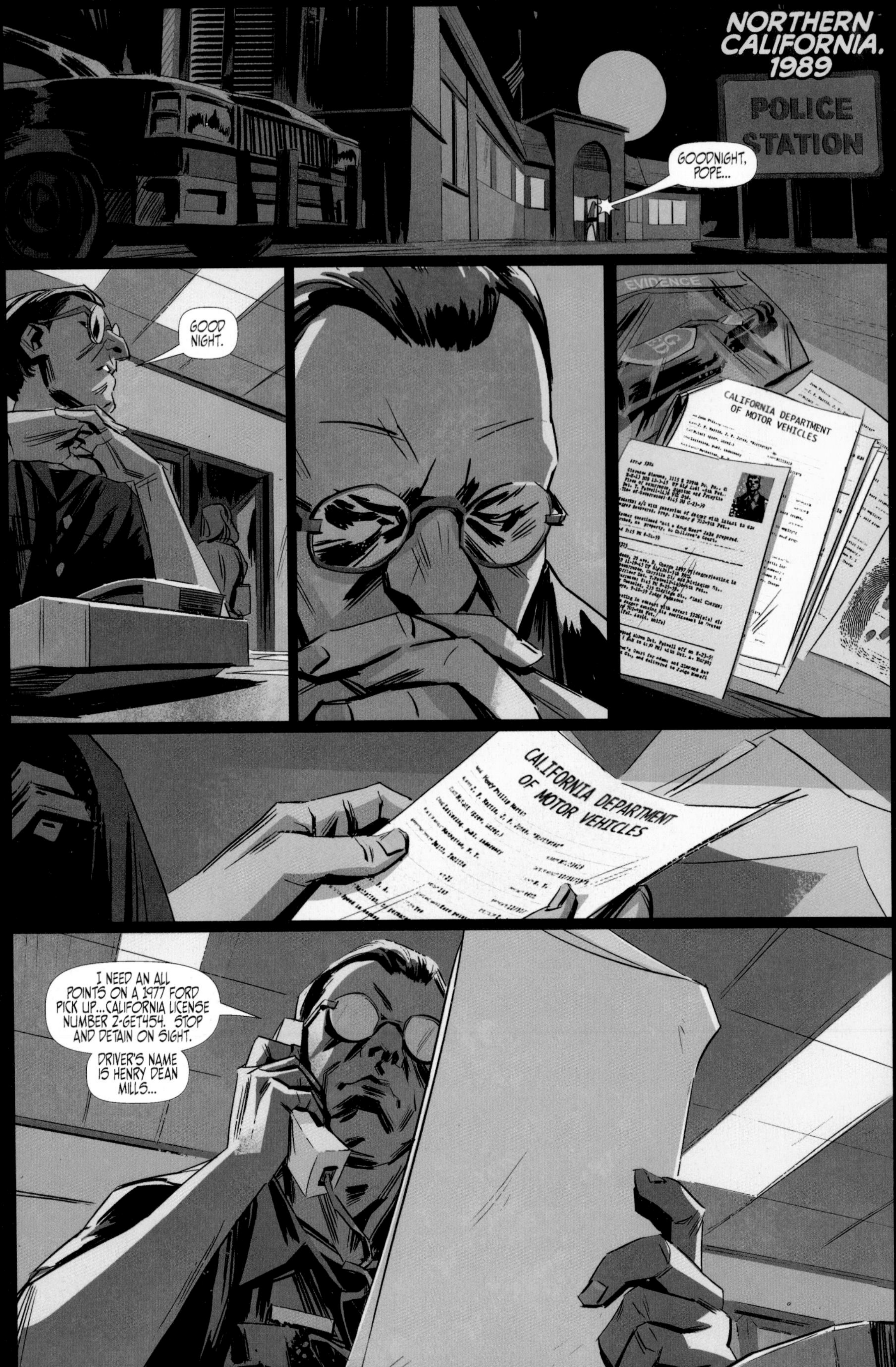
NORTHERN CALIFORNIA. 1989
POLICE STATION
GOODNIGHT, POPE...
GOOD NIGHT.
EVIDENCE
CALIFORNIA DEPARTMENT OF MOTOR VEHICLES
CALIFORNIA DEPARTMENT OF MOTOR VEHICLES
I NEED AN ALL POINTS ON A 1977 FORD PICK UP...CALIFORNIA LICENSE NUMBER 2-GET454. STOP AND DETAIN ON SIGHT.
DRIVER'S NAME IS HENRY DEAN MILLS...

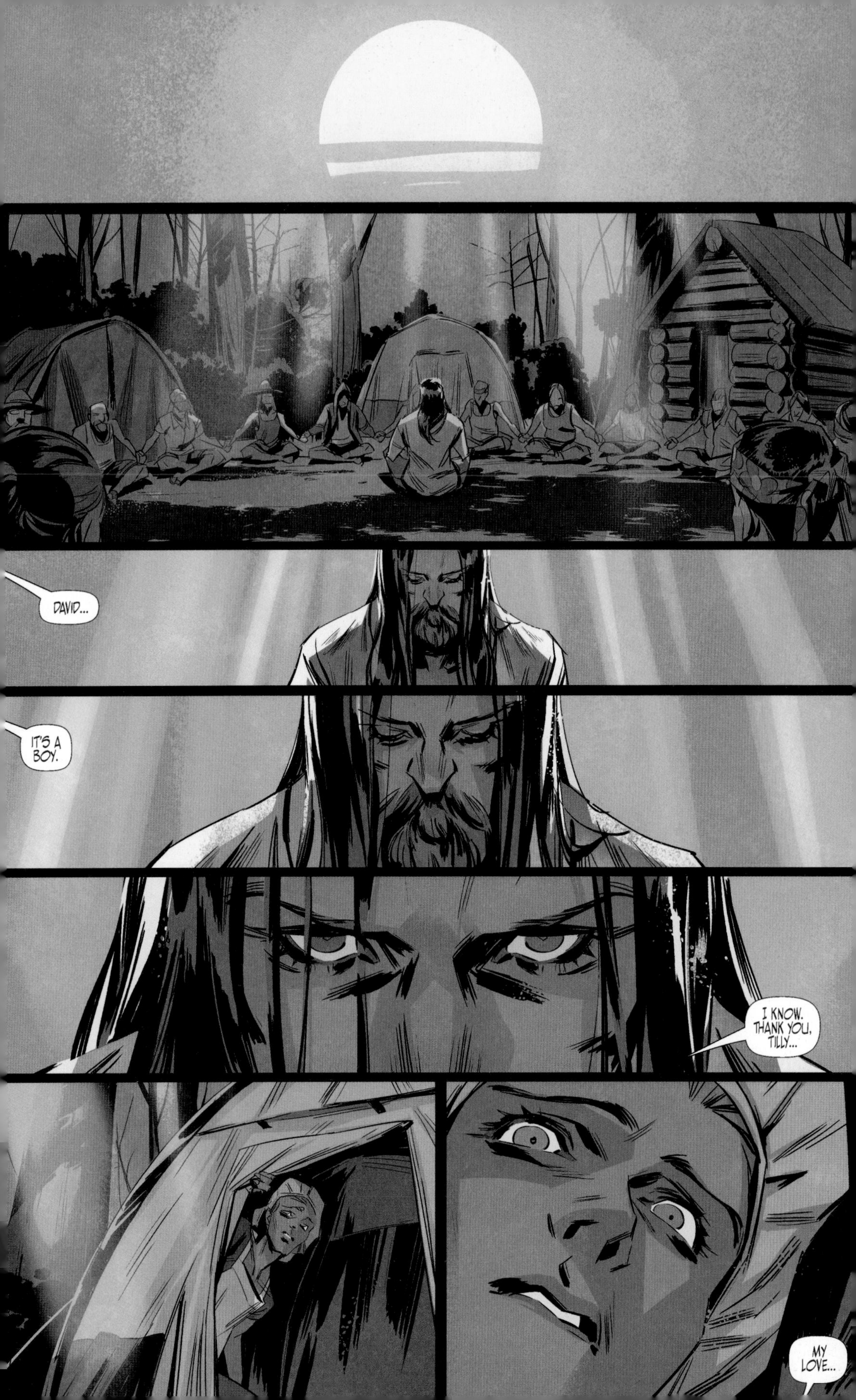
DAVID...
IT'S A BOY.
I KNOW. THANK YOU, TILLY...
MY LOVE...

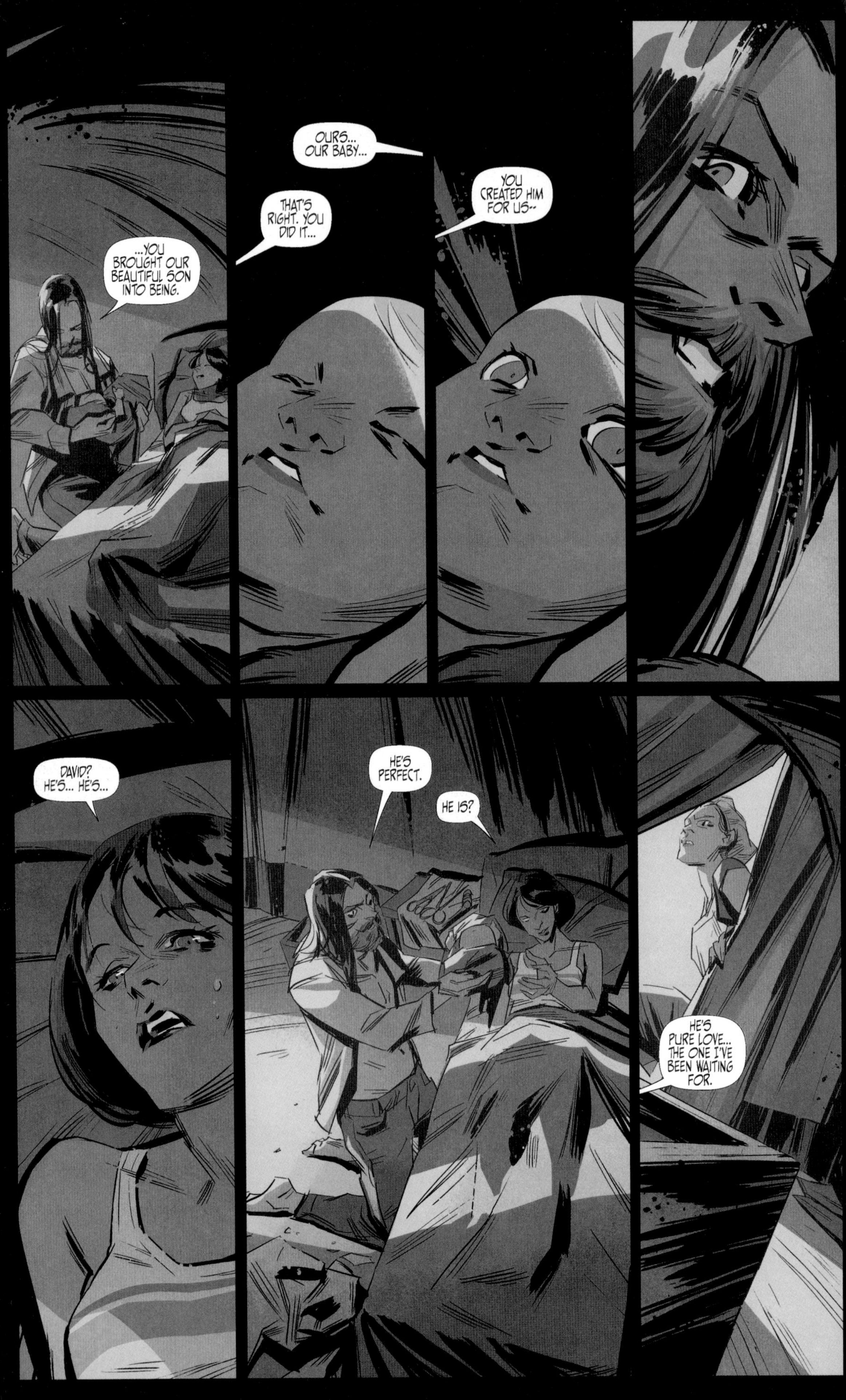
...YOU BROUGHT OUR BEAUTIFUL SON INTO BEING.
THAT'S RIGHT. YOU DID IT...
OURS... OUR BABY...
YOU CREATED HIM FOR US--
DAVID? HE'S... HE'S...
HE'S PERFECT.
HE IS?
HE'S PURE LOVE... THE ONE I'VE BEEN WAITING FOR.

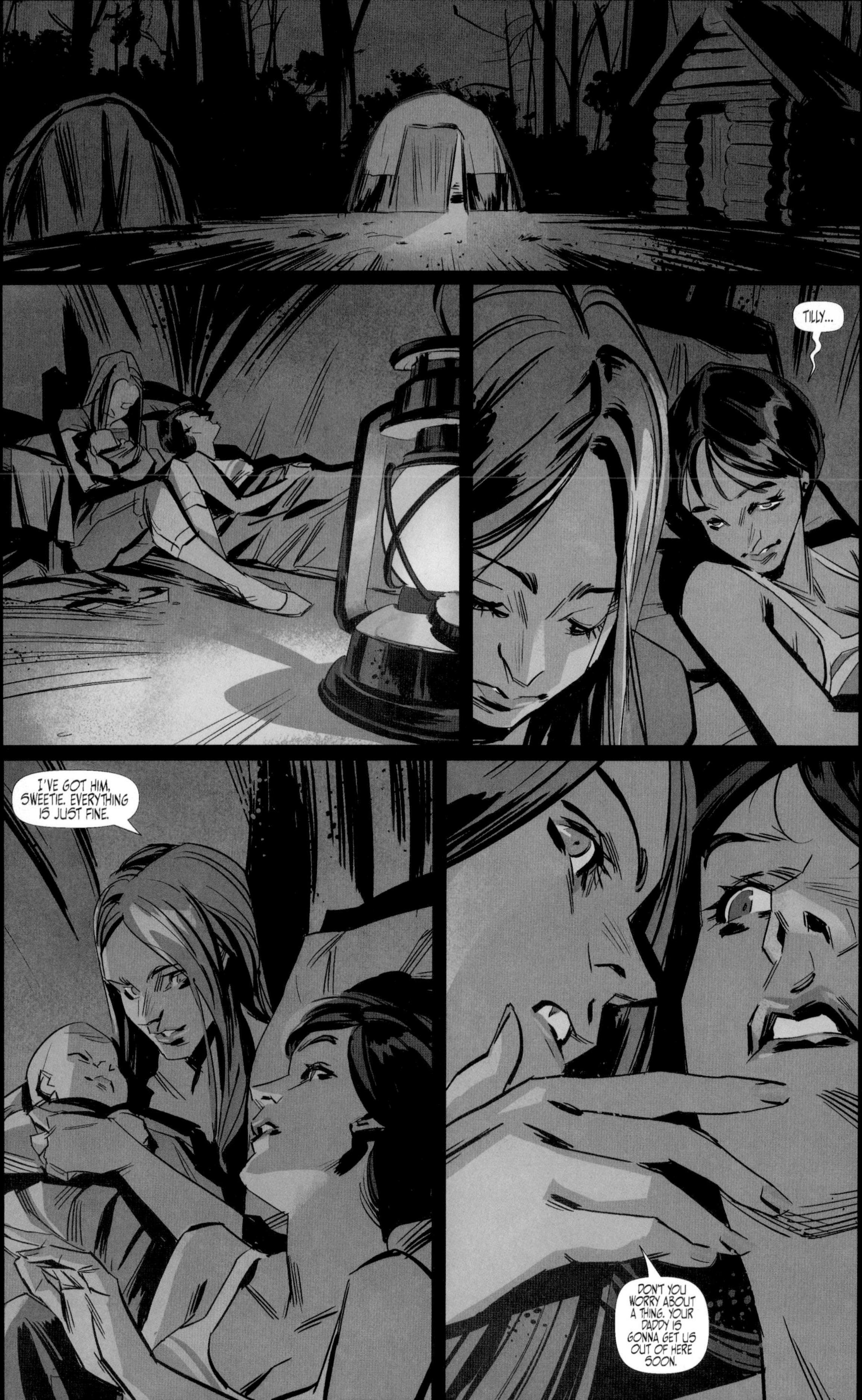
TILLY...
I'VE GOT HIM, SWEETIE. EVERYTHING IS JUST FINE.
DON'T YOU WORRY ABOUT A THING. YOUR DADDY IS GONNA GET US OUT OF HERE SOON.

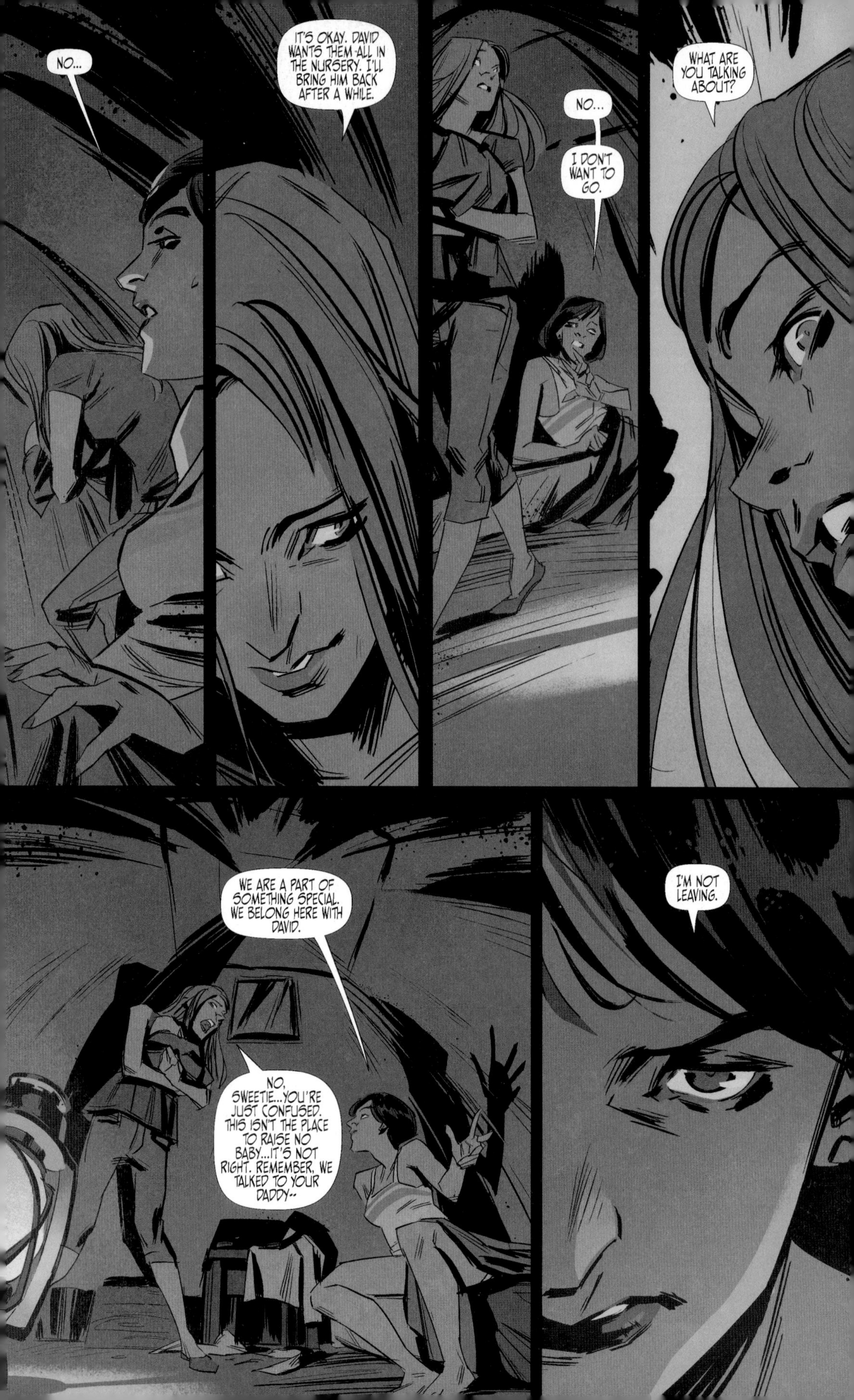
NO...
IT'S OKAY. DAVID WANTS THEM ALL IN THE NURSERY. I'LL BRING HIM BACK AFTER A WHILE.
NO...
I DON'T WANT TO GO.
WHAT ARE YOU TALKING ABOUT?
WE ARE A PART OF SOMETHING SPECIAL. WE BELONG HERE WITH DAVID.
NO, SWEETIE...YOU'RE JUST CONFUSED. THIS ISN'T THE PLACE TO RAISE NO BABY...IT'S NOT RIGHT. REMEMBER, WE TALKED TO YOUR DADDY--
I'M NOT LEAVING.

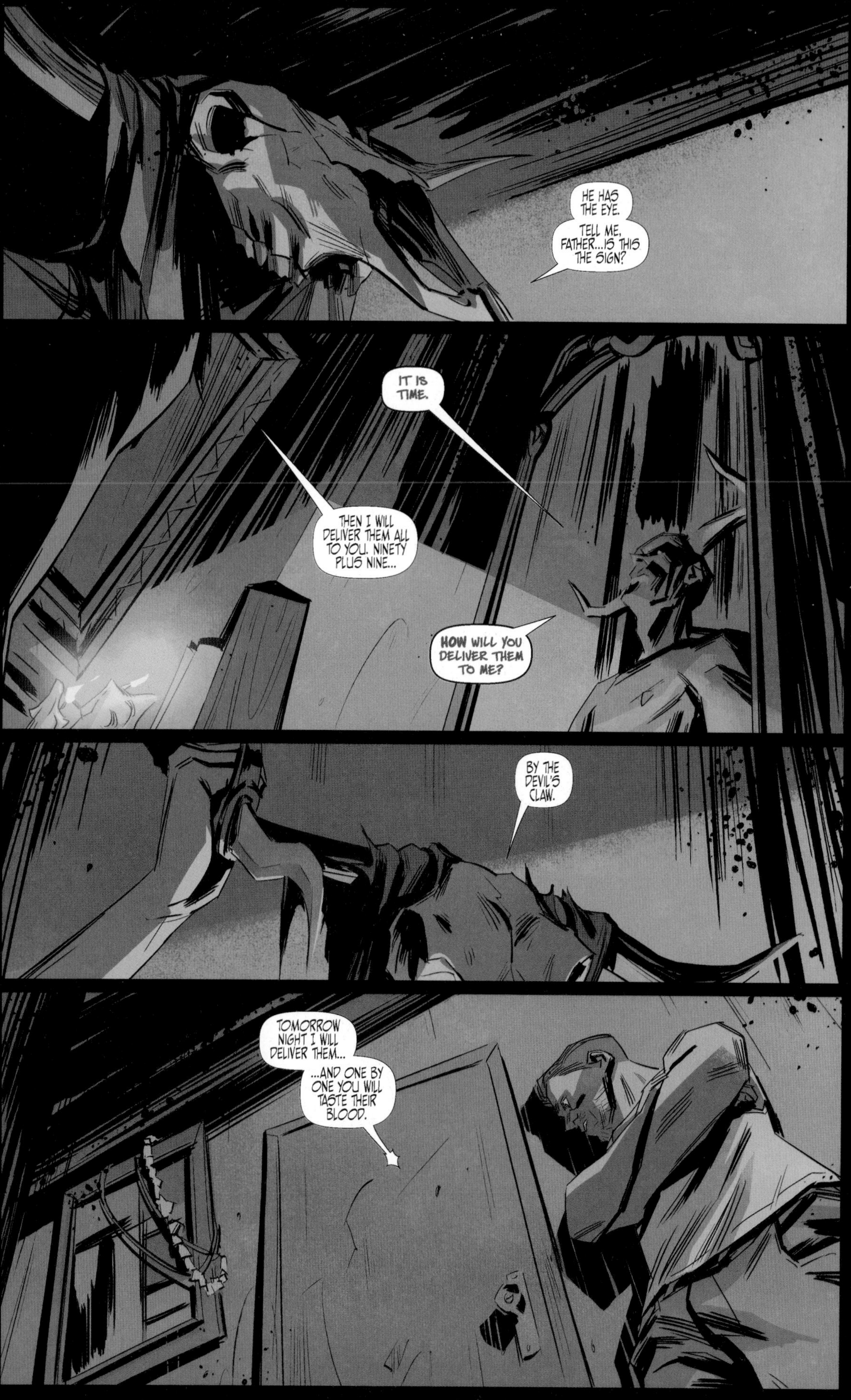
HE HAS THE EYE.
TELL ME, FATHER...IS THIS THE SIGN?
IT IS TIME.
THEN I WILL DELIVER THEM ALL TO YOU. NINETY PLUS NINE...
HOW WILL YOU DELIVER THEM TO ME?
BY THE DEVIL'S CLAW.
TOMORROW NIGHT I WILL DELIVER THEM...
...AND ONE BY ONE YOU WILL TASTE THEIR BLOOD.

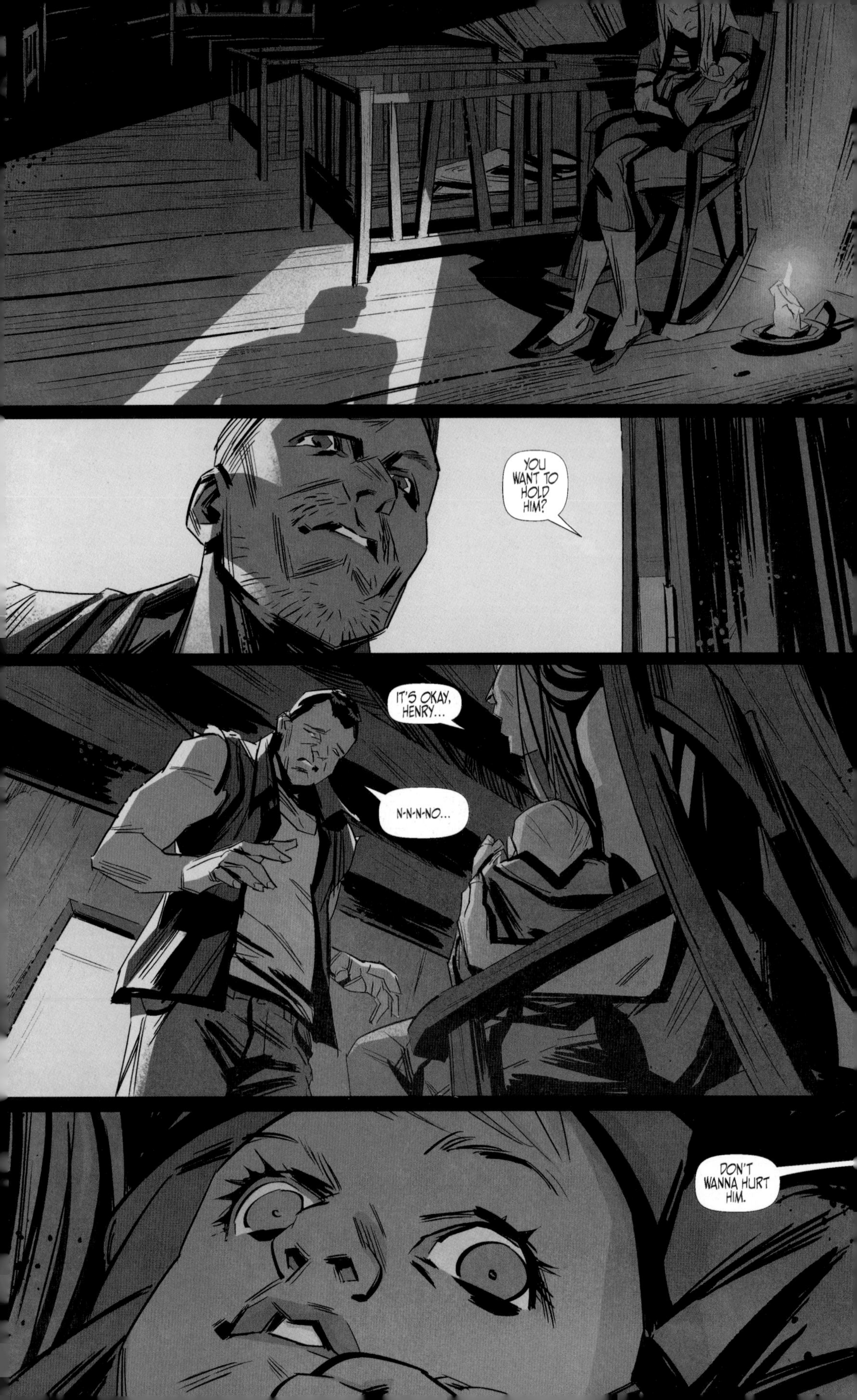
YOU WANT TO HOLD HIM?
IT'S OKAY, HENRY...
N-N-N-NO...
DON'T WANNA HURT HIM.

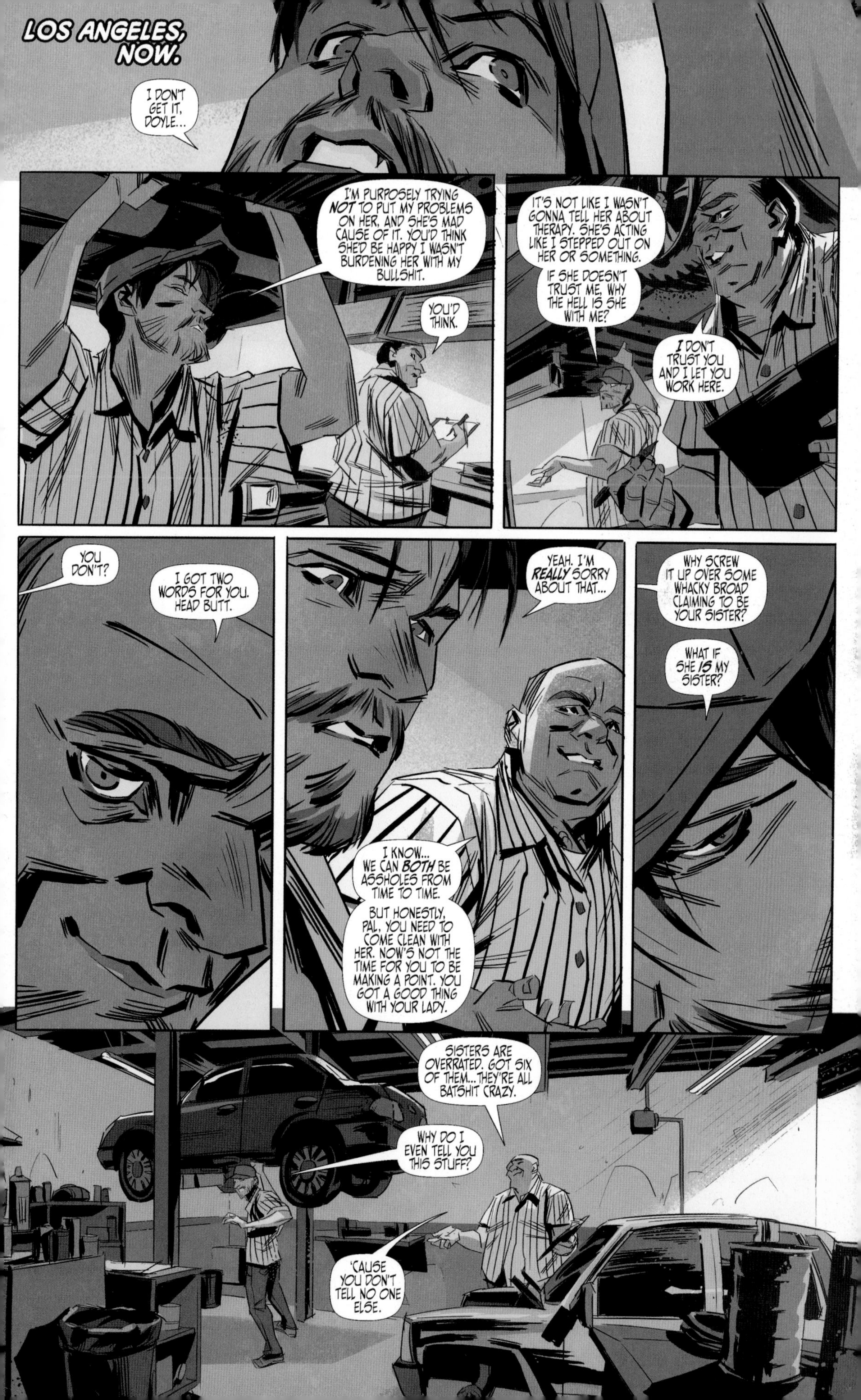

LOS ANGELES, NOW.
I DON'T GET IT, DOYLE...
I'M PURPOSELY TRYING NOT TO PUT MY PROBLEMS ON HER, AND SHE'S MAD CAUSE OF IT. YOU'D THINK SHE'D BE HAPPY I WASN'T BURDENING HER WITH MY BULLSHIT.
YOU'D THINK.
IT'S NOT LIKE I WASN'T GONNA TELL HER ABOUT THERAPY. SHE'S ACTING LIKE I STEPPED OUT ON HER OR SOMETHING.
IF SHE DOESN'T TRUST ME, WHY THE HELL IS SHE WITH ME?
I DON'T TRUST YOU AND I LET YOU WORK HERE.
YOU DON'T?
I GOT TWO WORDS FOR YOU. HEAD BUTT.
YEAH. I'M REALLY SORRY ABOUT THAT...
I KNOW... WE CAN BOTH BE ASSHOLES FROM TIME TO TIME.
BUT HONESTLY, PAL, YOU NEED TO COME CLEAN WITH HER. NOW'S NOT THE TIME FOR YOU TO BE MAKING A POINT. YOU GOT A GOOD THING WITH YOUR LADY.
WHY SCREW IT UP OVER SOME WHACKY BROAD CLAIMING TO BE YOUR SISTER?
WHAT IF SHE IS MY SISTER?
SISTERS ARE OVERRATED. GOT SIX OF THEM... THEY'RE ALL BATSHIT CRAZY.
WHY DO I EVEN TELL YOU THIS STUFF?
'CAUSE YOU DON'T TELL NO ONE ELSE.

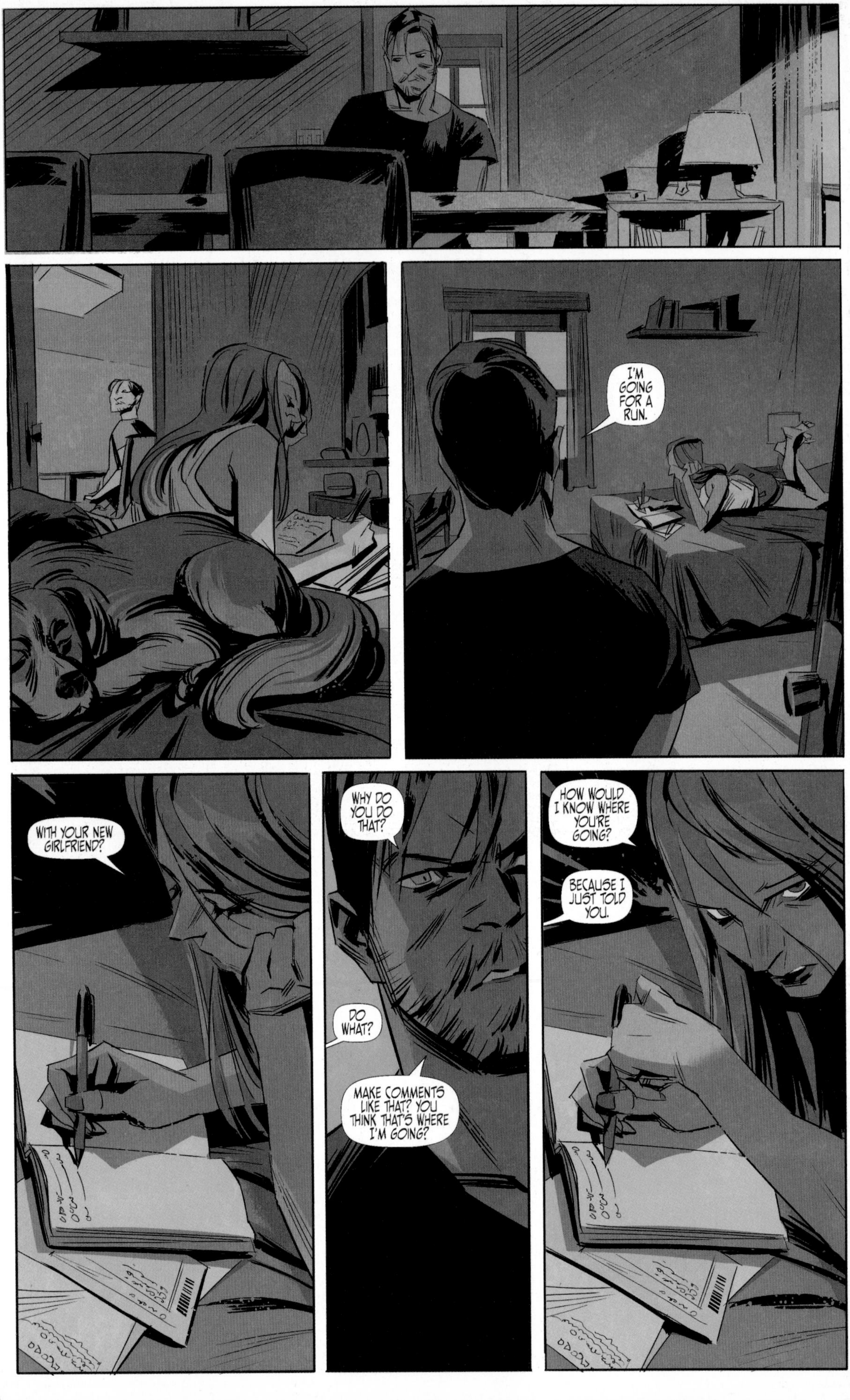
I'M GOING FOR A RUN.
WITH YOUR NEW GIRLFRIEND?
WHY DO YOU DO THAT?
DO WHAT?
MAKE COMMENTS LIKE THAT? YOU THINK THAT'S WHERE I'M GOING?
HOW WOULD I KNOW WHERE YOU'RE GOING?
BECAUSE I JUST TOLD YOU.

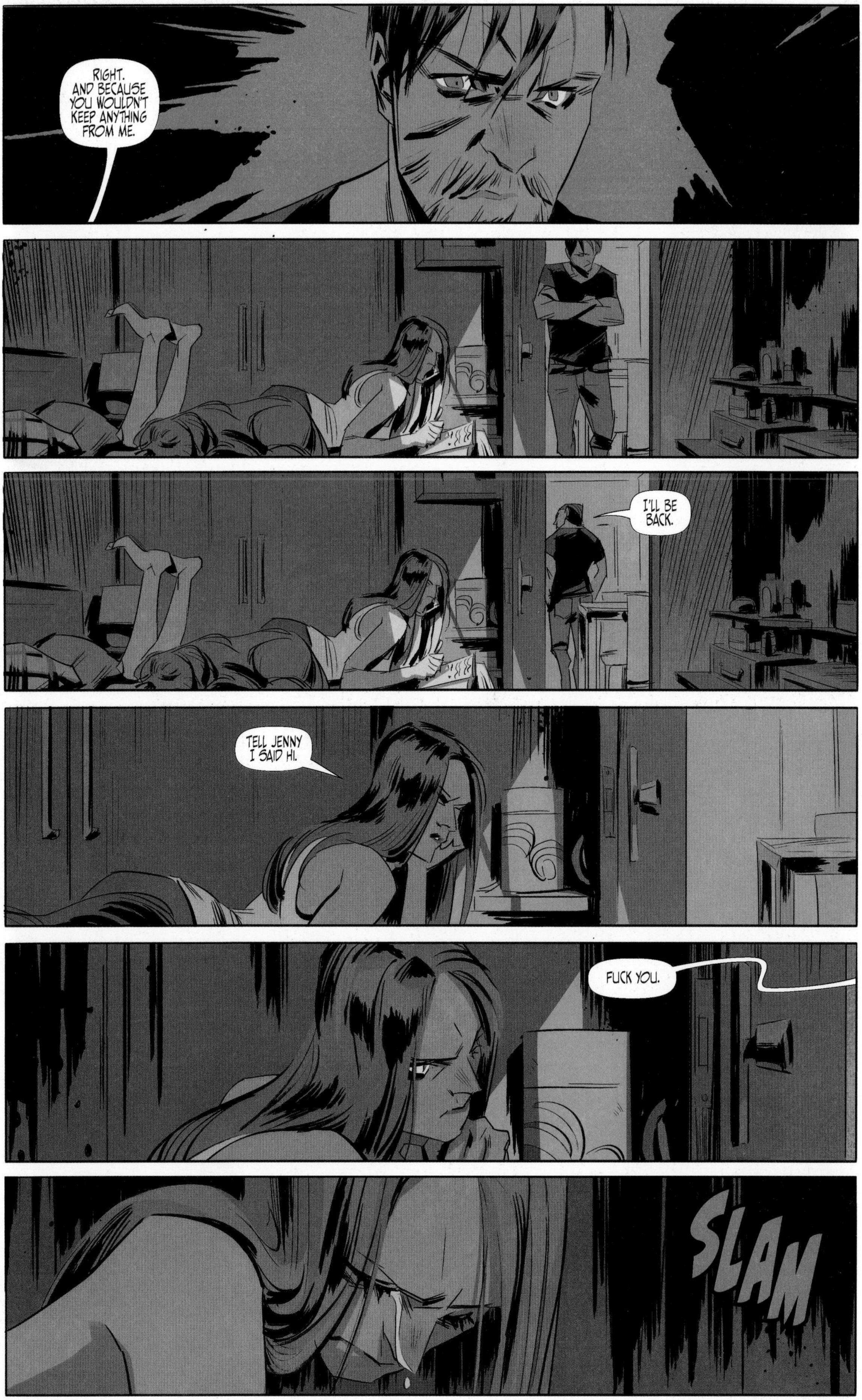
RIGHT. AND BECAUSE YOU WOULDN'T KEEP ANYTHING FROM ME.
I'LL BE BACK.
TELL JENNY I SAID HI.
FUCK YOU.
SLAM

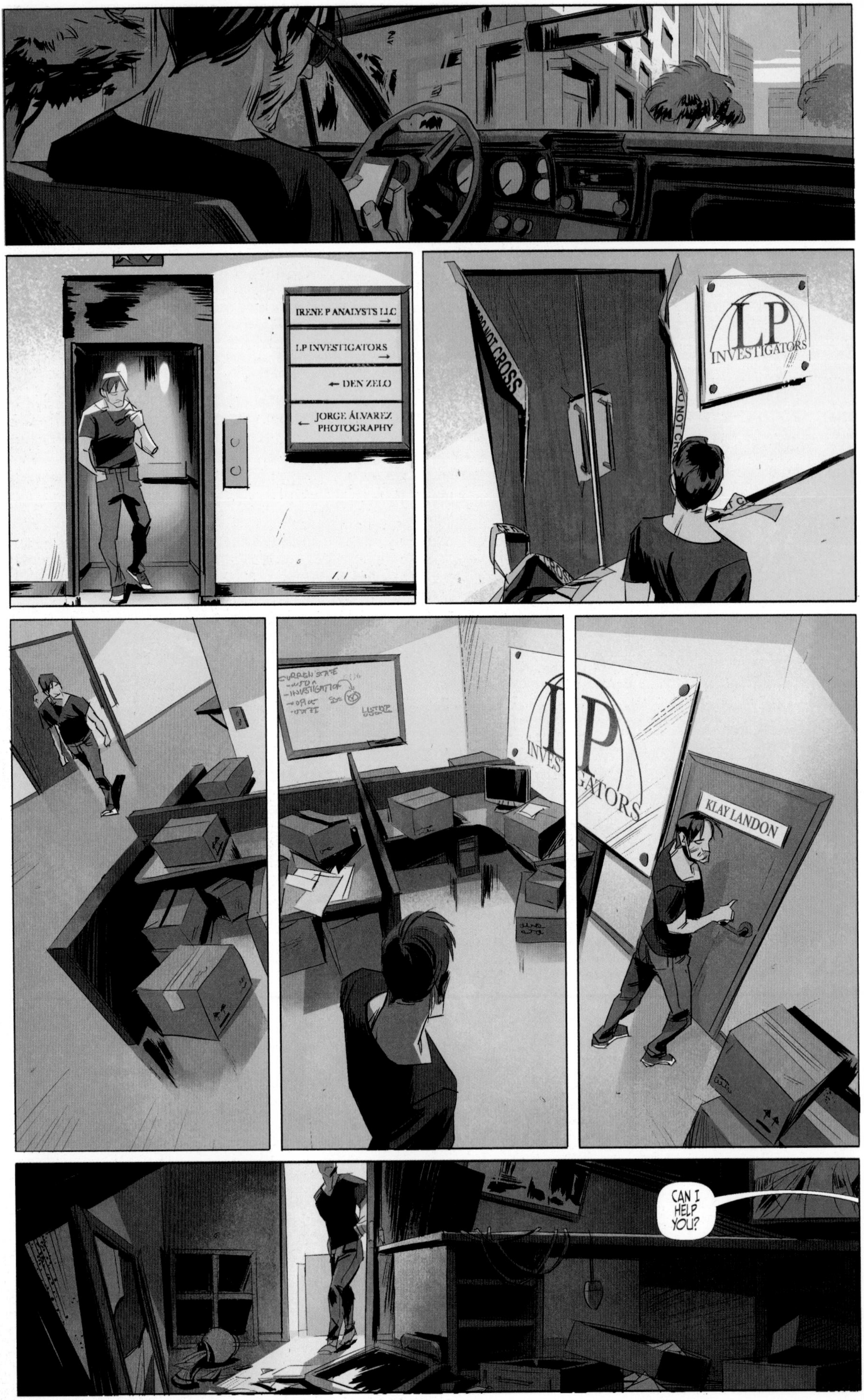
IRENE P ANALYSTS LLC
LP INVESTIGATORS
DEN ZELO
JORGE ÁLVAREZ PHOTOGRAPHY
DO NOT CROSS
LP INVESTIGATORS
LP INVESTIGATORS
KLAY LANDON
CAN I HELP YOU?

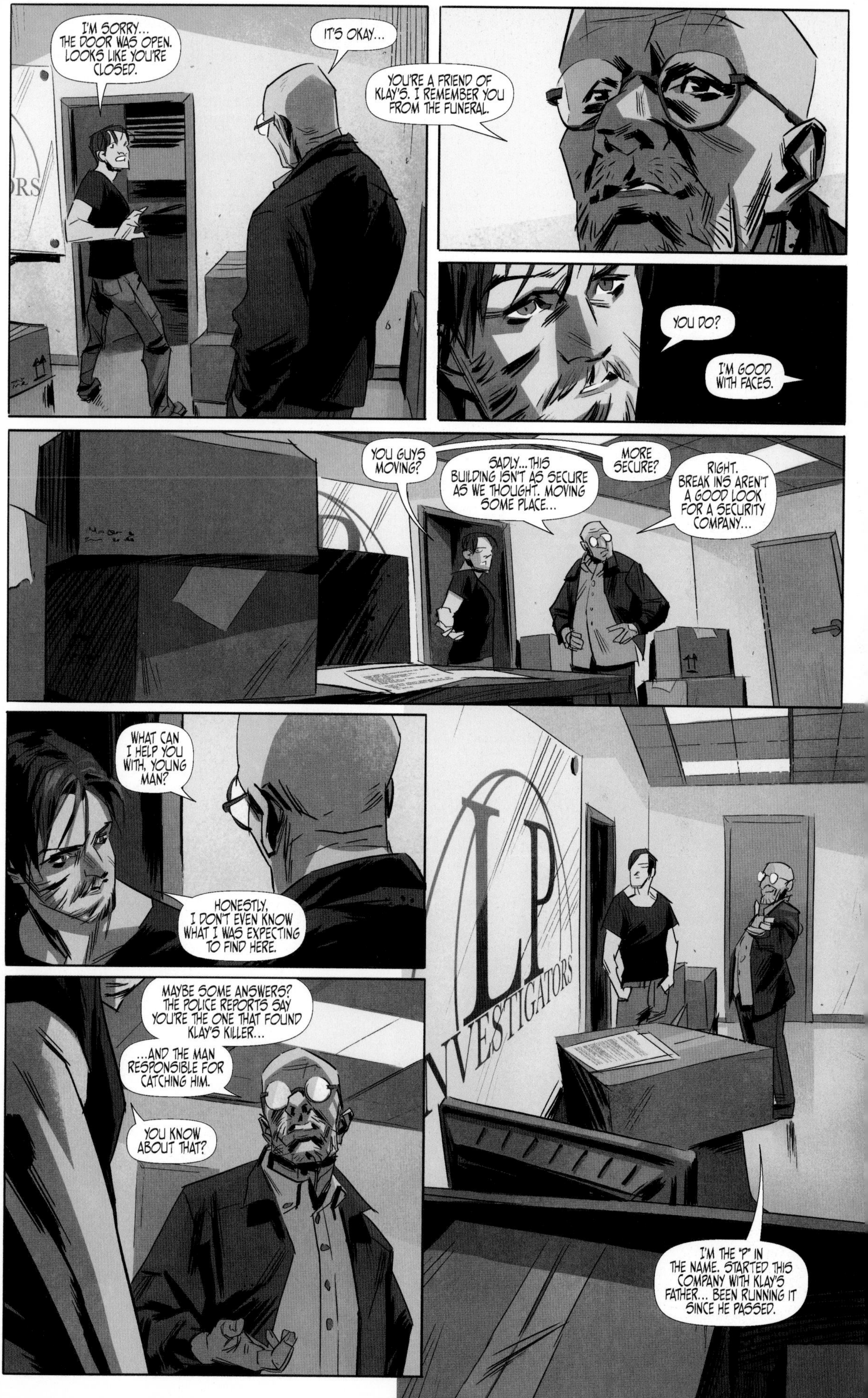
I'M SORRY... THE DOOR WAS OPEN. LOOKS LIKE YOU'RE CLOSED.
IT'S OKAY...
YOU'RE A FRIEND OF KLAY'S. I REMEMBER YOU FROM THE FUNERAL.
YOU DO?
I'M GOOD WITH FACES.
YOU GUYS MOVING?
SADLY... THIS BUILDING ISN'T AS SECURE AS WE THOUGHT. MOVING SOME PLACE...
MORE SECURE?
RIGHT. BREAK INS AREN'T A GOOD LOOK FOR A SECURITY COMPANY...
WHAT CAN I HELP YOU WITH, YOUNG MAN?
HONESTLY, I DON'T EVEN KNOW WHAT I WAS EXPECTING TO FIND HERE.
LP INVESTIGATORS
MAYBE SOME ANSWERS? THE POLICE REPORTS SAY YOU'RE THE ONE THAT FOUND KLAY'S KILLER...
...AND THE MAN RESPONSIBLE FOR CATCHING HIM.
YOU KNOW ABOUT THAT?
I'M THE "P" IN THE NAME. STARTED THIS COMPANY WITH KLAY'S FATHER... BEEN RUNNING IT SINCE HE PASSED.

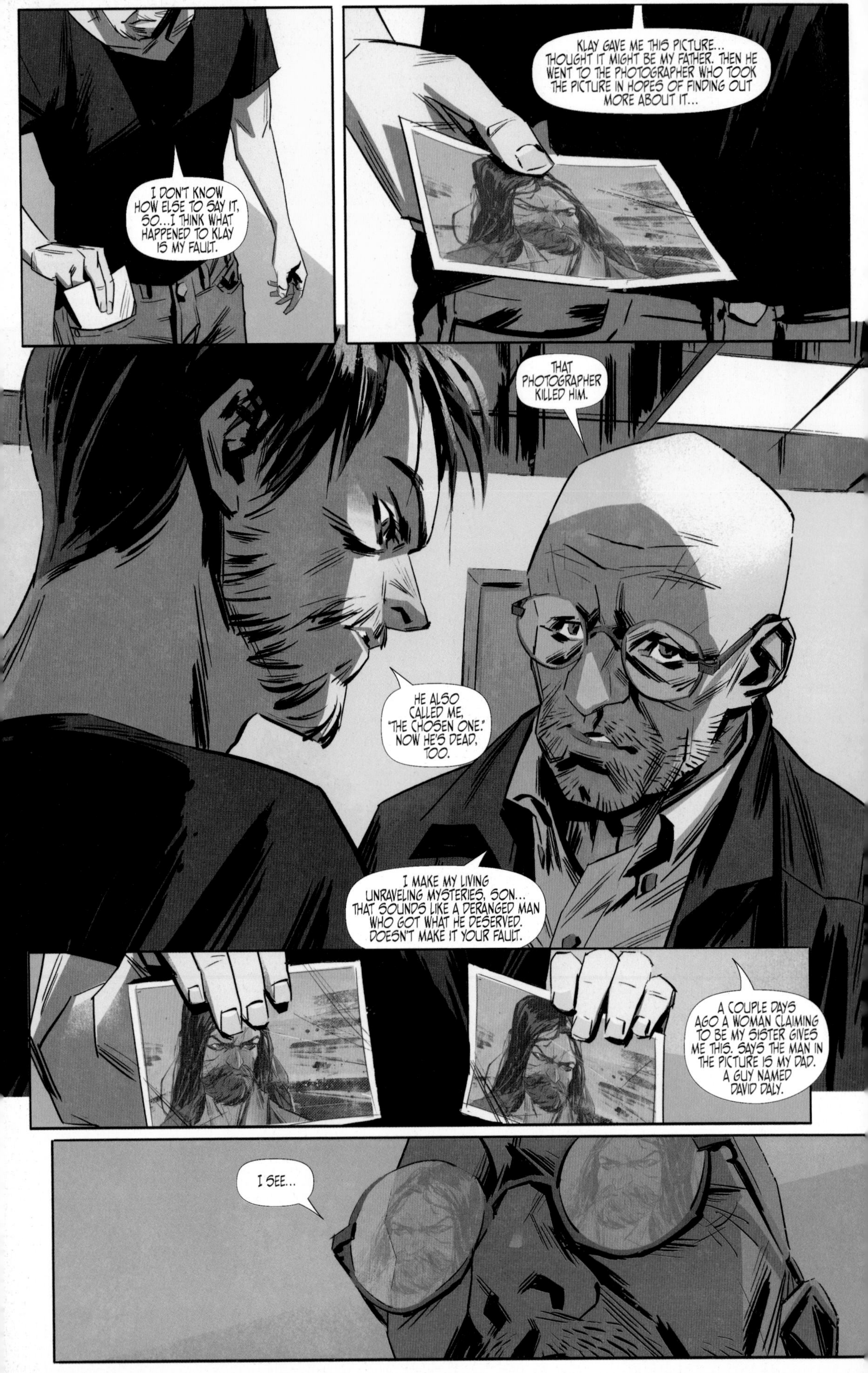
I DON'T KNOW HOW ELSE TO SAY IT, SO...I THINK WHAT HAPPENED TO KLAY IS MY FAULT.
KLAY GAVE ME THIS PICTURE... THOUGHT IT MIGHT BE MY FATHER. THEN HE WENT TO THE PHOTOGRAPHER WHO TOOK THE PICTURE IN HOPES OF FINDING OUT MORE ABOUT IT...
THAT PHOTOGRAPHER KILLED HIM.
HE ALSO CALLED ME, "THE CHOSEN ONE." NOW HE'S DEAD, TOO.
I MAKE MY LIVING UNRAVELING MYSTERIES, SON... THAT SOUNDS LIKE A DERANGED MAN WHO GOT WHAT HE DESERVED. DOESN'T MAKE IT YOUR FAULT.
A COUPLE DAYS AGO A WOMAN CLAIMING TO BE MY SISTER GIVES ME THIS. SAYS THE MAN IN THE PICTURE IS MY DAD. A GUY NAMED DAVID DALY.
I SEE...

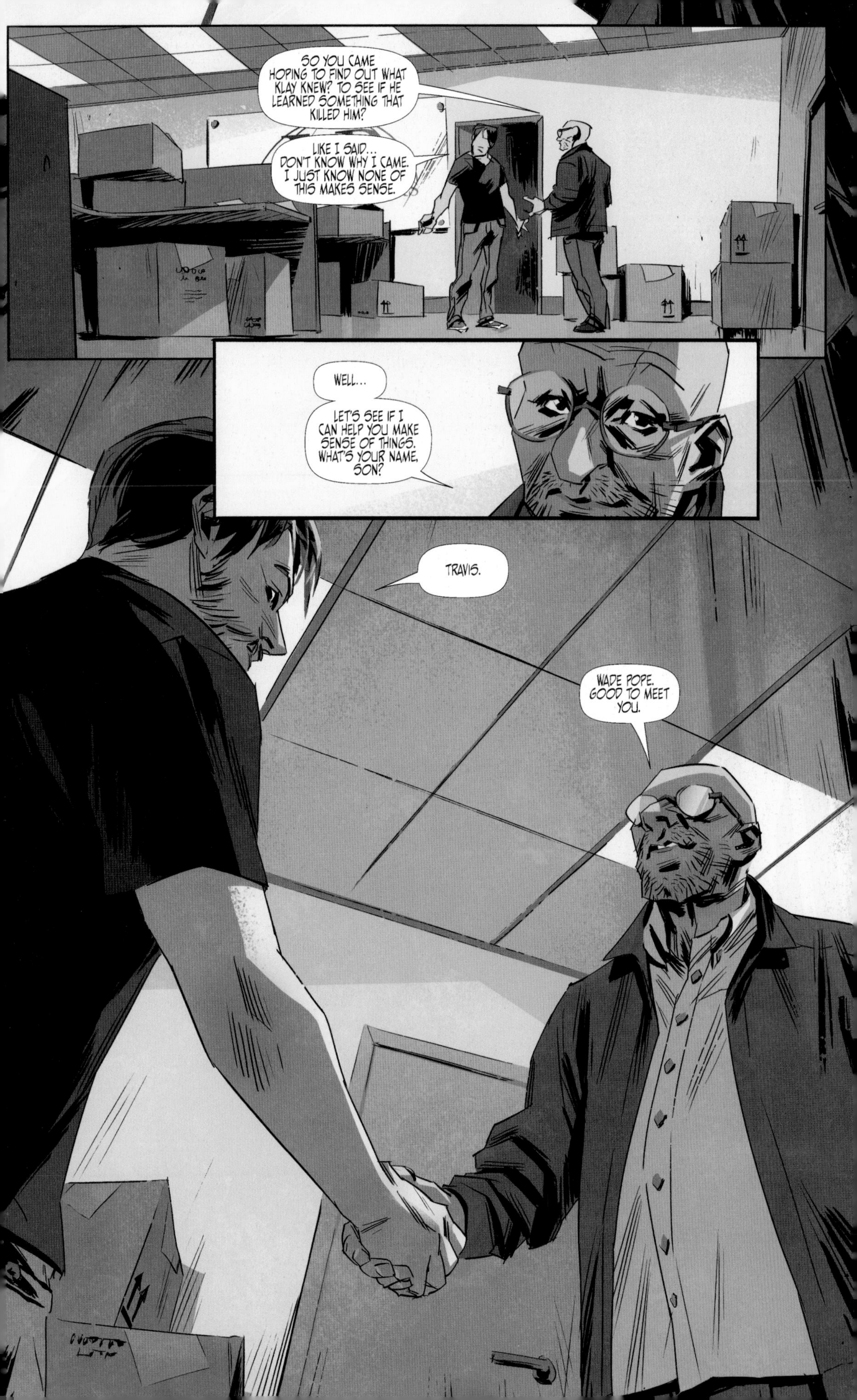
SO YOU CAME HOPING TO FIND OUT WHAT KLAY KNEW? TO SEE IF HE LEARNED SOMETHING THAT KILLED HIM?
LIKE I SAID... DON'T KNOW WHY I CAME. I JUST KNOW NONE OF THIS MAKES SENSE.
WELL...
LET'S SEE IF I CAN HELP YOU MAKE SENSE OF THINGS. WHAT'S YOUR NAME, SON?
TRAVIS.
WADE POPE. GOOD TO MEET YOU.

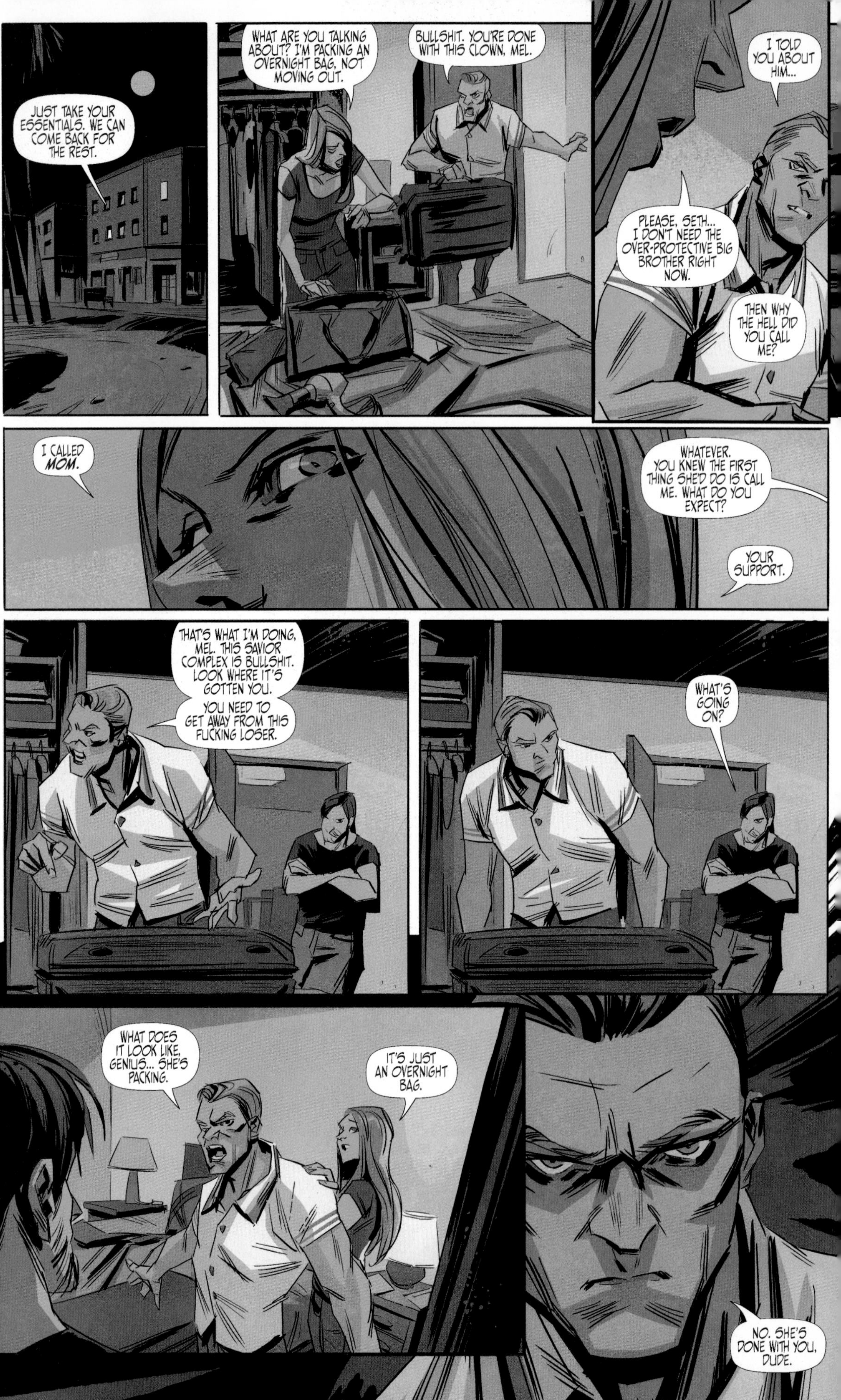

JUST TAKE YOUR ESSENTIALS. WE CAN COME BACK FOR THE REST.
WHAT ARE YOU TALKING ABOUT? I'M PACKING AN OVERNIGHT BAG, NOT MOVING OUT.
BULLSHIT. YOU'RE DONE WITH THIS CLOWN, MEL.
I TOLD YOU ABOUT HIM...
PLEASE, SETH... I DON'T NEED THE OVER-PROTECTIVE BIG BROTHER RIGHT NOW.
THEN WHY THE HELL DID YOU CALL ME?
I CALLED ***MOM***.
WHATEVER. YOU KNEW THE FIRST THING SHE'D DO IS CALL ME. WHAT DO YOU EXPECT?
YOUR SUPPORT.
THAT'S WHAT I'M DOING, MEL. THIS SAVIOR COMPLEX IS BULLSHIT. LOOK WHERE IT'S GOTTEN YOU.
YOU NEED TO GET AWAY FROM THIS FUCKING LOSER.
WHAT'S GOING ON?
WHAT DOES IT LOOK LIKE, GENIUS... SHE'S PACKING.
IT'S JUST AN OVERNIGHT BAG.
NO. SHE'S DONE WITH YOU, DUDE.

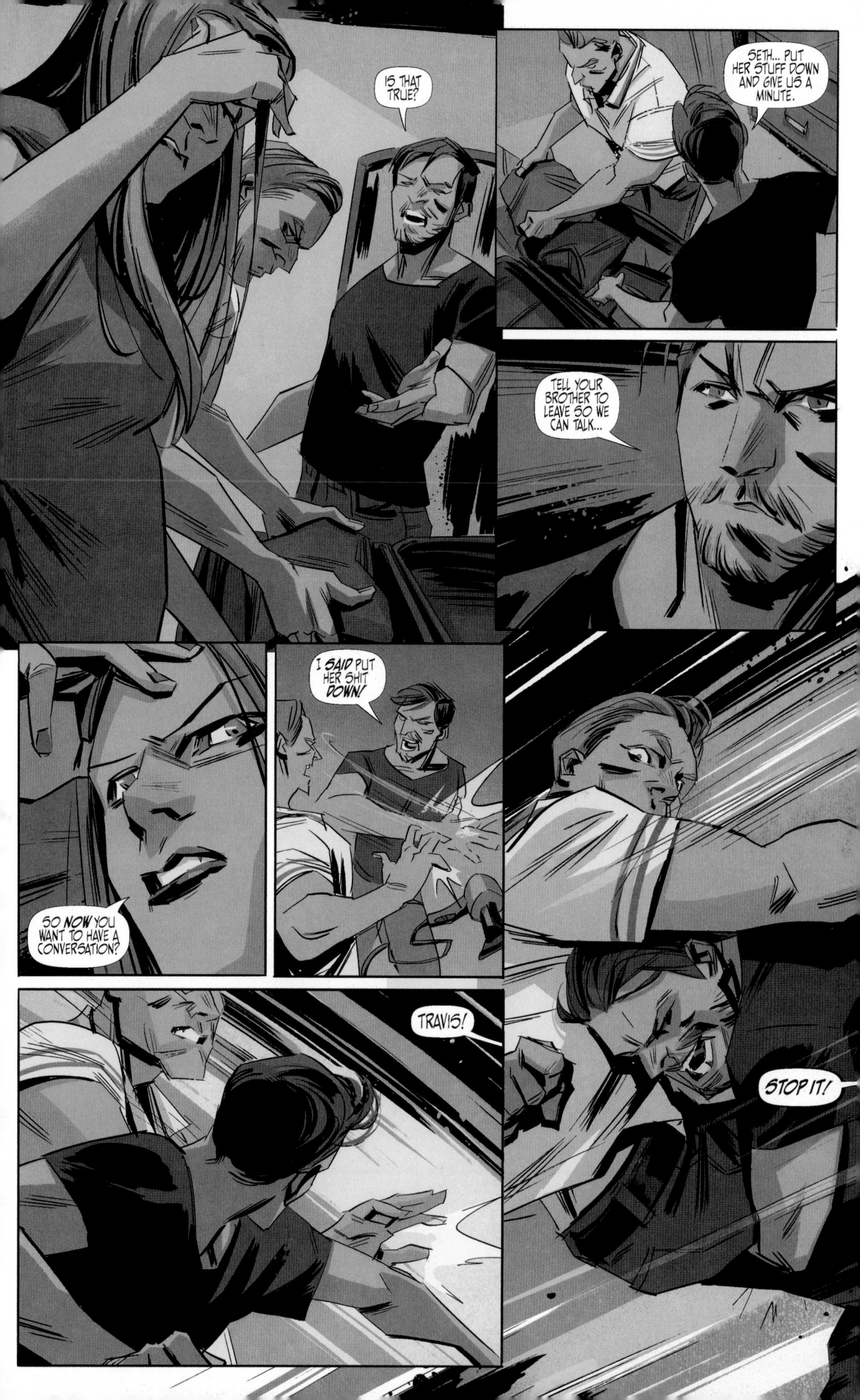
IS THAT TRUE?
SETH... PUT HER STUFF DOWN AND GIVE US A MINUTE.
TELL YOUR BROTHER TO LEAVE SO WE CAN TALK...
SO NOW YOU WANT TO HAVE A CONVERSATION?
I SAID PUT HER SHIT DOWN!
TRAVIS!
STOP IT!

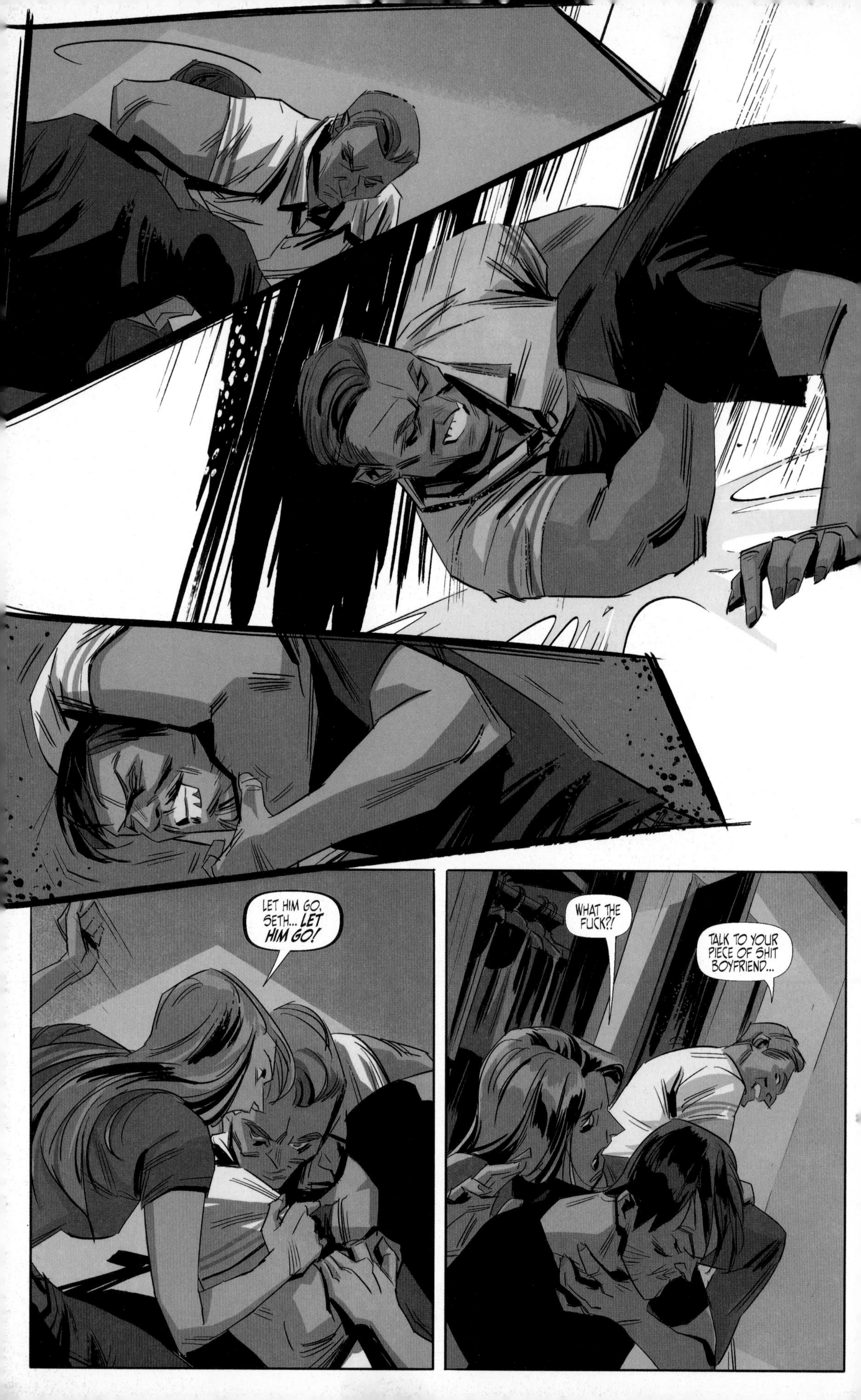
LET HIM GO, SETH... LET HIM GO!
WHAT THE FUCK?!
TALK TO YOUR PIECE OF SHIT BOYFRIEND...

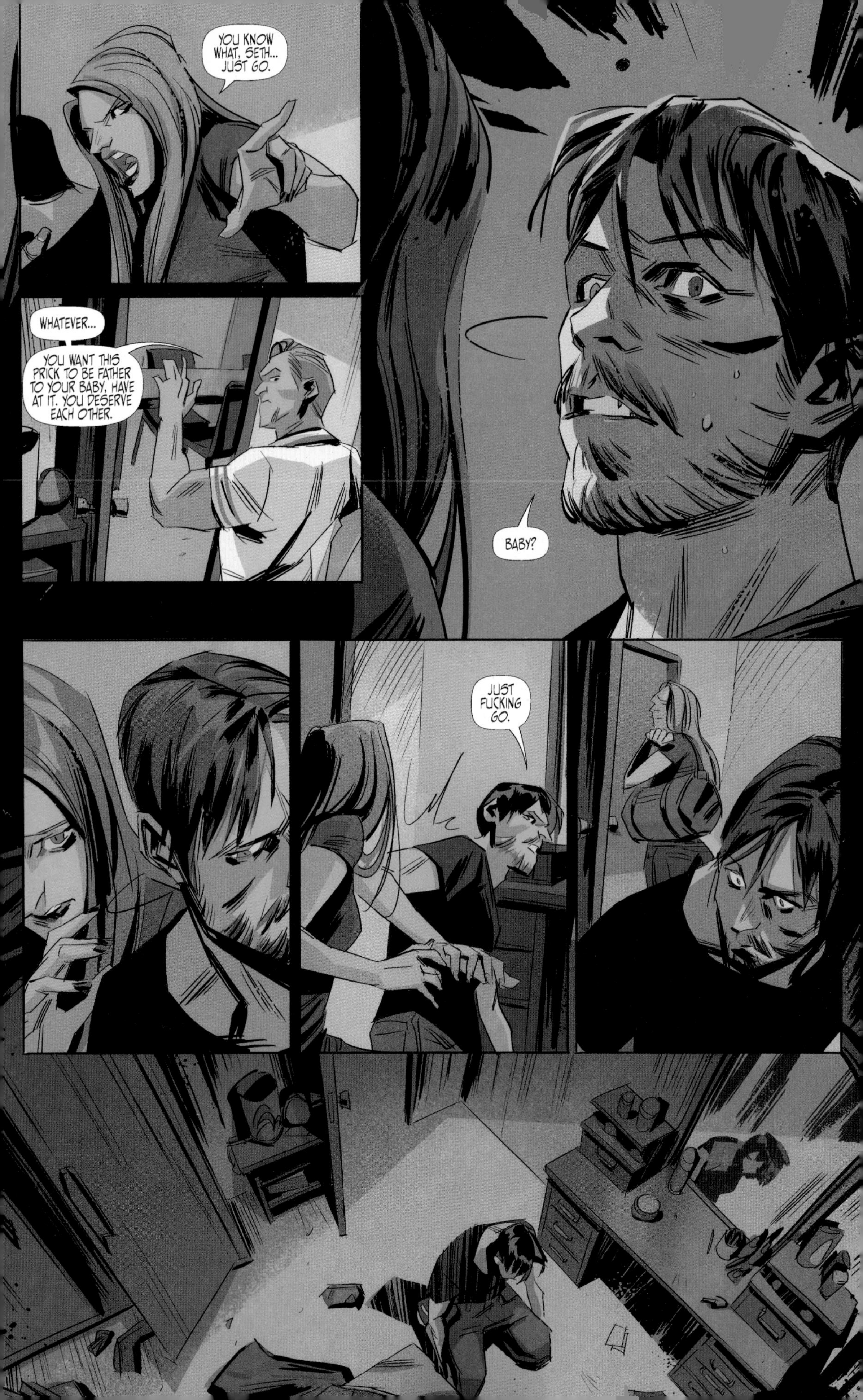
YOU KNOW WHAT, SETH... JUST GO.
WHATEVER...
YOU WANT THIS PRICK TO BE FATHER TO YOUR BABY, HAVE AT IT. YOU DESERVE EACH OTHER.
BABY?
JUST FUCKING GO.

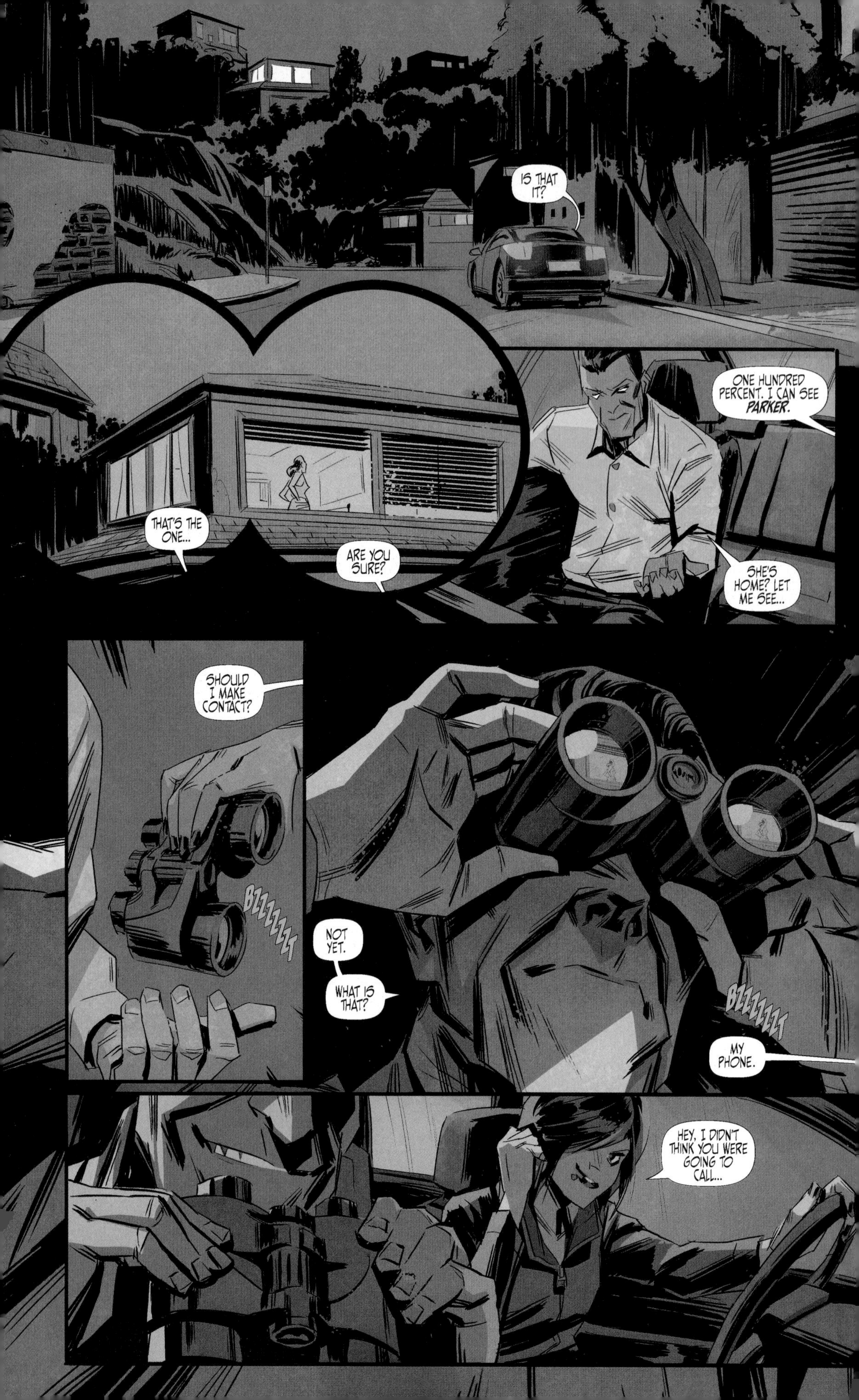
IS THAT IT?
THAT'S THE ONE...
ARE YOU SURE?
ONE HUNDRED PERCENT. I CAN SEE PARKER.
SHE'S HOME? LET ME SEE...
SHOULD I MAKE CONTACT?
BZZZZZZT
NOT YET.
WHAT IS THAT?
BZZZZZZT
MY PHONE.
HEY, I DIDN'T THINK YOU WERE GOING TO CALL...

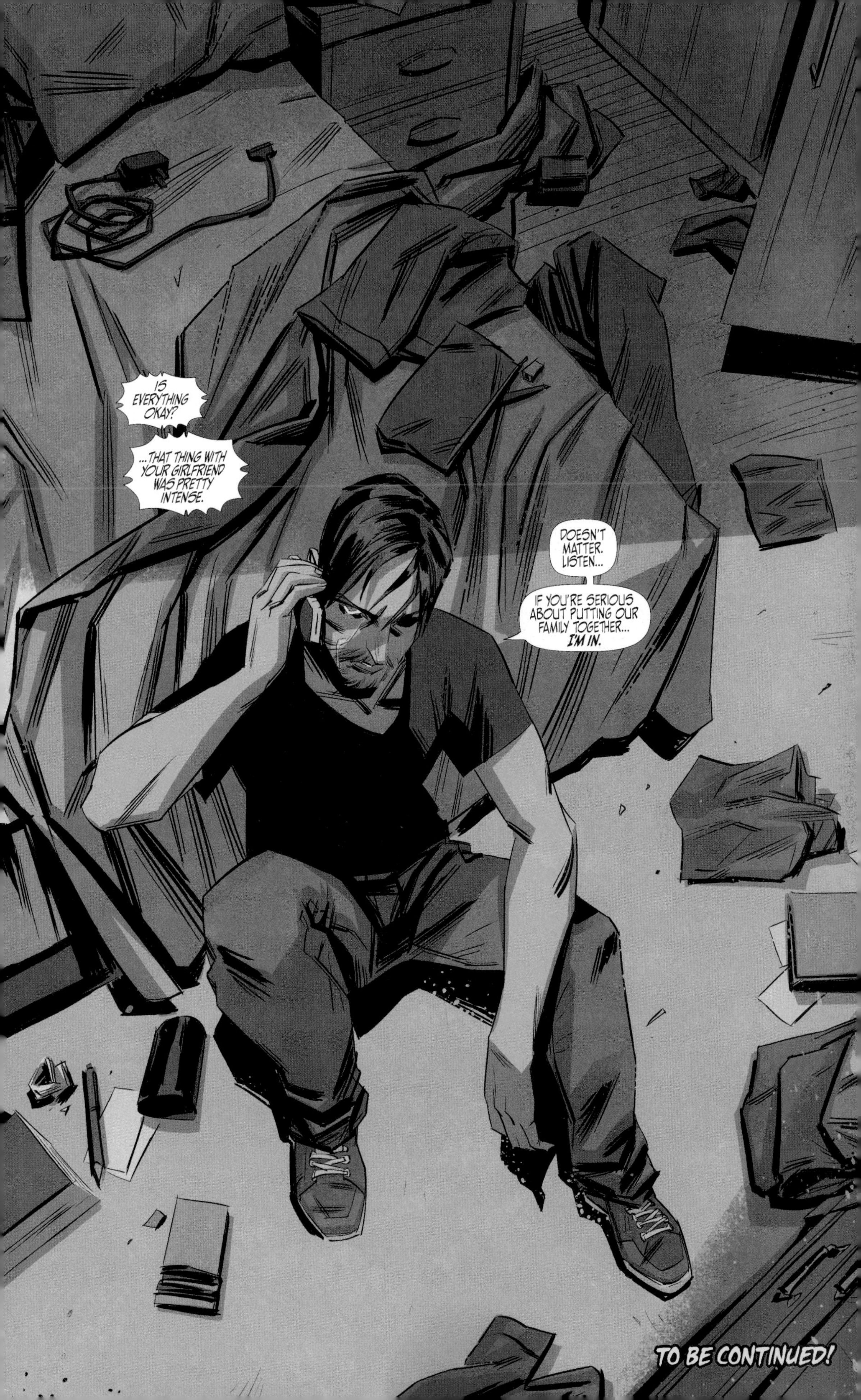
IS EVERYTHING OKAY?
...THAT THING WITH YOUR GIRLFRIEND WAS PRETTY INTENSE.
DOESN'T MATTER. LISTEN...
IF YOU'RE SERIOUS ABOUT PUTTING OUR FAMILY TOGETHER... *I'M IN.*
TO BE CONTINUED!

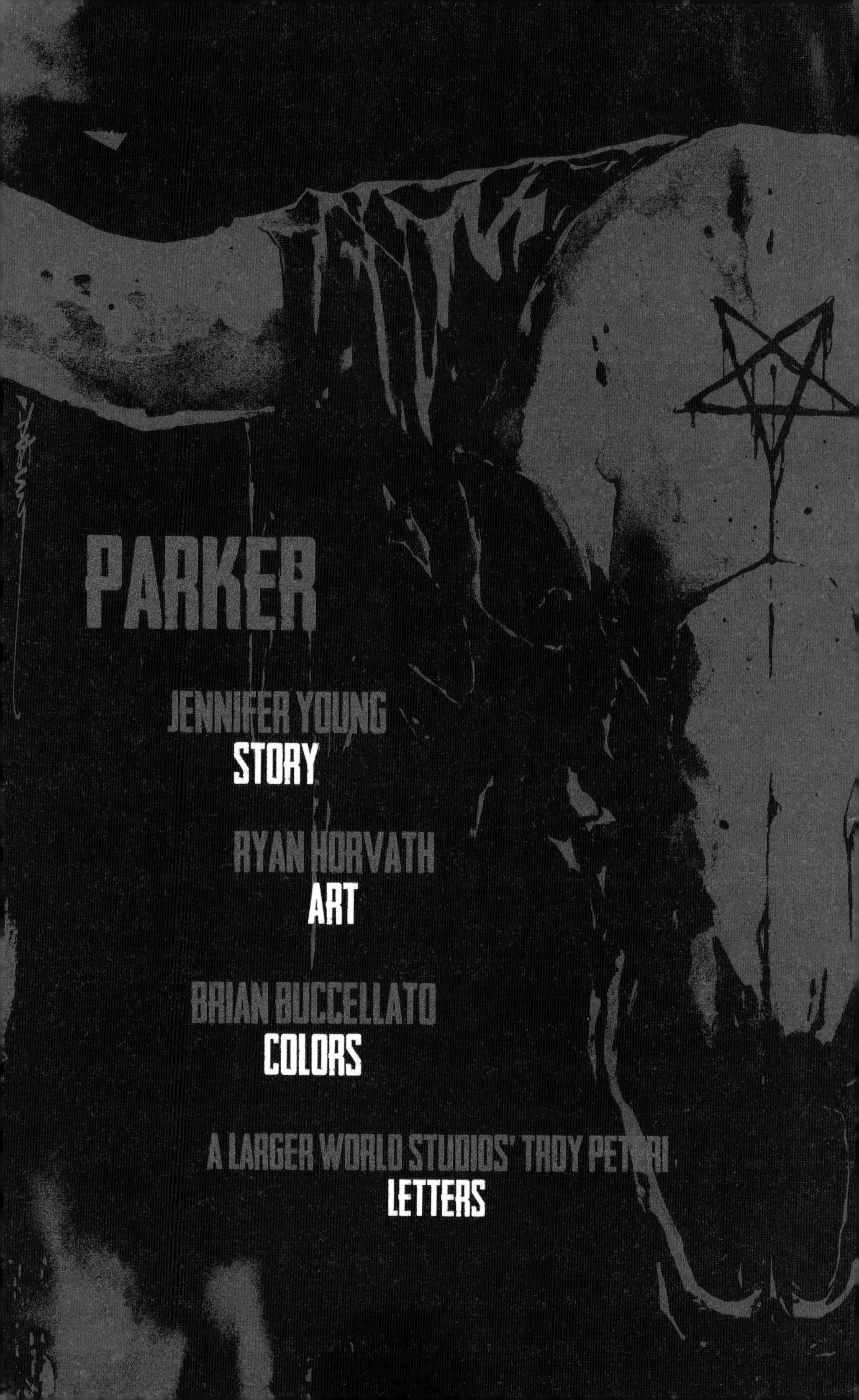

PARKER

JENNIFER YOUNG
STORY

RYAN HORVATH
ART

BRIAN BUCCELLATO
COLORS

A LARGER WORLD STUDIOS' TROY PETERI
LETTERS

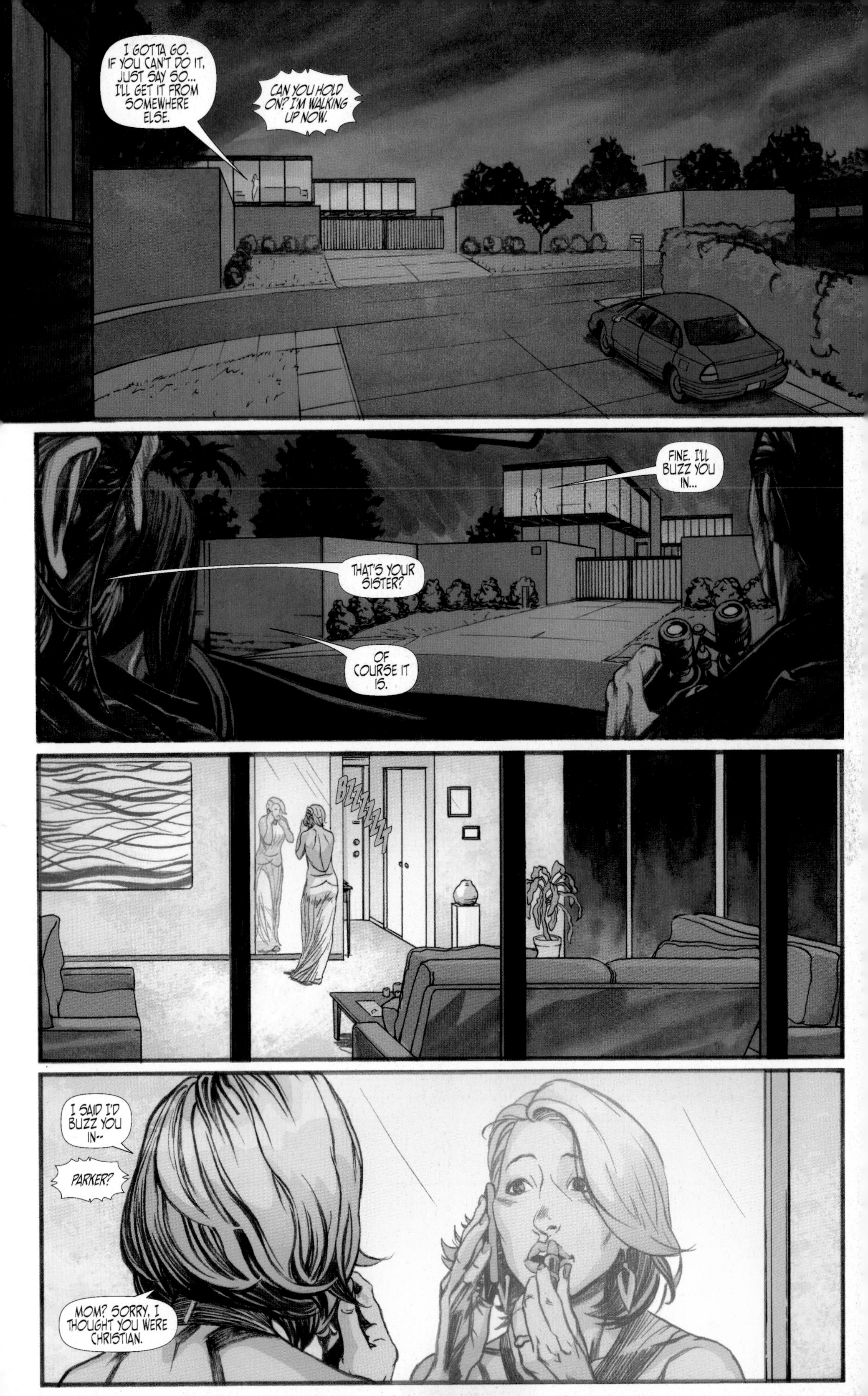
I GOTTA GO. IF YOU CAN'T DO IT, JUST SAY SO... I'LL GET IT FROM SOMEWHERE ELSE.
CAN YOU HOLD ON? I'M WALKING UP NOW.
FINE. I'LL BUZZ YOU IN...
THAT'S YOUR SISTER?
OF COURSE IT IS.
BZZZZZZZT
I SAID I'D BUZZ YOU IN--
PARKER?
MOM? SORRY, I THOUGHT YOU WERE CHRISTIAN.

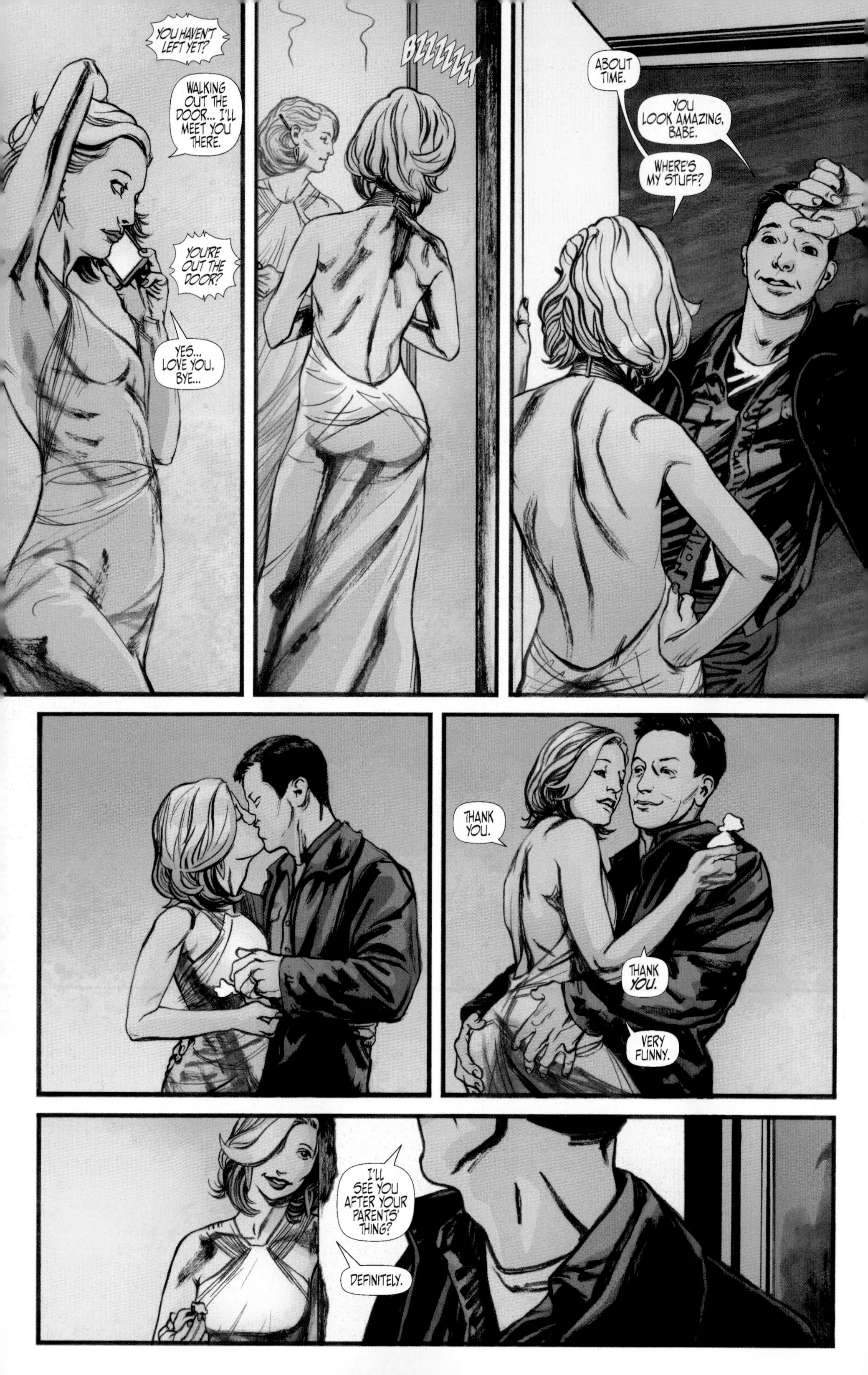
YOU HAVEN'T LEFT YET?
WALKING OUT THE DOOR... I'LL MEET YOU THERE.
YOU'RE OUT THE DOOR?
YES... LOVE YOU, BYE...
BZZZZZZT
ABOUT TIME.
YOU LOOK AMAZING, BABE.
WHERE'S MY STUFF?
THANK YOU.
THANK YOU.
VERY FUNNY.
I'LL SEE YOU AFTER YOUR PARENTS' THING?
DEFINITELY.

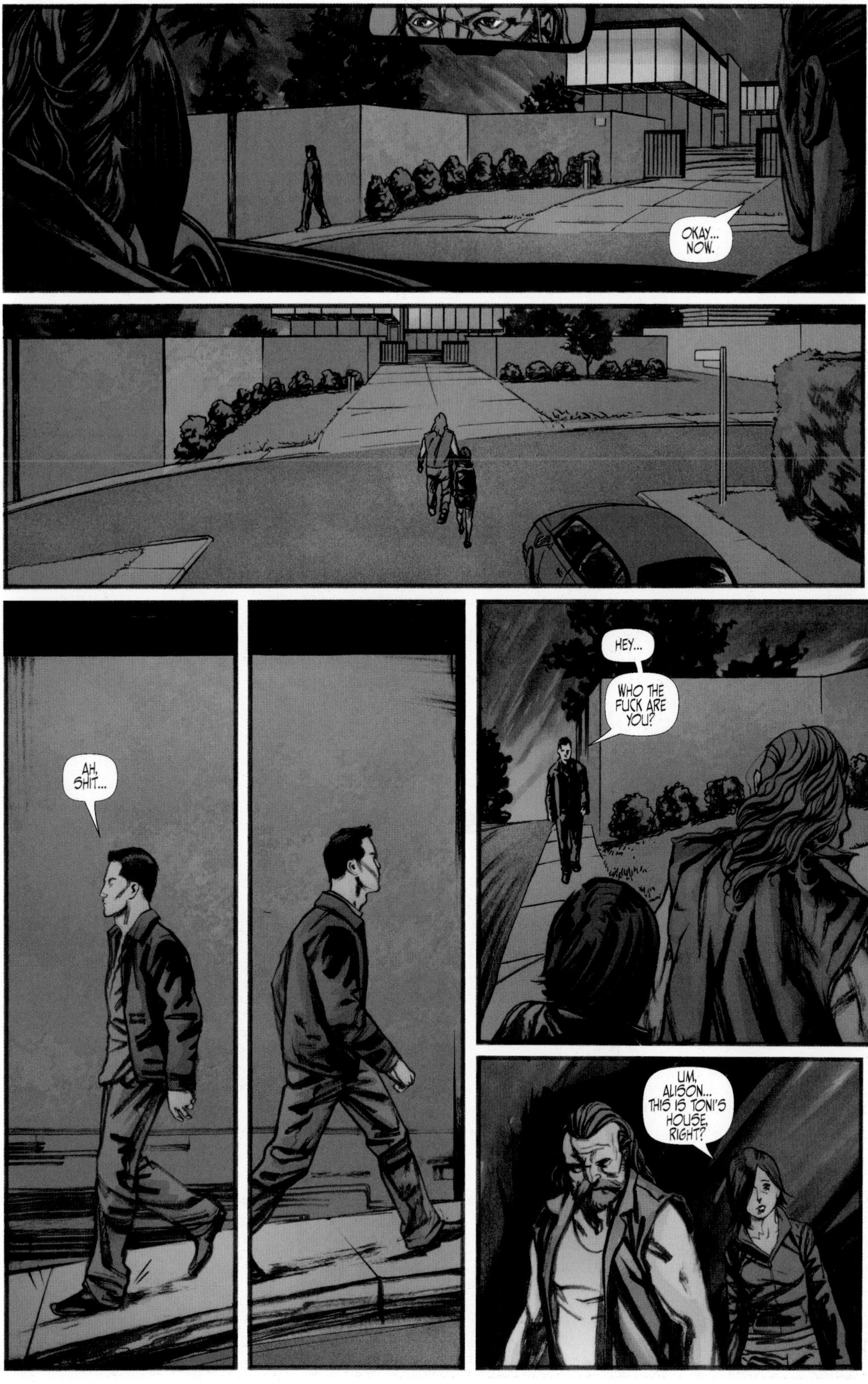
OKAY... NOW.
AH, SHIT...
HEY...
WHO THE FUCK ARE YOU?
UM, ALISON... THIS IS TONI'S HOUSE, RIGHT?

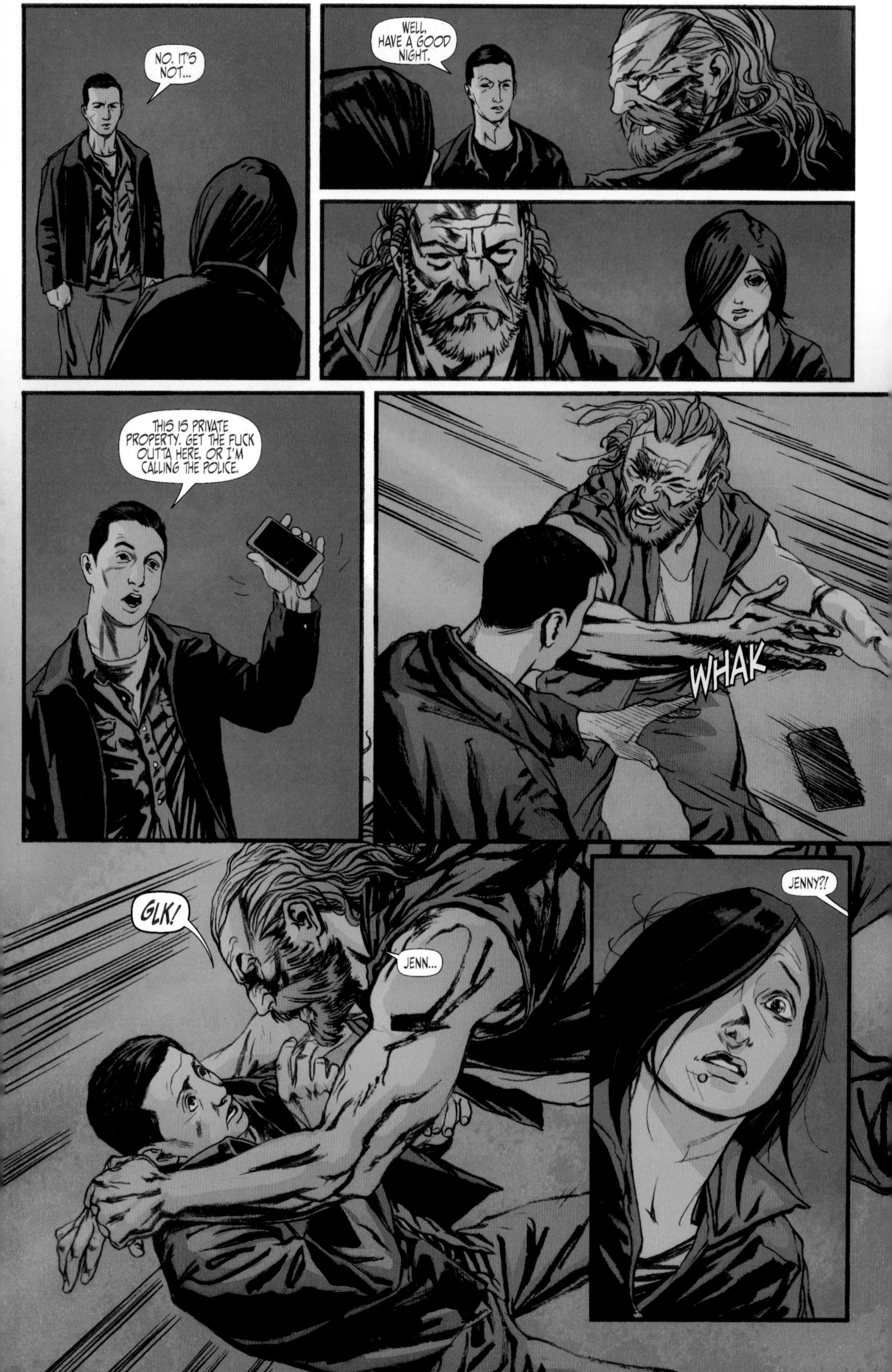
NO. IT'S NOT...
WELL, HAVE A GOOD NIGHT.
THIS IS PRIVATE PROPERTY. GET THE FUCK OUTTA HERE, OR I'M CALLING THE POLICE.
WHAK
GLK!
JENN...
JENNY?!

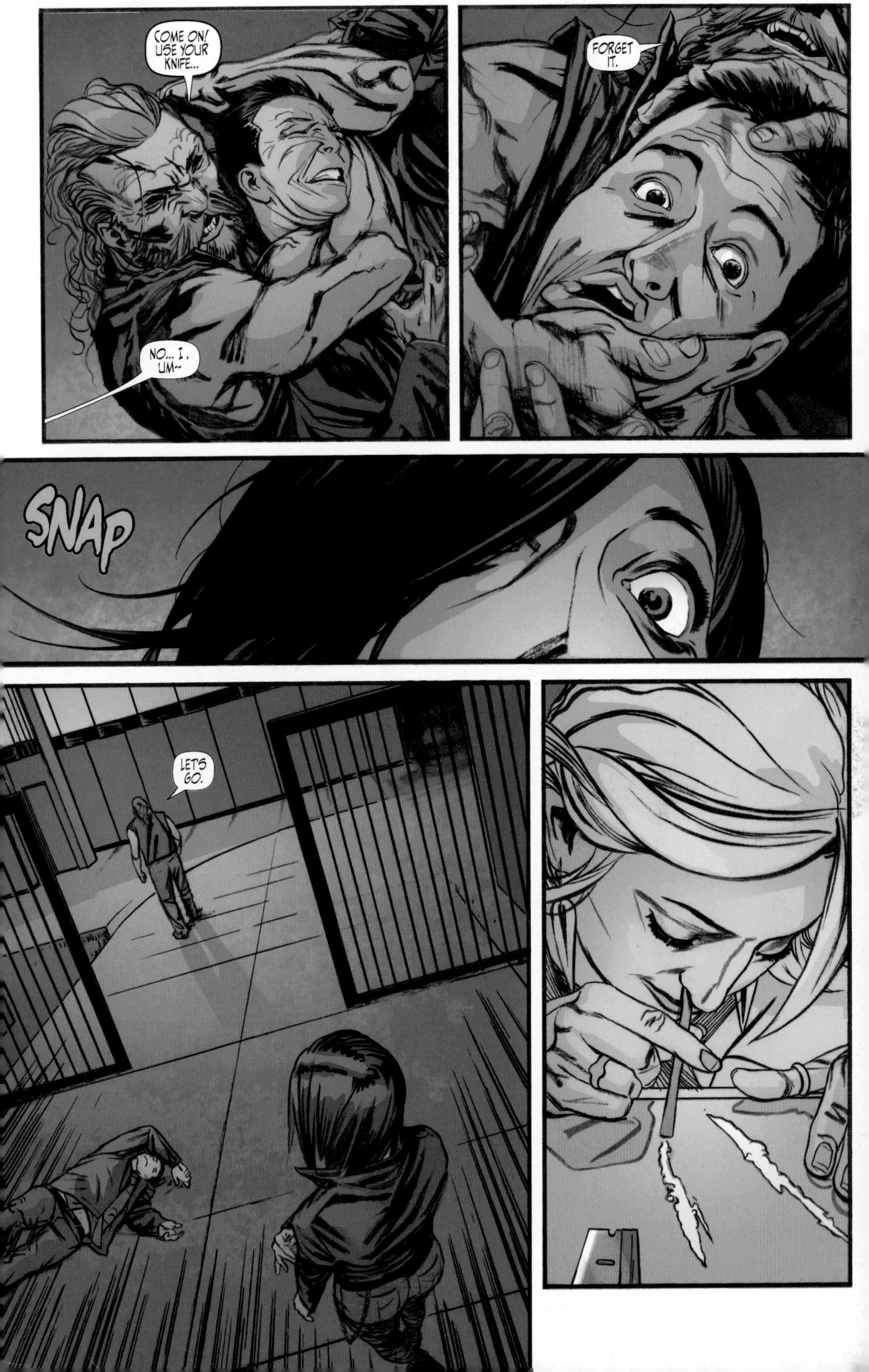
COME ON! USE YOUR KNIFE...
NO... I, UM--
FORGET IT.
SNAP
LET'S GO.

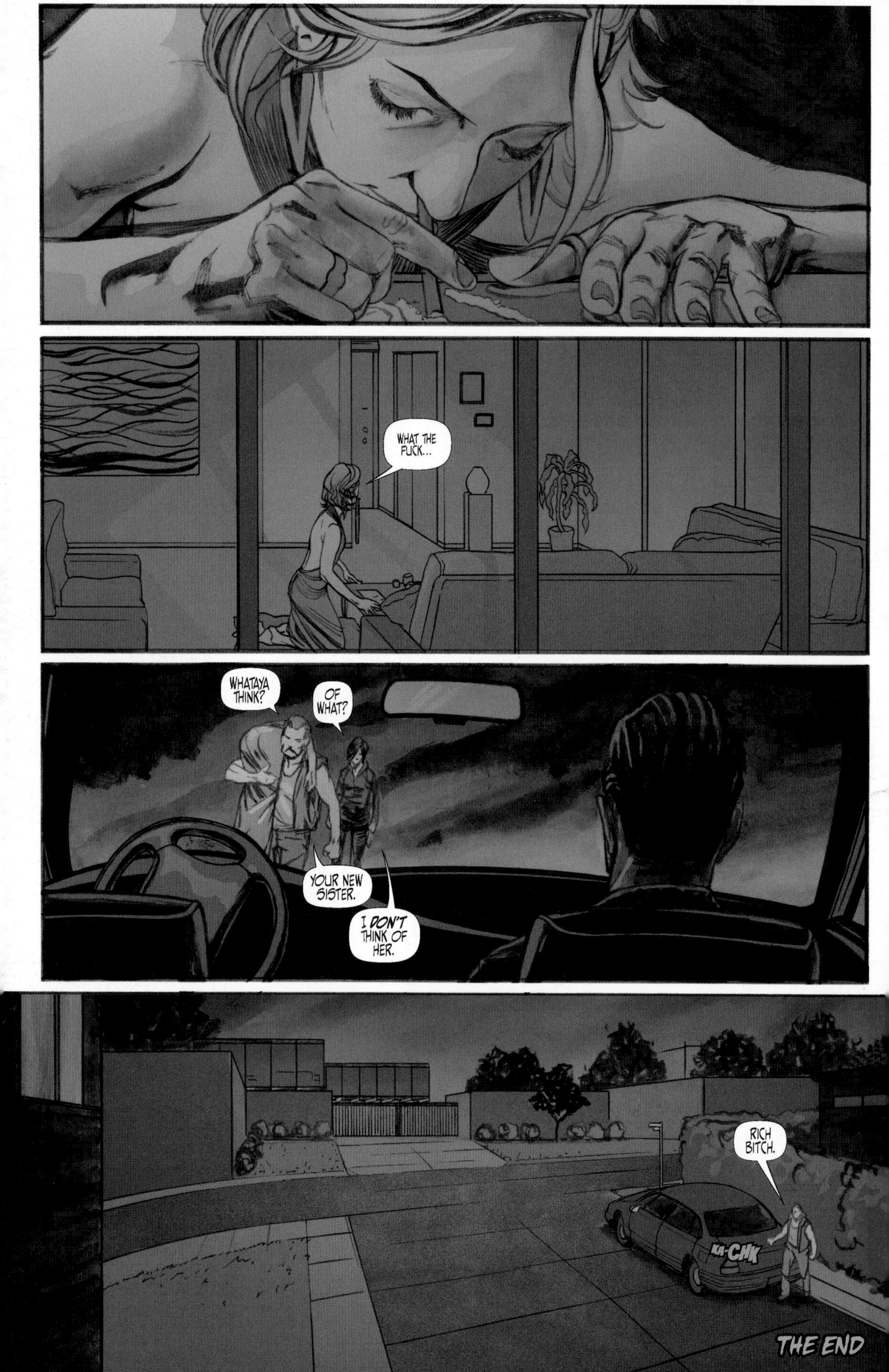
WHAT THE FUCK...
WHATAYA THINK?
OF WHAT?
YOUR NEW SISTER.
I DON'T THINK OF HER.
RICH BITCH.
KA-CHK
THE END

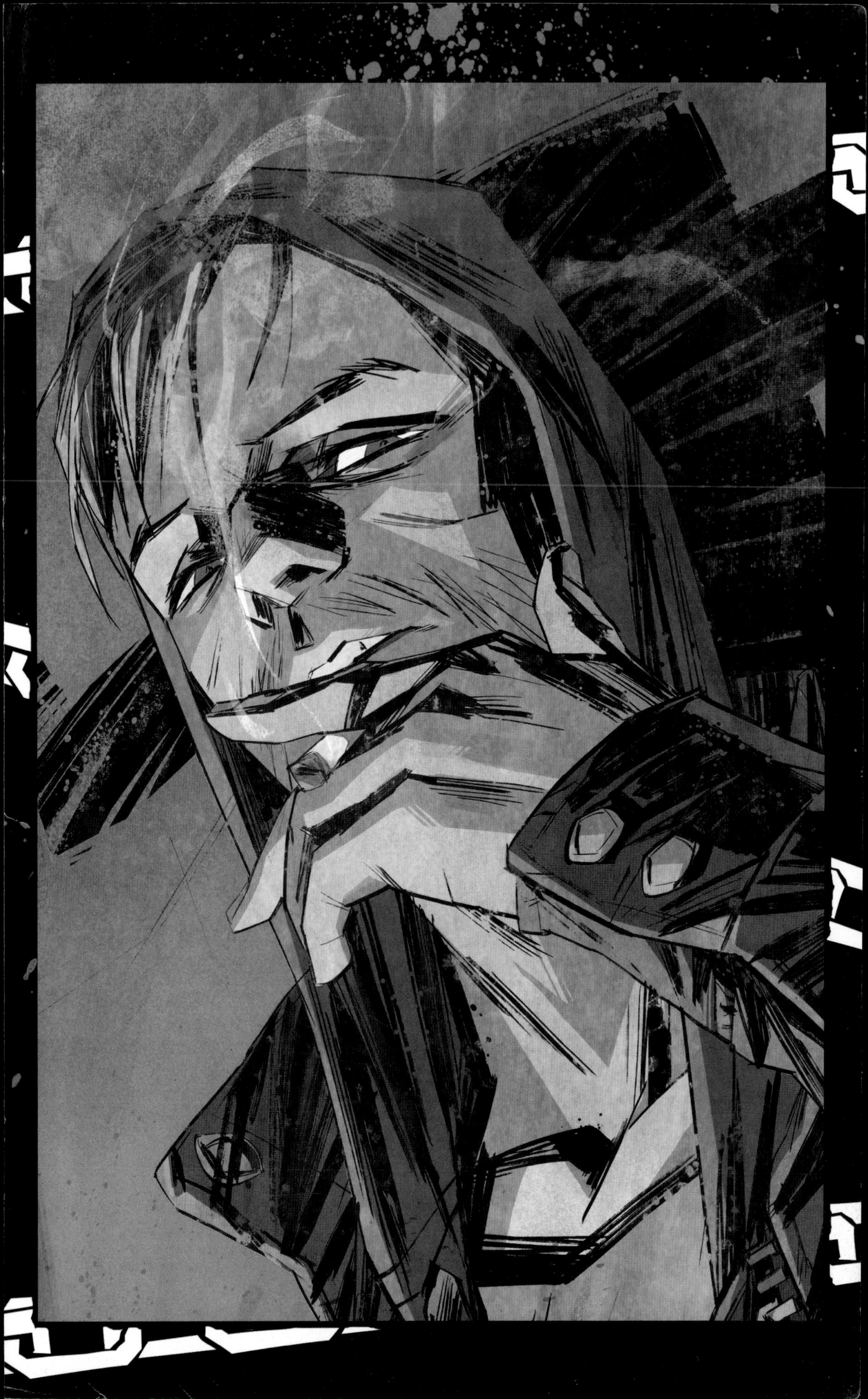

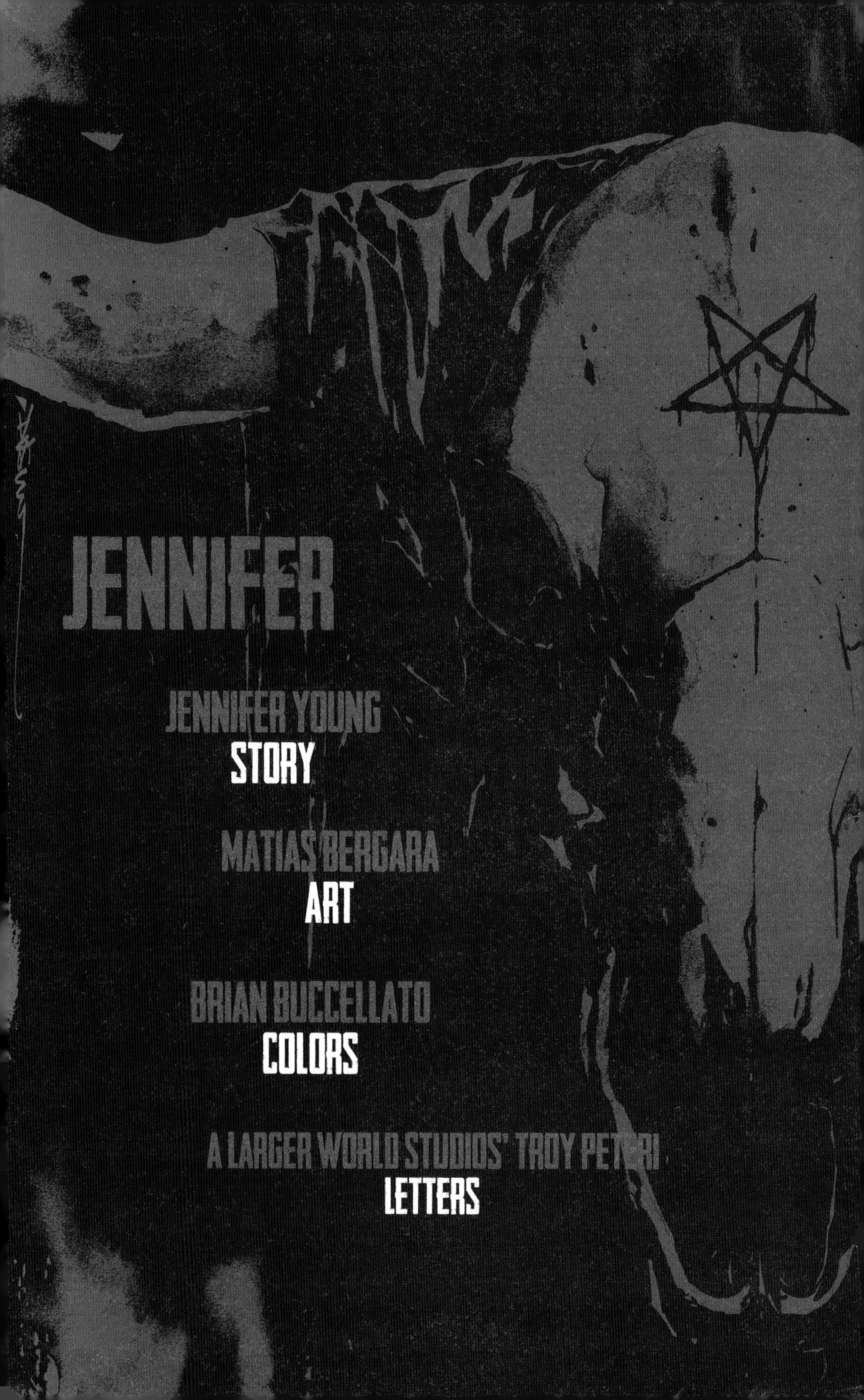
JENNIFER
JENNIFER YOUNG
STORY
MATIAS BERGARA
ART
BRIAN BUCCELLATO
COLORS
A LARGER WORLD STUDIOS' TROY PETERI
LETTERS

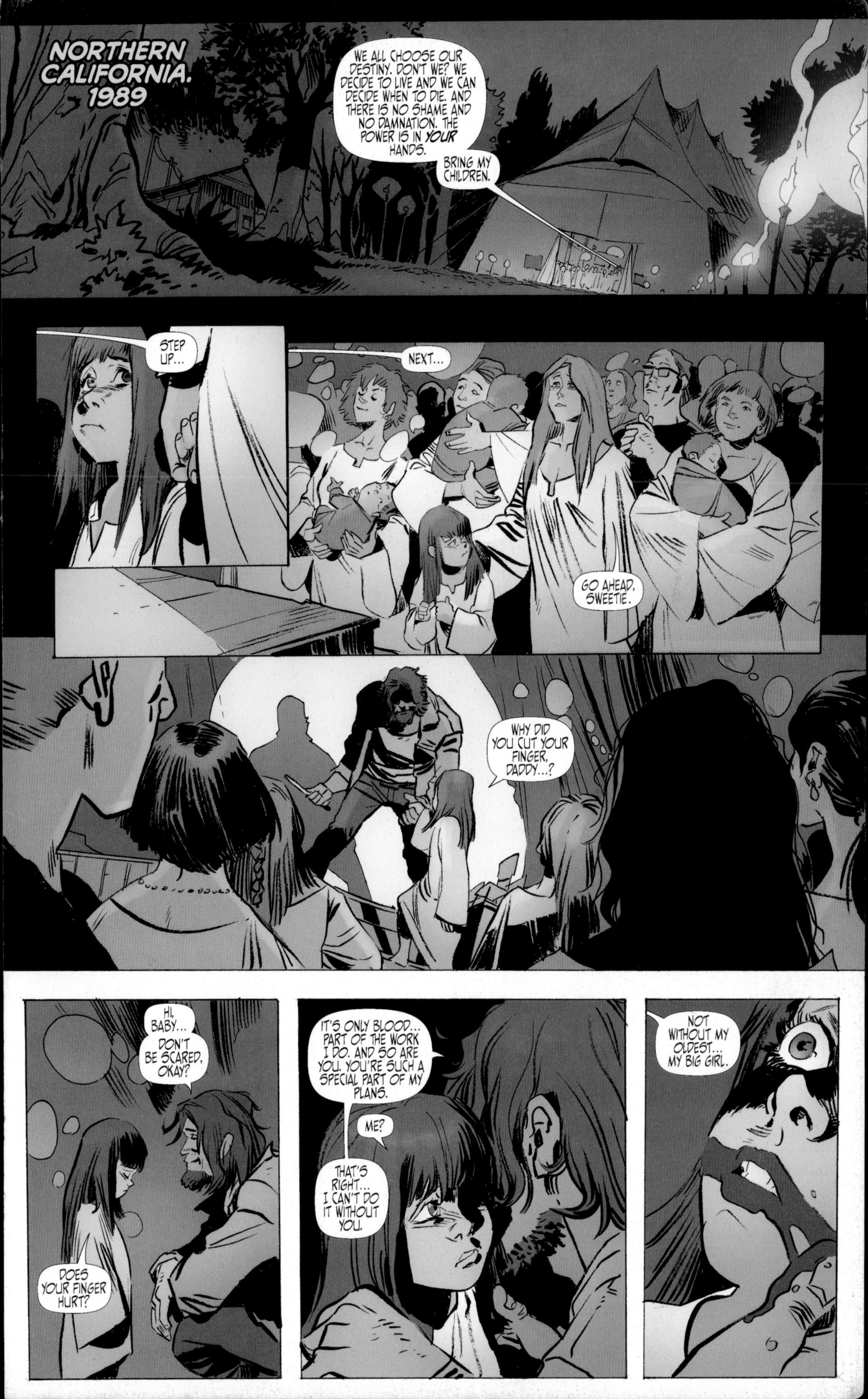
NORTHERN CALIFORNIA. 1989
WE ALL CHOOSE OUR DESTINY. DON'T WE? WE DECIDE TO LIVE AND WE CAN DECIDE WHEN TO DIE. AND THERE IS NO SHAME AND NO DAMNATION. THE POWER IS IN YOUR HANDS.
BRING MY CHILDREN.
STEP UP...
NEXT...
GO AHEAD, SWEETIE.
WHY DID YOU CUT YOUR FINGER, DADDY...?
HI, BABY...
DON'T BE SCARED, OKAY?
DOES YOUR FINGER HURT?
IT'S ONLY BLOOD... PART OF THE WORK I DO. AND SO ARE YOU. YOU'RE SUCH A SPECIAL PART OF MY PLANS.
ME?
THAT'S RIGHT... I CAN'T DO IT WITHOUT YOU.
NOT WITHOUT MY OLDEST... MY BIG GIRL.

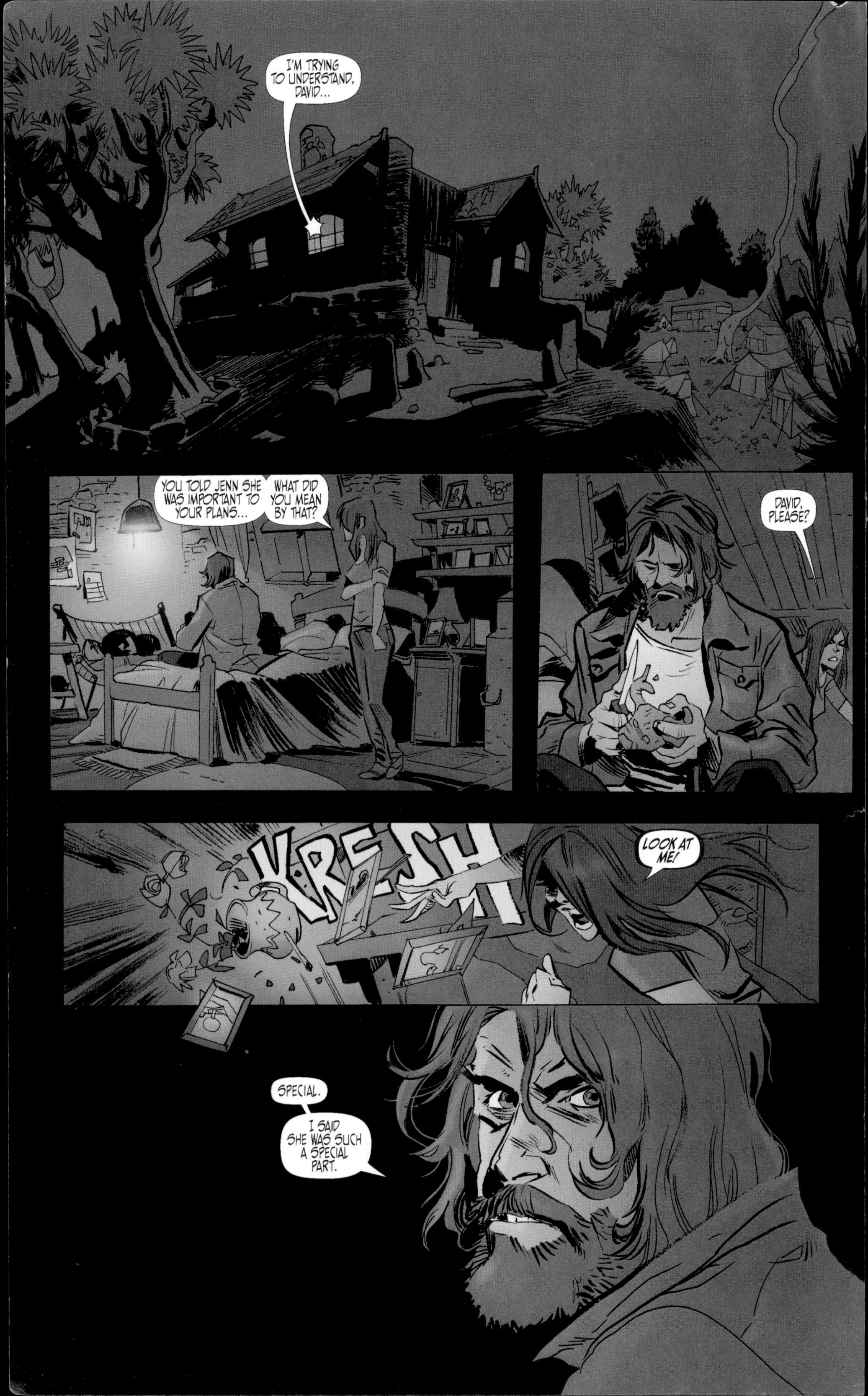
I'M TRYING TO UNDERSTAND, DAVID...
YOU TOLD JENN SHE WAS IMPORTANT TO YOUR PLANS...
WHAT DID YOU MEAN BY THAT?
DAVID, PLEASE?
KRESH
LOOK AT ME!
SPECIAL.
I SAID SHE WAS SUCH A SPECIAL PART.

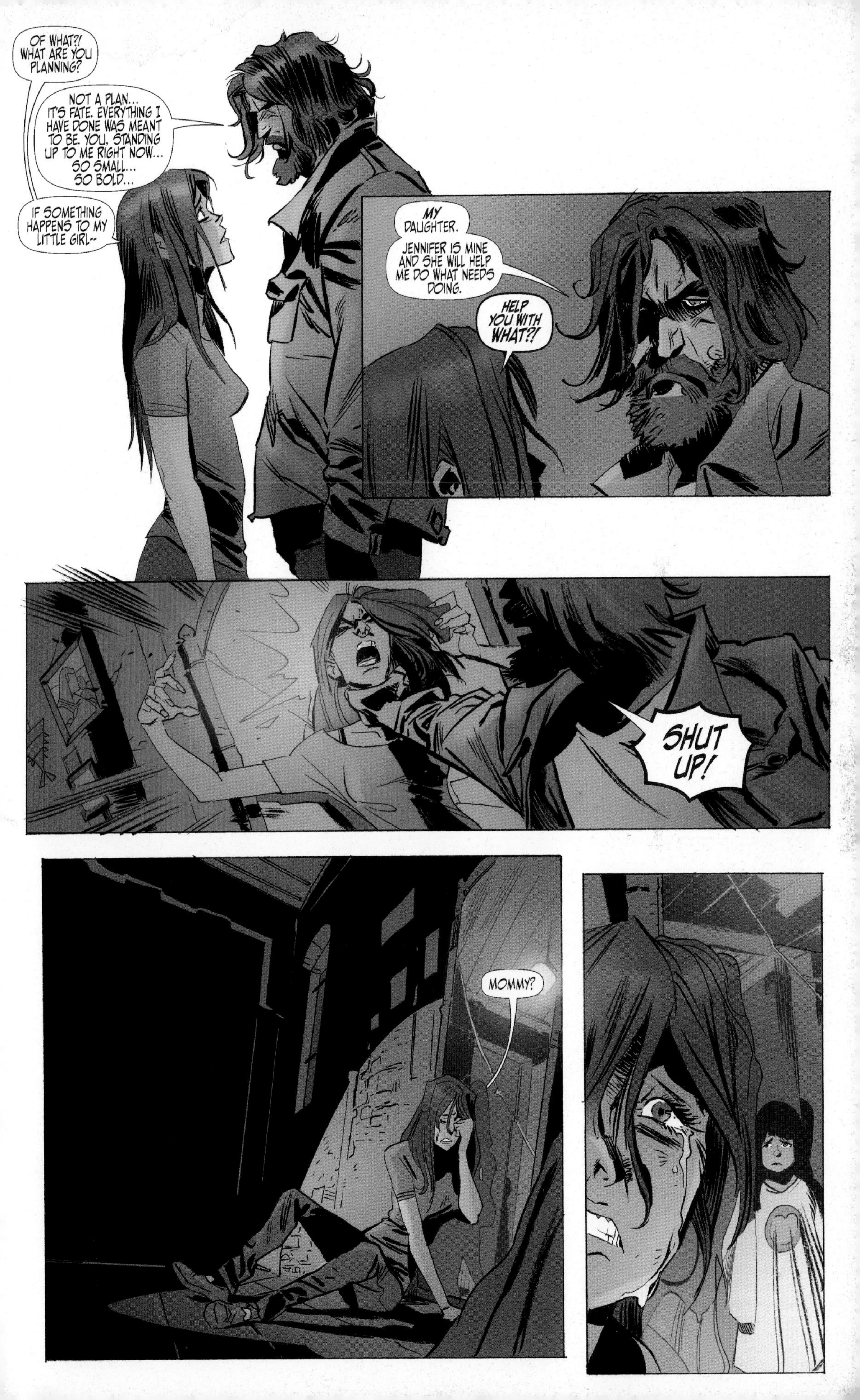

OF WHAT?! WHAT ARE YOU PLANNING?
NOT A PLAN... IT'S FATE. EVERYTHING I HAVE DONE WAS MEANT TO BE. YOU, STANDING UP TO ME RIGHT NOW... SO SMALL... SO BOLD...
IF SOMETHING HAPPENS TO MY LITTLE GIRL--
MY DAUGHTER.
JENNIFER IS MINE AND SHE WILL HELP ME DO WHAT NEEDS DOING.
HELP YOU WITH WHAT?!
SHUT UP!
MOMMY?

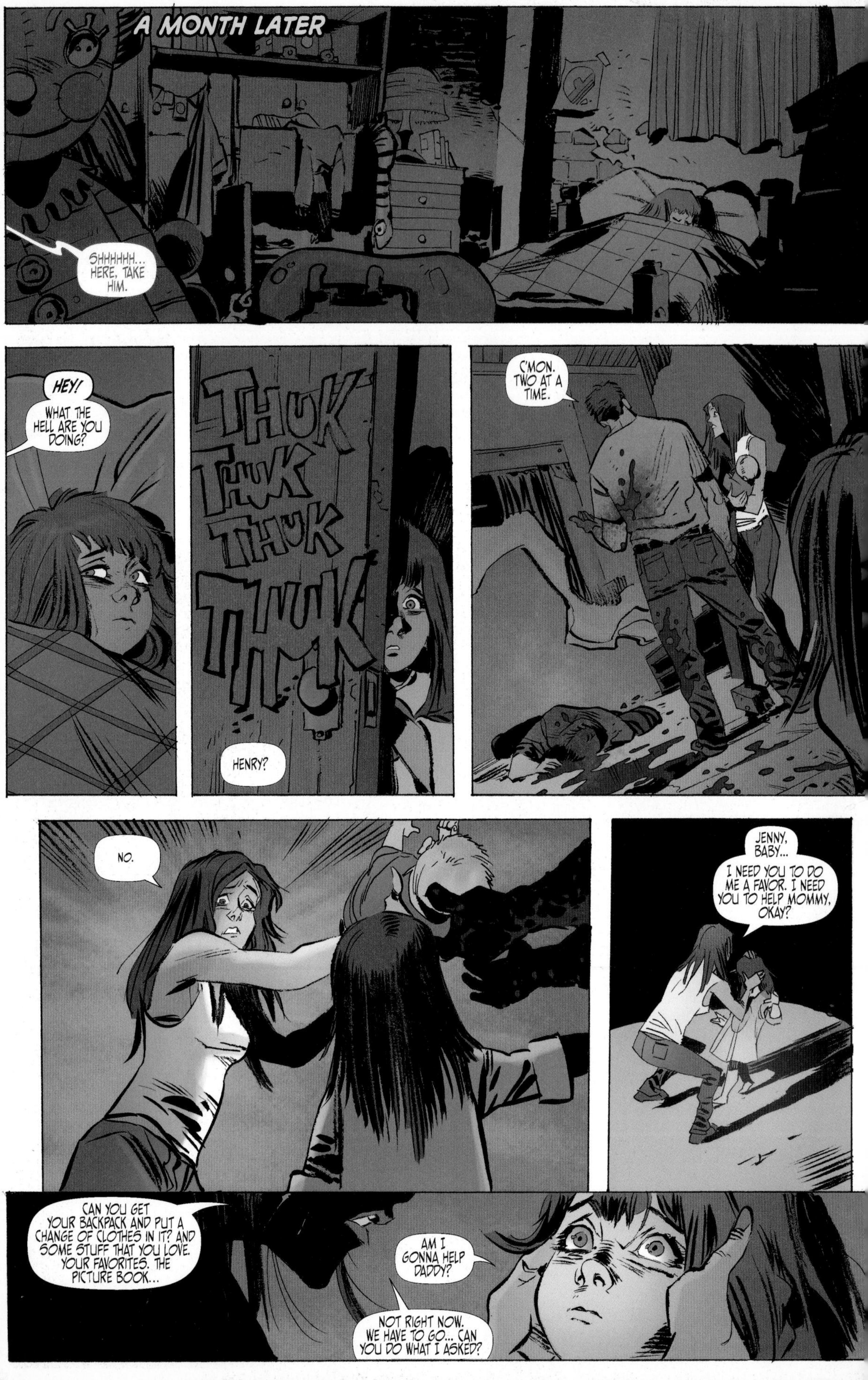
A MONTH LATER
SHHHHHH... HERE, TAKE HIM.
HEY! WHAT THE HELL ARE YOU DOING?
THUK THUK THUK THUK
HENRY?
C'MON. TWO AT A TIME.
NO.
JENNY, BABY... I NEED YOU TO DO ME A FAVOR. I NEED YOU TO HELP MOMMY, OKAY?
CAN YOU GET YOUR BACKPACK AND PUT A CHANGE OF CLOTHES IN IT? AND SOME STUFF THAT YOU LOVE. YOUR FAVORITES. THE PICTURE BOOK...
AM I GONNA HELP DADDY?
NOT RIGHT NOW. WE HAVE TO GO... CAN YOU DO WHAT I ASKED?

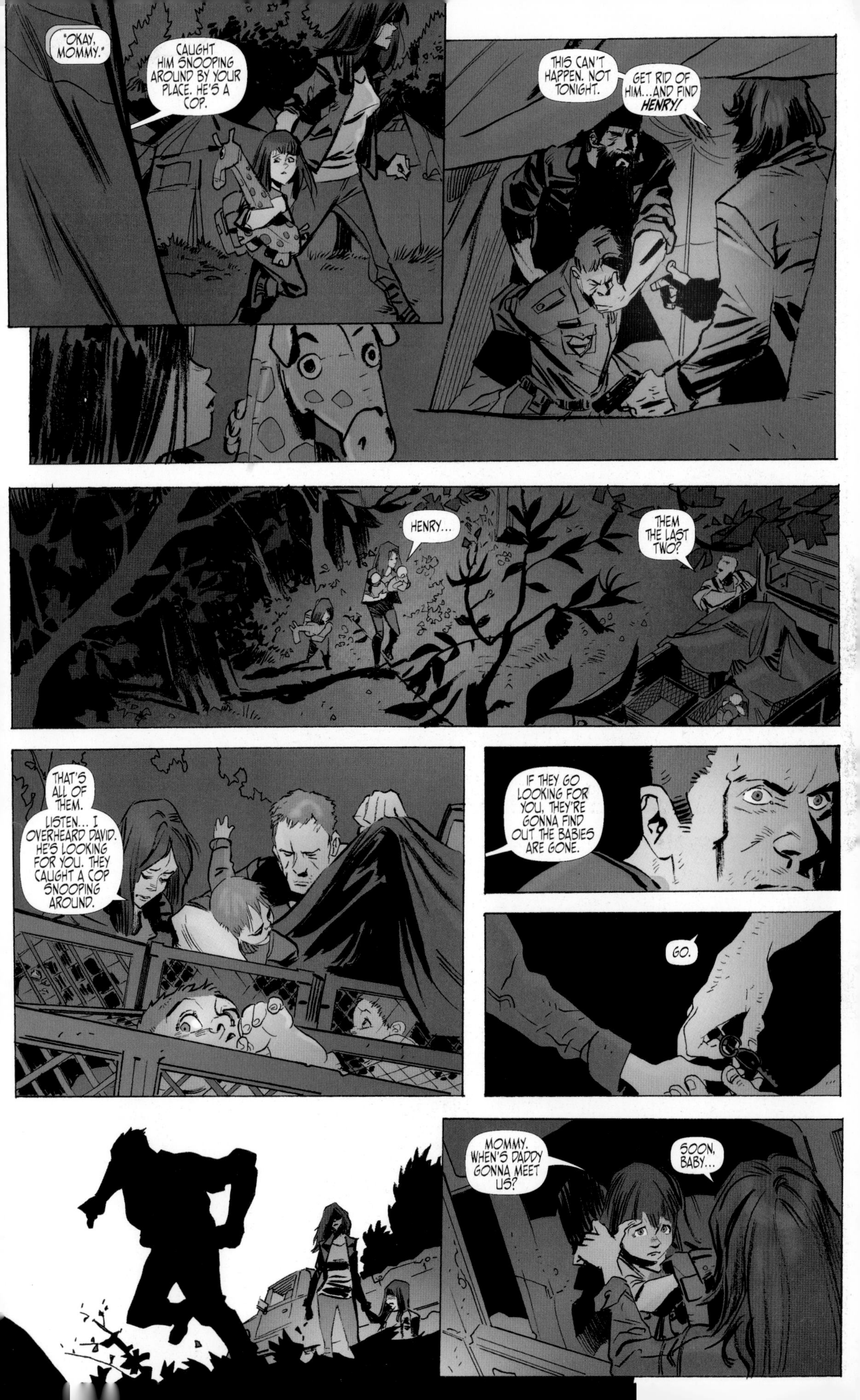
"OKAY, MOMMY."
CAUGHT HIM SNOOPING AROUND BY YOUR PLACE. HE'S A COP.
THIS CAN'T HAPPEN. NOT TONIGHT.
GET RID OF HIM...AND FIND *HENRY!*
HENRY...
THEM THE LAST TWO?
THAT'S ALL OF THEM.
LISTEN... I OVERHEARD DAVID. HE'S LOOKING FOR YOU. THEY CAUGHT A COP SNOOPING AROUND.
IF THEY GO LOOKING FOR YOU, THEY'RE GONNA FIND OUT THE BABIES ARE GONE.
GO.
MOMMY. WHEN'S DADDY GONNA MEET US?
SOON, BABY...

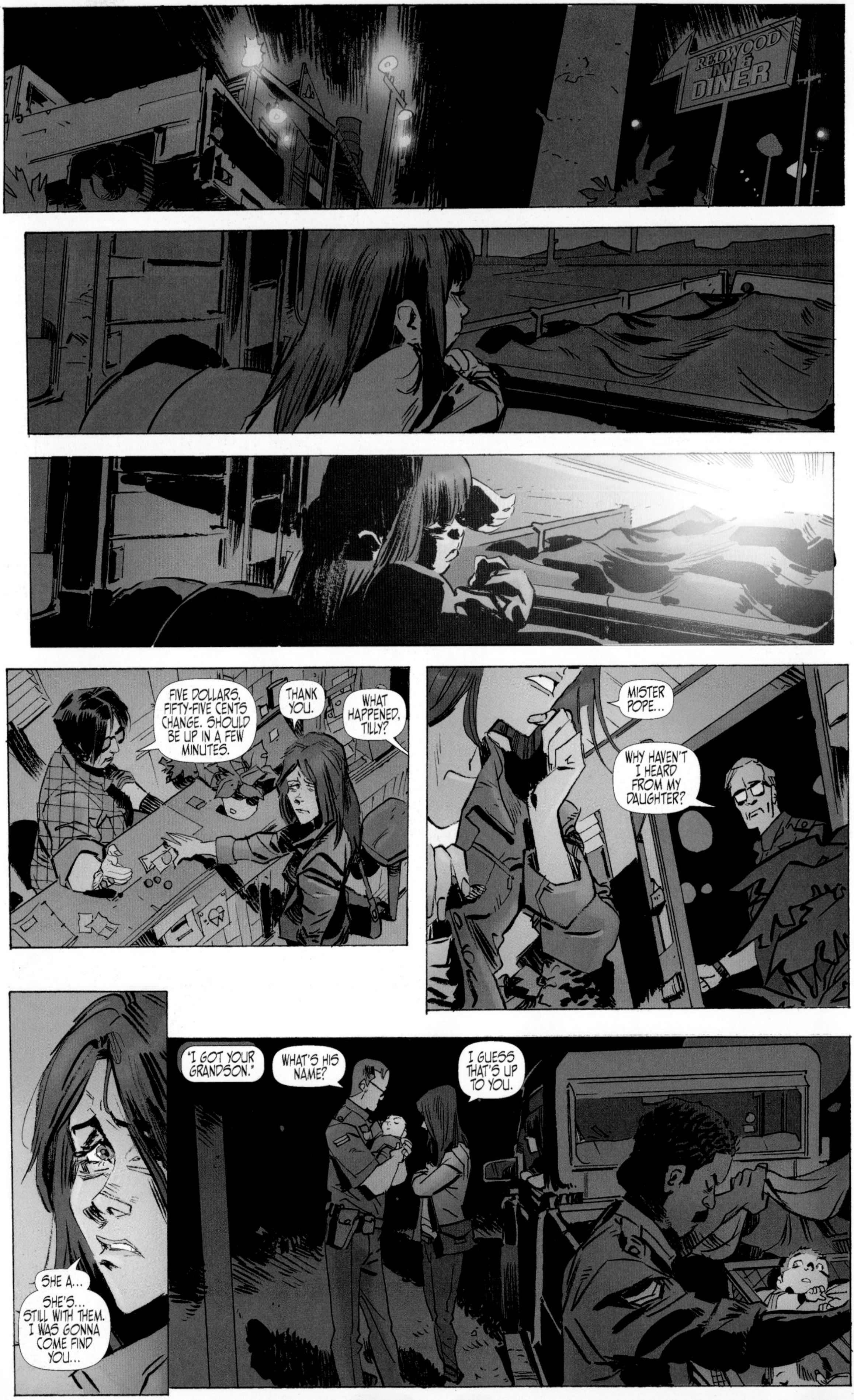
REDWOOD INN & DINER
FIVE DOLLARS, FIFTY-FIVE CENTS CHANGE. SHOULD BE UP IN A FEW MINUTES.
THANK YOU.
WHAT HAPPENED, TILLY?
MISTER POPE...
WHY HAVEN'T I HEARD FROM MY DAUGHTER?
SHE A... SHE'S... STILL WITH THEM. I WAS GONNA COME FIND YOU...
"I GOT YOUR GRANDSON."
WHAT'S HIS NAME?
I GUESS THAT'S UP TO YOU.

SEX CULT ENDS IN FLAMES

UM... JUST TO BE SAFE...

GONNA HAVE TO GIVE YOU A NEW NAME AND EVERYTHING. ANY, UM... IDEA WHAT YOU WANT?

DOESN'T MATTER.

SEX CULT ENDS IN FLAMES

I DON'T WANNA CHANGE MY NAME!

IT'S OKAY. YOU DON'T HAVE TO.

THIS IS AGENT GILES. HE'S GONNA GET YOU ALL SET UP...

MOM, I WANNA GO HOME.

IF YOU LIKED THIS, JENNY... YOU CAN KEEP IT.

SAY THANK YOU, JENN.

THANK YOU.

SIERRA POLICE DEPARTMENT

WADE S. POPE
Sergeant

Office: (409) 730
421 Opal St.
Sierra, CA 9

SURE.

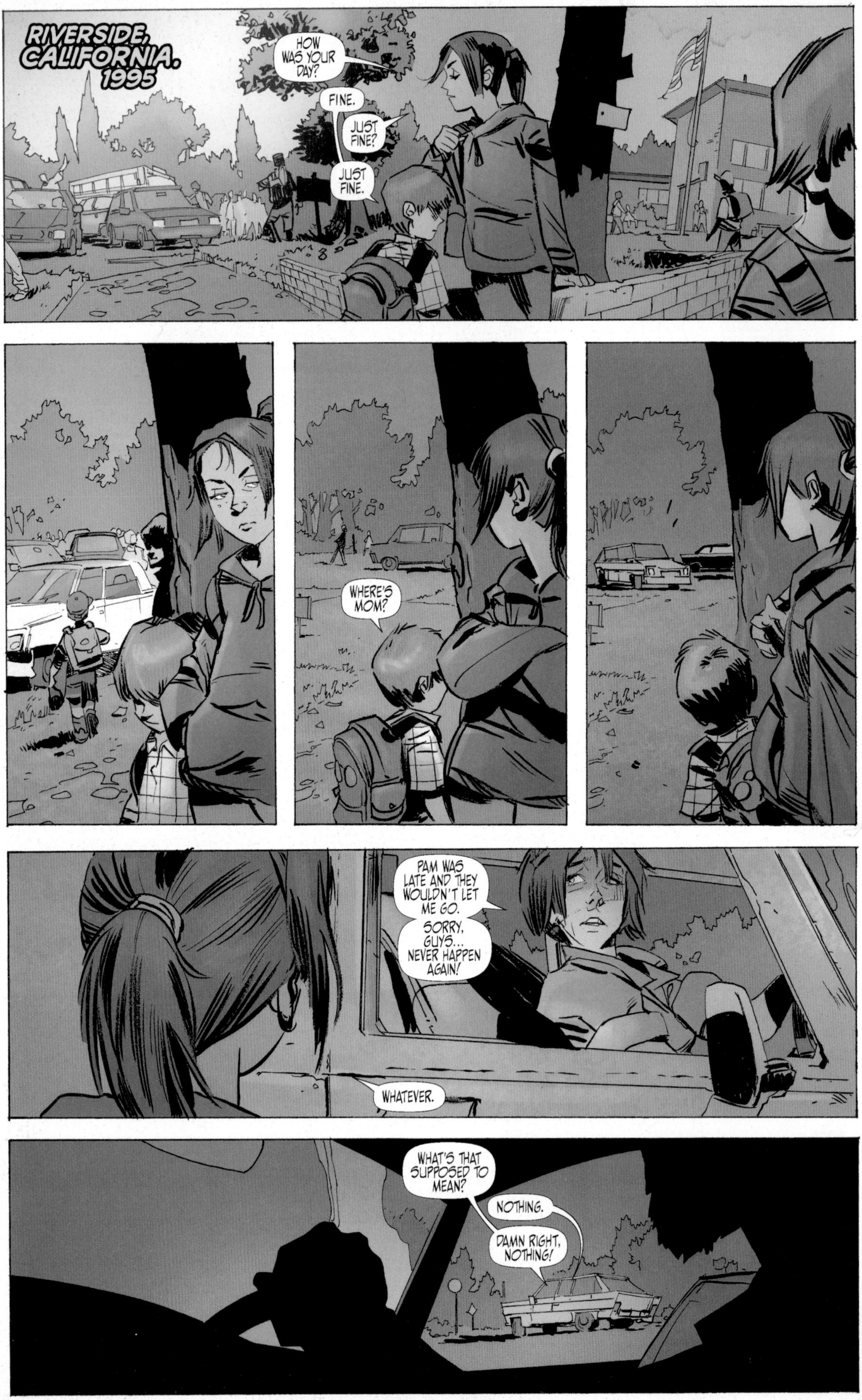
RIVERSIDE, CALIFORNIA. 1995
HOW WAS YOUR DAY?
FINE.
JUST FINE?
JUST FINE.
WHERE'S MOM?
PAM WAS LATE AND THEY WOULDN'T LET ME GO.
SORRY, GUYS... NEVER HAPPEN AGAIN!
WHATEVER.
WHAT'S THAT SUPPOSED TO MEAN?
NOTHING.
DAMN RIGHT, NOTHING!

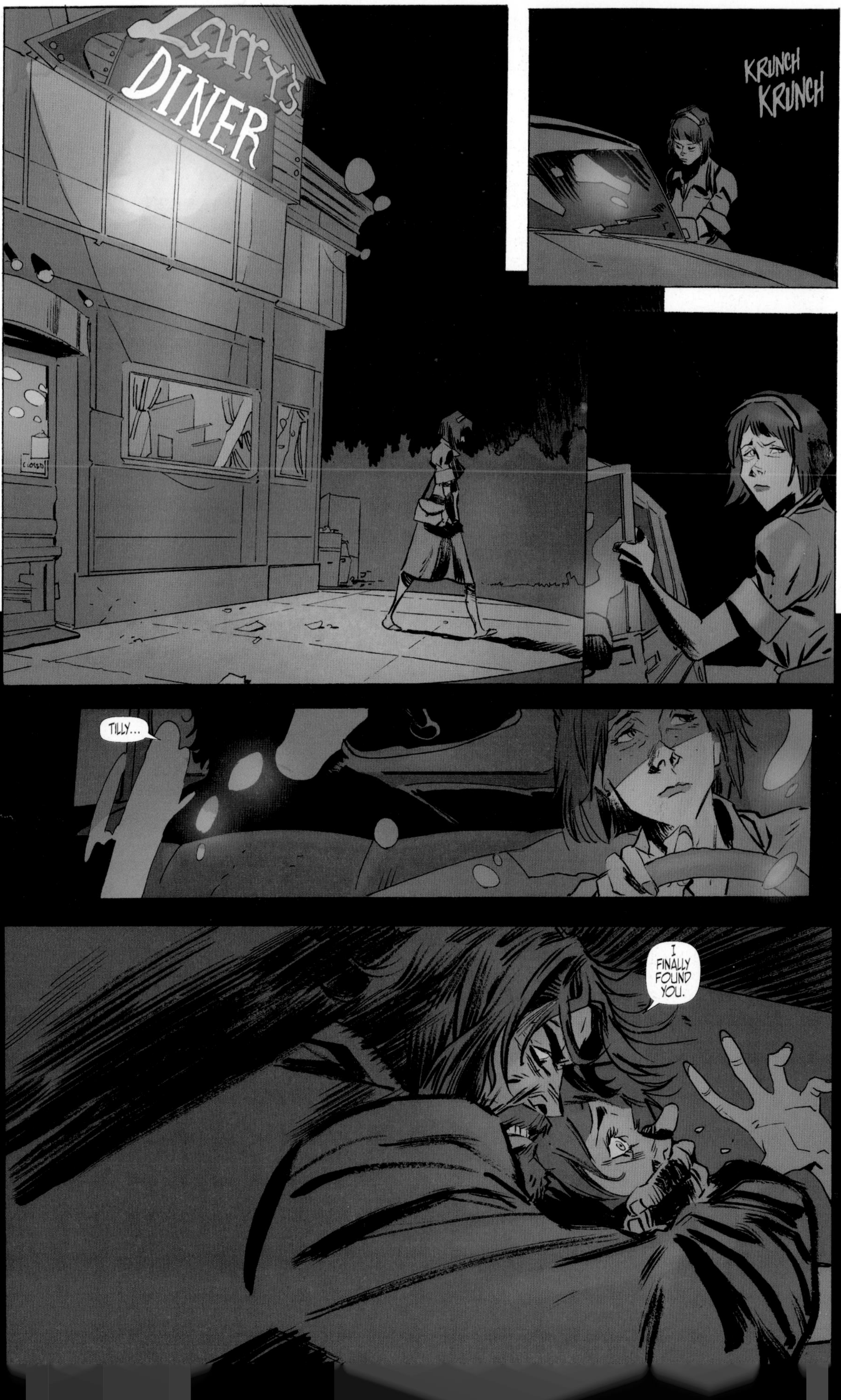
Larry's DINER
CLOSED
KRUNCH
KRUNCH
TILLY...
I FINALLY FOUND YOU.

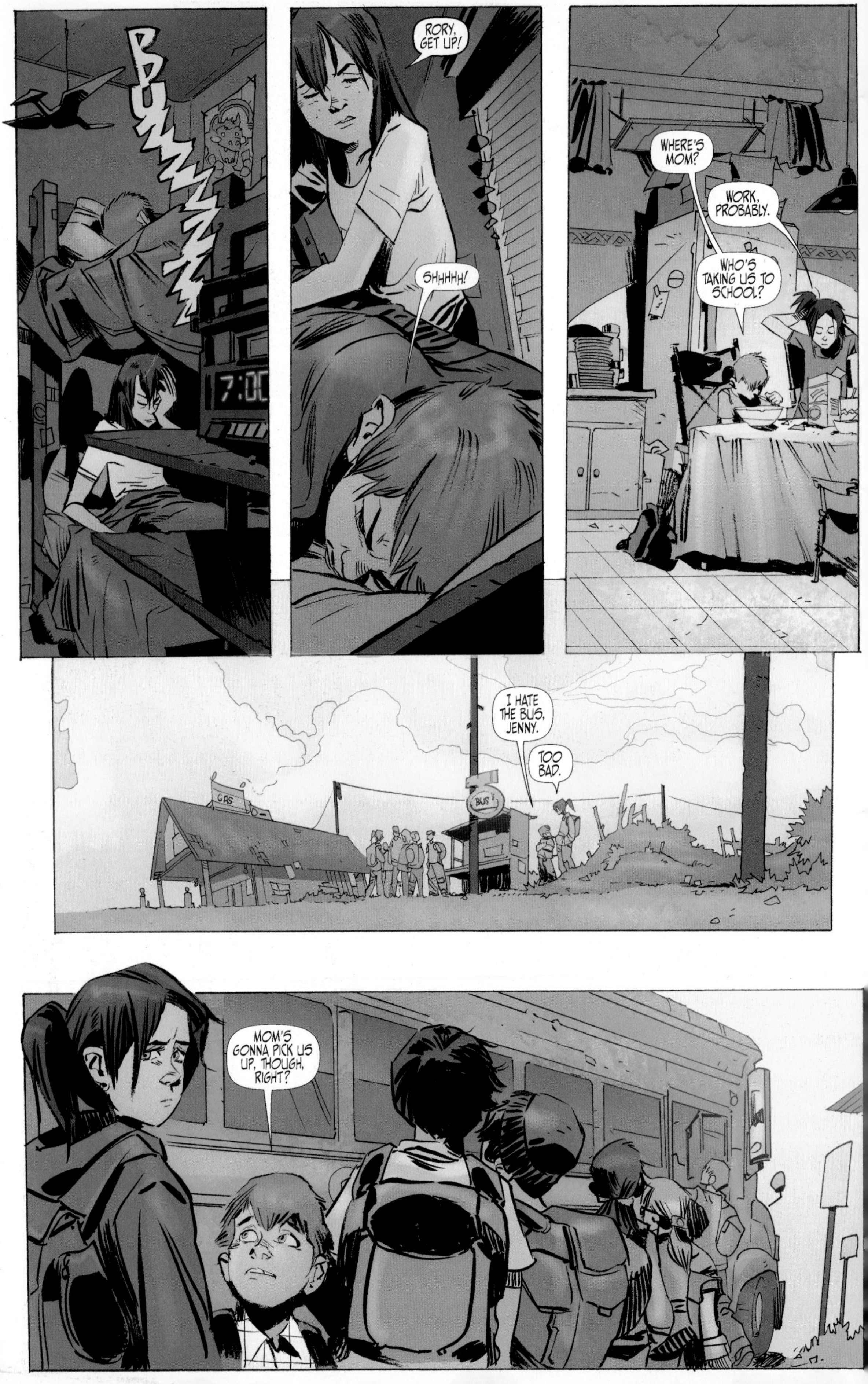
BUZZZZZ
7:00
RORY, GET UP!
SHHHHH!
WHERE'S MOM?
WORK, PROBABLY.
WHO'S TAKING US TO SCHOOL?
I HATE THE BUS, JENNY.
TOO BAD.
GAS
BUS
MOM'S GONNA PICK US UP, THOUGH, RIGHT?

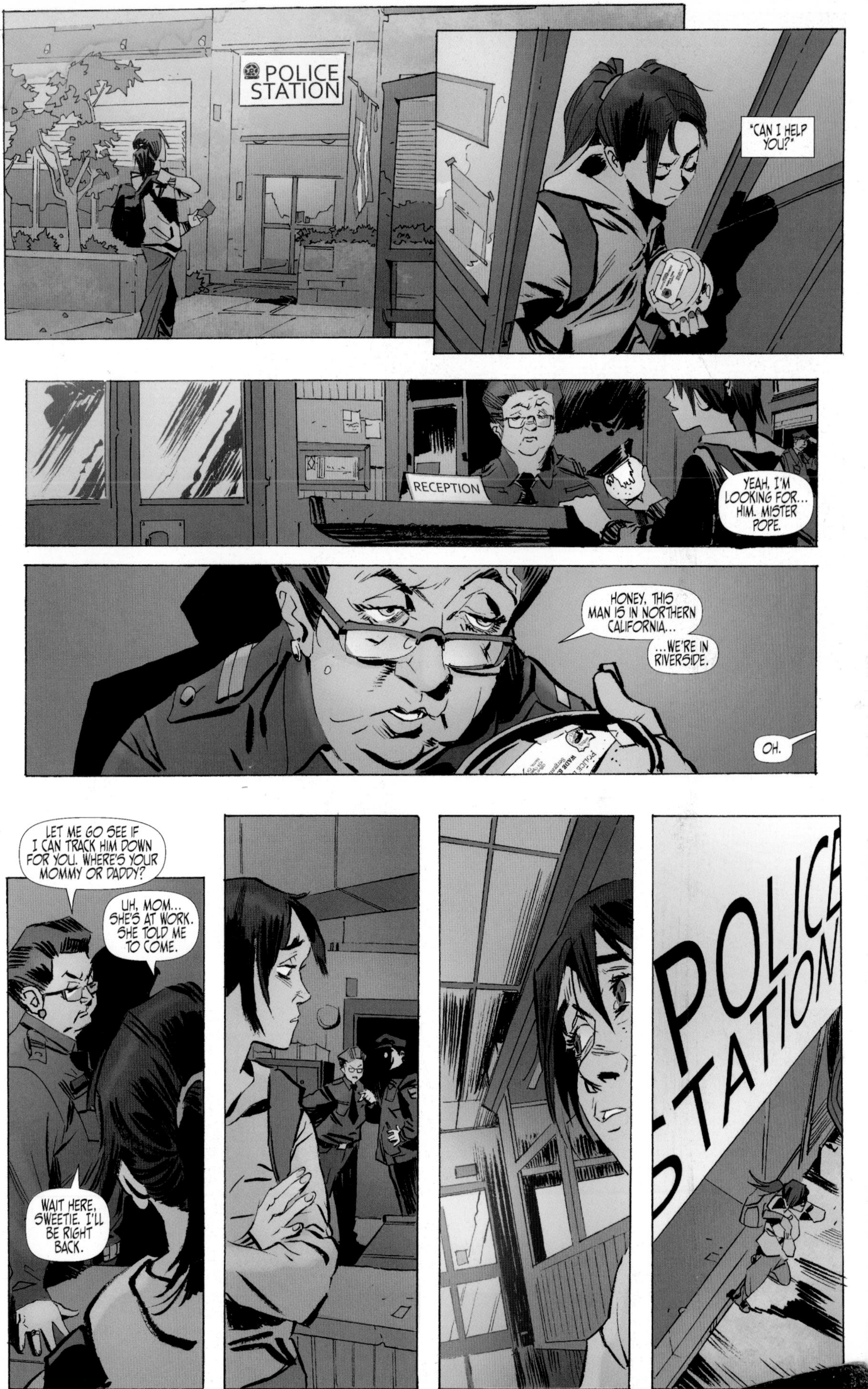
POLICE STATION
"CAN I HELP YOU?"
RECEPTION
YEAH, I'M LOOKING FOR... HIM. MISTER POPE.
HONEY, THIS MAN IS IN NORTHERN CALIFORNIA...
...WE'RE IN RIVERSIDE.
OH.
LET ME GO SEE IF I CAN TRACK HIM DOWN FOR YOU. WHERE'S YOUR MOMMY OR DADDY?
UH, MOM... SHE'S AT WORK. SHE TOLD ME TO COME.
WAIT HERE, SWEETIE. I'LL BE RIGHT BACK.
POLICE STATION

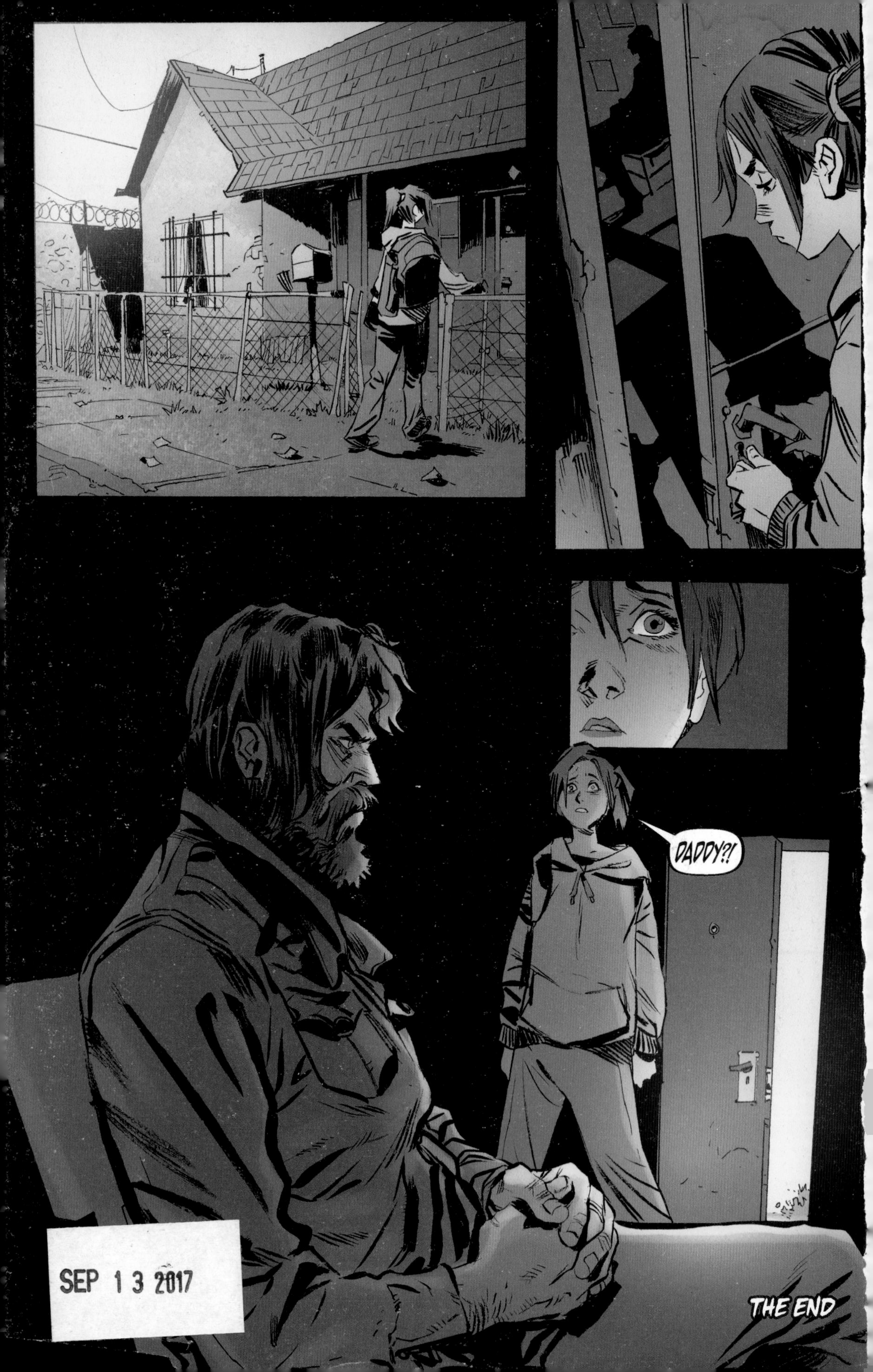
DADDY?!
THE END